ALONG CAME YOU

by
A.L. Stephens

Published by Rock Creek Press

Copyright © 2020 by A.L. Stephens

All rights reserved. No part of this publication may be reproduced, distributed or transmitted in any form or by any means, including photocopying, recording, or other electronic or mechanical methods, without the prior written permission of the publisher, except in the case of brief quotations embodied in critical reviews and certain other noncommercial uses permitted by copyright law. For permission requests, contact alstephensbooks@gmail.com

First Edition. Printed in the United States of America.

Books may be purchased in quantity by contacting:
alstephensbooks@gmail.com or Rock Creek Press at 541-580-4717

PB ISBN: 978-1-946353-05-4 (pbk.)
PB ISBN: 978-1-946353-04-7 (EPUB)

Publisher's Note: This is a work of fiction. Names, Characters, places, and incidents are a product of the author's imagination. Locales and public names are sometimes used for atmospheric purposes. Any resemblance to actual people, living or dead, or to businesses, companies, events, institutions, or locales is completely coincidental.

In loving memory of my husband, Rick Stephens---
When you came along, I finally experienced
the real meaning of true love.
You are missed deeply but will never be forgotten.
I love you, Love-Love, my Big Bear- always.

CONTENTS

Along Came You
Copyright

Chapter 1	1
Chapter 2	25
Chapter 3	44
Chapter 4	63
Chapter 5	86
Chapter 6	113
Chapter 7	132
Chapter 8	140
Chapter 9	165
Chapter 10	186
Chapter 11	204
Chapter 12	226
Chapter 13	243
Chapter 14	259
Chapter 15	274
Chapter 16	288

Chapter 17	304
Chapter 18	324
Chapter 19	345
Chapter 20	358
Chapter 21	379
Chapter 22	397
Chapter 23	414
Chapter 24	430
Dear Beloved Readers,	453
A special thank you to my Beta readers:	455

Chapter 1

"Hurry Elainah or all the seats will be taken," SaraLee hollers back at me.

I had decided at the last minute to bring my bag and book. I agreed to come to the rodeo with SaraLee but I hadn't agreed to watch, so I'll be reading. I have a hard time watching people get hurt and a good portion of the people here tend to do just that.

"I'm coming, I'm coming. And what do you mean by 'the seats'? You won't be sitting very much," I nudged her with my hip. Even though my hip comes to just below hers. She is quite a bit taller than me.

SaraLee is the type of girl you'd see at a rodeo. Long legged and big boobed, and she liked to show those two things off the most. Which is why she wore a mini skirt, cowboy boots she only wore to rodeos, and a very tight belly shirt. She's confident in herself and that's great and all but I can never understand why wearing a mini skirt to a rodeo would be comfortable. But then again, she never sat long enough to worry about her who-ah showing. Her blue eyes stood out against her beautiful auburn red hair that she liked to wear in big curls down her back. Her makeup is done perfectly. She is beautiful. I knew that if she could ride a horse at all, she could have been on the rodeo court. But then again, rodeo queens and princesses need to be a little less selfish than my good friend here.

I, on the other hand, am pretty much SaraLee's opposite. I am short with brown hair. I do have curves going for me, even though when I was younger, I always wished them away, especially while playing sports. As an adult, I've come to appreciate them. My eyes change colors from green to hazel to brown, depending on my mood and what I'm wearing. I only wear mascara and eyeliner, everything else makes me feel itchy. I'm wearing my go-to jeans, boots, and tank-top. My hair was braided into a side braid but I'm wearing one of my favorite ball caps. I dress for comfort.

"Whoooot-whoooo!" a whistle sounds behind us.

"Hey pretty lady!" calls after we don't turn around.

I nudge SaraLee thinking she hadn't heard but looking up at her I see that she has, she's smirking. I can see she's started her 'walk'. Her hips wiggle a little more when she walks this way. I know he's whistling and 'hey pretty lady'-ing to her.

She glances behind us and gives a smile and look that says, "I know."

I glance back and see a talk, dark, and handsome cowboy. Again, typical to see here. His dark brown hair was a little long under his cowboy hat. He wore a white long sleeve and a black hat. His jeans looked worn but new, they fit him well but not tight in the Wrangler way. I caught his eye for a split second and the look on his face made me look away quickly. He'd caught me gawking.

Great! How embarrassing.

SaraLee found some of her rodeo friends and headed straight to them. I followed.

I wonder how long I'll have to stand here before it's not considered rude of me to go sit somewhere and read. I think to myself.

After 20 minutes of standing awkwardly by, saying hi and answering the all too familiar, 'how are you doing' questions, I decided I had waited long enough.

"I'm going to go get a drink and find a seat, you know, before they're all filled up," I say to SaraLee half sarcastically. I knew she wasn't concerned about seating, I probably wouldn't see her again for the rest of the day and night for that matter. I was just a ride for her to get here.

"Uh, huh, sounds good, bring me one if you come

back this way, would you?" she asks, not looking at me.

Shaking my head and rolling my eyes, I walk away. She can be a good friend at times but when she's in her 'zone' she's... well... she's SaraLee.

I go stand in the drink line.

"What can I get for you?" the guy asks when I get up to the front.

"Diet whatever, please," I respond, politely.

"That'll be one token," he says.

"Aww crap, I forgot tokens. I'm sorry, I'll be right back," I say, stepping out of line.

I go stand in line for tokens. It's a bit longer than the other so I pull my book out and read a little. The line moves quickly and before I know it, I'm at the front.

"Twenty-dollar's worth please," I say.

"You don't have a wristband on, you need to go get your ID checked," the lady says.

"Oh man, seriously?" I ask.

"Yeah, over 21 gets a certain band so we know which tokens to give for beer and under 21 gets different tokens for soda-pop," she says.

"But I just want a diet soda for now, can I just buy some of those tokens?" I ask, getting a little annoyed.

"Sorry, I was told not to sell tokens unless they have a wristband, whether it's a 21 and older or an underage one," she says looking like she didn't like it either but it's what she was told.

I can't get upset with her, she didn't make the rules, even if they were stupid.

"Okay, no worries," I say as I step out of line yet again.

When I get in line to get my ID checked, I see familiar faces manning the booth.

"Hi Burt, hi Amy," I wave as I get to the front.

"Hi Hun," Burt says.

"Do I need to actually show you my ID since you know me and my age?" I ask Amy as I reach for my wallet.

"No sweety, you're good," she says laughing.

"Kind of annoying having to go to every booth, huh?" Burt asks as he puts an over 21 band on my wrist.

"Yeah but I get it. They want to make sure underage kids aren't given tokens by accident. I just haven't been to an event like this in a while so I forget the process. How long are you guys doing this for?" I ask as I step aside so the next person in line can get their ID checked.

"Until 4 o'clock, just in time for the bulls, did you hear who's here?" Burt asks excitedly.

"No," I answer.

But before he can answer, the guy behind me is standing in front of him for his band to be put on and the line is starting to stack up from Amy checking ID's.

I wave a goodbye and move back over to the token line. Luckily it goes quickly and I get enough tokens for a couple soda-pops and a couple for beers for later.

I get back in the drink line and a couple scoot in front of me, cutting.

No big deal, I can wait. I silently say to myself.

A tall cowboy stands in front of me.

Cough-**Cough**. I make the sound loud enough the cowboy turns around.

"Oh, sorry about that," he moves out of my way and stands behind me.

I just shrug, hoping he understands that to mean 'no worries'.

"Hey, I remember you," the cowboy says.

"Oh?" I say skeptically. No way does this cowboy know me.

"Yeah from earlier, in the parking lot. I was the idiot whistling," he says sounding embarrassed but I can't be sure, I can't see him.

Still not turning to look at him, I say, "Oooh yeah. My friend is somewhere over there. Her name is SaraLee." I gesture over in the general direction of where I'd left SaraLee with her rodeo groupies.

"She didn't seem too interested," he says, sounding like he wants to laugh.

"She plays that way... you know, hard to get... You better not tell her I told you that," I say, turning now to face him.

Wow... but wow!! My eternal thoughts are luckily

silent. He's so tall, at least 6'4". He is very good looking- very, very good looking. His eyes are a piercing blue and his skin is dark from being out in the sun. I can see his hair better now, a nice chocolate brown.

He laughs which pulls me out of my mental ogling. I laugh out an embarrassed laugh but also one to go along with what I'd said about SaraLee.

"My name is Dalton, Dalton Young," he says a little on the expectant side.

"Umm, it's nice to meet you, Dalton," I say, a little confused as to why he's still standing here talking to me as I had told him where I left SaraLee.

A few awkward moments pass and I turn back around.

Why is he staring at me? I wonder to myself.

"Can I get your name?" Dalton asks, half laughing.

"Why?" I ask before I can stop myself but I'm just surprised he's asking.

"So I know what to call you besides 'pretty gal'," he says now laughing fully.

I turn and look at him incredulously.

"You don't need to smooth your way in to get info about my friend. I already told you where she is and her name." I gesture again where I had left her and say, "Go get her."

Dalton tilts his head to the side a little and smiles, "What if it isn't her I'm interested in anymore?"

"Then you have a small attention span," I say a little snarkily. I realize I've said it out loud and look up quickly, "I'm sorry, that was rude."

He just laughs and says, "No, you're being honest." The most heartbreakingly gorgeous smile spreads across his face.

Before I can respond, I'm at the front of the line.

"Diet whatever, please," I say, holding up a token

"Diet whatever? No beer?" Dalton asks with an eyebrow raised.

"Not drinking yet, it's too early for me."

"Now I feel like an alcoholic."

"No, no! I'm just a lightweight. If I'm going to last until the dance, I can't start drinking now. Plus, I've got family watching," I nod towards Burt and Amy. Dalton looks over and sees them staring, they wave. We wave back.

"So I can buy you a beer later?" he asks.

"I guess," I shrug. The guy hands me my diet fountain drink and I start to walk away.

"Hey, I still don't know your name!" Dalton hollers over the heads of the other people in line.

I turn, shrugging again, and holler back, "You can figure it out."

I'm just messing with him. I know he won't waste his time trying to figure out my name. He'd find SaraLee and completely forget about me.

I walk along the bottom of the bleachers, looking up, trying to find a spot to sit. I see one in the top left corner, the entire area is empty. It's the furthest seating away from the action which is probably why it's still available. I make my way to it, excusing my way through the people already seated. Once I get to my spot, I sit and pull out my book.

I'm quite a few chapters in, maybe an hour has gone by when I feel a tap on my shoulder. I look over, and up, and see Dalton sitting here.

"Anyone sitting here?" he points to the seat beside me where my bag is lying.

I shake my head no.

"May I?" he asks.

I nod, still not able to talk. I'm stunned and surprised to see him again.

"Sooo, Elainah... why the hoops?"

"You went to SaraLee?"

"Well yeah, Elainah, I wasn't going to ask your parents."

Sigh "I go by Lainey, only SaraLee calls me Elainah. And they aren't my parent-parents."

It's quiet for a minute and then Dalton says, "It's nice to finally meet you Lainey but I don't understand. What do you mean by not your parent-parents?"

"They're my in-laws, my father-in-law and mother-in-law."

"Oh, you're married. I'm sorry. I didn't see a ring," he says as he glances at my hand.

"I'm... not married, not anymore."

He looks confused, "Divorced but still close to your in-laws?"

"Widowed and still very close to my in-laws."

Face falling he says, "Oh, I'm sorry."

"It's okay. It's been about a year and a half now."

"Can I ask what happened or still too painful to talk about?"

"He was killed in an accident."

"I'm so sorry. What was his name?"

"Jayce and it's okay. It's better some days. Some days it feels like it's starting all over again."

"I can understand that. Did you two have kids?"

"Yes, a boy and two girls. They're the reason I'm here. I wouldn't have been able to make it without them."

"You seem to be a strong person, I bet you could have handled it just as well."

"Thanks. So what about you?," I deflect the topic back to him. "Someone like you has to have a wife or at the very least a girlfriend. Which is one-hundred percent the reason for the... what did you say? Hoops? I don't like talking to taken men, their women tend to take it the wrong way."

Dalton laughs and says, "What do you mean by someone like me?" Looking down at himself.

"You shaved," I say as I reach up and touch his face. I didn't consciously think about doing it, my hand just has a mind of its own, I guess. "Sorry, I didn't intend to touch you, but--," I shake my head, "You look at yourself in the mirror when you do that, right?"

Still laughing, he touches where my hand had touched, "Ummm, yes."

"Then you know what you look like, and your confidence to whistle, and call out to women you don't know also shows you know what you look like."

"Are YOU saying I'm good looking?" he raises an eyebrow as he asks this.

My cheeks go pink and feel warmer, I say, "Well the whole world knows it, why would it be any different for me?"

"So you think I'm good looking?" he asks again.

"That's beside the point," I say, my cheeks full on red now. "My point is, you of all people here, would have a lady friend."

"Well, I don't."

"Whatever," I shake my head and look away.

"I don't. I broke it off not quite two years ago," he says with so much honesty, I look back up at him.

"Okay, so you don't have an official lady friend but you're a cowboy, you have a 'friend' in every town you go to, to rodeo."

"You don't have high opinions of cowboys, do you?"

"Some are fine but most are, 'slam, bam, thank ya ma'am', types," I say, remembering all the times

SaraLee has called crying that this cowboy never called or this cowboy won't even look at her anymore. Other friends have similar stories.

Laughing again, Dalton asks, "They're what?"

"Sorry, maybe the saying is, 'hit it and quit it', nowadays," I say, rolling my eyes. "It all means the same."

Dalton, still laughing, says, "Well, I'm neither. I'm a 'one girl at a time' type of guy."

"Really?" I'm truly surprised by this and not fully believing it.

"Yup. I don't like being played, so why would I do that to someone else?" he asks earnestly.

"Hmmmm… well this is… different," I concede.

"How so?" he's laughing again.

"A cowboy who doesn't sleep around…"

"Maybe it's because I'm not a true rodeo cowboy," he says winking.

I look skeptical at him, "How so?"

"I'm a cowboy because it's my job title. I'm also a farmer and rancher. I was here visiting and decided to enter because my buddy said this little rodeo was one of the most fun in all of the Western States."

"Huh…." stunned silent, I can't think of anything else to say.

"Doesn't feel good to assume things wrong, does it?"

I don't say anything and look away. Of course

he's right, I had been assuming all the worst things possible about him.

"Didn't think so," he says as he nudges me with his shoulder.

"I just don't know why you're here talking to me when you were already over with SaraLee," I say to him and then think to myself, *deflecting it back on him again, good idea Lainey.*

"She caught my eye first, yes, but you stole it a second later," he says earnestly again.

"Uh? When?"

He sighs and says, "Okay, back to your honest comment about my attention span. I did see your friend first, yes that's true. Only because she's so obviously pretty--"

I cut him off and say, "Obviously, which is why I'm saying you should be talking to--" Dalton cuts me off by putting a finger to my lips. The feeling of his touch, sends a delicious shiver down my spine.

"But when you glanced behind to see who had whistled and our eyes locked for that split second, I knew I had to talk to you. But then you disappeared into the crowd. I had looked for you for a while when I had decided to quit and get a beer and there you were."

"But... I'm nothing like SaraLee," I say, still skeptical.

"You don't see yourself clearly, do you?"

"I don't know what you mean."

"You hide under a hat but I see you."

"You don't know what you're talking about."

"Mmmm hmmm just like that."

"Whatever…" I pick my book up and act like I'm reading. I don't want to believe what he's saying is true. Jayce is the only one who has ever said things like this to me, said he 'saw' me. He's the only one that's ever made me feel like this, until Dalton.

"You come to a rodeo and read?" laughter in his voice again.

I shrug, "I don't like to watch and I brought SaraLee and I am meeting my best-friend at the dance later."

"SaraLee isn't your best-friend?"

"No, she's a good friend, but tends to only worry about herself, which is fine but Emily cares about me and checks in quite a bit. She talked me into coming here today and to the dance later."

"I'll have to thank her," he smiles a crooked smile at me.

I smile back, I can't help it. That smile could get a stone to smile.

"So why don't you like watching?"

"I don't like seeing people get hurt."

"Even people you don't know?" he asks in surprise.

"Even people I don't know," I answer.

"Will you watch when I ride?"

"What are you riding?"

He looks down at me in surprise, "Bulls." He says it like I should know.

"Of course you are, all you crazy cowboys love the bulls," I say shaking my head.

"Will you watch?"

"Are you any good?" I ask, teasing but actually really wondering. If he was good, maybe he wouldn't get hurt and I can watch.

"I'm okay," he's got an eyebrow raised. Is that confusion?

Cringing a little, I say, "I really don't want to see you or anyone get hurt."

"I won't get hurt."

My eyebrows go up.

"I'll try my best not to get hurt. Will you watch?" he asks again.

"I'll try my best," I say, copying him.

Dalton laughs and I smile.

"Stay here. I have to go check-in, bulls are next. Stay here and I'll be back after my ride."

"Okay..."

Dalton takes off down the bleachers. Everyone turns and looks at me.

Weird... I think to myself.

SaraLee passes him as he walks by, he nods, a polite gesture. She shakes her hair out, pushes her barely covered boobs out but he keeps walking. She slumps a little and turns slightly to watch him walk away.

She looks up at me and stomps her way up the bleachers to me.

"I saw Dalton Young talking to you, what was that about?" she asks snarkily.

"I honestly don't know," I say. Truly, I still can't figure out why he's talking to me.

"Did he ask about me?"

Crap, now she's going to get pouty. I think to myself.

"No, not really."

"Then what was he talking to you about for so long?" she asks skeptically. She can't fathom anyone not talking about her. I love the girl but my goodness...

"Me... He was asking me things about myself."

"Why?" she asks a little rudely.

I just look at her with my eyebrows raised.

"Well, I'm sorry but that's Dalton Young."

"Okay..." is all I can think to say, why would that matter?

"Do you even know who HE is?"

I shrug. I guess not. I thought I was just talking to some random cowboy, rancher, farmer guy.

"He's won multiple World Championships for bull riding. He has one of the biggest ranches in Montana. He's mega rich and mega hot," she says the last two things like they were the most important things she could have said about him.

"Huh... He's humble about it all then because he didn't say anything about it to me."

"Well, he probably assumes everyone at a rodeo would know him," she says snarkily again.

"I doubt he assumes very much about anything. He seems very nice," I say, starting to get annoyed with her attitude.

SaraLee pouts and says, "I can't believe he was talking to you... no offense."

I really hate when people say that, especially when they've already said the offensive thing. Do they really expect it to be 'okay' just because they say 'no offense' before or after?

"I don't know why," I say.

"You aren't ready for a relationship yet, are you? I mean it's been, what..." she stops and thinks for a minute and then gives up. "However long it's been since Jayce's accident."

Shocked and a little stung, I say, "It's been a year and a half, SaraLee. And whether I'm ready or not, doesn't mean I can't have a conversation with someone and get to know them. You're supposed to be my friend, that was really hurtful."

I grab my book and bag and stand up and make my way down the bleachers. I glance back up to see what SaraLee was doing. She's pouting with her arms crossed over her chest.

Of course she would act all butt hurt. I think to myself. I'm going to have to rethink this friendship or whatever it is. I've been a little blind to her selfishness but it's becoming all too blatantly obvious.

I find another spot and sit. It's closer to the chutes, closer to the 'action'. I go back to reading but keep an ear alert for Dalton's name. A couple chapters in, I hear the announcer giving a long speech and then he says, 'Dalton Young' extremely, and unnecessarily, loud.

The crowd erupts into a roaring applause. I look up and watch Dalton get situated on his bull, whose name is Life Insurance.

Of course... Just watch... if it looks like he's going to fall off or get hurt, close your eyes. You told him you'd try. I think to myself.

Dalton nods and I watch in awe. I've never seen anyone ride like him. It looks more like a dance, rather than a rider on top of a bull. The 8 seconds seem to last 8 minutes before the buzzer is going off. Dalton dismounts so gracefully that it looks like he's sliding off the side of something standing still, not a bucking, twisting bull, trying with all it's might to get him off.

He stands up smiling and looks over to where I had been sitting. His eyebrows crunch together a little and his smile isn't as big or genuine as it was before he looked over there.

Can he really be disappointed that I'm not sitting

over there anymore?

He waves to the crowd and then sees me again and his smile widens and beams. He points back behind the chutes. I shrug and nod quickly, agreeing to meet him back there.

I make my way behind and find him surrounded by a bunch of buckle bunnies. I hear one say to her friend, "Just think, if he can ride a bull that well, think of how well he could ride us!" she giggles, I roll my eyes.

Dalton sees me and makes his way to me.

"Did you watch?"

"Yes, you're a great rider," I state. He truly is the best rider I've ever seen.

"Thanks, I really do enjoy it."

"I can see that. I can also see how you could have won muiltiple World Champions."

His face falls a little, "You knew?"

"No, SaraLee told me right after you passed her."

He nods, "She knows her riders."

"Yup."

"When I looked for you and saw her, I thought you left."

"No, just found a different spot to sit," I say. I look around and see the buckle bunnies are starting to converge around us. "I'll let you get back to your fans. It was great meeting you... and nice ride."

"Wait, Lainey..." he hollers.

"No, it's okay. You're busy. We can catch up

later… or whenever," I turn and walk away. I can hear him call my name again but I just keep walking. I don't know how to feel about this, his attention, my feelings.

I get over to the beer garden entrance again and pull my phone out. It's too loud to call Emily, texting will have to do.

Me- *On ur way?* 4:02pm

Emily- *Still at work, on break* 4:03pm

Me- *I need you here ASAP* 4:03pm

Emily- *Y? What's happened?* 4:03pm

Me- *Kind of met someone. We've been talking. I need to talk to you about it.* 4:04pm

Emily- *I'll get there as soon as I'm off. It's slow, I'll see if I can leave now.* 4:04pm

Me- *Please do. Don't think I can wait for the dance to talk.* 4:04pm

Emily- *SaraLee not there to talk it through til I'm there?* 4:04pm

Me- *SaraLee is being SaraLee. She's upset he's talking to me and not her.* 4:05pm

Emily- *WTF? Is she really that selfabsorbed?* 4:07pm

Me- *I didn't think so but…* 4:07pm

Emily- *This is big… BIG for u and she's being a bitch…* 4:10pm

Me- *It's not that BIG* 4:10pm

Emily- *Yes it is. You haven't shown interest in anyone. This is BIG and so good. What's his name?* 4:12pm

Me- *Dalton* 4:12pm

Emily- *Dalton?* 4:14pm

Me- *Dalton Young* 4:14pm

Emily- *O!* 4:17pm

Emily- *M!* 4:174pm

Emily- *G!!!!* 4:17pm

Me- *So you know who he is?* 4:17pm

Emily- *Yes! Didn't you?* 4:17pm

Me- *No, I had no idea. I just thought he was some cute cowboy. He told me he was a rancher/farmer.* 4:18pm

Emily- *He's not just some 'cute' cowboy. He's THE fucking hottest cowboy ever.* 4:18pm

Me- *He seems really nice.* 4:18pm

Emily- *I'm talking to my supervisor to see if I can leave. Standby.* 4:20pm

I close out of Messages and look at the time. It's 4:20pm. The dance doesn't start until 9 o'clock. I have time to eat. Emily wouldn't be here for an hour if she gets off early. She was scheduled until 7 o'clock anyways.

My phone buzzes.

-New message from Emily-

Emily- *Sorry, Sweets. Pam says there was a wreck on the freeway. We've got four ambulances coming our way. I'll get there ASAP.* 4:21pm

Me- *No worries, be careful.* 4:21pm

Emily- *Will do* 4:21pm

I put my phone in my pocket and head towards the burger stand. Food would be a good thing. It's a long line. Sighing, I pull out my book and start reading again. I keep my peripheral vision on the line in front of me, moving whenever they move.

I'm really into the chapter when the person behind me taps my shoulder and says in a deep voice, "You can move up if you'd like."

I look up and see that I'm about three spots behind. I hurry and move forward.

"Thank you and sorry about that," I say as I look behind me for the first time since getting in line. Surprise spreads across my face and my mouth falls open but I can't help it, Dalton is standing behind me.

"It's okay," he says smiling. "You're really into that book."

"Yeah, I tend to get submerged at times," I say, a little embarrassed. I look behind Dalton and see a lot of people in line behind him.

"How long have you been in line?" I ask.

"A couple minutes after you."

"What?" I say a little too loudly.

"You really didn't know I was behind you?"

"No, I really didn't, I would have said something to you. I guess I was more into my book than I thought."

We are almost up to order.

"Will you let me buy you dinner?" Dalton asks.

"How about I buy dinner?"

"Or I buy dinner, you get us beer? You can have a beer now, can't you?"

Laughing, I say, "Yes, now would be okay."

"What do you want to eat? I'll order, you can go get in line for beer."

"Cheeseburger and curly fries please, with extra pink sauce."

Dalton smiles, "A girl that'll eat, I like it."

"I like food. It's too exhausting to pretend to be someone I'm not. I am who I am," I shrug and walk away to stand in the beer line.

I look up and see that Brandy is serving. She waves at me. Luckily the beer line goes quicker than the food line.

"Lainey! It's so good to see you. How are you?" she asks with her head tilted to the side like everyone does around here when they ask me how I'm doing.

"I'm doing good, thanks Brandy. How are you?"

"I'm doing good too. How are the kids?" she asks, sounding more normal.

"They're great. Really excited for summer break to start."

"That's good! What can I get for you?"

"One regular beer and one strawberry mango lemonade beer, please," I say.

Brandy grabs two from each bucket and hands them to me.

"Just pay for two, I'll get the others. I'm so happy

to see you out. And by the looks of it, with someone?" she asks with a little too much eagerness. She's a nice lady but the rumor mill tends to run right through her.

"Just met and just talking," I say quickly.

"Well that's great! Just two tokens then, Hun," she says. I hand her two tokens and step out of line. I put two cans in my bag and turn and find Dalton waiting for me between the food stand and beer line.

"Where to?" he asks.

"Did you bring a pickup?" I ask.

"Of course."

"I know a place, it's not too far. Wanna go for a drive and eat when we get there?"

"Sure," he smiles at me.

"I'll follow you," I say smiling back.

Chapter 2

Dalton leads us through the crowd. Some are staring at him but a lot are waving and saying hi to me. We get to the parking lot and a thought comes to me.

"Hang on a second. I want to put my book and bag in my rig."

"No problem."

We wind our way through the vehicles until my Tahoe comes into view. I grab my phone, ID, debit card, and cash out of my wallet, and the two beers, and then put my bag on the floor in back. I use one of my kids' discarded hoodies to cover it. I take the remote off my key ring and put my keys in the middle console. I put my phone in my back pocket and everything else in my front pockets. I put a can in the crook of each elbow and carry one in each hand.

"Okay, ready," I say turning towards Dalton.

He smiles his crooked smile and starts walking.

"What?" I ask.

"Nothing," he says with a small laugh.

"No, what's funny?"

"It's not funny, it's... fascinating... refreshing..."

"What is?"

"You."

"Me? How?"

"You only take what you need. You use your child's hoodie to hide your bag like a thief wouldn't look underneath it."

"The hoodie is so my bag isn't out in the open, hopefully making it hidden so anyone looking through the window won't see it. Use the mess the kids leave behind for something," Dalton laughs again. "And I don't like carrying a bag or purse or whatever, around if I don't have to, less to keep track of."

"I like that... like I said, it's refreshing."

We get to a new, fancy pickup and he unlocks it. He puts the food on the hood and then opens the door for me. I get in. He hands me the food and shuts the door. He walks, half jogs, around to the other side and gets in.

"This is a nice pickup. It's my favorite color too, charcoal grey."

"Glad you like it. Happy to see you aren't someone against Fords, seeing as you drive a Chevy Tahoe."

"I like all makes. Each one has their own special

thing."

Dalton laughs again, "Where to?"

"How familiar are you with the area?"

"I've come here quite often."

"Okay, head back to La Grande."

"Yes, ma'am."

I look at him with raised eyebrows.

"Yes, dear? Is that better?" he laughs.

"Being called 'ma'am' makes me feel old, is all."

"Well, I say it to be polite, nothing else."

"I know, just my own issue."

We are quiet for a minute. Just as something occurs to me, he speaks.

"Okay, let's start with basics."

"Well first, let me say if you plan on murdering me, everyone saw me leave with you, so there's that..."

Dalton laughs out a big belly laugh.

"If you're worried about me murdering you, why did you come?"

"I didn't think about it until now."

"Are you afraid I'll hurt you?" he asks seriously.

I think for a minute before answering. I stare at Dalton as he drives.

"No, no I don't think you will," I finally answer him.

"Good, because I won't."

"Good," I say smiling at him.

"Okay, let's start again. Basics. What's your full

name?"

"Elainah DeEtte Richardsen. You?"

"Dalton Edward Young. What's your birthday?"

I wrinkle my nose, "April 3rd."

"Year?"

"1984," I say reluctantly.

"Really?"

"Yes, why do you sound surprised?"

"Relieved actually. I thought you were quite a bit younger than me."

"What's your birthday?"

"January 24th, 1983."

It was my turn to be surprised, "Really?"

"Yes, why?" he was mimicking me but in a serious way also.

"You look younger than that, which is why I was reluctant to tell you my age."

"I guess we both have that going for us and plus, age is only a number."

I laugh, "I guess so."

"What's your kids' names?"

"Max, he's 10. Janey, she's 8. And Nelly, she's 4."

"Good ages."

"They're fun."

"Where were they today?"

"Staying with my sister. She lives in Idaho and takes them for the first week or so of summer. Nelly is old enough this year that she got to go. They'll be back before Max's birthday."

"I bet they're having fun."

"So far, so good."

"How are you doing with them being gone?"

"So far, so good," I laugh a little. "No, I'm... okay. I miss them and I'm ready for them to be back already but it's good for us. They enjoy playing with their cousins."

"I bet they do."

We're pulling into La Grande so I tell him, "Go through town like you're going to the fairgrounds."

"You got it."

"So you said you broke off your relationship with your girlfriend about two years ago?"

"Yeah."

"Did you guys have kids?"

"No... had we, I would have tried to work things out."

"Can I ask what happened or is it too personal? I'm too out of practice with this getting to know someone, that I don't remember what's too personal and what's not."

"Nothing is too personal when you're getting to know someone, don't you think?"

"Well, that's how I feel but I don't usually have the same views on things as other people," I admit.

"We agree on this," he says, smiling at me. Then he takes a breath and says, "Umm... to put it simply, I caught her, Sally, with another man on Halloween in 2019."

"What?" I ask, stunned.

"She tried to claim she was drunk and thought it was me but I was dressed as Zorro, she was dressed as my, Zorro's lady.. errr wife. The guy she was screwing was dressed as a werewolf."

"Oh my gosh! That's awful!"

"Luckily, we were at a friend's house, so I left. Sally came home in the morning, trying to apologize but I told her I don't tolerate cheating. She said it was a mistake and she was really drunk. I decided to give her another chance but the guy called me a week later and told me they'd been dating for months. He didn't know about me, he was done with her. She got home that night and I told her she had to pack her clothes and get out. I had my head guy, Frank, who works for me, stay while she packed. I went into my best-friend's house in town. When Frank called the next day, he'd taken her to Bozeman, to her sister, and I went home. I hadn't realized how much stress she was causing in my life until she was gone."

"That's awful. I'm so sorry she did that to you."

"It happens, I guess. I never thought it would happen to me but... you know that feeling better than most, don't you?"

"That I do... Still sucks, both of our situations."

Dalton looks at me in awe. I look out the windshield as a distraction from his stare and see we're sitting at a red light and close to where I was having us go.

"Just go straight and follow this road. We'll just be pulling off to the side at the top of the hill."

"Sounds good," he says, finally looking away from me.

We sit in silence for the rest of the drive. We get to the top of the hill and I see the pull off.

"Just park anywhere here. If you back in, we can sit on the tailgate."

Dalton just nods and then maneuvers the pickup so that the rear is facing the view and the front is facing the road.

"I didn't even know this was here," Dalton says as he opens his door.

"I've driven by a lot but have never stopped."

Dalton grabs the food boxes from the back seat where I had put them. I grab the drinks from the floor. I open my door and step out.

"I was going to get your door," Dalton says standing beside me.

"It's okay, I got it."

"Well, that's not really the point. I know you can do it."

"I appreciate the gesture."

We walk to the back of the pickup and before Dalton can put the food down, I put all the drinks in my left arm and open the tailgate.

Dalton shakes his head, smiles, and says, "You're something else."

"Why's that?"

"Sally always expected me to do everything for her. She never offered to help or anything."

"Well, I am not like that... at all."

"I'm figuring that out," he chuckles.

I hop up on the tailgate, Dalton hesitating a moment, looking like he was going to help me, but shakes his head again, laughs, mumbles something quietly, and then hops up beside me. Only his 'hop' was more of a tip-toe sit down than an actual jump hop like mine. We eat in silence for a minute, enjoying the view and the food. I reach to my right side and grab our drinks. I hand him his beers.

"You trying to get me drunk?"

Laughing I say, "No, I knew the gal serving. She gave me two for free." I pull one of mine out and crack it open. "Cheers!"

"To new beginnings," Dalton says, tilting his can towards mine.

"To new beginnings," I agree, holding my can up and letting him tap his to mine.

After another quiet few minutes, Dalton asks, "So you and your late husband, you were close?"

"Yes, very close. Like any relationship, we had our arguments but we always worked through them. He was everything to me. Learning to live without him...

Coming to terms with the fact that the person I thought I was going to spend the rest of my life with was gone, and never coming back, is the hardest thing I've ever done. It took a while to really become okay with that but I have and I truly am okay. Again, my wonderful kids have really helped me, more than they will probably ever know."

"Wow... I can't even imagine, nor do I want to... Tell me about your kids."

"My oldest, Max, he's one-thousand percent his dad. He's already built like him. He enjoys everything his dad did. He's just a mini-Jayce. My middle, Janey, is a complete sweetheart. She's such a helper, always wanting to help. I told myself right after Jayce's accident that my kids would continue to be kids. I would not allow anyone to tell Max he was the man of the house now, he was only 8, he didn't need that level of stress put on him. I wasn't going to allow myself to put responsibilities on Janey that were my responsibilities, such as taking care of her brother and sister. Janey also loves animals, boy does she love animals. I'll be really surprised if she doesn't end up in an animal field of work when she's older. She gives the best hugs and I used to be afraid she would be easily bossed around but she is slowly showing her inner strength. Nelly is my little love bug. She's only four but she already shows so much empathy, it's astonishing. She also gives the best hugs. She can always seem to tell when I need some snuggles, it's truly amazing. They are still so young, I'm excited to see how they grow and change into themselves as they get older."

Dalton just stares at me.

"What?" I ask.

"Your kids sound amazing. I'm one-hundred percent certain that is because of you."

I just shrug, "They have a lot of their dad in them." I smile.

"I have no doubt about that," Dalton says, smiling back. "Enough of the heavy. What's your favorite food?"

Laughing at his switching of topics, I say, "I honestly love food, I can't pick just one thing."

"Not even if someone said it would be the last thing on Earth, the only thing left to eat."

"Well, I guess I'd have to really think about it."

"Mine is pizza."

"I love pizza but I also love burgers... and salads... oh and fruit during the summer is an all-time must. Oooh, but I'd miss Chinese food, LOVE Chinese! And I can't forget about Mexican food, not just tacos, but enchiladas and taquitos and chips and salsa. Nelly loves chips and salsa. Shoot, popcorn is a must for evenings... mmm ice cream..." Dalton interrupts my food monologue with a laugh. My cheeks turning red, I say, "See, I love food. I seriously can't pick just one."

"Okay, what about candy? Mine is anything

sour."

"I love any of the Reese's, except Reese's Pieces, there's not enough peanut butter. But I also love fruity candies... like Skittles, Sweet-Tarts- the chewy kind, Starburst... See... FOODIE!" I say as I point to myself.

Dalton laughs and asks, "What's your favorite Skittle and Starbursts? Mine is the red."

"Yellow in both, all the way."

"Really?"

"Yup," I say smiling. It always surprises people when I tell them this, for whatever reason.

Dalton hops down and grabs the food containers and empty cans, as he does, I check the time on my phone. It's 7:52pm. We still have an hour before the dance. And there's still no text from Emily.

Dalton walks back over with a more serious look on his face. "Can I say something... a little... forward.. I guess is the word."

"Sure," I say hesitantly.

Dalton stands just to the side of my left leg, takes my left hand, and turns to me. I'm really nervous now.

"I know we've only just met but I'm feeling very drawn to you. I think I'm really starting to like you, and honestly, I didn't think I would ever find someone after Sally."

He keeps holding my hand, turning it over in his, running his fingers over mine.

"I know. I feel the same. It's just, Dalton, I

haven't... Jayce was the last person I was with, the last person I kissed in a romantic way," I take a breath. Dalton gets closer. I can see the moon reflecting in his eyes. "You'll have to be patient and really understanding if this goes anywhere. There might be emotions that flare up that I can't control that have nothing to do with you and me."

"I can do that," he whispers. He moves closer, his nose touches mine. "Do you want me to stop?"

I move closer, our heads tilting automatically, our lips barely touching. "No," I whisper and then push my lips into his.

Dalton lets go of my hand he was holding and runs his hand up my arm until he's cupping my face. His other hand goes to the other side of my face. Our kiss deepens.

I grab a hold of the front of his shirt and pull him towards me. He stumbles a little as he positions himself to stand in front of me, between my legs, as I'm sitting on the tailgate. He never broke our kiss.

I haven't felt like this in a really long time. 18 months to be exact. Nobody has made me feel like this since Jayce. To be fair, I never gave anyone a chance to try. I was never ready. But this fire, this need, this want, I remember this feeling.

Our lips part and when our tongues touch, it's like the fire intensifies 100 times hotter. The kissing becomes even more intense.

After what seems like no time at all, Dalton pulls away.

"You're vibrating," he says, breathlessly.

Blushing, I say, "I know but that doesn't mean I was done kissing you."

Dalton laughs and kisses me swiftly, and then says, "No, I think it's your phone."

Sighing, I lean to the side and pull my phone out of my back pocket.

-New message from Emily-

Emily- *I'm here. Where are you?* 9:22pm

I close out of Messages and look at the time. *Crap!* It's 9:22pm.

Me- *Be there soon.* 9:22pm

I put my phone away and turn to Dalton, "Emily is at the dance."

"What time is it?" he asks and starts to reach for his phone in his pocket.

"9:22."

"Wow... time flies-"

"-when you're having fun."

We start kissing again. It's hard to stop once we start. I haven't felt like this in a long time.

BUZZ-BUZZ

I pull away reluctantly.

Dalton says, "We probably should get you back to the ball, Cinderella."

We laugh. He helps me down from the tailgate by putting his hands on my hips. My tank-top has slid up a little and where his hands are touching, there's fire on my skin. He slowly puts me on the ground, barely, my tip-toes barely touch. My hands on his shoulders wrap around his neck. He shuts the tailgate with one hand but it goes instantly back to my hip.

"I don't want to let go," he whispers huskily.

"Me either," I breathlessly agree.

We start kissing... again. Our bodies smooshing into each other. Dalton leans into me, pushing me into the back of his pickup.

A small moan escapes my mouth, he groans, and starts kissing down my neck.

"Dalton..." I say his name breathlessly but also in a moan.

"Yeah," he mumbles into my neck.

"If we don't stop, we might end up doing something I'm not sure I'm ready for," I say breathing hard.

With a low growl, Dalton steps back, and says, "You shouldn't say things like that."

Taken aback a little, I say, "I'm sorry." Tears start

to form in my eyes. Embarrassing.

"Oh... no, Lainey, no that's not... don't cry. I just meant I was thinking the same thing and hearing you say my thoughts aloud makes me want more. Of course you aren't ready for more. I'm not saying not to say that, you can always tell me to stop if it's getting to be too much, I will always do as you ask."

"I'm sorry, I'm just out of practice. I don't know the right things to do or say," I say, wiping a stray tear away.

"You're doing great. I'm just as much out of practice," he says.

"You haven't been with anyone since Sally?" I ask, surprised.

"No, I haven't. I told you, I don't sleep around. If I'm going to be with someone, I'm going to BE with them," he says looking deeply into my eyes.

"Wow... okay then."

Dalton lets me go as my phone buzzes again. I stumble a little.

"See... lightweight. Two beers and I'm stumbling," I say embarrassed again.

"I thought it was my kissing skills," he says with a cocky grin.

I pretend to think hard for a minute, putting a finger on my chin. "That could be it too," I finally say. We both laugh.

Dalton takes my hand and walks me to the side

of the pickup and opens the door for me.

"Thank you," I say.

He kisses me, "You're welcome." He kisses me again before shutting the door and jogs to the other side to get it.

"Are you good to drive?" I ask as he slides into his seat.

"Oh yeah, I'm fine. I only had the one before I rode and then the two here."

"Okay, if you're sure."

"I would never drive drunk, especially with you in here with me."

I laugh a little as I put my seatbelt on. I get my phone out as well.

-New message from Emily-

Emily- *U left? Where'd u go?* 9:23pm
Emily- *Hello! Lainey!* 9:35pm
Emily- *Lainey?* 9:55pm
Me- *I'll explain later. It's ALL good.* 10:12pm
Emily- *Patiently waiting...* 10:12pm
Me- *:)* 10:12pm

"Everything okay?" Dalton asks.

"Yeah, just Emily checking on me."

"She seems like a good friend."

"She's the best. She's also another reason I'm doing as well as I am. She's really been there for me."

Dalton reaches over and offers me his hand. I take it. The small fire erupts again. Strange how a small action like holding hands can make butterflies explode in my stomach.

We drive in silence for a while. We're about a mile out of Union before either of us says anything.

"How long are you visiting for?" I ask just as he asks, "Do you live around here? I never asked."

We laugh.

"You first," I say.

"I never asked before, do you live around here?"

"Not here-here, but about 20 minutes South-West."

"Over by Baker?"

I laugh a little, "I forget you're familiar with the area. Yeah, I live outside of Haines."

He nods in acknowledgement and says, "You asked how long I'm visiting?"

"Yeah."

"Well, I was supposed to go back Sunday, but I might extend my trip now," he squeezes my hand.

"SaraLee said you have a big ranch in Montana. Do you have to be back for something going on there?"

"Farming has started but Frank and the guys can handle it for a little while longer. I'll have to be back when we move cattle to grazing pasture though. I'll call Frank in the morning and check in with him."

I don't want Dalton to go, I'm enjoying his company and getting to know him, but I don't want to cause problems with his work either. We pull into the parking lot and quickly find an empty spot.

"Wait..." Dalton says.

Confused, I wait. He opens his door and runs around to my side. He opens my door.

"Okay... Go," he says, smiling.

I laugh, "That was silly."

"Would you have waited for me to open the door?"

"Probably not. I'm not used to it."

"Well, when you're with me, you'll have to get used to it."

"But..." I start to protest.

"Nope, that's how it is," he says teasingly, offering me his hand.

"Okay..." I say, shrugging. I take his hand and step out of his pickup.

He doesn't let go, only pulls me off to the side, and shuts the door. He takes his cowboy hat off and puts it on top of the pickup cab. He takes my ball cap off and puts it up with his hat. He stares at me, reaches up and grabs a stray hair and puts it behind my ear. He bends down and kisses me, meaning to be soft and slow. But before we know it, he's pinned me to the side of his pickup, and we're kissing passionately again.

"Yeah get soooome!!!" a stranger yells from close by.

I jump a little and laugh in embarrassment, Dalton steps away slightly.

"Thanks for that man," Dalton says, a little out of breath.

"I got you, Bro," a man in a dark shirt and white cowboy hat says as he walks by.

"Drank ass," Dalton whispers, watching the man over the top of my head.

"Come on, I need to find Emily."

Chapter 3

After grabbing our hats and putting them back on, we head towards the clubhouse where we can hear country music being played. We get to the booth to get in and Dalton insists on paying. When we walk in, it's wall to wall people, and it's extremely loud.

"Do you see her?" Dalton yells into my ear.

"No, she might be out back in the beer garden," I yell back. I grab his hand and pull him through the crowd.

We get to the beer garden and I look around. I can't see her anywhere.

"I can't see her," I say, standing on tip-toe, trying to see over the crowd.

"Send her a text, I'll go get us drinks. You want another one of those strawberry mango lemonade beer things?" he asks.

"You noticed what I was drinking?" I ask, shocked.

"Of course," he says.

"Yes, please, another strawberry mango," I say, surprised. He kisses me swiftly and walks away. Still in shock, I shake my head, grinning like an idiot, and pull out my phone.

I open Messages and send a text to Emily.

Me- *I'm here, where are you?* 10:42pm

I know she's here, she wouldn't have left without telling me and she would want to know what the heck was going on. I don't have to wait long for her reply.

Emily- *Brayden showed up. I'm out in my car talking to him. I think we're going to give it one more shot.* 10:48pm
Me- *Do you need me to come out?* 10:48pm
Emily- *No, we'll come in..* 10:48pm
Me- *We're in the beer garden.* 10:48pm
Emily- *We?* 10:49pm
Me- *Me… and Dalton :)* 10:49pm
Emily- *We're on our way in* 10:49pm

I put my phone back in my pocket, smiling.

A couple minutes later, Dalton walks up to me holding our drinks.

"Your strawberry mango lemonade beer is pretty good," he says, winking at me.

"You tried it?" I ask.

"Yeah, is that okay? I guess I should have asked before I went ahead and took a drink," he said, not sounding sorry at all, and then winks at me.

"Yeah it's okay, just surprised is all," I say as I take a drink.

"We've already swapped spit a couple times tonight, I figured trying a drink and having you drink after me wouldn't bother you too much," he whispers into my ear, kissing it lightly.

I choke on what little fluid that was still in my throat. Not because of what he said, but because of the effect that little kiss on my ear does to me.

"You can't kiss me like that," I say.

"How come?" he asks, whispering into my ear again, and kissing it just the same.

A shiver runs up my spine, "Because it's driving me crazy."

"Why don't we find a cozy corner?" he asks.

"Because," I say and step a little bit away from him, "I'm not the type of girl to make out in a corner in public, especially with someone nobody here knows I've gotten to know."

"So you're worried about what people will think?"

"Well, yes in a way. I do live around here. I don't really want rumors being spread and getting back to family and close friends. I would like to be able to tell them the good news," I say, putting my hand on his upper arm.

"And I'm good news?" he asks with a wink.

"I think so... maybe..." I say a little unsure. "I mean, we just met but I feel like we're getting to know each other pretty well."

"I think so too," Dalton says.

"Lainey?" Emily's voice comes from behind me.

I turn and see Emily standing behind me with Brayden.

Emily is about the same height as me, a little taller. But so much prettier. She has blue eyes and blonde hair. She doesn't have to cake her face in makeup, her natural beauty is what cosmetic companies strive for when making new products.

"You're here!" I shout and hug her.

"Yup," she laughs.

I step back, looking at Brayden, I say, "Hi, Brayden."

He's a handsome guy too. Light brown hair and light green eyes. He's nice but I wish he'd make up his mind about what he wanted. I don't like Emily being pulled along on his indecision rollercoaster ride.

When I step all the way back and stand next to Dalton again, I introduce them.

"Emily, Brayden, this is Dalton Young. Dalton, this is Emily Thomas and Braden Lowell," I say.

"It's nice to meet you," Dalton says.

Emily and Brayden just stare.

"Guys?" I ask questioningly.

"Sorry... Hi... It's nice to meet you also...," Emily stammers out. "I'm sorry, it's just. You're really him."

Dalton gives a polite smile and shrugs. Humble.

"You really are him? The World Champion bull rider?" Brayden asks, dumbfounded.

"Yeah, among other things," Dalton confirms with a shrug.

"That's so cool," Brayden says.

"Nice," says Emily, winking at me. I make my eyes go wide, hopefully conveying to her to behave and not say anything crude that'll embarrass me.

"You wanna dance?" Dalton asks in my ear, offering me his hand.

A nervous laugh escapes me, "I can't dance." I look over at Emily for help, she just grins.

No help at all! I think.

"I can," he says. He takes my hand and starts to pull me back through the beer garden, back inside to the dance floor.

"No, really, Dalton, I can't dance," I holler over the noise.

"Lainey, don't worry, just relax and have fun, I'll take care of the rest," he whispers into my ear as we've gotten onto the floor.

It was a swing dance song and I've never been good at this type of dance. Honestly, the type of dancing I'm good at is in my house, when nobody is watching.

Dalton starts flinging me around, knowing exactly where my hand is going to be, and always catching it before I can go spinning out of control or fall to the floor. I do as he suggested. I relax and let myself feel the fun in the dancing. And it is fun!

The song smoothly changes into a slow song and he twirls me until I'm up against his chest. My right hand in his left, his left hand around my back, and my left wrapped around his right shoulder.

"You really think you can't dance?" he asks, again whispering in my ear. Even though it was a slow song, it was still too loud to speak at a normal volume and hear each other.

"You're just that good," I answer. "Don't let that go to your head."

He laughs, "I won't. But really, you are a good dancer. You followed my moves perfectly, like you'd done the dances before a million times."

"Again, you're just that good. I've never danced like that before, you're hand just knew where to go," I say.

As I finish talking, Dalton runs his hand up my back. "My hands tend to have a mind of their own."

That delicious shiver is back, goosebumps cover my arms. "I'm okay with that."

"Really?" he asks, his hand sliding back down, starting to inch closer to my ass.

"Well, no, not in public," I say, squeezing his hand that's holding mine. His other hand stops just at the top of my pants waistline. A little bit of my skin is bare again, from all the twirling and flinging around we'd just done. His fingers find a little skin and the burn is back.

I put my forehead on his chest and let out a huge sigh.

"What's the matter?" he asks.

"Nothing," I say quietly.

"Something," he says. "Come on, let's go outside and talk."

I let him pull me off the floor. As we pass Emily and Brayden, she touches my arm.

She mouths, *Are you okay?*

I nod.

We go through the front this time, away from the crowd in the beer garden. We walk for a minute to find a quieter place to talk and find the perfect place, the empty picnic tables in front of the burger stands

Dalton sits on top of one and pats the spot beside him. I sit.

"Okay, spill," he says.

I shake my head, "I don't even know where to begin."

"How about what you were feeling when you put your head on my chest? You don't think I missed your huge sigh, do you?"

"It's just all a little overwhelming," I admit.

"What is?"

"All of this... these feelings... being able to talk to you so easily. Sometimes I feel like I'm saying too much," I say, putting my face in my hands. "I honestly didn't think I'd feel this way again... ever."

"Is that so bad?" he asks so earnestly that I look up at him. His face looks concerned but hopeful.

"No... not at all... just... unexpected? We just met."

"Some things... some people... just click and have a connection. This is a first for me but I've heard about it."

"I want to believe you. I want to trust you. Something inside me is saying that I can... that I can trust you with everything. I guess I'm just scared to let my guard down. I know what true pain feels like, true heartbreak, and I never want to feel that again. I'm not talking about breakups, yes those hurt and suck but... what I've gone through... not only was it an emotional and mental pain, it was physical as well. I don't want to lose another person that I fall in... I care about deeply," I catch myself before I say the word love. I can't love him. I can see how I could but we. just. met. I need to reel my feelings and emotions back in before they get too carried away.

"You can trust me. I wish you knew me longer so that you would know that but please, please believe me when I say that you can trust me. I would never do anything to hurt you. Again, why would I put someone I care about, through pain. I'm not that kind of guy," Dalton says, reaching for my hand as he speaks. I put his hand in both of mine and feel his warmth coming from just one hand. "What else are you afraid of?"

I take a minute before I respond. He squeezes my hand.

"You can trust me," he whispers.

With a sigh, I say, "I'm afraid that this," I wave my hand at myself. "This will all be too much for you once you realize my level of crazy."

He laughs. "What do you mean by crazy?"

I shrug, reluctant again.

"Don't stop now, keep talking to me. Explain so I can understand, so that I can put your fears at ease," he says, squeezing my hand once again.

"My crazy is my emotional rollercoaster. Like I said, some days... most days are good. But then some days aren't. Some days I feel like I can't do this, that I'm failing my kids. That I could be a better mom... that I'm not doing all I possibly can for them. Most days I feel like I have fully come to terms with Jayce being gone but then some days, Max will do something that reminds me SO much of his dad that it hits like a wrecking ball. Or one of the girls says something that sounds exactly like how Jayce said it, again, wrecking ball. It's like my defenses get used to everything but then those little things sneak through and I get hit, hard. I can usually handle it in the moment but come nighttime, it all comes crashing down. Nighttime is the hardest because that's when I physically miss him the most. I miss being held. I do all the holding now and I love my snuggles with my kids but I SO miss having arms big enough to hold me. I miss the late night talks. Falling asleep next to someone or in his arms. Just holding hands," this time I squeeze his hand. "I miss it all so much. Which makes me feel guilty. For wanting it all again."

"Wow..." I look up at him. He sounds so forlorn.

"See, crazy... And I've probably said too much," I say, letting go of his hand and putting my face in my hands.

"No, Lainey... please... look at me," he's trying to pull my hands away. I feel him stand up and get in front of me.

He gently grabs hold of my hands again and pulls at them, I let him pull them away. He squats down in front of me. He's tall enough that his eyes are in line with my nose.

"I said 'wow' because I'm shocked that you can feel all that," he says. He takes his hat off and sets it beside me, so that he can look at me better. He takes my hat off too, probably so I can't hide under it, which I'm trying to do. "Lainey, I don't have kids but I can say, even with the small amount of time we've spent together, that you are a great mom. I can also say for certain that a typical mom, who hasn't had to go through what you have, feels the same as you. Being a mom is one of the hardest jobs out there, I know this, I put my mom through hell as a teenager, but she was one of the best. Your kids know how much you love them. They'll look back on their childhood and only see the love and support you gave them. You shouldn't waste any more time worrying about what kind of mom you're being or should be. I can tell, you are a great mom, just by the fact of you worrying about if you are or not." He kisses my hands. "And as far as your roller coaster ride of emotions about Jayce. That's to be expected too. The fact it's only been 18 months and you average more good days than bad, shows your true strength but even if it was 18 years from now, you'll still have those feelings. You loved Jayce, he was taken from you suddenly and unexpectedly, those scars never go away. But if you let someone in to help with the phantom pain they leave behind, you can learn to live with it better. It'll become a dull pain, not so much a sharp and demanding pain. Let someone hold you when you feel like you're falling apart."

I just stare at him. He tilts his head to the side.

"Am I wrong?" he asks quietly.

I shake my head no. He wipes a tear off my cheek. I didn't know I was crying. I put both hands on his face and lean forward and kiss him softly on the mouth.

"Thank you," I say. "I don't think anyone has

understood me lately, quite as well as you do."

"Are we interrupting something?" Emily asks. Dalton stands up and I look over at her. "Lainey, are you okay?"

"I'm fine, just spilling my guts out to Dalton and scaring him away," I say, laughing a little as I wipe my tears away.

"Not scaring me away at all," he says, pulling me up with one hand so that I'm standing on the seat of the picnic table. It's sad that I'm so much shorter than him that his head just comes to my chin.

"It's starting to get rowdy in there so we were just talking about going back to my house," Emily says, smiling up at me.

I look at Dalton, he says, "Sounds good to me but I need to call my buddy and tell him he's on his own tonight. I'll go get the pickup and bring it around, wait here?"

"Yup," I say, smiling at him. He kisses me deeply and then walks away. I stare after him, smiling like an idiot again.

"I'll go get my car," Brayden says, he also kisses Emily before he walks off towards the direction of the parking lot.

"He's so dreamy," Emily says in a high pitch voice. She jumps up on the picnic table and sits down. I sit beside her. "Spill girlfriend!"

With a huge sigh I say, "I don't even know where

to begin. It's kind of been a whirlwind."

"Start from the beginning, don't leave anything out," she suggests.

So I tell her about when I first saw him. About bumping into him at the beer garden. About him finding SaraLee and asking her my name. He tracked me down. We talked. He rode. How we spent our dinnertime. Dancing. And then the talk we just had.

"Holy shit!" she says. "Sorry, but holy shit!"

"I know... what do I do?" I ask.

"What do you want to do?" she counters.

"I know what my body wants but I don't think I should. I don't know how it'll affect me emotionally... mentally," I say, looking down at my hands.

"Then don't think," Emily says, nudging me with her shoulder. I look at her in surprise. "I'm serious. For once, just do something for yourself because you want to and because it'll feel sooo good."

"You act like I don't do anything for myself, ever."

"You don't," she says as I look at her doubtfully. "Okay, tell me one time you did something because you wanted to and it was something YOU wanted to do."

"Today... tonight."

"Wrong and wrong. You went to the rodeo today because SaraLee needed a ride and you only agreed to come to the dance because I asked you to come with me."

"Okay..." I try to think of a time to tell her that I did something for myself.

A few minutes go by and she says, "You can't think of a time, can you?"

"There has to be, let me think."

"If it doesn't come to you right away, it's been WAY too long since it happened. I bet it was pre-Jayce."

I try to think harder but there isn't anything that comes to mind. I've done things for my family since the moment Jayce and I started dating and then when the kids were born. Was there seriously not a time that I did something for myself because it's what I wanted to do?

"Don't think about it... just do what feels right, what feels good," Emily says, wagging her eyebrows at me. I bump into her shoulder, laughing. But then she gets a little more serious as she says, "Just think of it as a 'right now' thing. Nothing serious. Just something fun and casual."

"Oh there you are Elianahhh!" SaraLee says from the corner of the burger stand that's closest to the clubhouse.

"Hey, SaraLee," I say.

"Where did you run off to? I didn't see you after the rodeo," she pauses for a second and leans in, squinting her eyes at me. An evil smile spreads across her face and she laughs just as evilly. "What's the matter? Have you been crying? Did Prince Cowboy decide to find someone more... how do I say this nicely... more his caliber?"

My mouth actually pops open. Before I can say anything though, Emily is standing up.

"You jealous, selfish, bitch! Just because he wanted nothing to do with you, doesn't mean he's ditched Lainey!"

"Oh really, Emmmily? Where is he then?" she asks, putting her hands on her hips.

"I'm right here, actually," Dalton walks up behind her. "You ready Lainey?"

"Yeah," I say. I walk around SaraLee, but then turn and say, "You'll need to find a different ride home."

"What? But Elainah!" she starts to protest and then sways.

"And maybe lay off the alcohol you drunk ass ho," Emily says.

Just as we're turning the corner, Brayden pulls up in his car, right next to Dalton's running pickup.

"Seriously Lainey, if you don't smack her next time, I will," Emily says, she's seething.

"She's drunk and her ego is bruised," I say. Emily looks at me like she's about to say something, so I change course, "Okay, okay, I won't excuse her behavior. I'll have a talk with her. If she doesn't start making some changes, I'll be done hanging out with her... errrr giving her rides places at least."

We get to the rigs and Dalton says, "We'll follow

you."

I stand with my hands behind my back and let him open the door, he smiles in approval. I get in and put my seatbelt on while he jogs around the pickup once again.

When he's in and situated, I say, "We'd be driving right now if you'd let me get the door for myself, you know?"

"We can spare a minute or two for some chivalry. It's a dying courtesy but I will be damned if I allow it to disappear while I'm able to still do it."

I just stare, again.

"Am I wrong?" he asks, smiling at me.

"No," I answer truthfully.

"Well then, stop trying to get me to not be chivalrous for you," he offers me his hand as he pulls behind Brayden. I take it and he squeezes gently before he pulls it to his mouth and kisses it.

A vibration runs down my spine, yet again. And I think about what Emily said about doing something just because I wanted to, to follow what feels good.

Dalton kissing me feels good. I wonder what it would feel like if he kissed up my hand, up my arm, across my collarbone, and up to my neck?

I get visible goosebumps on the arm of the hand he's holding and I shiver.

"Are you cold?" he asks, surprise in his voice.

"No," I say before I can stop myself, before I can

think of something better to say.

"Then why the goosebumps and shiver?"

"I don't know," I say, my face turning an embarrassing bright red.

"Why are you turning red?" he asks, leaning forward to look at me better. "If you don't know."

I turn my face away, acting like I'm looking out the side window. No way was I going to tell him about what I was just thinking.

"Why won't you tell me?" he laughs. "I'll just think it's something you thought that was naughty... something dirty." He waggles an eyebrow at me.

"You wouldn't be wrong," I mumble but not silently enough.

"What!?" he laughs out. "You were thinking something naughty?"

I cover my face, it's so much warmer than I ever remember it being.

"No! No! I wasn't."

"You're a bad liar," he's laughing hard now. He pulls at my hand. "It's okay, Lainey. I've probably thought it and most definitely have thought worse."

I look up in surprise, "Really?"

"You won't tell me what it was you were thinking but I am a guy. We tend to have naughty, errant thoughts most of the time. We can, usually, control what we say, but our thoughts, they're a little harder to control," he smiles a devilish smile at me.

My heart stops, I know it did because it picks up pace trying to make up for the beats it just missed.

"I think you'd be surprised how dirty a girl's mind can be. If you could spend time in one, you'd look at us differently," I say smiling back and then laughing at the look on his face.

"Really?" his turn to be incredulous.

All I answer with it, "Yup!"

"Well, now you have to tell me what you were thinking about and what you have thought about in the past!"

"No, you need to concentrate on driving. If I told you, you might wreck."

He purposely swerves a little, "Is that so?"

"Without a doubt," I say.

"Gaaaaaahhhh," he growls. "Not knowing isn't better. Now you've got me thinking."

"You weren't already?"

"Not in the moments leading up to now, no."

I laugh and look out the front window. We're almost to La Grande.

"I'm going to text Emily and tell her we're making a quick stop. If you don't mind?"

"Not at all," Dalton says a little too enthusiastically and wiggles his eyebrows at me.

I laugh, "Not for anything close to what you're thinking."

"Oh man... I was just following our train of

thoughts," he laughs and winks, letting me know he's kidding.

"Actually, I want ice cream. DQ sounds good, don't you think?"

"You know, I can't think of the last time I had a DQ ice cream," he admits, thinking hard.

"No way, I have one at least every other week," I laugh. "Let's fix that."

I pull out my phone and send Emily a quick text about our detour. I ask if they want anything and that we'll meet them at her house.

She replies back quickly.

Emily- *2 cookie doughs please, the smallest they have.* 12:47am

Me- *U got it.* 12:47am

We pull into DQ and place our order.

As we pull out towards the main road, I say, "Head up towards the college. She lives not too far from there."

Chapter 4

We eat our ice cream in silence. Just enjoying each other's company and DQ of course.

"After the stop sign, turn right. The yellow house on the right is hers. You'll see Brayden's car in the driveway. You should be able to park behind him."

"Yes, ma'am."

Something else I'll have to get used to if we spend much time together.

He's just polite, that's all it is, nothing about age.

We pull in behind Brayden's car and park. As I reach for my door, he clears his throat.

I laugh and sit back, waiting. He jumps out and walks, deliberately slow, around the pickup. I laugh again.

"You'll get used to it," he says as he offers me his hand as I slide out.

"Maybe," I say playfully and then get on my tiptoes and kiss his cheek.

He turns his face quickly and kisses me on the lips. I put Emily and Brayden's ice cream on the pickup bed frame, at least I thought I was, I hear them splatter as they hit the ground.

Ohhh well....

I wrap my arms around Dalton's neck and pull him into me. He pushes me into the back door of the pickup, pinning me between it and him.

I can feel a hardening in his groin area, I smile.

"What?" he asks, kissing down my neck to my collarbone. My earlier fantasy is coming to fruition.

I gasp, "Nothing..."

"Mmmm, nothing like before?" he groans out into my neck.

"Something like that," I breathlessly say.

He kisses back up to my mouth and kisses me deeply.

"Hey Lainey, you out here?" I hear Emily ask from the front door.

Dalton and I jump apart like a couple of teenagers getting caught by their parents. We laugh, I blush.

"Over here," I holler over to her. "There was an accident with your ice creams, though."

"Did you eat them again?" she asks, laughing.

"Rude... but no, they fell," I say, laughing. She was never going to let me forget about the ONE time I ate her ice cream I was bringing her. To be fair, it was more milk than anything when I ate it, it was such a hot day that day.

Dalton picks up the now mostly empty ice cream cups and we walk around the pickup towards the house.

"Here, put those in here," Emily says, holding up her little porch trash can. "We're in the back."

We walk through the house and out the back door. She's got a cute little patio set setup. Her outside cooler is open.

"You guys want something to drink? I have beer and harder stuff in the house," she says.

"I think I want to make a drink. You know how beer gives me a headache if I drink too much of it," I say.

"I'll have whatever you make," Dalton says.

"You sure? She has everything," I say, looking up at him.

"Yeah, just make two of whatever you make," he says, kissing me on the cheek and then he goes and sits across from Brayden. They start talking, or Brayden starts asking Dalton questions about bull riding.

I follow Emily into her house, to the kitchen, I'm grinning like an idiot, yet again. I've been smiling like this so much today. I should probably be worried about myself, but I can't find that worry, just... happy.

Echoing my thought, Emily says, "You look happy. Like really happy. Happier than I've seen you in… well you know how long."

"Emily, I haven't felt this happy since before Jayce's accident. I thought I had, had happy days this last year and a half but this happiness… it runs deep."

"But we're keeping our feelings casual, right?"

"Oh yeah, emotionally, I'm in check. But physically…?" I grin.

"Really?!"

"Yeah, I think so… If the opportunity comes up," I wink at her and waggle my eyebrows suggestively and laugh. "Then I'll take it. Casual… I can do casual… One time… A one night stand? I've never had one of those, if that's what he wants…"

"Wow! Good for you!" Emily says while she pulls glasses out of the cupboard.

My thoughts instantly start to spiral.

"Emily…" she turns at the change in my voice. "What if I CAN do this? Does that make me a slut? A ho?" Panic really starts to creep into my voice.

"Breathe, Lainey," she says, coming to stand in front of me. "Having one one-night stand, if that's what happens, in your 37 years of life does not make you a slut or a ho. If you were to do this every night with a different guy, for your entire life, than maybe, but a couple fun nights are okay."

"What if I CAN'T do it?" I ask, still a little panic in my voice.

"Then you have a fun night of making out. You

two seem to enjoy that," she winks.

"Yes, yes we do," thinking of Dalton kissing me simmers me down in one way but excites me in another.

"Remember, don't think too much about it. Just go with the flow and have fun. You deserve some fun," Emily says as she gently shakes my shoulders. "You feel tense. Let's make you a drink so you can relax a little."

"Just do a V-cran, those always taste good," I say getting the cranberry juice out of the fridge.

"A V-cran so your V-can!" Emily says wiggling her eyebrows and thrusting her hips. She laughs as she stops and reaches for the vodka. I can't help but laugh too.

We get back outside with our drinks, Dalton moves the blankets that were on the chair next to him so that I can sit beside him.

"Thanks," I say as I hand him his drink.

He takes a drink and then asks, "Vodka cranberry?"

"Yeah, is that okay?" I ask back,

"Yeah, they're a good summer drink. Good choice," he says as he puts it on the table in front of us. He puts his hand on my leg and squeezes gently.

Breathe, Lainey. His hand on your leg isn't anything to get this excited about. Chill. I think to myself.

"I was just asking Dalton about his ranch, it sounds huge," Brayden says, thankfully interrupting my thought process.

"How big is it?" Emily asks and she looks sideways at me and winks the eye closest to me, so that only I can see it. I hit her leg with mine but hide my smile by taking a drink.

"Umm, pretty big," Dalton says. I spit some drink out and a small laugh bursts out, Emily does the same.

"What?" Brayden asks cluelessly.

"Nothing... it's nothing," I say.

Dalton looks at me with his head crooked to the side a little, eyes narrowing playfully, "Nothing like before when we were on our way here?"

I pick my drink up to my mouth and shrug and mumble, "Maybe," as I take a drink.

"Interesting," he says. He squeezes my leg again, only a little more intensely. I have to take a deep breath but do it in a way that no one notices. Luckily Brayden draws their attention.

"It's over a million acres," he says.

"What?" Emily and I exclaim together.

"I said it was huge," Dalton says and then squeezes my leg again. I smile and let out a small laugh.

Now who's being suggestive? I ask myself.

"Is it all farm ground?" Brayden asks again. Thank goodness for Brayden. His curiosity is saving me from too much embarrassment.

"Over half is forest, where we take the cattle late spring, early summer, and where they graze during the summer. We have pastures for all the horses and farm ground. We feed on most of the farm ground during the winter months," Dalton says.

"That's cool," Brayden says.

They talk about Brayden's job for a little bit. Brayden asks again about Dalton's rodeo career.

"I'm not sure how much longer I'll be riding. I enjoy it but I'm not getting any younger and I do have a ranch to run, I can't do that if I'm in a full body cast," Dalton says laughing.

"I guess not," Brayden says. "I wish I could have seen you ride today, I bet that was one hell of a show."

"Lainey watched him, didn't you Lainey?" Emily says. I can see her eyes glinting with excitement which is her sign that she's getting tipsy which means she's going to become all sorts of crude. "How did he look riding?"

I give her a 'stop it' look but smile and I say, "He looked like he knew what he was doing." I can't help my smile getting bigger, I know where that would take Emily's thoughts.

"I bet he does," she waggles her eyebrows at me. Dalton squeezes my leg again, he saw her brow waggle.

Shaking my head I look away from them all because I'm smiling like an idiot again.

"What's the trampoline for?" Dalton asks. "Do you have kids?"

"No, no kids yet. I got it for when Lainey and

her kids come over," Emily says, smiling at me warmly. She's always loved my kiddos like her own.

"I haven't been on a trampoline in years," he says. He stands up and walks over to it.

"Go," Emily whispers to me.

I stand up and walk over to him.

"Wanna jump with me?" he asks, a childlike excitement shining in his eyes.

"Sure," I say.

We kick off our boots and crawl up the ladder and start jumping slowly. We both laugh and start jumping higher. I can see what Dalton is going to do before he does it but I can't stop myself before he does it. He double bounces me and I fly into the air. My direction isn't what he was expecting and I crash into him on my way back down. We tumble to the trampoline. Laughing until we stop. He's on top of me. One of my legs is bent up, while he lays on the other.

"You planned that, didn't you?" I ask, teasingly.

"No, this was a happy mistake," he says. He leans down and kisses me. He moves his body just a little so that he's not lying directly on my leg anymore but he's more straddling it. He puts a hand on my bent knee.

Once again my body takes over before I can control it and I pull him down on top of me even closer. Our kissing intensifies and the fire in my stomach erupts. A small moan escapes my mouth. Dalton lets out a similar sound.

CHAPTER 4

His hand slides down my bent knee, down my thigh. He runs it over my ass for a second before he slows his progress. Maybe waiting for me to tell him to stop? I don't say a thing, I just keep kissing him, opening my mouth a little wider, wanting more of his mouth on mine. He slowly moves his hand up the side of my stomach. His thumb running over my ribcage. His breath catches a little as his thumb slightly rubs the bottom of my breast that's encased in my bra. His hand runs up the side of my breast, not stopping too long but it slows enough that I notice. I'm aching for more. To feel the touch of his hand on my skin.

His hand keeps moving upward until it's wrapped around the back of my neck, pulling my mouth closer to his, if that's even possible.

"Soooo, we're gonna go inside, here's some blankets if you guys want them," Emily says from the edge of the trampoline. I jump... caught yet again. I keep forgetting there are other people in the World when Dalton and I start kissing.

"Thaaaanks," I say, embarrassed.

"No problem," she laughs. "Carry on."

Shaking my head and laughing, I reach over my head and pull the blankets towards us.

Dalton rolls off of me to the right, his left arm slings over his face.

"What's the matter?" I ask, rolling to my side and into him. It's hard to lay on a trampoline with someone and not roll into them.

"Nothing, just need a minute," he says, breathing hard.

"A minute for what?" I ask, smirking.

"To calm down," he says, peeking at me from under his arm.

"Oh…" I say. I run a finger from his elbow down to his shoulder. "Why do you need to do that?"

I see and feel him shiver. He puts his arm down and looks at me. "If I don't, I'm going to keep doing more. Wanting more and I don't think you're wanting that."

"What makes you think that?" I say as I slide my left leg up and over his legs.

He takes a deep breath before saying, "Uhhhh.. I just assumed…"

"How does it feel to assume wrong?" I ask teasingly. I slide all the way on top of him, straddling him, and start kissing him again.

He runs both his hands from my knees, up my thighs, and puts them on my ass. He leaves them there for a minute, lightly, like he's waiting for me to tell him to get them off, but again, I don't. I suggestively push my hips into his.

"Ugh," a groan escapes his lips. I kiss down his neck this time. Hoping it drives him as crazy as it did me when he did it. His hands start moving again, this time they go under my tank-top. They move up my back until he touches my bra strap.

I sit up, his hands pause at my shoulder blades. I grab the top of his shirt and look at him questioningly. He nods and a small smile spreads across his face. I pull gently and the button let loose. I slowly pull at the buttons, all the way down until I get to where it's tucked into his pants. I pull on it until it's completely untucked and finish unbuttoning it. He sits up and lets me pull it over his shoulders and then lifts his hands up over his head so I can pull it completely off. He never takes his eyes off of mine. I stare at him, smiling, until I look away to toss his shirt to the side.

Fuuuuuuck..... I think as I look back at his bare upper body.

He's so fucking hot. His shoulders are nothing but muscle. As he lays back down, I can see them ripple. I run my hands from his elbows, up his massive biceps, and up to his shoulders. I lightly touch his muscles there and then place them on his pecs. He breathes in slowly, his eyes shutting. I run one finger between his pec muscles down to where his abs start.

Is a ten pack a thing for abs? I think to myself.

I place my palm on his abs, he catches his breath. His eyes pop open. He leans up, wraps his arms around me, and then rolls us until he's on top again.

"You have got to stop touching me like that," he growls.

"Why?" I ask, running my hands up and down his

arms.

"Because, Lainey, I want..." he takes a deep breath. "I don't think you're ready for this. I think..."

"Stop thinking..." I whisper as I lean up and kiss him passionately. I lay back down and say, "I want this. I want you, right now. That's all I'm thinking about. That's all I'm going to think about right now. Everything else... I can deal with it later."

Dalton exhales and leans down into me, kissing me deeply.

"Are you sure?" he asks as he kisses my neck again. Sending fire soaring from there to my toes.

I reach down and grab my tank-top and pull it off. He gasps.

"Yes... please... just please... stop thinking and kiss me," I plead out between breaths. I don't know where this bravado is coming from but it's giving me the encouragement to keep going.

Dalton doesn't waste any more time. He bends down and starts kissing me. This time I maneuver myself so that my legs are on either side of his hips. A groan deep in his throat comes up through his lips, which causes them to part. I again take advantage of that and slip my tongue in slightly. Another deep groan but this time it rumbles in my mouth. Our kissing becomes more intense. He blindly reaches to the side and grabs a blanket and flings it over the top of us.

Dalton takes his right hand out from behind me

and runs it over my stomach, until it's cupping my left breast.

"Mmmm," I moan out and pull my mouth away from his. Goosebumps popping up all over my arms from the shiver of delight running through me.

I bite my bottom lip as he starts to kiss down my neck again. Instead of stopping at my collarbone, he continues kissing down to the top of the breast he's cupping, squeezing it lightly. I arch my back, pushing my breast into his hand and lips more. Another moan from him and he slides my bra cup down and pulls my nipple into his mouth.

"Oh god," I say, breathlessly.

He reaches behind me and skillfully unclasps my bra. He pulls it down, exposing both of my breasts. My nipples harden from the cool night air and from him sucking on one and holding the other between his fingers. He wraps his hand around it, his palm pressing into my nipple.

He grinds his hips into mine, I feel his hardening bulge press into my pelvic bone. He lets out a long moan.

"Do you have a... a condom?" I breathlessly ask, slightly embarrassed for asking but happy to know that a portion of my brain was still thinking coherently and responsibly.

"Would you think I was presumptuous if I said yes?" he asks into the skin between my breasts.

"No… I'd think you're… prepared… and… responsible… and I'm… grateful…" I say while breathing hard.

"Good," is all he says before he sticks my other nipple in his mouth and starts to flick it with his tongue.

"Oh fuuuck," I moan. Hot pleasure shoots through my chest and down to my core.

"Mmmmmm," is his only reply.

He kisses back up my neck, taking my mouth with all of his. His tongue and mine doing a type of dance. I can feel him reaching for the button of my pants, I reach for his as well.

We somehow shimmy out of our pants, quite the task on a trampoline, but we do it and are laying in our underwear.

I run my hand, palm down, down his back, over his ass, and then run the back of it up his stomach. He shivers. I run it back down his stomach, slower this time, I get to the top of his underwear and slide two fingers in between the band and his skin.

He moans and pushes his hips closer to me. I slide my fingers further into his underwear and feel the tip of his throbbing erection immediately.

Damn!! I mentally shout. I reach my hand all the way in and try to wrap my hand around the pulsing shaft but my thumb and middle finger are far from touching. *SHIT!!*

I slowly start to rub it up and down, trying to hit the base before going back up to the tip. He moans deep in his throat again, thrusting into my hand.

He moves his mouth to my breast again, while moving one of his hands down to my undies. He slowly starts to rub my mound.

"Shit..." I say loudly and then cover my mouth with my free hand. *Fuck it* I think. "Get them off and get that thing on." I reach down and start to pull my undies off.

He grunts out, "Yes, ma'am!" He rips his underwear off faster than I would have thought possible. He reaches over me and pulls something out of his pants pocket. I hear the sound of a wrapper ripping open and realize he'd gotten the condom.

Breathe... Just breathe... It'll all be fine... STOP THINKING!!!

"Are you sure?" he asks. "We can stop, right here, right now."

"I'm sure," I whisper out.

He hesitates, looking me in the eyes. I bite my bottom lip again before reaching up and pulling him towards me, kissing him deeply. I wrap my legs around his hips and use my heels to push his ass down towards me.

With a moan of surrender, he pushes his hips down. I reach down and place the tip of him to me. Another moan escapes him.

I don't have to tell him to go slow, he does it on

his own.

Oh the pain! Oooooh the pleasure!

I try not to show the pain on my face, only the pleasure, but Dalton can probably feel how tense I'd gotten because he slowly pulls away and then pushes back in even slower.

I breathe in sharply.

"Are... you... okay?" he asks through clenched teeth. Oh yeah, he was holding back.

"Yes, don't stop," I whisper.

Dalton slowly pulls back and then comes back down. He gets a rhythm going, picking up speed slowly. After a while of this, I relax completely, then he pushes all the way in. I hadn't realized he hadn't been completely in.

I gasp and then follow immediately with a moan.

"Oh yes," I whisper out.

Dalton takes that as the 'go ahead' to speed up and thrust a little harder. His moans and grunts get more aggressive and louder as he goes. He slides a hand back down and starts rubbing my mound again.

Just a little lower... oh god, just a little lower... please... Dalton... a little... OH!!! I was mentally giving directions when Dalton's fingers found the spot I was aching for them to find. Pure, hot, delicious fire of ecstasy shoots through my body. Starting at my core and spreading out to my toes and fingers. Had pleasure had flames, it would be coming out the top of my head and the tips of my toes.

"Oh shit Dalton, yes... harder... faster..." I scream into my hand which I had clamped down over my mouth the second he'd found the spot. He keeps rubbing, adding a little more pressure and going a little faster. My inside walls squeeze around him as he thrusts in again and I hit my climax.

A deep, from my gut, groan rolls up my throat.

"Oh god Dalton!" I scream into my hand.

"Oh... shit... Lainey..." Dalton moans out. He's buried as deep as he can get. His mouth is pressed against my neck, muffling his growls of his own ecstasy and climax.

We shiver and jerk against each other for a minute before he slowly lowers himself so that he's lying fully on top of me. The trampoline gives enough that he's not squishing me. It's actually very comforting, having his weight on me.

"You okay?" I ask, slightly laughing but breathing hard.

"Better than okay," he says, kissing my neck. "Are you?"

"I think so," I answer truthfully. "I'm still riding the high."

"I know what you mean," he says, kissing my cheek. "By the way, you have a potty mouth."

I turn my head in embarrassment. "I know, my

ever so careful self-control and lady like behavior kind of goes out the window during sex."

"I noticed," he says laughing but pulls my face back towards him and he kisses me deeply again. "I like it."

"Yeah?"

"Oooh, yeeeah!"

"Well good," I laugh, kissing him.

After a minute of kissing, he rolls off of me but pulls me with him so that I'm lying half on him, half on the trampoline.

"This is a first for me," he says and then pats the trampoline when I look at him questioningly.

"Oh, yeah, me too," I say. The high from my climax is starting to dissipate and the reality of what just happened is starting to set in.

I just had sex... I just had sex with someone that wasn't Jayce... I just had sex with someone I just met today... What the actual fuck was I thinking?

Dalton must have felt the change in my body, he must be good at reading people, because he says, "Lainey.... Lainey? Hey, are you okay?"

I hadn't realized I was crying until a tear ran across my nose into my other eye. Dalton sits up the best he can on his side and wraps an arm around me.

"Hey, it's okay," he says, shushing me.

"It's just..." I take a deep breath. "It's just the first time, you know. I told you I'd be an emotional rollercoaster."

"And I said I'd be here to hold you when they hit," he says, pulling me closer to him. That genuine gesture and the feel of his strong arms around me, sends me over the edge and I burst out bawling

I'm not sure how long we lay like this, me bawling, him just holding me and rubbing my back. But soon, the tears stop and I hiccup myself into silence.

"Better?" Dalton asks.

I shrug. He leans back like he's going to lay down but reaches up and over his head. When he comes back, he's got his shirt in his hand. He wraps it around me and then pushes all the buttons closed. He then reaches above our heads and grabs his pants and awkwardly puts them on. He then rearranges me so that I'm lying on him with my chin on his chest.

"Now?" he asks, smiling that heartbreakingly beautiful smile I was starting to love.

Love? No, not love... adore... Do not start thinking about the word love, Lainey... Casual... Keep it casual...

"Yes, thank you," I say, kissing his nose.

"We should talk," he says.

"About?"

"What just happened and how you feel about it."

"It was amazing and then I completely ruined it by melting down."

"Why did you melt down so hard?"

I sigh and take a couple deep breaths before answering him.

"Honest, full answer?" I ask.

"Yes, always. I always want the full answer."

"Okay" I say, *You asked for it.* "Because you were... are... you are being so sweet and genuinely caring. And the feel of your arms around me... I've missed that... probably more than anything. I have missed being held. I hold my kids daily but I have missed being the one to be held. I've missed the feel of a man's body lying beside me. Just the presence you guys have, the warmth you put off, I've missed that... Add that to having my first sexual encounter and climax in 18 months... And then add that to the thought that I just had sex with someone that wasn't my late husband... AND add all that to me having sex with someone I just met today... something I have never done before, ever... like ever, ever... it all kind of hit. I thought I'd be able to handle it all better and I probably could have if you weren't so damn great."

As I was talking, Dalton had started to rub my back, rub my arms, all subconsciously.

"All very reasonable to have a meltdown," he says, very understandably.

"See that right there. Are you a therapist as well as a ranch, slash farmer, slash bull rider?"

"No?" he says it like a question.

"Most guys wouldn't be this understanding... this caring... this sweet..."

"Lainey, when are you going to believe me when I say I'm not like most guys?"

"When you tell me what's wrong with you?"

"What do you mean?" he asks laughing. He knows I'm joking but kind of not.

"You can't be this perfect."

"Come move cows with me and you'll see just how NOT perfect I am," he laughs.

I laugh too but say, "No but seriously…"

"I don't know what to tell you Lainey… I was raised by parents that taught me morals and how to treat people… not just women, but people… My dad was a huge inspiration to me, he treated my mom like she was the reason the sun came up in the morning and the moon shone at night. And he wasn't afraid to show it. My mom, she taught me it was okay to be a man but to also be soft and caring… I don't know… maybe I was raised differently than most the guys you know."

"Well, I can say one thing for sure… your parents raised one hell of a man."

"Thank you, I appreciate that," he kisses me.

"Speaking of your parents, do they live in Montana too?" I ask.

"No, they passed away about seven years ago. First my mom and then my dad a couple months later. Mom died from cancer, it took her pretty quickly. Dad, I think he died from a broken heart. Doctors couldn't really give me and my sister a reason why he'd passed.

They called it natural causes."

"Oh, Dalton, I'm so sorry."

"It's okay, now... it was a rough couple of years but my sister and I got through it."

"Sister?"

"Yeah, Darcy. She's eight years older than me and still thinks she has to protect me from everything. You should have seen her when she found out what Sally had done. She wanted to drive to Bozeman and rip Sally's hair out," he laughs. "She's sweet but a spitfire. She's a nurse and she and her husband, Phil Davis, have a ranch in Wyoming. Their three boys, Craig, Tony, and Liam are in high school. Craig is about to graduate."

"Do you get to see them often?"

"Yeah, they come up every spring to help move the cattle. Darcy won't let holiday's go by without us all getting together. We still do all the family traditions Mom used to do."

"Wow, that's great."

He nods and then says, "Okay, no more heavy stuff." He situates himself back underneath me so that we're both comfortable. "What's your dream breakfast?"

Laughing again at how quickly he can switch topics, I say, "Well, being the foodie that I am and you have to understand that I wouldn't be able to finish all this food but I would say a breakfast sandwich from Mickey-D's with their hash-browns, a cinnamon roll, hash-browns and sausage gravy, and a side of bacon."

"Nothing to drink? Orange juice maybe?"

"No, if I'm going through a drive through coffee shop like D-Bros or Antlers here in La Grande, I usually get the sweetest coffee they have and then ask for half the espresso. I love the effects of coffee, I just don't like the taste of it. But if I'm running into a store or gas station, I really, really like the cold SB Caramel flavored coffee."

"I like the way you think. That breakfast does sound good," he says hugging me tightly.

We talk like this until the sun starts to come up.

Chapter 5

And that's the last thing I remember, was the sun coming up before I fell asleep. Now, as I stretch awake. I find that I'm alone on the trampoline.

"Dalton?" I ask out loud.

I sit up and see that he's gone but I still have his shirt on. I reach for my undies and pull them on, as well as my bra, pants, and tank top. I put his shirt over my arm and slide off the trampoline.

I put my boots on as I reach for my phone that's still in my pants pocket. And see that I have no new messages. Well of course he wouldn't call or message me, we didn't exchange numbers but I see that it's just after 7 o'clock. I must not have slept long.

I walk into Emily's house and holler, "Hello?"

"Lainey?" Emily says, sounding confused. I can tell where she's at... in the living room.

"Hey," I say, as I walk in and slump onto the couch.

"I thought you left," she says.

"Nope... Why did you think that?"

"Well... when I looked outside, it didn't look like anyone was on the trampoline and when Brayden took me to my car back at the clubhouse, we saw that Dalton's pickup was gone from my driveway."

I put my elbow on the arm of the couch and rub my face with my hand. I gloomily ask, "Oh, when was that?"

"He got called into work and had to leave at 5:45," she said, turning to look at me.

"Oh, okay" is all I say.

"Soooo, how was last night? Did you and Dalton...?" she leaves the last question open but she knows, I know what she's asking.

"Yes we did," I can feel my cheeks going red and despite my mood, a small smile crosses my face.

"You did!?" she asks. But, before I can answer she asks, "How was it?"

"Yeah... and it was great... really, really great," I say gloomier than before but still smiling.

Emily is quick and doesn't miss a thing so my mood doesn't take long for her to pick up on, "If it was so great, why so sad?"

"Because... because I tried really hard to keep it casual... to remind myself that it was a one night thing... nothing serious... but..."

She groans, "Did you catch feelings?"

I cover my face with the pillow beside me and scream into it, and then muffle out, "Yes..."

"Oh Lainey," Emily says. She sounds disappointed but also like she feels sorry for me.

I lay down on the couch and put the pillow on my lap and say, "I know... I knew I wasn't a 'one night stand' type of girl but I had to try, right?"

"Right!" Emily says, jumping at the chance to make me feel better. "And next time... NEXT time," she wiggles her eyebrows at me. "It won't be so hard or confusing. You had to get one under your belt... Wait, he was nice to you, wasn't he? He didn't try any weird shit with you, did he?"

I laugh, "No, he was absolutely amazing which I think is part of the reason I'm so thrown this morning. I thought we connected on a whole different level... not just the 'one night stand, just for sex' level... which is probably my problem as to why I'm so... blah about it now... I let myself believe it was something else, when he was thinking it was just a one night thing... And there will be no, 'next time'. I can't do this. I can't put my feelings aside just to have sex."

"It'll take some practice but you could," Emily says. "I'm not trying to talk you into becoming a hobag but you, Lainey, need an outlet for stress. I can see that you're upset about how this turned out but the sex was good for you, not in the 'ooh baby-baby' good for you... which maybe it was..." she looks at me hopefully, like I'm going to totally gush about last night but I just wink and nod. She giggles and claps her hands and then continues saying, "buuuut I can see a light in your eyes I haven't seen in a while. I can see you're relaxed more now. That sex-ipaide was good for you."

I just shrug. I did feel lighter in a way but I knew sleeping with random guys was not going to become a normal thing for me. I actually shudder at the thought.

KNOCK-KNOCK-KNOCK

I look over at Emily when the knocking at the door stops. She just shrugs and gets up to go answer the door in the other room.

"Oh, hi," she says, extremely cheerful. And then she hollers, "Lainey, it's for you."

Confused, I slide off the couch and walk to the door. I skid to a stop when I see who's standing there with bags in one arm and a drink carrier in the other.

"Good morning," Dalton says, smiling that smile that makes my heart sputter.

"Uhhh hi… errrr good morning," I mumble idiotically.

"Come on in, you know where the kitchen is," Emily says, sweeping her hand out in front of her for Dalton.

Dalton walks in but before he passes me, he kisses me sweetly on the cheek.

Emily walks after him but turns to me, claps silently, smiles, points at Dalton's back, and mouths, *OH MY GOD!*

I mouth back, *I KNOW!* I wave her on.

Dalton sets everything on Emily's huge kitchen island counter and turns towards us as we're walking into the kitchen.

He says, "I was trying to make it back before you woke up but seeing as you're awake, I failed at that… but hopefully this-" he points to the bags on the counter and drinks, and smiles. He then continues to say, "-will make up for that."

We walk over and see iced coffee and food containers in the bags.

"I wasn't sure what you drank… if you drank coffee… Emily, so I just got you the same thing I got Lainey, hopefully that's okay," he says to Emily, as she's looking in the bags.

"Oh, you are a saint, that'll work just fine," she grabs one of the drinks and takes a sip. "Well, I took a morning shift when I thought you two had left, so I need to go get ready for work."

"Okay," I say. I turn to Dalton and say, awkwardly, "Hi."

"Hi," he says smiling hugely at me.

"So you went and got food, coffee, and…" I look him up and down, "Changed?"

I didn't think he could look any hotter but in his

jeans and t-shirt, that was tucked into his pants a little in the front to show off his belt buckle, and a ballcap, he looked even better than in his cowboy clothes from yesterday.

"I did. My buddy lives outside of Imbler so I ran there really quick and took a shower and changed into my normal clothes. And then stopped by to get food and coffee on my way back," he says. "Is that okay?"

"Yeah, it's totally fine," I say. Inside, I'm soaring, so much happiness going on inside. But on the outside, I'm trying to keep it cool. I have GOT to get these damn emotions in check. I ask, mainly to distract myself, "Normal clothes?"

"Yeah, I don't normally dress like I did yesterday, that's only if I'm riding. I have to keep up the appearance of a bull rider," he laughs and winks at me. Then tilts his head to the side a little and bumps his shoulder into mine as he walks over to the other side of the counter and asks, "You thought I ditched you, didn't you?"

"No," I say, turning pink.

"You did too," he laughs.

"Well, what would you think?" I ask, giving him a mischievous look, as if I could leave him in the morning as he slept. *Psssh yeah right.*

"I would think the same, I suppose," he says, smiling apologetically at me.

Dalton offers me one of the coffees, another apology in his eyes. I take the coffee and smile. There is nothing he needs to apologize for, my emotional self just needs to simmer down.

"Mmmmm, this is good," I exclaim after taking a drink.

"Oh, I'm happy to hear that, I really didn't know what to order," he smiles, takes the last cup and takes a drink. "It is pretty good."

"How do you usually take your coffee?" I ask.

"Black."

"So why did you get that?"

"I wanted to see if it was any good."

I was about to respond when my phone buzzed and dinged.

"Sorry, it might be my sister," I say, reaching for it in my back pocket.

"Oh yeah, no worries," Dalton says, waving his hand like it was no big deal.

-New message from Emily-

"Or not," I say and look towards the door Emily had disappeared through. I whisper, "It's from Emily."

Dalton whispers back, "What's she have to say?" Curiosity blanketing his tone.

I open my Messages.

Emily- *I LIKE him. He's so nice. FUCKING HOT too.* 7:22am

CHAPTER 5

I read it out loud for Dalton. He laughs.

"THANK YOU!" he hollers towards her bedroom door. I stifle a laugh.

BUZZ-BUZZ

Emily- *U TOLD HIM WHAT I SAID!?!* 7:22am

"Yes!" Dalton answers her question by hollering it towards her again.

BUZZ-BUZZ

Emily- *Bitch...* 7:23am

I laugh because I know she's only kidding.

I reach over and grab the bag that has a big yellow 'M' on it and pull out two of the sandwiches and hash-browns. I offer one of each to Dalton.

"No thanks, I ate already," he says, waving me off.

"Oh," I say, setting it down.

"I'm sorry, I was going to wait but I get hangry when I don't eat breakfast first thing. I didn't want you to see that side of me just yet," he says and then his gorgeous smile spreads across his face.

"Oh, okay. That, I totally get."

"So what do you want to do today?" he asks.

"I don't know, I assumed you would want to go to the rodeo."

"No, not really. I would like to spend it with you, if that would be okay," he says as he slides a to-go container to me. I open it and see hash-browns and sausage gravy and a side of bacon. I reach for the other box and find a huge cinnamon roll.

He got everything. I think to myself.

Smiling, I say, "I'd like that."

"Okay, so what would you like to do?"

"Hmmmm... " I take a minute to think so I eat a little while I process our options. After a couple minutes, I say, "When's the last time you were up at Wallowa Lake?"

"I've never actually been up there. I've meant to go but have never had, or made, the time to go up."

"Why don't we go up there then? I haven't been in years."

"Sounds good to me."

"Do you mind if I call my sister real fast? I don't remember how good the cell service is up there and I'd like to check in on my kids before we head up."

"Oh, definitely, go for it," he says.

I open video chat on my phone and hit my sister's name.

"It'll only take a minute, then I'll get ready..." I look around, "Shoot... I left my bag in my Tahoe."

My phone starts connecting a call out.

"Well, I kind of got you some things," Dalton says, looking a little sheepish.

"What do you mean?" I ask.

"I... well... I looked at your clothes while you slept and got your sizes. I noticed they were all from Maurice's but since it's so early and they aren't open yet, I stopped in Wally World and got you the same size jeans and a similar color t-shirt. I also got a pack of socks and a pair of undies for you... Which by the way, was a lot of fun. I really enjoyed picking them out for you," he says, winking at me. And then, probably from the look on my face, he says in a rush, "Please don't be upset. I know some girls have issues with their clothes sizes, I just wanted to do something nice for you."

"I'm totally fine with that... I'm just not used to anyone going out of their way for me."

"Really?"

"Yup... Usually it's me doing thoughtful things. I actually prefer it."

"Why am I not surprised by that?" he says, shaking his head and laughing.

I just shrug.

"*Hello?*" comes my sister's voice from my hands.

I jump. I forgot I was calling her.

"Oh, Lucy! Sorry! Hi!"

"*Hey! You're up early. I would have figured you would be taking advantage of kidless mornings.*"

"Yeah, not this morning."

She tries to look behind me.

"*Where are you? That doesn't look like your house.*"

"I'm at Emily's."

"*Oh! Rough night last night? How was the rodeo and dance?*"

I look over at Dalton, he's smiling his devastatingly beautiful smile at me.

"*Who are you looking at? Is that Emily? Tell her to come say hi.*"

"It's... not Emily," I say.

"*Why are you smiling like an idiot? Who is it?*"

Dalton looks at me with a 'should I come over' look, I nod and wave him over. He walks over and stands behind me. I angle the phone so she can see him better.

Lucy's mouth falls open for a second but she recovers quickly. She looks at him and then at me.

"Lucy, this is Dalton Young. Dalton, this is my sister, Lucy."

"It's nice to meet you," Dalton says, smiling.

Lucy doesn't say anything. She just stares.

"Lucy?" I ask, trying to prompt her to speak.

"*But you're Dalton Young... the bull rider...*"

"Does everyone know who you are?" I ask, looking at him dumbfounded.

"Everyone but you," he says and then winks.

"*That's because Lainey doesn't like to watch things where someone might get hurt. She can't even watch those funny videos of people doing funny, stupid stuff, and getting hurt from it,*" Lucy says rolling her eyes and laughing.

"I can't laugh at things when people get hurt. I can only imagine how much it would hurt," I say, giving her the, 'stop saying embarrassing things', look.

"*Momma?*" I hear Nelly's voice from beside Lucy. Dalton steps to the side and back around to the side of the counter, where he was standing earlier.

"*Is that my momma?*" Nelly asks.

"*Yeah, you wanna say hi?*" Lucy asks. She lowers the angle down so that Nelly's adorable little face shows up.

"Hi Baby Girl," I say.

"*Hi Momma!*" she exclaims.

"How are you?" I ask, smiling.

"*Good,*" she says and adds, "*I don't miss you no more.*"

"That just means you're having fun at T-T's, doesn't it?"

"*So much fun! T-T painted my nails, look,*" she says as she holds up her little hands to show me her bright pink fingernails.

"Oh, Nelly, those are beautiful," I say.

"*T-T did them,*" she says smiling up at Lucy.

"She did a great job," I say, then ask, "Where's Bubba and Sissy?"

She looks over her shoulder and then says, "*Sleeping. Just me and T-T are up.*"

"That sounds fun. Are you being a good girl for T-

T and Uncle Peter?"

"*Yup,*" she says matter of factly.

"Good! Will you give Bubba and Sissy a hug for me when they wake up?" I ask.

"*Yup,*" she says cutely.

"T-T, will you give Nelly a hug for me?" I watch as my sister holds the phone out so I can see her give Nelly a big, one handed, hug. "Thank you." Lucy smiles at me. "Alright Nelly-Bug, I gotta go but I'll call again, probably tomorrow, okay?"

"*Yup. Love you, Momma!*" Nelly says sweetly.

"I love you too, Baby Girl!"

Lucy's face is back on my screen.

"*Tell Dalton it was nice meeting him,*" then she whispers, "*You have to call me and tell me all about how this happened.*"

Dalton smiles, he heard her.

"I will," I say, smiling. "Bye, Sis."

"*Bye,*" she says and then I end the call.

"You will?" Dalton asks as he walks over to me.

"Well, I have to now that she's seen you."

"You wouldn't have told her about me had I not shown my face?"

I think for a second, teasing him, and then I smile widely. "No, I would have told her. She wouldn't have believed me, though."

"Why not?" he asks as he wraps his hands behind my back and pulls me towards him.

"Because stuff like this doesn't happen in real life, at least not in my life," I say, looking up at him.

"This is your life and this is real," he says and then he kisses me.

My body, acting on its own again, closes whatever little space there was between us, and presses up against him.

"I'd say get a room but this IS my house," Emily says from behind us.

"Stop doing that," I say, jumping and stepping away from Dalton slightly.

"Doing what?" she asks innocently.

"Interrupting us," I say, laughing.

She shrugs and laughs too, "Here to help."

"Very helpful," I say, laughing harder.

She's got her scrubs on and her hair in a wet messy bun. She grabs her purse off the table and walks over to the counter.

"Anything left to eat?" she asks.

"Yeah, take half the cinnamon roll, that bag of sandwiches, and the rest of this," I say as I hand her what's left of the hash browns and gravy.

"Thanks and you know you can feel free to make yourself at home," she says. She laughs and then pauses and adds, "well, not TOO at home." She winks at me.

I shake my head, my cheeks going red for the hundredth time in less than 24 hours.

"Thank you," I say, sarcastically.

Emily smiles and then looks at Dalton, "And you... you keep doing what you've been doing. I haven't seen my best friend this happy in a long time."

"I can do that," Dalton says as I say, "Oooookay... thank you..." to Emily, pushing her to the front door. She smiles and hugs me when we get to the door.

She whispers in my ear, "Have fun! There's condoms in the bathroom, bottom drawer."

"Oh. My. Gosh! Emily!" I whisper-shout.

"I'm just sayin'," she whispers back and quietly laughs.

"Thank you," I say, yet again, sarcastically.

She winks and walks out the door laughing.

I walk back into the kitchen and see that Dalton is cleaning up.

"I guess I'll go jump in the shower," I say. "TV remote is usually on the coffee table, if you want to watch something."

"Sounds good," he says as he throws the last bit of garbage away.

I walk through Emily's room, to her bathroom. She always has better shower products in her bathroom and her shower is so much better than the guest shower. Emily's bathroom is huge. The shower itself is at least six feet by six feet. Two of the walls are rock and the others are glass.

I start the shower and then strip off my clothes. I am starting to take my hair out of my braid when there's a knock on the door.

"Yeah?" I ask.

Dalton mumbles something but between the roar of the shower and the door, I can't hear him.

"Sorry, what was that?"

The door opens and Dalton steps in, saying, "I said that--"

He stops dead in his tracks and stops talking. I freeze with my hands behind my head, my fingers half-way through taking my braid out.

"Woooow..." is all Dalton says, causing me to turn bright red. His eyes travel down my naked body, stopping here and there for noticeable extra moments before they travel back up to my face. "Just... wow!"

I can't help but smile. I let my hands fall to my sides. He's already seen everything, no reason to cover up now. He takes that as an invitation and steps up to me and kisses me passionately.

I wrap my arms around his neck and pull him down to me. His hands push on my lower back, pulling me into him.

His hard bulge has returned. Again, I smile.

I step away and slowly pull my hair the rest of the way out of my braid, I never take my eyes off of his. I see Dalton swallow hard.

"I know you've already showered, but..." I turn and walk towards the shower. I look over my shoulder, trying to flirt with my eyes. I smile slyly and continue,

"You can join me, if you want to."

I open the shower door and step in.

"Ooooh, I want to," I hear Dalton say.

I look over and see him taking his clothes off. I step back into the water, letting my hair get drenched, and close my eyes.

I hear the shower door open and I open my eyes. I see Dalton stepping in.

"Damn," he says, looking at me.

"My thought exactly," I say, looking him up and down.

Seeing him in the light, made him more handsome. His muscles flex as he moves towards me. I look down and see his erection standing hard and strong. Now it's my turn to swallow hard.

The ache and the want are back but in higher demand. It's like my body remembers what happened only a few hours ago and it's demanding more… needing more.

I run my hands, wet from the water, up his arms. I glide them over his shoulders and down his pecs, marveling at his strength and beauty.

I slide one hand down his abs but stop just before the base of his erection. He shivers.

He shivers again and says, "You have no idea how good that feels."

I look down and grin. I look back up and slyly say, "I can tell."

His crooked smile is back on his face as he steps into me and starts kissing me deeply again. Our tongues start their dance. I can feel his hardness on my stomach.

As much as I don't want to stop kissing him, I make a decision and turn so my back is towards him. I push my ass up against him and I hear him exhale sharply and then moan. His lips are on my neck.

I reach behind me and grab his ass. He pushes into me as he runs a hand down my chest, stopping to gently grab one of my breasts.

Dalton's other hand slides around on my stomach and slowly moves down to the spot that has the most demanding need for his touch.

His fingers find my spot immediately and I gasp. He starts rubbing hard but slow. I rock my hips into his hand and back into him, feel his cock get even harder against my lower back.

"Oh... shit... Dalton," I moan out as heat builds even more in my core.

He slides his middle finger into me, using the heel of his hand to keep pressure on THAT spot.

"You're so wet," he moans into my ear.

"We ARE in the shower," I tease.

He growls into my ear, "That's not what I mean." He licks my ear and nibbles it a little. I shiver this time. He then starts to slowly slide his finger in and out, while rubbing me.

"Mmmmm...." I moan again. My head rolls back

against his chest. Dalton's fingers on my breast go to lightly pinching my nipple between his thumb and pointer finger.

I push my hips into his hand, in rythym with his fingers. He speeds up, adding another finger, pushing hard with his hand and pinching my nipple a little harder. All of that and the hot water hitting my front, sets me on the edge. When he sucks on my neck, I lose it. I climax hard and loud.

"Oh fuck, Dalton!" I scream, not bothering to cover my mouth.

I feel his cock twitch at my exclamation.

"Ughhh... Lainey... I want you," he groans into my ear.

"Hold that thought," I pant. I step out of the shower, on shaking legs, and quickly grab a condom out of the drawer Emily said they'd be in. I rip the wrapper open and toss it in the trash as I dash by it, back into the shower.

"Here," I say. Handing it to him. As he's putting it on, I turn him so he's standing in the stream of water now.

I run my hand up his sides until they're around his neck. I run my fingers in his hair, at the base of his neck. Then, I lean up and kiss him, pressing my breasts into him, feeling his erection press into my stomach again.

I run my hands through his hair, pulling him

down to me a little more so I can kiss him harder.

I slowly stop kissing him and then I run my tongue down his neck, to his collarbone. He shivers again. He runs his hands over my hair. I kiss across his upper chest and then down to one of his nipples where I flick and tease it with my tongue for a second. I then pull it into my mouth with my lips and suck on it hard for just a second before moving over to his other nipple and doing the same thing.

"Oh god, Lainey," he moans, rocking his hips into me harder.

I kiss back up to his mouth and kiss him passionately before turning my back to him again.

With my ass right up against his thighs, I bed over, slowly. Holding on to the little built in bench with one hand, I reach back with the other and gently grab hold of his cock. I slide it down until it's at my entrance.

Dalton has to bend down a little to get the angle right but when he does, his tip slides in easily.

"Awww...." I moan.

Dalton echoes my pleasure.

"Fuck, Lainey, you're still so tight," he moans out.

"Mmmm...." is the only reply I can manage.

He slides his erection further into me, causing me to take an involuntary half step forward. He moves his hands that were on my back, down to my hips, and pulls me back to him. When he does this, his full length enters me.

"Ahhhhhh-awww!!" I scream in pleasure.

Dalton tries to go slow but that speed doesn't last long. Quickly, he speeds up. His grip on my hips tightening, holding me in place as he thrusts into me.

"Oh god... yes, Dalton... yes... yes... don't stop..." I plead.

As he starts pushing in and pulling out faster, harder, I reach down between my legs with my hand to my spot and start rubbing with my fingers, in time with him.

"Oh... Dalton... Oh... Yes... Yes..." I can feel my climax building again.

"Lain...ey.. I'm... I can't... I'm going to..." Dalton's panting and grunting and with one last hard thrust, we both explode in ecstasy at the same time.

"Awwwww!! FUCK ME!" I scream.

"Shhhhiiiiit..." Dalton groans out.

His thrusting slows and we both stand straight. I put my hands on the rock wall to steady myself.

"My legs... feel like jello..." I pant out.

"That's a good thing... right?" Dalton says breathlessly.

"A very good thing," I laugh.

He runs his hand down my back and then up to my hair.

"Can I wash your hair?" he asks abruptly.

Stunned, I turn to him. I counter ask, "Do you want to?"

"Yeah, I've always wanted to wash a woman's hair in the shower. I don't know why, I've just always been fascinated by it."

"Sure, go ahead," I say, smiling.

"Hang on, let me get rid of this," he reaches down and removes the condom. He steps out of the shower, wraps it in toilet paper, and throws it in the trash can.

How thoughtful. I think.

"Okay, get in the water, turn around and face me, and I'll get started," he says. He reaches for the shampoo as I turn.

He starts massaging soap into my hair, using his fingers to rub my scalp. He tilts my head up and lets the water wash the suds away. One hand stays in my hair, running his fingers through it, and the other pumps out some conditioner. He rubs his hands together and then is back to massaging my head. He rinses my hair again but slower this time. My eyes are closed so I don't see him bending down until his lips are on mine.

We kiss softly but as usual, that doesn't last. Our kissing becomes urgent, more passionate again.

Breathing heavily, Dalton pulls away slowly but keeps his nose touching mine. He says, "I better let you finish the rest or we'll never get out of this bathroom."

I laugh quietly and say, "Would that be such a bad thing?"

"No, not at all, I could spend days doing this," he says, and then he's kissing me again.

I feel him start to get hard again and I decide he's right. If we don't stop now, it would be hard to stop at all.

This time, I'm the one to pull away.

I look up at him and say, "I think you're right. And plus, Wallowa Lake is calling our names."

Dalton laughs, kisses my nose, and says, "I'll leave you to finish."

He steps out and finds a towel. I ogle him as he dries off. Mesmerized at how his back muscles ripple as he runs the towel over himself.

I silently laugh to myself as I notice for the first time the difference in the color of his skin. His ass is white as white can be, as well as his legs. But his upper body is a beautiful color of sun kissed tan skin. When he's outside, he must work with his shirt off.

Shaking myself and forcing my eyes away from Dalton's nakedness, I hurry and shave my armpits, and wash my body. He's just pulling on his pants and fixing his belt when I step out, reaching for a towel.

"You're so damn beautiful, Elainah," he uses my full name which has me staring at him. My cheeks are reddening, once again. "It's almost painful."

"Ummmm... thanks," I say embarrassed, as I wrap a towel around me.

"I mean that in a good way," he says, reaching out

with his hand, lifting my chin up with his fingers. He steps towards me and kisses me.

When he steps away, I breathlessly says, "I know what you mean. It's how I think you look."

He smiles that heart stopping smile at me and then holds up a bag.

"This is what I originally came in here for. I thought you might like your clothes."

"Oh yeah, thank you."

"I'll go make sure everything is cleaned up in the kitchen and let you get dressed. I don't think I can handle seeing you naked and keep my hands off you for long," he winks at me as he steps out and closes the door behind him.

I let out the breath I have apparently been holding. The thought of Dalton's hands on me starts to get me riled up again so I start thinking of everything we can do up at the lake. I get dressed as fast as I can. The shirt he got me is soft and light feeling. The pants fit perfectly. The undies are a silky, satiny, lacey combo, they are comfy and cute. I throw on some eyeliner and mascara. I brush my hair quickly and decide to braid my hair again, it helps to keep it out of my face.

I walk out of the bathroom as I'm putting my hair tie on the bottom of my braid.

As I walk into the kitchen, I say, "Okay, I'm all done. How's it going in here?"

"All done too," Dalton was bent over the garbage

bag, tying it. When he stands, he looks up at me. "That color looks amazing on you."

"Thank you," I say, embarrassed again. I'm not used to such earnest compliments.

"Ready?" he asks. "I thought I'd take the trash out on our way out."

"Yeah, I'm ready and that's thoughtful of you."

He winks at me as he steps around me, running his hand across my stomach. Fire is left behind from his touch. Embers flaring up inside.

My body needs to simmer the hell down. I growl to myself.

I grab my bag of yesterday's clothes, and the contents of my pants pockets off the counter, and slide my phone into my back pocket. I lock the door before we close it and make our way to his pickup. I wait while he puts the garbage in the trash can. It would upset him if I let myself into the pickup.

"Thank you for letting me do this," he says as he opens the door for me.

"You're welcome, I can be patient," I say, smiling at him.

As soon as Dalton is on the main road out of town, heading towards Wallowa Lake, he offers me his hand and I take it immediately. His touch… his warmth… is becoming very comforting and reassuring.

I've got to get myself reeled in.

We drive in silence for a while, me daydreaming… fantasizing really.

"Do you want to go to the dance again tonight?" he asks, breaking the silence suddenly.

Caught off guard, I just stare for a minute.

"Lainey?"

"Sorry… Uhhh yeah, that would be fun… as long as you'll be there."

"Of course I'll be there."

"Good."

"I had a lot of fun dancing with you last night, I thought we could do that again tonight."

"I had fun too, surprisingly," I laugh.

"You can dance, you really can," he says, squeezing my hand.

I smile back at him, "Thanks, but you honestly did most of it."

"You seriously don't understand yourself, your movements… your beauty… your goodness… do you?" he asks, so earnestly again it sounds like it's painful for him to say it.

I shrug and answer him honestly, "I really don't know what you mean."

"You can dance but you don't see it. I tell you you're beautiful and you look at me like I'm speaking gibberish."

I shrug. "Whether I think I am or not doesn't change me. I'd rather be a good, kind person, than believe I'm beautiful or have mooooves," I draw out the word and wiggle my hips the best I can while sitting, and smile at him.

"And that statement right there makes you the most attractive, most beautiful woman in the world," Dalton says, kissing my hand.

I blush and look out the window.

We're quiet for a while again. Dalton lets go of my hand for a second and turns on the radio. He takes my hand again and smiles at me. I smile back and then yawn.

"Are you sleepy? We didn't really get a lot of sleep last night, did we?" he asks with another wink.

"Yeah, but I'm okay."

"Take a nap. I'll wake you when we get there."

"Do you know where to go?"

"I can read signs," he laughs. "Lainey, take a nap. I'll be fine."

"No, I'll be okay."

He shakes his head and starts singing along with the radio. I lay my head back and just stare at him.

He. Can. Sing.

I close my eyes and listen to him sing the song, rather than the artist on the radio.

Chapter 6

I wake up to gentle touches to my face and my name being called quietly.

"Lainey… Lainey… Wake up Lainey…"

My eyes open slowly and I see Dalton staring at me, smiling.

He's always smiling.

"Shoot, I fell asleep?"

"You sure did. Are you still tired?"

"No," I say just as I yawn.

"I had an idea on the way up here," he says. I look out the front window and see us parked in a shaded area, facing the lake. "I have a sleeping bag in the back and a couple blankets in the back seat. We can make a bed in the back of the pickup and rest. We have a long day ahead of us, plus the dance tonight. A nap would be good."

I yawn again and smile, "Okay, that does sound good."

We set up the sleeping bag as a sort of mattress and spread a blanket out on top. We fold one as a makeshift pillow. I sit on the tailgate and take my boots off and then crawl over to the right and get under the blanket. The shade makes it just cool enough that the blanket is very much needed.

Dalton hops up on the tailgate and takes his boots off too.

"This isn't so bad," he says when he's gotten situated beside me.

"Not bad at all," I agree.

He pulls me to him so that my head is lying on his chest. He starts to rub my back and shoulders, humming a song as he does. Listening to his heartbeat, breathing, and the rumbling hum in his chest lulls me to sleep quickly.

I wake up and look around. The sun has moved so much that it's shining on us, we aren't shaded anymore. I look up at Dalton and see he's still sleeping but I see a sheen on his forehead, he's getting warm and sweating a little bit.

When I try to roll away, his arms tighten around me.

"Where you goin'?" he asks in a sleepy, husky voice.

"It's getting warm," I say.

"That's okay."

I roll back over and run a finger back and forth

over his chest. He inhales slowly and then exhales even slower.

"That feels good," he whispers.

"Yeah?" I ask.

"Yeah."

We lay like this for a few minutes. I think he's fallen back to sleep but he shifts the way he's lying so that I'm on him more.

I slide up onto him so that I'm straddling his hips. I don't mean it in a sexual way, just playful. I put my hands on his chest and then his stomach and pat out a rhythm of a song. He opens his eyes and sits up a little so his back is against the back window of his pickup.

"You're too good at this," he mumbles out.

"At what?" I ask.

He cocks his head to the side and says, "You don't know the effect you have?"

"No," I say. "I guess not."

"You honestly don't know how sexy you are?"

Blushing scarlet, I look down. "I really don't know what you're talking about."

"This little move," Dalton says, placing his hands on my hips. "Is about to send me into a frenzy. If we weren't out in the open, I'd take you right now, but I know since we are in the open, you wouldn't be comfortable with that so I am trying everything in my willpower to not think about you sitting on me. Not thinking of how sexy you look from this angle."

"I just sat like this so I can look at you better," I say. "I didn't mean to make you... uncomfortable." I can't help the small smile that crosses my face.

"You not knowing how sexy you are, makes you even more sexy. You have no idea," he slides his hands on top of my thighs.

"I guess I don't," I say in a more remorseful tone than I mean to use. I'm not sure why. I move to get off of him but his hold tightens.

"What do you think you're doing?" he asks a little roughly.

"I don't want to make you uncomfortable so I'm getting off you so we can talk."

"Don't be silly, I can handle it," he laughs. "What do you want to talk about?"

"Well... " I open my arms out and look around. "What do you want to do here?"

He winks and squeeze his hands on my thighs. I stiffen just barely but he notices.

"Relax Lainey, I'm just teasing, seeing what kind of a reaction I can get out of you. You reacted as I had expected," he laughs. "I don't know, what do you wanna do?"

I roll my eyes and smile at him before saying, "Ummmmm... well there's mini-golf... or go-carts... or we can ride on the tram up to the top... I think there's a little cafe or food shack where we can get lunch from up there."

"Are you hungry?" he asks.

"Dalton, I'm always hungry... or at the very least, I can always eat..."

"Let's go for that tram ride, get lunch, and then we can come back down and I'll kick your ass at some mini-golf and go-carts," he teases.

"Mini-golf is a for sure thing but go-karts, I might surprise you."

"Really?"

"Yup... maybe."

"Well, let's go then," he says as he gently lifts me up. "I wanna see your mad driving skills."

Laughing, I pull him up as I stand. He doesn't let go of my hands but pulls me to him and kisses me.

As soon as our lips touch, the fire that had been smoldering, flares. Caught off guard by it, I gasp and push myself closer to Dalton.

He runs his hand up my arms and I wrap mine around his waist. His hands get to my neck and I feel his fingers interlock into my hair, he pulls my face even closer to his, crushing our mouths together.

Breathing hard after a few minutes, we step away from each other.

"That was... intense." Dalton says, breathlessly.

I laugh but I'm out of breath myself so no sound comes out but I manage to whisper, "Uhhh yeah, I'd say."

Dalton steps around me and jumps off the tailgate. Before I can decide if I'm going to jump or sit and slide off, he reaches up and grabs my waist and lifts me up and starts to put me down.

Caught off guard, again, I gasp.

He slowly lowers me but I'm nearly smashed against him again. I look up at him and he's got his devastating smile smeared across his face.

Before we can get lost in kissing again, I reluctantly step away from him.

He laughs and says, "You should see your face. You look like someone that's trying to make a very hard decision."

"I am... I want to kiss you but I know if I do, I won't want to stop. So... I'm not going to let myself start."

I turn and start to walk away, towards where I think the gondola is located. Before I get too far away from him, Dalton grabs my hand and spins me back to him and is kissing me before I've stopped moving.

A few more minutes have gone by again before he slowly stops kissing me and says, "I wish I was as strong as you. I give in to my desires for you so easily."

I smile a disbelieving smile and say, "Guys don't talk like that, you know."

"Well it's a good thing I've proven that I am, huh," he says as he presses his pelvic area into me, revealing his hard bulge.

Fire flaring in the pit of my stomach, I bite my lip

and consider just turning back to the pickup but no... we came up here to hang out.

Smiling, I push back slightly and then step away, holding his hand.

"Let's go, Casanova," I say, laughing.

"Casanova?" he laughs. "I've never been called that before."

"To your face, maybe."

We laugh and then walk in silence for a few minutes. When we get to the tram, Dalton reaches for his wallet.

"If you pay for this, I pay for lunch," I say.

"Why won't you let me pay for it all?"

"I don't know, it doesn't feel right."

"You haven't been on a date in a while, this is how it works. It'll come back to you," he laughs slightly.

Sighing and resigned, I wave him on, nonchalantly on the outside, but totally freaking out on the inside. I think 'giddy' is the word. *A date?* I hadn't been thinking of it that way.

Dalton pays for us and we hop on. No one is behind us or insight, so the gondola attendant sends us up the mountain.

To distract myself from the height, I start asking Dalton questions.

"So did you grow up in Montana?"

"Yeah, my parents started the ranch and then

Dad and I became partners about 12 years ago and we grew and expanded the land and cattle."

"That's pretty cool."

"Yeah, it's been interesting."

"I bet. Ranching isn't for the faint of heart."

"It sure isn't. I guess I've never asked, what do you do?"

"I own a bookstore in Baker. I serve local bakery goods and coffee for breakfast, and pizza and local beer for lunch and dinner. I'm not as busy as you but it's enough to keep me occupied. I also help my in-laws on the farm when they need an extra equipment operator."

"That's really cool."

"It's pretty fun," I make the mistake of looking out the side window. I lean away and ask, "How long have you been riding bulls?"

Dalton's head is tilted to the side and looks out the window and smiles, "Are you afraid of heights?"

"Yes," I answer matter of factly. "I get vertigo pretty bad."

"Then why are we on this?" he's still laughing, more in disbelief than in humor.

"It's an experience and you've never been up here."

"But if you don't like it, we could have skipped this," as he says 'this', he waves around him.

"Don't be silly, I can handle it," I say it like he did

earlier.

He smiles and then says, "You asked me something but I was distracted by you... no surprise there. I'm always distracted by you... And once again, I say too much."

"Uhhh, I am the one that says too much," I say dumbfounded.

"You edit."

"Not by much," I smile. "And I asked how long you've been riding bulls."

"Oh... I started riding sheep, I was four, I think. Haven't really stopped. As I got older, the animals got bigger and more dangerous. Four year old me thought a sheep was terrifying. Had I known then, what I know now," he laughs.

"Have you ever been seriously hurt?"

"My calf got stepped on six years ago. They were worried about the muscle detaching from the bone but it wasn't. I just got bruised really bad. Luckily it was at the end of the season at a small rodeo. The World Championships were over. I was laid up most of the winter but made it work. By the time it was time to start riding again, I was good to go."

"Oh my gosh, that's crazy."

"I've been pretty lucky."

"I'd say."

"Have you ever been seriously hurt?"

"No, not yet anyways," I say. Then add, "Knock

on wood."

Dalton laughs.

Our tram ride comes to an end, luckily I can look out now. We step out and Dalton instantly takes my hand.

I don't know if it's because it's been so long since I've had a physical connection with a man, that I'm having such strong feelings at such a simple action like holding hands, or if it's because it's Dalton and it's something more than a fleeting thing? Whatever the reasoning, my body is reacting crazily. My pulse is racing and the fire is flaming again.

Trying to distract myself, I ask, "Are you hungry? Should we have lunch now? Or would you rather walk around a bit?"

"Let's get you fed," he laughs.

I laugh too, in agreement.

We walk over to the little restaurants and pick a picnic table that has a beautiful view of the lake way, way, way down below.

I sit on one side, Dalton sits on the other so we're facing each other.

"Are you okay sitting here?" Dalton asks, concern in his voice.

"Yeah, this is fine. Dangling on a wire over nothing, that's a different story," I laugh.

Dalton laughs, too.

A waitress comes up and says her name is Kara.

We tell her what we'd like to drink. She leaves menus and walks away. Dalton is looking at the menu but I'm glancing around, which is how I see Kara do a double take at him and then proceeds to tell the other waitress something, while pointing over at us... at Dalton. I smile because I can imagine what they're saying.

"What?" Dalton asks, he's looking at me in amusement.

"Nothing," I reply.

"Your smile says otherwise."

"I'm sure we'll find out soon enough."

"What?"

"Just wait and see. I'll tell you if it doesn't happen but I'm almost positive it will."

"Ooookay," Dalton says, laughing quietly.

Sure enough, when Kara comes back, she's smiling and almost giddy looking.

She puts my diet pop down in front of me without looking at me and is all googly eyed at Dalton.

"Are you... are you Dalton Young?" she asks.

He looks at me and I'm trying to suppress my smile and laugh.

He reluctantly looks up at her but smiles politely and says, "I am."

"Wow! I thought it was you. Amanda didn't believe me. Can I get your autograph?"

"Sure but I'm on a date so I'll leave it with the bill after we're done eating," Dalton says in a nice but stern voice.

"Oh, a date?" Kara says and looks at me. Her eyes blink fast, then she looks back at Dalton. She says quickly, "Oh yeah, of course. No problem. I'll be back to take your food order in a couple minutes."

"Thanks," he says with a hint of annoyance in his voice. He looks at me and I'm grinning at him. "What?" he asks.

"Nothing," I say, as I take a drink of my pop.

"Is that-" he waves nonchalantly towards where Kara has walked away, "-what you were smiling about?"

"Yes, I saw her and... Amanda, talking and pointing at you."

"I don't like how she was treating you..."

"Treating me?" I ask, surprised.

"Yes, like you weren't even here."

"Dalton, when you're around, no one notices anyone else."

"Is that so?"

"Yes."

"Is that how you feel? Do you forget we're sitting in public when you're sitting with me?" he's got his cocky smile plastered on his face.

"Frequently, especially when we're kissing," I say truthfully and then blush. I feel like I always say too much. Did I really have to add the kissing part. *UGH!*

"I feel the same way about being with you," he says, reaching for my hand. "We only sat down for a minute but when the waitress came up for the first time, she startled me a little because I, too, get lost in your company."

"Well, then you can't blame her for not seeing me," I say, jokingly.

"It's her job to be polite to everyone at the table."

"She's being polite. She's just distracted by you," I laugh.

Dalton shakes his head and goes back to looking at the menu, but one handed because he's refusing to let go of my hand. I don't mind, it feels good to hold hands.

Kara comes back a few minutes later and takes our order. I ask for the chicken sandwich with fries and Dalton asks for the beef dip.

We sit in silence for a while, enjoying the view, and being in each other's company.

"This is nice," Dalton says, quietly.

"It is," I agree, looking out over the valley below us.

"The view is beautiful but to feel content to sit and enjoy it without feeling the need to talk, that's what makes it nice. Don't get me wrong, I have so many more questions for you but it's nice and relaxing to just sit here with you."

"I know what you mean. Not everyone can sit in silence."

"Some definitely can't but I'm glad we can."

We sit in silence for a few more minutes before

Dalton sighs.

"Tired of the silence?" I laugh.

"Not at all but the questions keep accumulating in my head."

"Ask away," I encourage.

"I know we've only just met yesterday, but I was wondering when… if I'd get to meet your kids?" he asks, unsurely.

I take a drink of my pop before answering.

"I think there is a very good chance you'll get to meet them but I told myself I wouldn't bring anyone around my kids until I was sure he was going to stick around. I don't want my kids to get attached to someone who might not be planning on being around long and then getting their hearts broken when they don't get to see him again. They've been through a lot, processing the loss of their dad, I don't want to put them through anything like that again. I know I can't protect them from loss, I can't control that, but there are some things I can control and this is one of them. I told myself that I would have to feel like I could trust the guy with not only my heart, but with three little ones as well. I honestly never thought I'd meet someone willing to take it all on. It's a lot and I always figured it would be too much."

"I can respect that. Is that why you haven't dated much? Or at all?"

"Partly, yes."

"What's the other part?"

I look down at my soda and play with the straw for a minute.

"You don't have to tell me if you don't feel like it," he says, I look up and see him smiling comfortingly at me.

"I'm deciding on if I want to keep it light or let the heavy truth out," I say a little solemnly.

"I always go for the truth, no matter how heavy it is, sometimes keeping things light can cause things to be misconstrued or taken the wrong way."

"That's true," I agree. I take a breath and say, "I haven't started dating again because I never thought I would find someone that could love me... Me for who I am.. like Jayce loved me. I didn't think it would be fair for one person to get that kind of love, to get to experience that twice in one life, when some people don't get to experience it at all. So I focused on my kids and work. Another reason is because I feel like everyone I know was friends with Jayce and will always think of me as Jayce's wife, which equals off limits. I decided I wasn't going to move anywhere, keep my kids going to school here and close to our families. All of Jayce's family lives around here and I won't take my kids away from them. So pickin's are slim around here," I add, to try to lighten it up a bit.

"It's not your fault or your problem if John-Boy or Sally-May have never gotten to experience love like what you had with Jayce. Don't feel guilty for wanting that again. Why do you feel people only deserve to be happy with one person?"

"I guess I believed in soul-mates."

"Believed? You don't anymore?"

"I don't know... If I do, then I got the shortest amount of time with who I thought was my soul-mate. And selfishly, I don't think that's fair."

"Do you think there could be multiple people we could be meant for?"

"Like multiple soul-mates?"

"Yeah, I guess you could say it that way. But think of it this way, what if you and Jayce never got together. You met someone else, would that love be more or less than what you and Jayce had?"

"I wouldn't know the difference because I wouldn't have known the love that Jayce and I had, the love he showed me. It wasn't just about him loving me for who I was, it was like we thought the same way. At times, I'd be thinking something and then he'd say it. We'd be driving home from being out with friends and we'd be silent for a while and I'd have a thought but before I could speak it, he would... he would say exactly what I was thinking. We were different enough that we equaled each other out but the same enough, that we were compatible. I can see what you're saying though, like there could be more than one person out there for someone, it just depends on the time and place on who you meet?"

"Exactly. And what you're describing about yours and Jayce's relationship sounds a lot like two people that were friends with similarities and then became a couple."

"I guess," I say. I don't know how to explain to Dalton how mine and Jayce's relationship felt deeper than that, that it felt soul deep.

"Here's your food, would you two like refills on your drinks?" Kara startles the both of us as she puts our food down in front of us.

"That'd be great, thank you," I say, handing her my cup.

She walks away and I look over at Dalton, he's looking at me weird.

"What?" I ask.

"I just can't believe you think you don't deserve to find love again. I've known you for what," he pretends to look at a watch that doesn't exist on his wrist and says, "a little over 24 hours and I can tell you this, you definitely deserve all the good things that life has to offer and that includes love."

"Stick around and I might change your mind," I say teasingly.

He laughs and asks, "How so?"

"Oh I don't know, we all have our obnoxious habits and what not, don't we?"

"What could you do that could be obnoxious?"

"Hmmmm I tend to be a homebody. Don't get me wrong, I love going out and doing things but home is one of my favorite places to hangout."

"That is not obnoxious. It's great that your home is a place that brings you peace and allows you to relax."

"I'm sure I can think of something," I say pretending to think hard.

"Well, don't hurt yourself thinking too hard, I have a feeling you are one of the least obnoxious people on the planet."

I shake my head and then take a big bite of my sandwich. After chewing and swallowing I say, "I like food a little too much. I'll never be a size 2."

"Again, not a bad thing."

"You'll discover something about me that drives you crazy."

"Have you already found something about me that drives you crazy?"

"Well, you are abnormally good at everything you do but that doesn't really drive me crazy."

He rolls his eyes at me before taking a bite of his beef dip. We sit in silence for a few minutes, eating. It really is nice knowing we don't have to fill the silence with forced conversation just so it's not quiet.

We finished eating at the same time but Dalton talks first.

"Where to now?"

"Wanna go for a little walk around up here before we head back down?" I ask.

"Sounds good to me."

We gather our garbage and head to the trash can.

"Don't forget to leave an autograph for Kara," I say, nudging him with my shoulder.

"Ugh… I did forget. Do I have to?"

"You said you would."

We walk back over to the table where Dalton takes a clean napkin out of the little holder and writes his name quickly and then adds, 'To Kara, have a great day.'

"That should work," he says, a little red around the ears. He puts it under the cash he's left for the bill and tip.

"Are you embarrassed?"

"A little, I honestly have never gotten used to this," he says walking over and taking my hand in his, squeezing lightly.

"It would be pretty strange to be recognized by everyone, everywhere you go."

"Well, almost everyone," he says, bumping me with his arm.

I laugh as we find a small trail to follow, that wraps its way around the trees.

Chapter 7

Leaning my head back against the headrest, my hand out the window, letting the cool air flow through my fingers, I think back over the last couple of hours.

Dalton and I had walked around at the top for about an hour, after lunch. He made fun of me on our way down, he noticed I didn't look out the window very much.

We decided to play mini-golf first. He, as I expected, won. The last couple of holes, I could tell he was trying to let me win so that he wouldn't kick my ass too bad, but I told him I would make up for it at the go-carts. All he said was, "Yeah, okay."

Our first go-kart race he again seemed to be taking it easy on me but I soon proved I could hold my own. Because of him throwing the race and me actually being able to drive, I smeared him. The second race I could tell he was actually trying. But I, again, won by a couple lengths. We decided on one more race, if I won, we'd be done. He said his ego couldn't take it anymore. I could tell he was teasing but also impressed with my driving skills.

After I won the third race, we decided to walk down to the lake. Dalton teased that there wasn't anything down there he could lose at to me.

We thought about renting a boat or something but after touching the water, we decided the air wasn't warm enough for how cold the water was today.

We walked around the gift shop, where I bought Max, Janey, and Nelly a couple stuffed animals. Not that they needed them but it had started to be something I did anywhere I, or we, visited.

"What are you thinking about?" I hear Dalton say as he brushes his fingers down my arm.

A delicious shiver runs down my body and warmth follows where his fingers touch. I open my eyes, I hadn't realized I had closed them, and look over at him.

"Just today," I say, smiling.

"Oh yeah? Thinking about how I could give you some golfing lessons?" he laughs, teasing again.

"Sure, right after I give you some driving lessons. You wanna pull over and I'll drive and give you your first lesson?" I say, equally teasingly.

"Touché," he says, laughing hysterically.

After a few minutes of quiet, Dalton speaks

again.

"The dance is starting right now. Are you wanting to go straight there or would you rather go get dinner first?"

"How do you feel about getting a burger there? It's one of the things I actually enjoy about rodeos."

"You go for the food, not the rodeo itself, or to watch the riders," he laughs.

"Well, yeah, the best burgers are sold there," I smile at him.

"They are pretty good."

"Are you put off about my love for food?"

"The opposite actually, I like that you like to eat," he takes my hand and squeezes.

I look out my side window so that he can't see the tears filling my eyes.

I never thought I would... ever... find another man that would accept me for me like Jayce did. He loved me for me, all of me. Dalton is making me feel like Jayce did, like I could be loved again.

After Jayce's accident, I resigned myself to the fact that Jayce was it. He was my one and only. The only man alive that could love me. I wasn't lying when I told Dalton I couldn't be lucky enough to find true love twice, one person couldn't be that lucky.

Thinking back to our conversation early has me pondering again. Soul-mate. Doesn't that mean only one person is truly meant for you? Jayce was that for me. We truly did have enough similarities and opposites that we balanced each other out. My anxiety to keep everyone safe was balanced out by his reassurance that everything would be okay. Life was meant to be lived, not kept in a safe little bubble all of the time.

Learning how to reel in my anxiety and remind myself of how Jayce lived and how we lived as a family before his accident, was something I had to work on and still work on to this day.

"What are you thinking about now?" Dalton asks, breaking through my emotional inner monologue.

I sniff and wipe my face quickly with my right hand and say, "Nothing."

"Hey, are you okay?"

"Oh yeah, I'm fine. Just overthinking."

"Overthinking about what? I really do love how you like food."

"Nothing about food."

"Jayce?"

I look at him, stunned again about how in tune he is to me already.

"Yeah, I'm sorry. I don't mean to get emotional but…"

"You can't help it."

"Nope."

"You wanna talk about it?"

"I was just thinking about how lucky I was to

have gotten the time with him and how he got me so well. I didn't think I'd ever find it again, which is why I haven't been with anyone since him, like I said earlier. But then, along came you, and..." I stop talking abruptly.

Stop talking! You met him yesterday. I scream at myself in my head.

"And what?" Dalton asks, squeezing my hand.

"It's nothing," I say, looking down at my hand in my lap.

Stupid! Stupid!

"It's something, you can tell me... Talk to me," he urges softly.

"You seem to understand me and accept me like Jayce did," I say a little too shyly.

Dalton surprises me with a laugh and says, "I hate to burst your bubble but you aren't very hard to understand. You are by far the easiest person to talk to or not. The silence is never awkward, it's peaceful. You're easy going and down to earth. I've known you for a little over 24 hours and I can already tell you are the most genuine person I've ever met."

"I'm just me."

"See that right there. You don't see yourself clearly at all. You say you're just you but you say it kind of like it's not a big deal. You are... you are the most incredible woman I know."

Blushing, I look down again.

"I'm serious, Elainah," at my full name, I look up at him and see him staring at me intensely. "You are amazing."

"Well thank you, I appreciate that but please watch the road," I say to lighten the mood.

"Psh... I'm a great driver," he says smiling but looks back at the road.

"Says the guy who lost three races to a girl."

"Any other girl, I probably would have beat or at least had to let win. But you... again, amazing," he smiles his crooked smile, that I love, at me.

I yawn again, then laugh, "Sorry, I haven't yawned this much in a long time."

"Take another nap, we've still got a solid hour and a half before we're back to Union."

"No, I'll be.. *yawn*.. Okay."

"Lainey, I'll be fine. I promise. Close your eyes. I'm hoping for another repeat of last night so you'll need your rest."

I look at him with my eyebrows raised and a surprised look on my face and ask, "A little presumptuous, don't you think?"

"What?" Dalton asks, surprised. Then he understands and laughs and says, "I meant dancing. What are you thinkin'?"

"I was thinking of dancing too. You think you can get me out on the dance floor again?"

"I know I can."

"Oh really?"

"I'm sure I can persuade you," he says as he picks my hand up and kisses the inside of my wrist and up my arm a little, as far as he can with my arm stretched out as far as it'll go, without me leaning clear over the middle console, into his lap.

I swallow embarrassingly loudly and say, "You play dirty."

"You have no idea," he says with a wink.

The fire in the pit of my stomach flares.

"Really?"

"Mmmhmmm," he says kissing my hand.

"Interesting," I say with exaggerated thinking.

"How so?"

"Just thinking."

"Of?"

"What I could get away with if I played dirty."

This time I see Dalton gulp, his Adam's Apple goes up and back down, slowly.

"Oh yeah?" he says, a little more high pitched than usual. "How so?"

"Oh… I don't know," I say. I let go of his hand and put it on his leg closest to me. I run it down to his knee and then back up to his crotch where I find a bulge straining against his zipper.

Interesting… slightest touch… or how long? I wonder to myself.

"Ohhh you…" he takes a deep breath.

"I bet I can persuade you not to take me out onto the dance floor," I say, running my hand back down to his knee.

"Oh, no doubt about that," he whispers and smiles over at me.

I laugh and place my hand in my lap with my other one.

"I'll behave."

"Good, I can't concentrate when you do that and I need to get us back in one piece."

"That would be a good thing."

"So why don't you be a good girl and take a nap? That should keep us both on our best behaviors."

I laugh and then yawn again.

"You might be right."

Dalton turns the radio on and starts to sing. It really should be against the law of nature for someone who looks like him and obviously athletic, to be able to sing like he can, it doesn't seem fair.

Ignoring my inner debate on fairness, I close my eyes and let him sing me to sleep again.

Chapter 8

"SHIT!!!"

The sound of screeching tires fill the air. I jump awake, almost out of my seat but my seatbelt keeps me locked in.

"What?! What?!" I ask, confused.

"Sorry, Lainey... A bunch of damn elk crossed right in front of me."

"Did you hit one?"

"No, luckily I saw them in time. Just scared the shit out of me."

I look around, "Where are we?" I look behind us, it's really dark so I can't tell where we are in relation to which town we're close to.

"We're in between Elgin and Imbler."

"Oh, okay."

"And you're still set on having burgers at the clubhouse?"

"Yes, they're the best burgers around. Are you

wanting to eat somewhere else?"

"No... No, the clubhouse will be fine. The burgers are pretty good, I just wanted to make sure you really want to eat there. Just seems like it's too easy for a dinner date."

"Dates don't have to be complicated. At least not with me."

"I'm starting to get that," he says, smiling over at me.

We're quiet for a bit, just listening to the radio.

Soon, we come to La Grande and make it through town until we hit Hwy 30.

"I'm going to check in with my sister, if that's okay?" I say, not asking for permission but not wanting to be rude.

"Oh, yeah, that's absolutely fine."

I pull my phone out and turn it on. I don't get very good service when I'm out of the area so I had turned it on to airplane mode so my battery would last.

-New messages from Emily-

Emily- *You having fun?* 1:13pm

Emily- *You guys going to the dance?* 2:02pm

Emily- *I just got home. Sex in my bathroom?* 6:53pm

Emily- *In the shower perhaps? NICE!* 6:54pm

Emily- *We're goin' to dinner if you guys wanna join us.* 7:48pm

I silently gasp, turning bright red. I quickly send a reply.

Me- *Had fun.*
Yes, going to the dance, eating there.
How did you know about...??? 9:02pm

While I wait for her to reply, because I know she will. I send a message to Lucy.

Me- *Hiya Luce! How are my kiddos? We're almost back to Union.* 9:03pm

BUZZ-BUZZ

-New message from Emily-

I open her message, cringing at the thought of what she has said.

Emily- *I didn't dig through the trash but the wrapper was visible.* 9:05pm
Me- **Facepalm emoji* Crrrap... sorry Em.* 9:05pm
Emily- *No worries at all. I was proud.* 9:06pm
Me- *Oh my gosh!!!* 9:06pm

CHAPTER 8

Emily- *We're about done eating. Where are you sex craze maniacs?* 9:06pm

Me- *STOP THAT!*

    We're almost to Union. 9:06pm

Emily- *OK, see you in a couple.* 9:07pm

BUZZ-BUZZ

-New message from Lucy-

Lucy- *Hi Lainey! Kids are doing great. In bed. I told them we'd call tomorrow when they're all awake.* 9:07pm

Me- *Thank you. Love you!* 9:07pm

Lucy- *Love you too! You know you have a long conversation ahead of you with me, right?* 9:07pm

Me- *Yes… yes I know* 9:08pm

Lucy- *Ok good, have a fun night. *winky face** 9:08pm

    Ugh… I close my phone and look out the windshield. We were just pulling into Union.

    "Everything okay?" Dalton asks.

    "Yeah it's all fine. Kids are in bed. I'll talk to them tomorrow. Emily and Brayden are going to meet us at the dance."

    "Oh that'll be fun. They're pretty cool."

    "Mmmm… yeah, fun."

"What's wrong?"

I laugh a little and then say, "Nothing."

"Something."

Do I tell him Emily found the condom wrapper? Would he be embarrassed or think it's funny? Only one way to find out.

"Emily found the wrapper."

"The wrapper?" he asks, confused.

"In the bathroom…"

He still looks confused but after a second, he starts to laugh hysterically.

"That's awesome! Is she mad?"

"No, she said she was… proud," I laugh.

"She's awesome," he says, patting my leg before taking my hand.

Of course he'd find it funny. I guess it is funny. I start to laugh a little harder.

We pull into the parking lot and Dalton parks by my rig.

"Oh good, it's still here," I say half serious, half kidding.

"Were you worried about it?"

"I'm always a little worried but I figured it would be fine. It's why we have insurance, right?"

"Yeah, I guess," he laughs quietly.

We hop out and as I walk around the back of his pickup, I see him with his hands on his hips, looking at me.

"What?" I ask.

He gestures back towards my door.

I laugh and say, "Ooops, sorry. I forgot."

"Tsk-tsk... We'll just have to get you used to it," he scoops me up and throws me over his shoulder

"AGH! Dalton!" I holler.

"I'll just carry you to the burger shack."

"NO!"

"Yup! My chivalry knows no bounds."

"Dalton! Put me down please! I'll work on remembering you opening doors for me."

"Promise?"

"Yes! Yes! Please!"

He gently puts me down but before I can catch my breath, he's kissing me.

Caught off guard, I gasp and pull him to me tightly. A piece of paper couldn't have been slid between us.

"Yeaaah! Get some! I've got seconds!" a drunk guy says from behind me.

Dalton stops kissing me and glares.

"Like hell **hiccup** you do, **hiccup** I'm next," another guy says, sounding even more drunk.

"Why don't you guys go sleep it off in your trailer?" Dalton says as he pulls me behind him.

"Oh damn **hiccup** it's Dalton **hiccup** mother-fucking **hiccup** Young," drunk guy #2 says.

"Shit, yeah it is," drunk guy #1 says.

"Come on, let's get food," I say to Dalton, I can feel him stiffening.

"Yeah **hiccup** go get something to eat **hiccup** I bet her puss is a real nice treat..." drunk guy #2 says.

"Hey!" Dalton hollers, stepping towards him.

"Dalton, please, let's just go. They're drunk assholes, they're not worth it," I say.

"I'll show you worth it," drunk #1 says as he grabs his crotch.

Dalton finally looks down and then nods.

"Yeah, okay, let's go," he says, pushing me in front of him so that I'm blocked from the drunk assholes' view.

"We'll see you later baby," drunk #1 says.

I grab hold of Dalton's hands that are on my shoulders, and force him to keep holding on, and keep moving forward. I can feel him turning to look back.

"Ignore them, they'll be passed out in an hour," I say, pulling him forward.

"I hate guys that talk that way to women, no matter if they're drunk or not," he says, seething.

"I know, I do too. But you can't argue with them when they're that far gone. It just turns into a physical fight and I'd rather not spend the night telling the police why you kicked their asses," I say, stepping to the side so I can hold Dalton's hand.

"You think I can kick their asses?" he asks,

puffing his chest out a little more than normal.

"Look at you... look at them... You definitely can. Even on their best day, you could. It really wouldn't be a fair fight," I say as I squeeze his hand. I wasn't trying to boost his ego, he really is huge, a very, very strong man.

"Well, I would hate to ruin your night," he says, nudging me with his arm, playfully.

We get up to the counter at the burger shack fairly quickly. While Dalton waits for our food, I go stand in line for ID check and then go get in the token line.

I'm sitting at a table by the time Dalton gets our food and he walks over to me.

"Bon Appetit, mademoiselle," he says as he places my burger and fries in front of me.

"You speak French?" I ask before taking a bite of my burger.

"A little. I can make do if I'm talking to someone or actually in France," he says, shrugging.

"Of course you can," I say, shaking my head.

He laughs, "What do you mean?"

"Is there anything you're not good at, honestly?"

"Painting... drawing... I'm awful."

"Well that's a relief," I laugh.

"What about you? What are you bad at? If anything?" he counter asks.

"Hmmm... carrying on a conversation with a

stranger... I feel awkward trying to think of things to talk about with adults and feel nosy if I ask questions about them and their life. I'm with my kids a lot of the time so they do most of the talking. At work, it's small talk, short and easy," I say.

"Ummm, I think you've been great to talk to," Dalton says, looking at me doubtfully.

"You carry the conversation."

"You carry your own."

"Maybe it's because you're so easy to talk to about everything."

"I feel the same about you. Like if you asked me anything, I'd probably answer truthfully without a second thought," he says, shrugging as he takes another bite of his burger.

"Probably would tell the truth?" I ask, putting a little emphasis on the word 'probably'.

"Well, if it was something embarrassing, I probably would be a little more hesitant to tell you this early in our..." he pauses for a minute. Then says, "whatever this is we're doing."

I'm not sure if he's asking me or just stating he doesn't know what we're doing, so I don't say anything.

But really, what are we doing? He'll be going home soon. Will I see him again? Will we stay in touch and see each other when we can?

The thought of not seeing him makes me sad and hurts my stomach a little more than what I'd like to admit. I push the rest of my burger and fries away and take a sip of my strawberry lemonade beer.

"What's wrong?" he asks, taking my hand.

"What ARE we doing?" I blurt out before I can stop myself.

"We're having dinner and then dancing... after that, only tomorrow will tell us."

"You're leaving soon."

"Not yet."

"And when you do, you'll be... what... seven to eight hours away? That's not a quick trip."

"It's not but it makes for good weekends away. And we'll talk, I mean I plan on exchanging numbers before I leave," he says, laughing.

"That's true, having somewhere to go for a weekend away would be nice," I laugh.

"I would love for you to come to the ranch, would you really come?" Dalton asks, excitedly.

"If I'm invited, yes," I say laughing at his excitement.

"Oh, you're invited," he says, squeezing my hand from across the table.

BUZZ-BUZZ

"Sorry, my phone is going off again," I say.

"You're fine," he says, shrugging.

"Why hasn't your phone gone off?" I ask.

"It's been off. I probably have a ton of voicemails and texts but oh well."

"You could have kept it on," I say, surprised.

"No, it's nonstop and I wanted some peace today while I was with you."

"Oh," is all I brilliantly say.

I look at my phone.

-New message from Emily-

Emily- *We're here. Where are you?* 10:22pm
Me- *Just finishing up our food. We'll be right in, get us a drink please.* 10:22pm

"It's Em, they're here now... in at the dance," I say to Dalton as I put my phone away.

"Are you finished?" Dalton asks, pointing towards my almost gone burger and fries.

"Yeah, I'm good."

He picks our food trays up and dumps them in the trash, we chug the rest of our drinks and throw the empty cans in the can bin.

As we walk back to the clubhouse, Dalton takes my hand and squeezes tightly. I look up at him and he smiles down at me and winks.

"I'm really happy to be here with you," he says.

"Me too... Thanks for stalking me yesterday," I say, laughing.

"Stalking?" he says in a fake offended voice. "I think it was investigative work I did. Had you not been so oblivious to my flirting, I wouldn't have had to work so hard."

"I didn't know you were flirting. I thought you were being nice," I say. "I've never been good at knowing when someone is flirting or not, so I always default to not, they're just being nice."

"Poor guys... but good for me. I guess it pays to be persistent," he laughs.

"I guess so," I laugh also.

We walk in silence to the clubhouse. Emily and Brayden are waiting just inside the beer garden for us.

"Hi," she and I shout at the same time. We laugh.

"Here's a couple drinks," Brayden says, handing Dalton a beer and me, a strawberry lemonade.

"Thanks," I say.

"Yeah, thanks man," Dalton says.

"There aren't as many people tonight as there were last night," I say, looking around. The beer garden is about half as full as it was last night. We easily find a table to sit at and take seats, girls on one side, guys on the other. I'm sitting across from Dalton.

"The barbeque feed fundraiser is going on in La Grande, there were still a ton of people there when we left," Emily says as she wraps her arm through mine.

"Oh I forgot about that, that was tonight?" I ask.

"Yeah," she says, taking a drink of her beer.

We sit in silence for a while, just drinking and people watching for a bit.

"Wanna go dance?" Dalton asks, offering me his hand.

"Wanna not dance?" I counter ask and then wink. I run my foot up his leg.

A wickedly sexy smile crosses his face and he says, "I'm always up for not dancing."

Emily looks at him and then at me, "I'd say get a room but the last room was at my house."

That brought my flirtatiousness to an end. I elbow her and shout, "EMILY!"

"Am I wrong?" she asks laughing. Dalton is grinning ear to ear.

"No, you're not wrong," I say quietly as I turn red.

"So maybe dancing it is," Dalton says, laughing now.

"Ugh… I guess so," I say. I put my beer down next to Emily and stick my tongue out at her as Dalton pulls me back towards the dance room.

"You really shouldn't protest so much about dancing, you're a really good dancer," he says as he twirls me and then pulls me into him.

"Thanks… it's more of people looking at me. I'd rather dance in private," I say, looking up at him.

"They look at you because you're a good dancer and people like to watch good dancers," he says.

I just shrug. It's a slow dance, so I lay my head against his chest and listen to his heartbeat and breathing. He kisses the top of my head and dances us around in circles. The next song is a swing dance song and he starts to twirl and spin and flip me in every direction possible. I just keep my hand out and he always knows where to grab it.

A couple fast paced songs were after and then, thankfully, another slow song comes on. Dalton once again, spins me into him and starts the slow circles again.

"I'm getting dizzy from all the spinning but having so much fun," I say, laughing.

"See, once you relax and let all the shyness go, dancing is fun," he says squeezing me tighter to him.

"I think it has a lot to do with you," before I know what I'm doing, I reach up on my tip toes and kiss him deeply.

COUGH-COUGH

"Can we cut in?" I hear from over my shoulder, an all too familiar voice.

I spin around and see the guys standing there. Jack, Lee, Dylan, Jay, and Alex.

"Ugh... hey guys," I say, feeling embarrassed for some reason.

They aren't looking at me, they're looking over

my head at Dalton.

"Oh... ummm, this is Dalton Young. Dalton, these are the guys. This is Jack and Dylan," Jack and Dylan nod. "This is Lee and Jay," they nod also. "And Alex, Jayce's brother." Alex just stares.

Dalton shakes hands with them all. Alex still hasn't really acknowledged that I've spoken or Dalton, other than shaking his hand.

"So it's true?" Jay asks. "People were telling us you were hanging around Dalton Young but we weren't sure if it was true or not. I'm a big fan, Dalton."

"Thanks man, appreciate that. You ride?" Dalton asks, I can tell he's being polite but I can also see him side glancing at Alex.

"A little in high school but I got hurt pretty bad and thought it would be better not to pursue it anymore," Jay says, shrugging.

"So were you going to tell us?" Alex finally asks, sounding pissed.

"Tell you what?" I ask, crossing my arms.

Alex waves his hands between me and Dalton, "You two."

"We just met yesterday. We've been hanging out," I say, starting to get pissed now too.

"It was just a surprise to hear," Dylan says.

"That I was getting to know someone or that it was Dalton?" I ask, really irritated now.

"Getting to know someone, is that what it's

called these days?" Alex asks, suggestively.

"Okay, enough, come with me," I say as I grab Alex by the forearm. "Dalton, I'll be back."

I pull him past the guys and Dalton and out towards the beer garden, back to a less crowded corner.

"What's your problem?" I quietly shout.

"What's yours? Have you forgotten about Jayce?" he shouts back.

I take a step back like he's slapped me. I close my eyes and take a deep breath before answering him.

"Of course I haven't," I open my eyes and can feel them starting to fill with tears. "Jayce will always be a part of my life, a part of me. How long is, me, being lonely enough time for you to be okay with this, Alex? Another 18 months? 18 years? I have finally found someone that makes me feel genuinely happy again. Makes me laugh. Understands me. Dalton and I only met yesterday but it feels like we've known each other for years. When am I allowed to feel like this again?"

Alex has gone a little white and lets out a huge sigh. "It's just hard to see you with someone other than Jayce."

"Believe me, Alex, it's not the easiest thing to navigate. I have had all sorts of feelings, emotions... thoughts... flying around in my head for the last 24 hours."

"Is it serious?" he asks.

"Serious how? Like are we going to get married?

No, we just met yesterday," I say, annoyed again.

"Has he met the kids? Does he know about the kids? Does he know about Jayce?"

Glaring up at Alex, I say, "He hasn't met the kids yet. And of course he knows about them and Jayce."

"Well, I don't know. Some girls don't tell guys about that kind of stuff because most guys don't want any part of that. Emily told us you guys were fucking."

"Well, it's a good thing he's not like most guys and I'm not some girl," so beyond pissed. "And who I decide to… fuck… is none of your business."

I turn to walk away, I can feel the tears really starting to fill my eyes. That's what happens when I get mad, I cry. It's really annoying.

When I walk past Emily and Brayden I say, "Thanks for that. Why did you have to tell them about me and Dalton? Did you really tell them we were… fucking? You know that's not at all what that was about and how hard it was for me to get close to someone like that again."

"No, Lainey, that's not what I said, that's not what I told them," Emily starts to stand.

I wave her off and says, "Whatever, I need some air."

I walk back out to the dance floor. The guys are all surrounding Dalton, at least they seem to be having a pleasant conversation. Dalton sees me and starts to take a step towards me.

I put my hand up to stop him and say, "I'm fine, just need some air and to use the bathroom."

The guys start talking to him again but I can see him watching me as I go towards the bathroom. The line is about 15 girls deep, so I decide to brave the port-a-potties outside.

When I get outside, the air has cooled just enough that it makes me shiver. For an early summer night, it's abnormally chilly. I let the tears fall, I have found that if I try to hold them in, I get a headache.

I make my way to the side of the clubhouse to where the long line of port-a-potties have been set up. I step over the decorative logs along the way and find a clean potty. I use some tissue to dry my face off and wipe my nose. Before I step out, I hear voices outside.

I step out and without looking around, step to the handwashing station.

"There you **hiccup** are," I hear from behind me. I turn slowly and see the drunk guys from earlier. Drunk guy #1 is leaning up against the furthest port-a-potty from me but closest one to the clubhouse.

"Told you we'd be seeing you later, baby," he says, winking.

"I'm not your baby," I say.

"Where's **hiccup** your **hiccup** boyfriend?" drunk #2 asks.

I'm about to say he's not my boyfriend but I don't think that will be good to tell these guys. "He's on his way out."

"See, I don't think he is. I watched you leave and he seemed pretty busy talking at the time," drunk #1 says, taking a step towards me.

"Whatever," I say as I start to walk to the clubhouse. My heart is starting to beat fast now.

Drunk #1 steps in front of me, "Where you goin'? Party's out here now."

"It's not... it's really, really not," I say, stopping a couple of feet away from him. "Please move, I'd like to go inside."

"Well, I'd like you to stay out here with me," he says, taking a step towards me.

"Nope, that's not going to happen," I say, sounding more sure than I feel.

"I think it is," he steps towards me and I step around him but he grabs my arm closest to him and spins me around into him so that my back is against him. "Mmmm you smell good."

A shiver of fear rocks through me.

"Let... me... go..." I say through clenched teeth.

"Why would I do that? You feel so good," he says as he pulls me closer to him.

"I **hiccup** don't feel **hiccup** so good, Elijah," drunk #2 says.

"Shut up, Phil, go sleep it off," drunk #1, Elijah, says. "I'm busy."

"No.. you aren't," I say, trying to get away from

him.

Elijah squeezes me tighter, I can feel him getting hard.

"Mmmm keep moving like that, it feels good," he mumbles into my ear. I can smell nothing but alcohol, not the beer they are serving in the clubhouse, but hard alcohol.

"Fuck off," I say.

Using one of his arms, he crosses my stomach, and holds both of my wrists in his hand. He reaches up and tries to pull my face towards his.

"Stop it, knock it off," I say, trying to squirm away.

As his hand slides down towards my chest, his arm across my stomach loosens, and so does his hold on my hands. I step back into him and then I pull forward hard and his grip slips. I step away but he's quick and his hold tightens on my wrists and pulls me back into him. I slam into his body. His bulge in his pants has gotten bigger.

"I like a little fight in my fillies, more fun to break," he whispers in my ear as he grinds his crotch into my lower back.

"Fuck... off!" I shout as I stomp on his foot and throw my head back into his face that's still at my head level. I hear his nose crack and I feel a small pain on the back of my head where I connected with his nose.

"Ughh, fucking bitch," I hear him shout from behind me but I'm already a couple feet away, I'm running towards the clubhouse. I'm just about to the stupid decorative logs when I feel his hand close around my shoulder. He spins me but before I've stopped moving I feel his fist hit me across the face, sending me spinning back the other way. I go flying and trip over a log and face plant into another.

Pain seers across my face, through my head, and down my neck.

I'm flipped over quickly and feel Elijah sitting on top of me before my vision is cleared from smashing my face into the log.

"I'll teach you a fucking lesson you'll never forget, you fucking bitch," he says. I can feel him trying to pull my shirt up over my chest. I cross my arms and start to scream for help.

He covers my mouth with one hand and says, "Shut up you stupid bitch, they'll hear you."

I bite his hand and shout, "That's the point you dumb ass. GET! OFF! OF! ME!"

"Lainey?!" I hear multiple familiar voices say from over by the clubhouse.

I'm seeing spots but can hear running footsteps.

"Get the fuck off of her!" I hear Dalton yell.

I feel Elijah getting pulled off me.

"Call the cops," I hear Lee say. "And an ambulance, Lainey's hurt really bad."

"Lainey?" I hear Dalton say from beside me.

CHAPTER 8

"Hey, open your eyes and talk to me."

I can hear fighting going on a few feet away. Punches connecting with bodies, grunts and shouts.

"Don't let the guys kill him, I don't want them to get in trouble," I whisper out. My head is really starting to hurt.

Dalton laughs a quiet but relieved sounding laugh, "They won't kill him but he deserves every ounce they're dishing him."

I feel him lay his jacket over me. I sigh. "That feels good, it was getting chilly out here."

"Can you open your eyes for me?" he asks, concern in his voice.

"They aren't open?" I ask, starting to feel sleepy.

"No they aren't, Honey," he says. He then shouts, "Hey, someone go get some towels from the clubhouse. We need to stop the bleeding."

"Shhh... too loud..." I say, trying to reach up to cover my ears but my arms feel really heavy. And then because it took a minute for what Dalton said to register, I ask, "Bleeding?"

"Yeah, you've got a pretty nasty gash on your forehead, right above your left eyebrow, can't you feel it?" he asks. I feel something being pressed where he was saying and I feel a sting. I open my right eye a little and see Dalton is shirtless. This concerns me more than the throbbing starting to intensify in my head.

"You're naked, you'll freeze," I giggle out. *Why*

am I giggling? A part of my mind asks myself. And then I say, "But you're nice to look at though."

"I'm not naked, I still have on my pants. I'm using my shirt to get the bleeding to slow. I don't know if we have time to wait for an ambulance..." Dalton says. I feel him moving around while keeping one hand on his shirt on my head but I've closed my eyes again so I can't be sure what he's doing. "Jack, take my keys and go get my pickup, use the panic button to find it. We'll have to take her."

"Cops are on the phone," Lee says.

"Tell them we're taking her to the hospital," Dalton says.

"What the hell?" I hear Alex say. "What happened?"

Irrational anger flares in me and I say, "Oh, nothing. Just Dalton and I about to fuck..."

"Lainey," I hear Dalton say.

"It's apparently all we do.. Fuck.. fuck... fuck... right Alex?" I can hear how belligerent I sound but I can't stop myself from talking.

"That's not what I meant," Alex says from beside me.

"Whatever..." I say.

"I'm gonna go get Emily," Dylan says from a few feet away.

"What happened?" Alex asks again.

"That bag of dicks over there was..." Dalton says,

CHAPTER 8

I can hear him swallow hard, trying to control his anger.

"Was what?" Alex asks again, sounding more pissed.

"Was trying to fuck me... that's all guys want from me... right Alex? And that's all I want? Right Alex?" I say, belligerent again.

"What?! NO! Lainey..." Alex starts to say. "Where is he?"

"The other guys already knocked him out," Dalton says. "Do we need to have a conversation about Lainey and me? She hasn't said 'fuck' this much, in the short time that I've known her."

"It's apparently--" I start to say and then puke everywhere. I feel Dalton roll me so that I don't choke on it.

"Shit, I think she has a concussion," Dalton says.

"Ouch... my head hurts," I say. All belligerence gone. I try to open my eyes but they feel really heavy.

"Lainey? Dalton? Alex? What the..." I hear Emily say in surprise. "What the hell?"

"Hang on Lainey, Jack just pulled up in my pickup. We'll take you to the hospital. Emily, get in the back with her, I'll tell you what I saw on our way into the hospital," Dalton says. I can feel him lifting me up but I feel like I'm floating.

"Lainey, are you okay?" I hear Emily asking but it sounds like she's in a tunnel.

"Mmmm," is all I mumble out.

"I'm going too," I hear Alex say.

"We'll wait for the cops and then we'll come in," Lee says. I can hear Jack and Dylan mumble an agreement.

"I'll bring your car in, Em," Brayden says from a few feet away.

Their voices sound like they're getting further and further away. I take a deep breath and let it out slowly and let the darkness take me.

Chapter 9

Before I open my eyes, I can hear beeping. And then I feel pain. A deep throbbing in my head and a sharp pain on my forehead and bottom left side of my mouth.

"Ughnah…" I moan.

"Lainey?" I hear from my left.

"Is she waking up?" I hear from my right.

"Mmmm…" I mumble.

"Lainey?" I hear from my right again. Emily.

"Mmmm hmmm…" I mumble.

I try to open my eyes but find that I can't open my left one. My right one slowly opens. It's bright in the room so it takes a couple tries before I can keep it open. I see Emily sitting but leaning onto my bed. She reaches out and takes my hand.

"Hi," she says, it sounds like she's been crying.

"Hey," I croak out. I cough to clear my throat.

"You feeling okay?" I hear Dalton say, on my left.

I look over and see him sitting like Emily but holding my hand.

"Hi," I say. Then answer him, "Yeah, I'm okay. My head hurts and my mouth." I reach up with my right hand and touch my bottom lip. It's swollen pretty bad and sore.

The nurse comes in and says, "Oh good you're awake. How are you feeling sweetie? Are you in much pain?"

"My head is hurting pretty bad," I say.

"Would you like a dose of Morphine?" she asks as she checks my monitors.

"No thanks, maybe just some Tylenol and Ibuprofen?" I say.

"Sure thing, deary," she says as she leaves.

"Morphine will kick in faster," Dalton says.

"I'm a lightweight when it comes to hard pain killers, they knock me out. Tylenol and Ibuprofen work best for me," I say.

"That could be why you've been sleeping so much," Emily says. "The Doc had them giving you regular doses of Morphine."

"How long have I been out?" I ask.

"About 18 hours," Emily says.

"Dang," I say.

"Do you want to talk about what happened?" Emily asks. "Dalton told us what they saw when they found you but that's all we know. He said the guy was one that was harassing you earlier in the evening?"

"Yeah... apparently his name is Elijah. The other one was Phil but I'm pretty sure he passed out before everything started to happen," I say. I tell them what had happened, what I could remember, which was up until Emily got there. I touch my mouth and say, "So this must be where he hit me and this is from hitting the log." I touch my eyebrow.

I hear Dalton slowly let out a breath. I look over at him and see he's pissed.

"Hey, you okay?" I ask.

"No... I... am not okay..." he says. "I need to go for a walk. I'll find the guys and tell them you're awake."

"Ooookay," I say. He stands and leaves the room. I look at Emily and she shrugs and raises her shoulders. I ask her, "The guys are here?"

"We've all been here since we brought you in," she says. "They just went to get something to eat."

"You guys didn't need to stay," I say.

"We did, Doc wasn't sure how severe your head trauma was going to be and we all wanted to be here when you woke up," Emily says, wiping her eyes.

"Hey, I'm going to be okay. It's just a bump on the head," I say, reaching my hand out for her.

"You could have been hurt far worse than this, Lainey, I'm so sorry," she says, putting my hand up to her face. "If we lost you... I don't know what I'd do."

"Don't be sorry, it's not your fault," I say, squeezing her hand.

"I'm sorry I told the guys about you and Dalton," she says sheepishly.

"Yeah, I was wondering, when did you see them to talk to them about that?" I ask, my anger with her is gone.

"At the barbeque dinner. They were there. They had been told by a couple different people that they had seen you with Dalton. The guys were getting all big brother about it so I told them to leave you alone. That you seemed happy and were smiling your true smile and actually laughing again. I might have left slip that you finally got a good lay in also but that was a total accident because I was explaining to them how much stress looked to be gone from you when I saw you the next morning," she says really fast. She tends to talk fast when she's excited about something or trying to explain something.

"I've been smiling and laughing these last 18 months," I say, a little taken aback that she would think I hadn't been.

"Yeah but it wasn't your true, deep down laugh or a fully genuine smile... I'm not saying it in a bad way... you've had a lot going on, Lainey. It was just nice to see you truly happy," she says smiling at me.

"Hmmmm..." is all I can say. After a few minutes of silence, I ask, "Are the guys in trouble for what happened to Elijah?"

"No, the officers took their statements and I guess when that Elijah guy woke up, he was running his mouth about you. One of the officers came here to get a statement from Dalton. They told him when you woke up to give them a call and they'd come take your statement. Basically, they just want your statement so that Elijah can't come back and say he didn't know what he was saying because he was drunk or whatever."

"He was definitely drunk but I'll give a statement. I wouldn't want him to try this with anyone else," I say, wincing a little at the pain.

"Deb will be back with your pain meds soon, she's probably getting you something to eat since it's been so long since you ate last," Emily says as she pats my arm.

"Is there any way to get a cold washcloth or ice pack or something to put on my head? My eye is starting to throb," I ask as I close my eyes and wish the pain away.

"I'll go get you one," Emily stands up and leaves the room.

I keep my eyes closed and listen to the beeping of the monitors. It's slightly calming. I hear the door open and close, I open my eyes, expecting Emily but see Dalton and the guys standing around me.

"Oh, hey guys," I say.

"How ya feeling, Lainey?" Jack asks, coming over and sitting in the seat Emily had been sitting in a few minutes ago.

"I'm okay, just sore, I'll be okay though," I answer. I notice his bandaged hand and ask, "What's that? Is that from the fight?"

"Yeah, just a sprained wrist," he says sounding embarrassed.

I look over at Dylan and Jay and see they have their own battle wounds. Dylan has a fat lip and Jay has a black eye.

"Oh, you guys..." I start to say but then change my mind. "Thank you."

"I know it's cliche to say, but, you should really see the other guy," Dylan says laughing.

"Yeah, we let him have it," Jay says.

"It looked like you had already taken care of his nose though," Jack says, patting my shoulder. "Good girl."

I laugh, "I tried."

"You did good," Jay says.

"Hey," Alex says, stepping forward. "We... well, I... wanted to apologize for how I talked to you last night. It wasn't fair of me and I'm sorry."

"No worries, Alex... we're good," I say, smiling at him.

BUZZ-BUZZ **BUZZ-BUZZ**

"Sorry, that's my phone," Dalton says. "I'll step

out and take it, and let you guys talk."

"Hey," I say before he leaves. "Thank you to you, too."

"Always," he says and winks before stepping out into the hall shutting the door behind him.

"I like him," Jay says.

"We know..." Alex says, slightly annoyed. "You wouldn't shut up about him all night and all morning."

"He treats Lainey great and they just met. He's been here since they brought her here. I really think he cares about her," Jay says, sounding defensive.

"I'm right here, you don't need to talk like I'm not, but thank you Jay, I like him too," I say, smiling over at him. "And I'm sorry I didn't tell you guys about him. I honestly wasn't sure if it was anything and we still aren't sure what... this... is either. We're taking it day by day but he's going to be going home soon and I don't know what's going to happen after that, which is why I didn't say anything. Why bring it up if it's a weekend thing?"

"I think it's more than that," I hear Lee say. "Just my opinion from watching him with you."

"I'm not getting my hopes up, guys. For once I did something spontaneous and out of the ordinary for myself and I've had fun," I say.

"You do look happy, like really happy," Dylan says.

"You do," Alex says, coming to sit in the seat

Dalton had been sitting in earlier. "I mean under the bruises and cuts and what not, you do look less stressed and more happy. Last night when we walked into the clubhouse and saw you guys dancing, the smile on your face made me smile. I haven't seen you smile like that in... well you know."

"I know, and Alex... actually, all of you...," I take a minute to look at them all before I continue. "If, or when, I do get into a new relationship, whether it's with Dalton or someone else... I will never, ever, forget about Jayce. He's a permanent fixture in my heart. My kids will know their dad. Dalton or whoever the guy ends up being, will not replace Jayce but he'll be an addition to our family... our big family, which is you guys. So don't feel threatened or jealous or whatever you might feel towards Dalton or whoever, help me pick a good one."

The guys all mumble in agreement and a couple turn their faces away and wipe their eyes.

Alex takes my hand and says, "We will. I'll do better, I promise."

"Thank you," I say, squeezing his hand.

The door opens and Emily comes in holding a cold compress and some water. She looks around the room and says, "Why are you guys crying? She's gonna be fine."

A couple of the guys mumble something about not crying but needing to go to the bathroom. Jay and

Lee leave, followed by Dylan.

"Here, I grabbed a bottle of water for you and this compress," Emily says. "Deb was heading this way with your pain meds. I passed Dalton in the hall. Any idea who he's talking to on the phone? He sounded pissed."

"Thanks," I say as she hands me the water and puts the compress on my eye. The coolness helps a lot. "Yeah, I don't know who he's talking to."

"Whoever it is, is getting an ear full," she says and makes a 'yikes' look on her face.

Deb walks in and Jack jumps up out of her way.

"Here darlin', take these, you'll feel better soon. The doctor will be in soon to go over a few things with you and where we go now that you're awake, okay?" she says as she checks my monitors again.

"Sounds good, thank you," I say and then swallow my meds. She brought me some chicken noodle soup and a sprite.

"We're gonna head out, but call us if you need anything," Alex says.

"Actually, would you guys go back to the clubhouse and get my rig and bring it here?" I ask. "I don't know how long they're gonna keep me but I'd like to have it here for when I'm released."

"Sure thing," Alex says.

"My keys were in my pants pocket, wherever they are and my phone. Shoot, I probably better call

Lucy and let her know what's happened," I say.

"I already told her and I called her when I went to find a cold compress. She says to call her as soon as you're feeling up to talking but maybe not video chat until you're healed a little bit, wouldn't want to scare the kids," Emily says.

"Thank you," I say, patting her hand that she had resting on my arm.

"I'll go get your phone and keys," she says and leaves the room.

"We'll go with her," Alex says.

"See you soon, Lains," Jack says.

"Thanks, guys," I say.

As they leave, Dalton walks in. He does look pissed.

"Hey, is everything okay?" I ask.

"No, not really… That was Frank on the phone," he says and sits down next to me.

"Something going on back on the homestead?"

"Yeah, the Vet refuses to come and work the cattle unless I'm there and we can't take them to forest land until they've been worked. I was hoping they'd be able to take care of it so I could stay here and help you out."

"Oh no, no, no, don't worry about me. I'll be fine. If you need to get back home, don't feel bad about that."

"I want to be here for you though," he says, taking my hand in his.

"I know but there's not much you can do right now and even when I get released, I'll probably be made to lay around and rest. So again, not much you can do there," I say, squeezing his hand.

BUZZ-BUZZ **BUZZ-BUZZ**

Dalton's phone is buzzing him again.

"See what I mean? It's never ending," he looks at the caller ID. "It's Frank again."

"You own and operate a huge ranch, your phone is supposed to do that. Go talk to Frank, I'm gonna eat my soup and drink my Sprite."

Dalton stands up and kisses my forehead, "You truly are incredible."

As he walks out the room I hear him answer his phone angrily.

I knew he was going to go home soon but the reality of it being now, doesn't make me feel good. I shouldn't have let myself get feelings for him but how can you stop yourself from getting feelings? No matter how many times you tell yourself to stop feeling, it doesn't change anything. You can tell yourself over and over how stupid you're being but it doesn't change anything. I just have to remind myself that this bad feeling is nothing compared to losing Jayce. There's still a possibility that Dalton and I can become something, even if it's later, and that is a better feeling than knowing

Jayce and I can never be again. Coming to terms with that, that was hard. This will be easy in comparison.

I eat my soup and lean my head back. Having food in my stomach makes me feel better and helps the pain meds kick in too. Soon I can feel the throbbing start to ease and the sharp pains are gone soon too. I hadn't realized how achy I was also, my muscles feel more relaxed.

Dalton walks in and startles me. I must have fallen asleep.

"Did I wake you?" he asks, sitting down and taking my hand again.

"Yeah but it's okay. Did you get things figured out with Frank?"

"Yes and no. I'm going to have to fly out tonight so that we can get things lined out for working the cattle tomorrow so that we can move them Monday. I'm so sorry, Lainey. I really wanted more time here with you."

"We'll talk on the phone... it'll be like high school all over again," I laugh. "It'll be fun. We'll make plans for weekend getaways. I'll come visit you, you can come back and visit me. If you want, this can work."

"I do, I really do," Dalton says. "I honestly didn't think a woman like you existed. So yes, I want to talk on the phone like high schoolers and I want to plan weekends."

"Then we will," I say, pulling his hand up to my mouth and kissing it but then wince immediately. "Well, kissing is off the 'can do' list."

"So maybe it's a good thing I'm having to leave, I tend to have a hard time not kissing you and keeping my hands off of you," Dalton says, teasingly.

"Maybe it is," I laugh.

Emily comes back in and sits down. "The guys left to go get the rigs. I told them to find me and give me your keys just in case you're sleeping."

"Thanks, Em," I say.

"Okay, it looks like you're in capable hands. I should probably go get all my stuff together. I fly out in a couple hours and I have to do a preflight check and all that too," Dalton says about to stand up. "But I need your number before I leave."

"Wait, preflight check? Are you a pilot?" I ask, astounded.

"I am, did I not tell you that?" Dalton looks confused for a second.

"Uhhh, no you did not... but I should have guessed..." I say rolling my eyes and laughing. "You're everything."

"Well, I was flying all over the country for livestock sales and looking at farm equipment and what not and it was getting expensive to keep flying. So I figured I could probably have my own plane and license paid off for the amount I was paying the airliners. I was right, it's way cheaper and quicker this way. Plus, it makes weekend getaways more fun," he winks at me.

I shake my head but laugh. He amazes me, I just can't get over it.

He pulls out his phone and I rattle off my number. Emily pulls my phone out of her pocket and hands it to me. In one second I have a new message from a Montana number, it's a kissy face emoji.

"Cute," I say but I'm grinning as widely as my hurt mouth will let me. I quickly add him to my contact list. "Will you call or text me when you make it back home?"

"I will," he says. "You rest and let me know what the doc has to say, okay?"

"I will," I mimic him. He smiles and kisses me on the top of the head. He says goodbye to Emily, then kisses my forehead one more time. We say goodbye and then he leaves.

I'm staring at the door when Emily says, "He's a good one, Lainey."

"But is he for real?" I ask out loud.

She laughs and says, "As real as you and me."

"There has to be something he's not saying that makes him not so damn perfect," I say a little irritatedly.

"Why does something have to be wrong with him?"

"I don't know, he's so... he's just..."

"Dreamy? Sexy? Amazing at everything he does and touches?"

"YES! Exactly, all of that," I say.

"Oh Lainey," Emily is laughing now. "I'm sure he does something that would drive me crazy but to you, he's perfect. Just like Brayden is perfect in my eyes but not in yours."

I look at her skeptically, but then understand what she's saying. She loves Brayden but he does things that I would have a hard time sticking around and tolerating. Maybe Dalton does something that would annoy someone else, but it doesn't annoy me. Hmm, interesting.

I close my eyes and find myself in a field full of tall green grass and wildflowers. I'm running my hand over the top of the grass, letting it tickle my hands and arms. I can hear someone calling my name from a distance. Emily's voice starts to get louder.

I open my eyes and I'm in the hospital room again. Weird how quickly I fell asleep.

"Was I given Morphine again?" I ask.

"Half a dose," Emily says.

"I didn't want anymore," I say sternly. "I don't want anymore. It makes me sleepy and I feel weird when I wake up. A loopy kind of feeling."

"Okay, I'll tell them no more, strictly Tylenol and Ibuprofen."

"Why'd you wake me up?"

"Deb came in and said the doc would be coming in shortly to go over a few things with you."

"Do you know what?"

"No, I'm not allowed to look at your chart unless you give them permission to let me look."

"Oh, well, I'll tell them it's okay if you do."

A second later, there's a light knock on the door and the doctor walks in with Deb the nurse.

"Mrs. Richardsen, it's good to see you awake. Emily, happy to see you as always," the doctor says, nodding in Emily's direction.

"Nice to see you too, Dr. Rhines," Emily says respectfully.

"Mrs. Richardsen-," Dr. Rhines starts to say

But I interrupt and say, "You can call me Lainey."

Dr. Rhines smiles and says, "Okay, Lainey... we're going to go over what I've seen and what we should do from here, Emily is welcome to stay if you wish her to or we can have her step out."

"No, I want her here and she has my permission to look at my charts as well," I say.

"Very good, Deb will put a note in your charts about that," Dr. Rhines says. "So, as you can see, visibly you have a couple good dings. We waited to run any tests until you were awake. Are you up for a couple? We'll do an x-ray of your face to check for any broken bones and then a CT scan to see if there is any significant brain injury."

"Yeah, I'm good with that. I would like to make sure that I'm not given Morphine anymore. I feel like I can sleep just fine and Morphine makes me loopy. Tylenol and Ibuprofen are good enough for me."

Deb looks slightly ashamed for slipping in the half dose but nods at me.

"Deb will get the orders for your tests sent up and we'll get you ready for that. Should be done with it all in about an hour, hour and a half tops," Dr. Rhines says. He nods at Emily and then leaves the room, with Deb following behind him.

Waiting for them to come and get me for the tests was the hardest part. The x-ray and CT scan were easy, I just had to lay still. I almost fell asleep during the CT scan. Deb let Emily wheel me back to my room. We had dinner waiting for us when we got back. Alex had dropped off my keys and some takeout from my favorite little drive-thru.

He left a note.

After eating a couple meals here myself, I thought you'd like some real food. Keys are on the table with your phone. Text or call if you need anything.
-Alex

Chicken strips and tater-tots. Probably the healthiest the place had but still delicious. Emily runs and gets us a couple of drinks. I wasn't allowed anything dark so I had another Sprite.

"When should I hear about my test results?" I ask Emily after we finish watching a rerun of 'Friends' on the tv.

"Dr. Rhines put a rush on them so you'll know tonight. If everything looks good, you'll get discharged tomorrow. You can stay with me for a couple days, if you want. Might be more fun than going home."

"Oh wow that's quick but nice. I hate waiting to find out test results. And yeah, I think it would be nice to hangout with you for a couple days."

We watch a couple more reruns, when Dr. Rhines comes into my room again.

"So, we'll get straight to it as it's getting late and you need to rest. The good news is you don't have a traumatic brain injury. You do have a slight concussion but nothing that looks too concerning. Bad news, your eye socket is cracked and there isn't a lot we can do for it, just be very careful for the next 4-6 weeks. It's not so bad that I'll suggest another x-ray but if it gets bumped pretty hard, we'll want to make sure it didn't crack to the point of splintering. It's not to that point right now, so don't worry about splinters. Your jaw is cracked also but not so bad that we need to do anything about it either, just be careful with it as well and watch what you eat. Nothing too hard for the next two weeks. So no apples or something that can put pressure on your jaw. If either area gets bumped and you experience severe pain, come in and we'll take a look but little bumps and minor pain, soreness, is fine. I'll put in your discharge papers so you can go home in the morning. I can put an order in for a Morphine prescription but from how you were talking earlier, you don't like the effect of it. So would you like a prescription of a high dose Tylenol and Ibuprofen?"

"Yeah, that would be great," I say, still stunned.

"Okay, I'll get that sent to the pharmacy. Do you have any questions for me?" he asks.

"Not right now, no," I say.

"Well, if you think of any, let Emily or Deb know and I'd be happy to answer them for you, have a good night," he and Deb walk out and shut the door behind them.

I look over at Emily, she looks as stunned as I feel.

"So basically I'm broken but not broken enough to need anything done about it. So… that's good?" I ask.

"In a way yes. You'll be sore as hell but at least your jaw isn't wired shut and you don't have to wear a face shield to protect your eye socket but on the other hand, you need to be really careful for the next couple of weeks about getting bumped. Anyways Lucy or the grandparents can take turns with the kids?"

"Oh, no, I can't be away from them for that long. They'll be fine. If I explain why they have to be careful with Mommy, they will be."

BUZZ-BUZZ

My phone goes off, letting me know I have a new message. Emily hands it to me.

-New message from Dalton-

"Eeehehe, it's from Dalton," I say grinning.
"Is he already home?" she asks, surprised.

Dalton- *About to take off. Wanted to say thank you again for an amazing weekend. I'll text when I land. *kissy face emoji** 10:52pm
Me- *Fly safe. And no, thank you, you have no idea. Best weekend I've had in a long time.* 10:52pm
Dalton- **kissy face emoji** 10:52pm

I read the text exchange to Emily. She's smiling like an idiot.

"I love how he uses emojis, it's so cute," she says.

"I love it too," I say giggling.

"I wish Brayden would use them, I'm lucky if I get a response at all from him," she says sourly.

"It's the honeymoon stage. You remember the beginning of any new... relationship... if that's what this is... anyways, everyone is all googly-eyed and whatnot," I say to make her feel better but secretly hoping it never stops.

"When do you think he'll get home? How long of a flight do you think it is?" she asks.

"I'm not sure, maybe an hour or two? I guess it depends on where he's flying into and then the drive home," I say.

"That's true," she says. "And you don't know where that is?"

"No, he just said he lived in Montana and I never asked specifically where in Montana," I say, grimacing and then yawn.

"Getting tired again?" she asks.

"Yeah, I feel like I've done nothing but sleep."

"Your body needs to heal and to do that, you need sleep. It's normal to feel tired even if you've been sleeping a lot already."

I adjust myself down onto my bed and pull the blanket up to my chin. "Well, then I'm gonna close my eyes. If I don't wake up when Dalton calls or texts, and you hear it, wake me up, please."

"Mmmmhmmm," is all she says.

I fall asleep to another 'Friends' rerun starting.

Chapter 10

Waking up this morning was a little rough. I had slept through the night which meant missing a couple doses of pain meds, which in turn meant for some pain.

"Feeling better yet?" Emily asks. It's been about 45 minutes since I took my first dose of the day. She doesn't have to work today or tomorrow, she asked to be put on the 'On Call' list, so that way she can babysit me.

"Yeah, the throbbing is a dull pain now and the stinging on my face has stopped," I say as I pull my shoes on. I've been discharged and can go home! Or at least to Emily's house.

I look at my phone for the 100th time this morning, still no call or text from Dalton. I'm starting to worry. Hopefully he made it home okay.

"Just text him... or call him," Emily says.

"I don't want to bother him if he's busy," I say.

"He said he'd get ahold of you once he got home, I think it's perfectly fine if you get ahold of him first."

"That was when he was here. What if he's changed his mind and doesn't want the trouble of trying to make this work?" I ask, worry and doubt coloring my tone.

"Then he's a good actor and a total ass-hat," Emily says as she hands me my keys to my rig and my overnight bag. She had Brayden run to my house and get me a couple things. "I could tell he was totally into you and he seemed genuine when he left last night."

"Alright, alright… I'll send him a text…" I say. I've never been one to like to play games. If you want to talk to someone, just talk to them. Call them. Text them. I really shouldn't have to wait for him, should I? No… no I shouldn't.

I pull out my phone and open my messages.

Me- *Hi, just wanted to check in and make sure you got home safe.* 8:48am

There, no harm in that. I put my phone back in my pocket.

"Better?" Emily asks, smiling.

"I guess so," I say. "I'll be better when we're back at your house. Let's get out of here before Dr. Rhines changes his mind and makes me stay longer."

Emily grabs her bag and walks out of the room. She had parked beside my rig so I let her lead us out.

"Hey, do you want a coffee?" she asks.

"Ohhh yes, a good coffee would be a welcome treat!" I say, enthusiastically.

"Head to my house, you know where the spare key is hidden. I'll go get us a couple coffees and maybe some doughnuts or something to go with them. I'll meet you there," she says as she gets into her car.

"Sounds good, thanks Em," I say. I get in my rig and head to her house.

I find the key where she has hidden it for as long as I've known her, in the garden gnome's hat that sits by her door, the hat twists off. It's so well hidden that you wouldn't know it comes off unless you've been shown and there's a trick to get the hat to twist so even if you were messing with it, it wouldn't work unless you knew the trick.

Sitting in Emily's living room should bring back every memory of all the fun times I've had in here with her but all I can think about is the other morning when I woke up and thought Dalton had bolted from a one night stand but was surprised by him coming back with arms full of coffee, food, and clothes. Who does that? Apparently Dalton does. But here I sit, wondering about if I'll ever hear from him again.

Ugh, I thought I was done with this crap. I thought that since I married Jayce, that I wouldn't have to worry about this type of thing again. I knew when I'd see or talk to him again. The worry of 'does he like me, does he not' was over. The 'game' of dating was over, I had found my person. But now, here we go again. Although, does it have to be this way? Why can't I just look at it as a casual thing? I can talk myself down, I've gotten really good at it over the last 18 months. I don't have to let this bother me. If Dalton texts me back or calls, great, if not, no worries. We had a great weekend, it can be left at that, right? I think I can handle it.

I put my keys and phone down and go into the bathroom and wash my face. I take a look at my bruises. My gash is healing nicely, thanks to the multiple stitches. My lip is still pretty bruised but it isn't as dark purple as it was yesterday, still pretty gnarly looking though.

I hear my phone going off back in the living room so I dry my face and walk back out.

-New message from Dalton-

Amazing how just seeing that notification can make my heart skip a beat and my stomach fall to the floor.

You're ridiculous! I think to myself.

Dalton- Hi Lainey!
I'm sorry I didn't get ahold of you last night.

I got in pretty late and didn't want to wake you. This morning started off with nonstop phone calls to the vet and employees to get them here so we can start working the cattle. We'll be starting that in about 20 minutes.

How are you feeling? 9:16am

Do I keep it cool and wait so it doesn't seem like I'm sitting on my phone waiting for him to reply or just reply?

Ugh... Lainey, stop. Just reply. You are setting your own self up for this stupid mind game. Stop. Just do what you want and to hell with anything or anyone else's view of the 'rules' of it all..... My inner monologue pep talks are getting good. If people could hear what I thought... or knew how much I talk to myself in my head... I'd probably be committed.

Me- *I'm so glad you made it home. I was worried. One of the things about me, I worry when people are traveling.*

I'm doing really good. Discharged this morning. At Em's house now. I'll probably stay here for a couple nights and then go home.

Have fun working cattle, it's my least favorite job but with the right people, can be fun. 9:17am

Dalton- *Happy to hear you're out. Hospitals are no fun. Tell Emily hi for me. I'll call you once we're done with the cattle, if it's not too late.* 9:17am

Dalton- *Frank just walked in. He's asking why I'm smiling like an idiot. It's because of you, you make me smile like an idiot.* 9:17am

Dalton- *Probably didn't need to tell you that but... even hundreds of miles away, I still say too much when I talk to you. Haha* 9:18am

Me- *I like it and hope you always tell me what you're thinking. *smile emoji** 9:18am

Dalton- **wink emoji* You want to know EVERYTHING I'm thinking?* 9:18am

Me- *Ummm yes...* 9:18am

Dalton- *Well, right now I'm thinking about Emily's shower and our last... visit to it... *drool face emoji** 9:19am

Me- *What a coincidence, I was thinking about the last time we were here at Em's house too.* 9:19am

Dalton- *Really?* 9:19am

Me- *Yup... the trampoline is looking awfully lonely... The shower... way too cold, it needs a little steam to liven it up a bit.* 9:19am

Dalton- *Not... nice... I'm supposed to go work cattle... like this?* 9:19am

Me- *Something to think about while working.* 9:20am

Dalton- *Evil... evil woman! *kissy face emoji** 9:20am

Me- *Bahaha You started it!* 9:20am

Dalton- *I know and now Frank looks really concerned for me. I better get to work. It's cool enough outside that it'll have to work as my cold shower.* 9:20am

Me- *That bad? *Laugh crying emoji** 9:20am

Dalton- *Always with you.* 9:20am

Me- *Bahaha Sorry!* 9:21am

Dalton- *Sure looks like you are... Haha* 9:21am

Me- *I am... sort of... hahaha* 9:21am

Dalton- *OK, I gotta go, everyone is showing up. TTYL *kissy face emoji** 9:21am

Me- *Bye *wink emoji* *smile emoji** 9:21am

As I'm putting my phone down, Emily comes in the front door.

"What are you all happy about?" she asks with a huge grin on her face. I can feel my sore lip starting to hurt, I am in fact smiling like an idiot. "Did Dalton message you back?"

"Yeah, he got in late and didn't want to wake me and has been busy on the phone with getting things lined out for work today," I say, still smiling.

"See, it's all good. I knew he wasn't an ass-hat," she says. She puts our coffee and doughnuts down and sits beside me, grabbing the remote. "What do you wanna watch?"

"Whatever you want, is good with me," I say, taking a sip of my coffee. I take a doughnut and grab a blanket from the back of the couch and snuggle in for whatever Emily chooses to watch. Turns out to be a movie we've seen at least a 100 times.

I start to feel sleepy again, how, I'm not sure. I feel like I've done nothing but sleep for the last couple of days but I close my eyes and let myself snooze.

◆ ◆ ◆

CHAPTER 10

I wake up to my phone buzzing on the table. I pick it up.

-New message from Dalton-

My idiot smile is back. I also see that I've been sleeping for a good two hours. I look over at Emily and see she's napping also.

Dalton- *Lunch time update:*
I'm questioning why I run cattle. Although I question myself about this every time we work them.
Frank keeps asking if I'm OK. Apparently I'm smiling a lot today.
It's not cold enough out here. A cold shower might be needed later. Might actually help if I STOPPED thinking about you and... well you... haha 12:17pm

Dalton- *How are you feeling?* 12:17pm

Me- *I'm feeling ok. I took a nap... again. I'm sorry it's not cold enough for you. How cold is it?* 12:17pm

Dalton- *It's in the low 60's right now... I'm needing freezing temps... 32 degrees would be great...* 12:17pm

Me- **Laugh crying emoji* Is it really that bad?* 12:17pm

Dalton- *It's a bit uncomfortable... yes* 12:17pm

Me- *Bahaha I'm sorry... I really am... I don't know what it's like but it can't be fun... *Laugh crying emoji** 12:18pm

Dalton- *Your laughing emoji contradicts your sorrowful words...* 12:18pm

Me- *Laugh crying emoji* 12:18pm

Dalton- Evil... I tell you what... 12:18pm

Me- I'm not doing anything. You need to control your thoughts. Haha *Laughing emoji* 12:18pm

Dalton- If it were that easy, I'd be having an easier time... Haha *Wink emoji* 12:18pm

Me- Would it help if I said we can talk this out later this evening when you're done working? 12:18pm

Dalton- Ouch... no... that makes it worse... but yeah, we should definitely talk this out later... *Wink emoji* *Drool emoji* 12:19pm

Me- Try not to think about it... hahahahaha 12:19pm

Dalton- Mmmmmhmmmm, that's not going to happen... 12:19pm

Me- I wish I could help... *Wink emoji* 12:19pm

Dalton- Stop saying things like that... 12:19pm

Me- LOL but it's true 12:19pm

Dalton- STOOOOPPPPP... *Cross eyed emoji* 12:19pm

Me- You're ridiculous... *Kissy face emoji* 12:20pm

Dalton- Don't even do that emoji... It makes me think of you kissing me... and... ouuuuuuch! 12:20pm

Me- You're just messing with me right? 12:20pm

Dalton- Hahaha yeah, kind of. I mean.... I am... uncomfortable but it's not as bad as I'm making it out to be. Just sucks cause you aren't here. 12:20pm

Me- You're a shit... lol 12:20pm

Dalton- *Wink emoji*... 12:20pm

Me- Eat your lunch and get back to work. 12:20pm

Dalton- Yes ma'am... we'll talk later this evening? 12:20pm

CHAPTER 10

Me- *I'm not going anywhere.* 12:21pm
Dalton- *Great, talk to you then...* 12:21pm
Me- *Bye *Wave emoji** 12:21pm

I set my phone down and think about how all this is so ridiculous. I need to reel it all in and keep my feelings and emotions in check... yeah right, like that's going to happen, I'm already too far gone. *Crap! Crap! Crap!*

Shaking my head at my own stupidity and lack of self-control, I get up and find my bag that has my pain meds. It's time for dose number two and I'm not going to let myself get behind on them again. Sitting back on the couch in my spot, I grab one of the doughnuts still in the box and eat it while sipping on my still warm coffee. I'd fallen asleep before I was able to finish drinking it.

I find something to watch on TV and reposition myself into a more comfortable position. I can tell my days were going to consist of a lot of naps, or at least today was turning out to be that way.

◆ ◆ ◆

"Lainey... Laaainey..." I hear Emily saying my name. I open my eyes slowly and see her leaning over me.

"Mmmm... what's up?" I yawn.

"It's 5:30, I'm hungry. Do you want something to eat?" she asks as she walks into the kitchen.

"Oh wow, 5:30 already?" I ask and grab my phone off the table. Sure enough it's 5:30pm.

"Yeah, we conked out," Emily says with her head in the refrigerator. "What sounds good? I don't have much."

"I don't know... wanna just order delivery?" I ask.

She shuts the fridge door and walks back into the living room and says as she sits down, "Sounds good to me."

"Chinese?" we say at the same time. We both smile at each other and nod.

"I'll call it in, same as usual?" she asks.

"Yup," I say. I get up and go into the bathroom. When I come out I stop in the kitchen and get some water. I'd slept through my Tylenol alarm but it was just time for Ibuprofen. I take both doses and sit back down on the couch.

"Dinner will be here in about 45 minutes," Emily says. "Brayden is going to come over when he gets off work. We might go out for a drink, if you think you'll be okay here alone... unless you want to go with us?"

"Oh, no, I'll be fine. I want to stay in," I say, laying my head back. It's starting to throb a little around my gash. "I need to make sure I wake up for my alarms, so

I can take my pain meds when it's time. I haven't been very good today, I've been sleeping so much."

"I'll set my alarms too, did you just take some?" she asks, picking up her phone.

"Yeah," I say, reluctantly. I feel silly having to have her set her alarms too but with how much I've been sleeping, it's probably a good idea to have a backup.

"If you want to go shower, I'll change your bandage," Emily says, leaning over and looking at my forehead.

"Yeees, I could really use one," I say, standing up.

BUZZ-BUZZ

I pick my phone up and see a notification.

-New message from Dalton-

Dalton- *Well that was the most interesting time I've ever had working cows.* 5:37pm
Me- *Hahaha Oh yeah?* 5:37pm
Dalton- *Very. How was your day?* 5:37pm
Me- *Not as interesting as yours, I slept for most of it... okay, for all of it.* 5:37pm
Dalton- *You need to get as much rest as possible. It's the best and fastest way for you to heal. What are you up to now?* 5:37pm

Me- *I'm not sure I should tell you.* 5:38pm

Dalton- *Why's that?* 5:38pm

Me- *Just with how your day's gone, I don't wanna make it worse.* 5:38pm

Dalton- *Well now you gotta tell me...* 5:38pm

Me- *You sure?* 5:39pm

Dalton- *Yes, you can tell me anything, Lainey... Should I be worried? I feel worried.* 5:39pm

I smile as I get up and head towards the bathroom.

Me- *No you shouldn't be worried it's nothing bad.* 5:39pm

Dalton- *Okay... soo... what are you doing?* 5:39pm

Me- *Just turned on the water to take a shower...* 5:40pm

Dalton- 5:40pm

Me- *Dalton?* 5:40pm

Dalton- 5:40pm

Me- *You OK? *Crying laugh emoji** 5:40pm

Dalton- *Yup... just give me a minute...* 5:40pm

Me- *You asked... *Laughing emoji** 5:41pm

Dalton- *I sure did...* 5:41pm

Me- *You gonna make it over there?* 5:41pm

Dalton- *You go take your nice, warm shower, I'm gonna go take a cold one...* 5:41pm

Me- *HAHAHAHA OK...* 5:41pm

Dalton- *I'm not kidding, I just turned the cold water on... you're killin me Smalls! *Wink emoji*...* 5:42pm

Me- *Don't take FOORRREEEVVVEEERRR in there...* 5:42pm

Dalton- *I see what you did there, nicely done, nicely done!* 5:42pm

Me- *Ok, I'm really gonna get in now or I'll run out of hot water. I don't want or need to take a cold shower* 5:42pm

Dalton- **Drool face emoji** 5:42pm

Me- **Wink emoji** 5:42pm

    I strip off my clothes and get in the shower. The hot water feels good on my sore muscles. Again, I hadn't realized how sore I was until they relaxed. I'm careful when I wash my hair so that I don't bump my bandage above my eyebrow or get soap in my little cut on my lip.

    "Lainey, I'm gonna put your bag on the toilet, you forgot it out in the living room," Emily says as she opens the bathroom door.

    "Oh shoot, thank you," I say.

    "No worries, talking to Dream-Boy can be distracting," she says laughing.

    "How did you know I was talking to Dalton?"

    "The look on your face... it lit up as soon as you said that he had messaged you."

    "Am I ridiculous?" I ask sincerely.

    "Not at all," she says seriously. "This is good, Lainey. Really good."

    "I hope so," I say as I turn the water off.

    I hear her shut the bathroom door. I reach out

and grab my towels, one for my hair and one for my body. I get dressed and brush my hair out, then whip it into a braid to keep it out of my face.

When I walk out, our food has been delivered, and Brayden is sitting in the living room.

"Hi Lainey, how are you feeling?" he asks.

"Hi Brayden. I'm a little sore but okay. Happy to not be in the hospital anymore," I say, grabbing my to-go box and sitting on a barstool.

"I bet. Are you coming out with us?" he asks and then looks skeptical at my outfit.

"No, I'm going to stay in, thanks for the invite though," I say, smiling. He just smiles and goes back to watching the show on TV. Emily must be getting ready. Sure enough, twenty minutes later she comes out of her room, dressed super cute.

"If you need anything, anything at all, call me, okay?" she instructs as she grabs her purse and heads to the front door, Brayden jumps up off the couch and walks with her.

"I will, you guys have fun," I say around a mouth full of food.

They wave goodbye and leave. I scarf down what I can finish of my food and go to the couch. I pull my phone out and call Dalton.

He answers on the third ring.

"Hey!" he says enthusiastically.

"Hi, did you have a good shower?"

"*I did. All better now,*" he says, laughing.

"I'm not sure I want to know how you got better but I'm glad you're more comfortable," I laugh out loud.

"*Well it wasn't that type of shower, it was actually cold, I wasn't kidding when I said I was going to take a cold one. I'd ask how your shower was but if I think too much about it, I'll be back to square one, so how about we steer clear from any conversation that might lead to... my uncontrollable thoughts about you and...*"

"Ha-ha-ha, can do," I say. "Well how about we play a game or something. 20 questions? We each take turns coming up with a question that we both have to answer? We can use these conversations as a way to get to know each other better. Sound good?"

"*That's a great idea because I do have some questions for you. Just things I'm curious about.*"

"Okay, you can go first then."

"*Alright... let's see... What is your perfect day off?*"

"Oh gosh, I don't know. It depends on my mood and energy level, I guess. I'm always up for going for a drive and doing something outside but I also enjoy just hanging out at home, watching movies and playing games. Vegging out. What about you?"

"*I'd say I'm the same. I enjoy fishing and hiking but also enjoy just spending the day at home not doing anything. Not having to be somewhere or do something in particular is always welcomed on days off.*"

"Yes exactly. Not HAVING to be somewhere or do something, is the best. Are you more of an introvert or extrovert?"

"*Hmmm I guess a little of both. I don't mind being around people and find that if I don't see people after a while, I get almost grumpy. I need to socialize on occasion but also don't mind being in the silence of an empty house. I bet you're more of an introvert, right?*"

I laugh. "Yeah, I tend to be more introverted but like you, I need some socializing to feel happy. But I don't need to be around a ton of people to feel that way. Even one adult to visit with makes my heart happy. I say adult because I have constant company with my kiddos and I love them but I can only talk and hear about Minecraft, horses, dolls, barbies, and be shown the newest LEGO creation so many times, before I need to have an adult conversation with someone."

"*Totally understand that, completely... Okay here's one... do you have a favorite sleeping position and side of the bed you HAVE to sleep on?*"

"I usually fall asleep laying on my side, spooning, well, hugging a pillow, it's really comfy. And the side of the bed... whichever side is closest to the door. I used to think that, that started from when my kiddos were infants. It was easier for me to get out of bed to go to them if I didn't have to crawl over Jayce but thinking about it now, I'm pretty sure I've always slept on that side of the bed. I don't like being right up next to the wall if the bed is pressed up against it."

"*Interesting but makes sense from your mom standpoint. Jayce didn't get up with the kids?*"

"No, he slept soundly and when they were babies, I didn't. My mom ears were always on high alert, so I just got up with them. What's your side of the bed?"

"*Right in the middle,*" he laughs. "*Which is why I have the biggest bed they make. Plenty of room on either side.*"

"A California King?" I ask. Laughing, I say, "I have that same size. Works out when all the kids want to snuggle in the morning."

"*Yup, that size! I bet that makes it more comfortable for you and builds wonderful memories for them.*"

And this is how we spend the evening, taking turns asking each other questions.

Chapter 11

Thinking back about the last year and what this weekend means, makes my heart skip a beat. Dalton and I kept having to cancel on each other every time we made plans to meet up.

I had told him that holidays weren't going to work this year, both my families were wanting to stick to their traditions and his sister was wanting to do their usual things too. There was a weekend before school started for the kids that I was going to go visit him but we had a last minute opportunity to have a wine tasting at the shop. It ended up being a very good opportunity as we were the only place in town to get to sell the certain wine and it's been a big hit.

There was a weekend Dalton was going to come visit me between Halloween and Thanksgiving but a freak snowstorm had him sticking around the ranch to double check they got all the cattle down from the mountain pasture.

We made the best of every conversation we had, whether it was a call, video chat, or messaging. And I don't think there was a day I didn't wake up to a morning text and there definitely wasn't a night that we didn't talk or text before falling asleep. Some days we didn't talk as much as the day before but we always had some sort of communication for the day.

I'm taking the kids to Lucy's tomorrow and then Dalton will be getting here Thursday afternoon. He isn't riding in the rodeo this year but he said he wanted to come down for it anyways. I had made arrangements with Lucy to keep the kids two weeks this year, just in case Dalton could spend a little extra time here.

I had introduced him to the kids over a video chat that the kids had interrupted one night when they were supposed to be in bed. Max said he could hear me laughing and had gone into his sisters room to find out if they knew who I was talking to so they decided to come ask. They all thought Dalton was the coolest and every time I talked to him, they had to say hi. In person meeting, I wasn't sure why but I wasn't ready for that just yet. Dalton is really understanding about it and doesn't push it. He says when I'm ready, it's fine by him. He wants to meet them but doesn't want me to feel pressured into it.

Thinking of the kids and Dalton brings up a funny memory about a sexting incident that happened about three months ago.

I had been messaging Dalton all day. He was feeding cows and plowing snow all day. I was at the shop, putting on my barcodes on the new shipment of books I'd gotten in and scanning them into my system. I'd gotten home and he said he was plowing the lane again, the storm wouldn't let up.

I had jokingly said I wish he could plow me multiple times a day and that got us into a sexting mode. It was getting pretty hot and hands on, Dalton had to stop the tractor before he wrecked, so he said. Anyways, we were just getting to the good part, when Nelly came crashing through my door, running into my room, and jumped on my bed, screaming and laughing hysterically. Max and Janey came in with silly masks on. They had made them out of boxes and they were pretending to be monsters, chasing Nelly around the house. Needless to say, I didn't get my happy ending. I called Dalton after I got the kids out of my room and back downstairs and explained why I abruptly stopped sending messages. He assumed it was because I was finishing, which he said thinking about what I might be doing, made him actually finish. He laughed when I told him that I hadn't been doing that, I had gotten bombarded by two monsters and their victim.

Now, I catch myself smiling and then laugh at myself, as I'm packing the last bit of Nelly's clothes, Max and Janey insisted on packing their own bags this year, when my phone starts to ring.

"Hello?" I answer, without looking at it.

"*Hi,*" Dalton's voice comes from the other end.

"Oh, hey!" I say more excited than before, heart beating 100 miles per hour.

"*What chya doin'?*" he asks.

"Finishing up packing the kids' bags," I say. "I'm excited to see you."

"*Yeah… about that…* " he starts to say. I put down the shirt I was folding and slump on my bed.

"You have to cancel? Really?" I ask forlornly.

"*Yes but I have a counteroffer…*" he adds quickly.

"Okaaay," I say skeptically and I can feel my heart sinking. We aren't ever going to see each other again at this rate.

"*You're taking the kids to your sisters tomorrow, right?*"

"Yes…"

"*How about this? You come to me…*"

I don't know what to say so I just sit here.

"*Lainey? Are you still there?*"

"Yes… Me, come see you? Come to Montana?" I ask, not sure why I need the clarification. In one of our earlier 20 questions conversations, I found out Dalton lives near Missoula, it's the biggest city near his ranch.

"*Yes, you come here. I really want to see you but the vet called today and said that he can only come out this weekend to work the cattle. His daughter just had their first baby, his first grandbaby and his wife said they were leaving*

Monday to go visit them and they weren't sure when they'd be back, a week or two."

"Oh... well... I guess I can see if Fern can handle the shop alone for a couple days. We don't have any events or anything like that anytime soon. I could head up your way after dropping the kids off at Lucy's."

"Offer two has a bonus, let me get you a plane ticket and you can fly out of Boise and not have to drive so far and you get to me quicker."

"Fly?"

"Yeah..."

"You don't have to get me a ticket, I can get one."

"I have frequent flyer miles I need to use, let me get it for you... especially since I'm the one changing our plans... again... let me do this for you?"

"Well, it would be nice to not have to drive all that way alone and I would get there quicker, that's true..."

"Is that a yes?"

"That's a yes," I say, laughing.

I have to pull the phone away from my ear because Dalton is hollering his excitement.

"Okay! I'll get it all figured out. All you have to do is pack your bag and give your information to the clerk at the ticket booth at the airport. What time are you meeting Lucy tomorrow?"

"I was going to meet her in Nampa at noon Idaho time but I will just take the kids to her, now that I'm flying out. I'll see if I can leave my rig at her house and ask her or Peter to drive me to the airport."

"*So an afternoon flight would work best?*"

"Yeah."

"*Okay, I'll let you know when you need to be at the airport. Get to packing and I'll talk to you in the morning... OOOOO-EEEEE I can't wait to see you!*" he's hollering again.

"I can't wait to see you either," I say, laughing.

"*Good night, Lains,*" he says.

"Good night," I say before we hang up.

Going to him now? This is crazy. This is bonkers. This is exciting!

I hurry and call Fern to make sure she doesn't have anything going on for the next week or two. Turns out she doesn't and would love to take care of the shop for me. I call Emily and tell her what's going on, she's excited for me. Then, I call Lucy and tell her about the change of plans, she's also very excited for me.

It took three hours to get through the whole story of mine and Dalton's weekend and how I got hurt, when I called and talked to Lucy after I'd gotten back home from spending a couple days with Emily. Lucy wanted every detail. It was fun to hear her excitement but also made me feel bad. Everyone seemed so certain that I hadn't sounded as happy or been this happy in a long time. I thought I had been happy or happy-like, but apparently not. Ever since Dalton came into my life, I feel lighter, like I can breathe again. It's a strange feeling because I never really felt heavy or like I wasn't able to breathe.

I finish packing Nelly's bag and get mine packed in record time. Trying to go to sleep is like how a kid tries to sleep on Christmas Eve.

◆ ◆ ◆

I sleepily roll over to turn the alarm off that's going off on my phone. I jolt up, wide awake all of a sudden, and full of excitement.

I get to see Dalton today! I think to myself.

I check my phone.

-New message from Dalton-

I read it as I run mine and Nelly's bag down to the front door.

Dalton- *Good morning, Beautiful. I know you won't get this for another couple of hours but I wanted to let you know first thing this morning that your flight leaves at 2:30 Idaho time. You need to be to the airport by 1, 1:30 at the latest.* 5:45am

Me- *Good morning, Handsome. Flight leaves at 2:30, got it.* 7:17am

Dalton- *Really can't wait to see you. *Kissy face emoji** 7:17am

Me- *I can't wait either. *Huge emoji** 7:17am

Dalton- *Text me when you leave your house and when you get to the airport. I have a few things to get done before you get here.* 7:17am

Me- *Okay, I will.* 7:17am

I close my phone and go into the girl's room. I lay with Nelly first.

"Good morning sweet girl, it's time to wake up... you get to see TT, Uncle Peter, and your cousins today," I say.

Nelly stretches her little arms above her head before she wraps them around my neck and yawns out, "Good morning, Momma."

"Hi baby," I say as I kiss her cheek.

"Good morning, Mom," Janey says from across the room. I give Nelly a big squeeze and then head over to Janey's bed.

I lay on top over her, pretending to squish her.

"Good morning my beautiful girl, did you sleep well?" I ask as I give her a kiss on the cheek.

"Mmmmm I did... but... you're squishing me," she giggles out. I lean up on my elbow and she grins up at me. I roll off her bed and stand. "Did you say we're going to Aunt Lucy and Uncle Peter's today?"

"Yup, today's the day. Summer break officially

starts!" I say, clapping my hands.

"Yay!" Janey says as she throws her blankets off of her and jumps out of bed. "My bag is all packed. I'll take it down after I get dressed. When do we leave?"

"In about an hour," I say as I walk out the room and head for Max's door.

I knock twice and open it, he's lying in bed awake already. I walk over and lay down next to him.

"Hey dude, how is my handsomely cool son this morning?" I ask, nudging him with my elbow.

"Fine..." he says.

"Did you sleep well?" I ask.

"Yeah..." he answers.

"You're so talkative, how long have you been awake?"

"I don't know, a little while," he mumbles.

"What's the matter?"

"Nothing..."

"Something," I say, sitting up to look at him.

"I didn't get my bag packed last night, will you help me finish it?" he asks sadly.

"Of course I will. There's no reason to be upset about it," I say, ruffling his hair. "We need to hurry though if you guys want to eat breakfast before we leave."

"Okay," he says but jumps up with a little more enthusiasm than he had a second ago.

I finish packing his bag as he gets dressed. I hand

it to him and tell him to add it to the ones by the front door. When I come into the kitchen, Janey has gotten her and Nelly cereal and Max is rummaging in the freezer for a breakfast sandwich. I make my coffee and start to take bags out to the rig. I then spend the next hour or so making sure everything is picked up, put away, washed, shut, and locked, before ushering the kids out the door.

"Everyone buckled up?" I ask after getting the kids in the rig.

"Yup!" they all three say at the same time.

"Okay, Idaho... here we come!"

I open my phone messages and send a quick text to Dalton.

Me- *Pulling out of my driveway. *Kissy face emoji** 8:24am

Dalton- *Drive careful. Let me know when you get to the airport. *Wink emoji** 8:24am

Me- *Will do.* 8:24am

◆ ◆ ◆

The drive seems to take five times longer than it normally does, even though the clock says we've been driving for two hours and fifteen minutes. Which means, I'm going to get to Lucy's about twenty minutes quicker than usual. Weird.

It's 11:52am when we pull into their driveway.

Lucy and Peter are waiting on the front porch for us. I had called her when we were ten minutes out.

I park and the kids all but fly out their door.

"TT!" Nelly yells as she flings her little body into Lucy.

"Hi sweety!" she says, picking Nelly up and hugging her tight.

"Hi Uncle Peter," Max says, sounding more mature than I'd like him to sound.

"Hey Max-Man!" Peter says, bumping knuckles with Max before he hugs Lucy. "Bye Mom, I love you," he says, giving me a hug and kiss and then heads into the house.

"Hi Aunt Lucy," Janey says, giving Lucy a hug and then Peter.

"Girls, give me loves and hugs," I say. They each give me big squeezes and kisses and then they run into the house.

I must look worried because Lucy says, "Don't worry about them. They'll be fine. Like the last three summers."

I smile at her and say, "I know, it's never easy leaving them though but it's good for us all."

"Especially this time," she says, nudging me. "Give your keys to Peter and throw your bag in my car, I'm taking you to the airport."

"Don't worry about the kids' bags, I'll get them later," Peter says. He hugs me, gives Lucy a kiss, and then heads into the house.

Once we're buckled in, Lucy pulls out of her driveway and we head for the airport. It's about a fifteen minute drive.

"Are you excited?" she asks.

"Nervous…. Excited… all of the above…" I answer truthfully.

"How come? You guys talk all the time," Lucy says as she enters the freeway.

"It's been a year since we've seen each other in person, what if I don't look like what he remembers?" I ask.

"You guys have video chatted, he knows what you look like, Lainey. And plus, video chatting isn't very flattering, which you look good on, but he'll be blown away by you. Don't worry about that," she says reassuringly. "Just relax and have fun."

"I'll try," I say. I lean my head back and close my eyes. My nerves are really starting to get to me.

Lucy lets me sit in silence, something I know is hard for her. I know she's got a million questions she wants to ask but I also know she can tell how nervous I am.

"Okay, I need to say something," she finally says, breaking the silence.

"What?"

"You ever think you and Jayce were meant to be so that he would know what true love felt like, to know the love of being a father before his time here was up? Maybe Dalton is your happily ever after? You can have more than one true love, the world isn't as black and white as we think it is or should be."

"Jayce will always have a piece of my heart."

"Did you give part of the love you had for him away when you had Max or did your heart grow?... What about Janey?... Nelly?... Did the love you felt for your family diminish when you added a new family member to your heart?... Don't you think your heart will grow for the right guy when he comes along?... You deserve to feel that love again, Lainey, you deserve to feel loved."

Wiping a tear away, and coughing to clear my throat, I say, "I never thought about it that way and I never thought someone would be able to put into words how I felt about Jayce. You're right though, my heart will grow because he, whomever he may be, will be a new member of our family. He won't be replacing or taking Jayce's spot in my heart, he'll be an addition to it."

We lapse back into silence. Lucy, quietly, letting me think about this little exchange.

The drive over from home seemed to take forever but the drive to the airport seems to go by in a second. Before I know it, I'm hugging Lucy outside of her rig with my bag over my shoulder.

"Got everything?" she asks.

"I think so, I'm supposed to go to the ticket counter when I get in there, he said they'd know where to send me," I say, shrugging.

"Text me when you land," she says.

"I will," I say, hugging her again. "Love ya, Sis."

"Love you, too."

I walk through the doors and head for the ticket counter. The guy standing behind the counter looks up and smiles.

"Hello and welcome to the Boise Airport, my name is Chris, how may I help you?"

I pull my wallet out of my bag and take my driver's license out and hand it to him and say, "I'm Elainah Richardsen, I was told to come here for my flight details. It's supposed to be leaving at 2:30pm, I'm a little early but I wasn't sure where to go or how long it would take."

"No problem. Just one second, Elainah," Chris says as he enters my information into his computer. He gets a look on his face and then looks at me.

"Is something wrong?" I ask.

"I'm sorry, just one more moment," he says and then gets on the phone to someone.

A few minutes later, an older woman dressed in a suit comes out from behind Chris, from a door I hadn't noticed until now. She introduces herself as Helen.

"Elainah, follow me please," she says politely but also sternly.

"Ooookay," I say, looking around. Other people waiting in line are looking at me oddly.

We walk up to TSA and I'm expecting to go through so I'm getting ready to take my bag off my shoulder but Helen holds up a badge and the TSA agent waves her and me through.

"Ummm.. excuse me, Helen, am I in trouble or something?" I ask quietly.

She turns with a smile on her face and says, "No, why would you think that, Hun?"

"Because you're escorting me through the airport," I say nervously. More people are looking at us as we walk through security without stopping.

"I'm just taking you to your lounge," she states matter of factly.

"My what?" I ask, confused.

"Your lounge, dear," she says a little more loudly. She must have thought I hadn't heard her the first time.

"Like the waiting area by the boarding gates?" I ask.

"No, the lounge that accompanies all private jet owners," she says, looking back at me with concern now.

"I'm sorry, I'm just confused. What private jet?" I ask, really confused now.

Before she answers me, we stop at double doors and a plaque on the right hand side says, 'Dalton Young'. She opens the door and gestures me inside. The room looks like a living room out of a catalog. Overstuffed chairs and couches. A big screen TV. A bar set up so that someone sitting there can watch the planes taking off and landing.

"Mr. Young's private jet," Helen says, smiling at me.

"Oh..." I have nothing more to say. I have nothing else I can say.

"Leave your bag here," she points towards a door opposite where we had just come in. "Your flight attendant, Brad, will take it aboard for you once it's time to board. Joe will be here shortly."

"I'm sorry, who's Joe?" I ask, looking around.

"Your server, dear," she says as she smiles kindly at me. "Have a safe flight and happy travels."

I pull out my phone and hit Dalton's name. He answers on the first ring.

"Hello?"

"Hey," I say, sounding a little more annoyed than I probably needed to be.

"Make it to Lucy's yet?"

"Yeah, I'm actually at the airport now," I say, trying to sound more chipper.

"Oh... really?" he sounds nervous now.

"MMMhmmm," I say.

"Have you checked in yet?" Yup, he's sounding really nervous now, which makes me laugh.

"Yes," I say and then thinking about all this again

has my tone stern again. "A private jet, Dalton?"

"*Okay, okay, yes... a private jet...*" he says in a rush.

"You did not have to get me a private jet," I start to say but he interrupts.

"*I didn't, I promise, I didn't. It's... mine... I got it for when I fly international. I'd rather sleep when I have to travel that far, not fly the thing myself. So I invested in a private jet,*" he says in a rush again.

"Oh... well I guess... you own a private jet?" I ask, surprised. "And never told me?"

"*It never came up in our conversations. How do you casually tell someone you have a private jet without sounding like a total pompous ass?*" he asks.

"You have a point," I say, reluctantly. "All of this is yours?"

"*Are you in the lounge?*"

"Yes."

"*Then yes, that's all mine. Joe, the bartender should be there soon. I told him to be there at 1:00pm so that he could get things set up for you but you're early. Brad, the flight attendant, will be there at 2:00pm to get you boarded.*"

"What's with all the guys? Are you against females working for you?" I ask, mostly joking but also, find it a little strange.

"*Well, yeah, kind of, in a way. I did have a female server and flight attendant but they were always flirting and trying to get into my pants. I told you, I'm not like that. So I decided to hire males so that it was less likely for it to hap-*

pen. Bob is the pilot, by the way. Zane is the co-pilot."

Interesting. He surprises me constantly.

"Well, I guess that's good," I say, not really sure what else to add. I hear Dalton say something to someone away from the phone.

"Lainey, Frank just got here. We're getting things set for tomorrow. If you're okay, I'm gonna get off here. If you need anything, call, I'll have my phone on me."

"I'm good."

"Okay, I can't wait to see you. Just a couple more hours. Bye, Lainey."

"Bye, Dalton, see you soon."

We hang up. I only have to wait ten minutes before someone shows up.

"Are you Joe?" I ask.

"I am. You must be Ms. Lainey," he says, walking over and shaking my hand.

"I am...Ugh, nice to meet you," I say. He nods and walks over to the bar and starts pulling things out of the little refrigerator and cupboards from underneath the bar.

"Can I make you a drink?" he asks.

"Sure, why not? Just a vodka cranberry, if you've got it," I say, smiling at the joke Emily had told this time last year.

"Sure do. Here's some nuts and pretzels. I can make you something to eat, if you're hungry. Mr. Young did suggest nothing too heavy as it'll be about dinner time when you get there."

"These are fine," I say, pointing to the nuts and pretzel mixture.

Joe whips my drink out and I ask, "Is it okay if I sit over there?" I point to one of the overstuffed chairs.

"Absolutely, make yourself at home."

I grab my drink and the bowl of nuts and pretzels and go sit in the chair. Not sure what to watch, I put on the weather channel. It says there's a fifteen percent chance of a freak snowstorm to hit the high mountains in the Western United States tomorrow.

I wonder if Dalton's place is considered high mountains, I'll have to ask him. I think to myself.

I take a couple pictures and then send them to Emily and Lucy in a group message. I tell them about the private jet and lounge. They're going to freak out.

I mindlessly watch the weather on the screen. After about the twentieth time of watching it repeat itself I decide to turn the channel until I find a sitcom. I relax into my chair, sip my drink, and eat some bar mix while I wait for it to be time to board the plane... sorry, jet.

After the second sitcom is over, I hear the door that leads out to the airport open and close. I look behind me and see an older gentleman standing there, he's dressed in a suit.

"Ms. Lainey, I'm Brad, your flight attendant for today. I'm going to take your bag aboard and check with the pilots, Bob and Zane, and see if we can get you up in the air a little sooner than planned," Brad says, smiling at me as he walks past and picks up my bag and leaves out of the door to the right of the bar, before I can say anything.

I down my drink and take it back over to Joe.

"Would you like another one?" he asks.

"No, thank you, that one was enough," I say.

I walk over to the window and watch a couple planes pull in and a couple start to taxi down the runway. It was beautiful to watch. They were synchronized and moving in a soothing way. I don't know how many times Brad had called my name but he was all of a sudden standing next to me, tapping my shoulder.

"Ms. Lainey, if you're ready, I can take you aboard your jet, Bob said he has clearance to take off so soon as we'd like," Brad says smiling at me.

"Oh, yeah, that'd be great. Thank you," I say as he leads the way towards the door.

"Thank you, Joe," I say, not wanting to be rude.

"No problem at all," he says from behind the bar.

I'm expecting a little jet but what I enter is a mid-size one. It would take four of my arms lengths to reach one side to the other. The seats are leather and recline and look more comfortable than any airplane seats I've ever seen.

"Take any seat you like, once we're up in the air and it's safe, Zane will turn on the light that says it's okay for you to move around. Feel free to do so," Brad says, pointing to a light over by the cockpit door, it was red right now.

I choose a seat halfway down the walkway and turn it so I can look out the window. Brad comes by and checks that I've got myself buckled in correctly and asks if I want something to drink.

"A Sprite would be great, thank you," I say.

"I'll be right back," he says.

A minute later he's back and then he goes and sits in the seat to the back of the jet. Another minute late and the pilots come out of the cockpit.

"Ms. Lainey, I'm Bob, your Captain for this flight. This is Zane, he's my co-pilot. We'll be taking off here in about two minutes and then we'll be on our way to Mr. Young's. It's about a two hour flight, about fifteen minutes after takeoff we should be able to turn on the light signaling you it's safe to walk around. You'll hear a ding and the light will flash red when it's time to take your seat and buckle up again There is no weather on our flight path so it should be a nice flight. Do you have any questions?" Bob asks.

"No, I don't, thank you," I say, smiling politely at him. He and Zane nod and then go back into the cockpit.

And exactly two minutes later we are taxiing down the runway. Take offs have always been my favorite. Watching everything on the ground speed past us and then once we're up in the air, it's like everything slows down to a crawl. I lay my head back and settle in for the flight. I don't really have a desire to get up and walk around but I ask Brad to let me know when there's a few minutes left before we start to descend so that I can use the bathroom if need be.

Watching the blue sky float by, I instantly relax. Nervousness is gone at the moment, just totally relaxed for now.

Chapter 12

"Ms. Lainey, we have ten minutes before we're going to be descending," Brad says.

"Oh, thank you," I say as I unbuckle for the first time and make my way to the back of the jet where the bathroom is located.

I use the facilities and then wash my face off and then head back out to my seat. When I get there my phone buzzes in my pocket.

-New Message from Lucy-

Lucy- *No freaking way!* 1:55pm
Emily- *Are you kidding me?* 1:57pm

Weird that I'm just now getting the messages since they were sent about two hours ago. Oh, well. I'll reply now.

Me- *I know! I couldn't believe it.* 3:43pm

Me- *I'm about to land. Text or call you when I can.* 3:43pm

I look out the window and see farm ground and forest. It doesn't look like there's an airport anywhere near here.

"Brad?" I call, getting his attention. He walks over to me. "What airport are we landing at?"

"Oh, it's Mr. Young's personal airport… airstrip… about five miles from the Home Place."

"Oh, okay," I say, dumbfounded again.

DING-DING

I look over at the light by the cockpit and it's flashing red.

"Better buckle up, we're gonna be descending now," Brad says. He checks my buckle and then walks over and takes his seat

I watch as the green pasture below us comes closer and speeds up. I can see the runway stretch out in front of us. A jolt of the jet's landing gear touches the ground and we screech to a halt. We taxi for a moment over to a little building where some men are wheeling out a moveable staircase. I see a familiar pickup pulls out from a parking spot and it drives out and parks in front of the stairs.

And then HE gets out. Dalton. I forgot how tall and strong looking he is, his head looks over the pickup easily. *What the hell does he see in me?* I'm instantly locked in place by fear, regret, nerves, and self-consciousness. *What am I doing here?*

"Ms. Lainey, you can unbuckle now and exit the jet, if you're ready?" Brad says, standing beside me, looking concerned.

"Th-thank you," I say nervously. On shaky legs, I stand and walk to the door. The sun is shining so that it hits me in the face when I step out.

I hear a gasp from down below, that draws my attention. Dalton is looking up at me. I can't tell what the look on his face means. Is he realizing he'd built me up in his head and I don't resemble anything he remembers me being in person? Is he disappointed?

Brad follows me down the steps and hands my bag to Dalton.

"Thank you, Brad," he says, nodding.

"You're welcome, Sir. Is there anything else I can do for you today?" Brad asks, stepping off to the side.

"No, this will be all for now, thank you," Dalton says, he hasn't taken his eyes off of me. I look away, turning slightly pink in the cheeks.

He opens my door and I slide into my seat. It smells the same. His cologne plus hay and dirt. He shuts the door and then walks around to his side, opens the back passenger door and puts my bag on the seat, shuts the door, and then opens his door and gets in his seat. He starts his pickup and we drive away in silence.

"How was the flight?" he asks, looking at me with concern.

"It was good, thank you," I answer, sounding a little too formal.

"That's good," he sounds unsure. "My house is just a couple miles away."

"Oh ok," is all I can say. *Why is this so awkward? Hadn't we spent every day this last year talking on the phone? Texting? Video chatting? What's wrong with me?*

The rest of the drive is a silent one. We turn off one dirt road onto a graveled lane. It's lined with white fences and trees. We turn a corner and his place comes into view. To say it's a house would be a massive understatement. It's not huge to the point of being a mansion but it's not a little farmhouse. It looks more like a cabin resort than a house. I can feel my mouth hanging open so I close it quickly.

He has a big, huge, red barn and dark wooden panel fences around the smaller pastures next to the barn. I'm guessing this is where the cattle get worked. It's easier to replace these types of fence panels than the white ones we drove past.

Dalton pulls up in front of his... house and puts his pickup in park. I can tell he's looking at me but I'm staring out my side window, up at his house. I hear him get out, I'm reminding myself he likes to open doors so I wait for him. Sure enough, he's at my door and opening it for me. I'm not paying attention to my footing when I step out, so I kind of slip off the running board. Dalton catches me and a zing of familiar electricity flies through my arms where he's touching and explodes in my stomach. Nervous butterflies gone momentarily.

"You okay?" he asks, sounding breathless too.

I take a deep breath and step, slightly, away from him. "Yes, thank you. Just missed the running board."

He nods and puts my bag down on the walkway. "Do you want a tour of the outside before we go in? Dinner will be ready in about an hour."

"Sure, a tour would be nice," again, I sound way too formal.

"Okay," Dalton says, still not sounding too sure, probably wondering about my sanity.

We walk around his property. He shows me the barn and all the horses inside, there's sixteen. He shows me where the cattle will be worked, I was correct in thinking the little pastures beside the barn. He shows me the back yard where I saw an awesome little sitting area and a covered patio. There's a pond back behind it where he has trout brought in so he can go fishing quite literally out his back door. He says it's for his nephews when they come to visit but I can tell by the way he's talking about it, he enjoys it also.

We walk back around the house and we stop at my bag. His phone starts to go off.

"Dinner will be ready in ten minutes," he says as he turns his alarm off. "Do you want to go inside now?"

"Sure," I say. I bend to grab my bag just as he's bending for it too. Our heads hit.

"Ouch!" we say at the same time.

"Sorry," we say again at the same time.

"I'll get it for you," he says, smiling his crooked smile at me.

"Thanks," I say.

He turns and leads the way up the walkway. We get to the front door, where I see the porch wraps clear around the house. I hadn't been paying attention on our walk to notice from the yard. He opens the right side of the double doors. It opens up into not what I was expecting. For some reason I was expecting a resort or hotel feel to the inside but I am instantly reminded of a comfy, warm cabin, tucked away in the mountains. The front door opens into the living room, a big living room, full of the same oversized chairs and couches that the lounge had back at the Boise Airport.

We walk through the living room, turn left and turn a corner, and find stairs leading up. The stairs look like they are made from logs, cut in half. Dalton starts up them, I follow. About halfway up, the stairs turn and go to the left and then continue up. We walk down a hallway and pass what looks like a game room on the right, it has a pool table and ping-pong table, and what looks like retro video games. Another open door on the right shows an office. And then the next door is on the left, which are french doors, and it's a bedroom. He steps inside.

"I wasn't sure... I didn't want to assume...," he looks around the room. "This can be your room," he says, setting my bag down on the bed to the left of the door.

"Thank you," I say. He didn't want to assume anything would happen between us or he's just saying that now that I'm here? Ugh... awkward overload!

"Umm... so you can hangout up here if you want or come downstairs... I need to pull dinner out of the oven," he says, unsure again.

"I'll come downstairs, if that's okay?"

"Of course it's okay," he says with a little more excitement. He turns and leads us out of the room and back down the hall. "After dinner, I'll give you a tour around the house, so you know where everything is, if you'd like?"

"That'd be great, thank you," I say, shyly.

I see Dalton glance over his shoulder, I instantly look down at the floor. *Uhh, am I the only one that thinks this is awkward? Am I making this more awkward than it needs to be?*

We get back downstairs and Dalton leads us through the living room. We pass a doorway that shows a long, beautiful dining room table. Down a short hallway and we walk into a huge kitchen.

"Oh… my… gosh!" I say, staring around.

"Not too bad, eh?" he jokingly asks.

"It smells really good, what's for dinner?"

"Lasagna, my mom's recipe. One of the few things I can cook well," he laughs.

"You cooked?"

"Yeah, why do you sound surprised?"

"I don't know, I guess I wasn't expecting that," I say, honestly.

"I enjoy cooking but I do have a cook, her name is Val. She's more of a loving grandmother than anything else. Mom hired her when I was 9."

"Oh that's nice," I say.

"She was a little annoyed with me when I told her I wanted to cook tonight, she's been wanting to meet you. I told her she could cook breakfast tomorrow, she seemed appeased by that," he laughs. He pulls the lasagna out of the top oven and garlic bread from the bottom. A double oven? This is starting to become my dream kitchen. "There's a salad in the fridge, if you wouldn't mind grabbing it. Also, a bottle of wine in the chiller below the island counter."

I grab the wine, it's one of my favorites. *Hmmm, that's interesting.* And then I get the salad. I follow him over to the little four seater table in the corner of the kitchen, I think it's called a breakfast nook. He's got two spots set up with plates, silverware, and wine glasses.

We take our seats and he opens the wine. "Go head," he says, gesturing towards the food.

"Thanks," I say. It smells so good, my stomach is starting to grumble. I haven't really eaten much today and I'm starting to feel it. I dish out some lasagna and scoop some salad out of the bowl. The garlic bread is still steaming a little as I break a piece off.

Dalton pours us some wine and holds up his glass.

"Here is to you being here, cheers," he says.

"Cheers," I say, as we clink our glasses together. He takes a sip and puts his down. I take a couple gulps and then put my glass down.

I take a bite of my food and *OH MY GOSH!*, "Wow, this is amazing!"

"You like it?"

"Mmmmm, oh yeah," I say around another mouthful. "It's delicious!"

"I'm glad you like it," he says with a big grin.

We eat in silence. Neither one of us knows what to say or how to start a conversation. I see Dalton look up and look like he's about to say something but then looks back down and eats. We finish eating in record time. I help clear the table and put the dishes in the dishwasher.

"Where's your dishwasher detergent? I'll get this

going," I say, looking around.

"Under the sink, I believe," he says, seeming to answer without thinking. I start to look under the sink and Dalton starts to walk over, "Oh, no I can do that."

I grab the little pod and stand up. I find Dalton standing right in front of me.

"Oh," I say. I look up into his eyes and the burning in my stomach flares. "Ummm, it's okay, I don't mind."

He looks like he's about to say or do something but then steps back. I move back over to the dishwasher and put the pod in, then start it up. When I turn to face him again, he's standing with his back against the counter, his arms are crossed, and he's looking down at the floor.

"You okay?" I ask.

"Oh yeah," he says startled a little. "I'm fine. Ready for the tour?"

"Sure," I say.

He leads me down the hall to the right of the kitchen. There's a big pantry, a guest bathroom and at the end of the hall, two big doors.

"This is my room," he says as he swings the doors open. I step in and see a huge room. I see his California King bed. A little sitting area, across from the door, by a fireplace in the wall. There are a couple bookshelves full of books, and on the other side, a door opening into a bathroom. I can see half of a huge jacuzzi bathtub.

"It's... nice," I say. What I wanted to say was that

it's amazing... Wonderful. The bedroom of my dreams but for some reason those words didn't compute from brain to mouth.

We walk back down the hall, past the kitchen, and into the living room. To the right is a short hallway that leads to another door to the guest bathroom and across from there is a decent size room of floor to ceiling bookshelves.

"A library?" I ask dumbfounded. "You have a library in your house?"

"Ha-ha, yeah or at least a little one. These were mostly my mom's collection, a few of my dad's, and another good amount of my grandparents. They were sitting in storage and I didn't like that, so I decided to build this addition to make into a small library. I've added some here and there when I've read a book I really enjoyed or found an author I really liked, I'd add their books to my collection."

Smiling like an idiot, I walk around the room. There's one wall of nothing but windows, I can see the silhouette of the mountains with the sunset just going down behind them.

"It's beautiful," I say.

"Very beautiful," he says. I turn and see him look quickly away from me, towards the windows. *Weird.*

We leave my now favorite room of the house and back through the living room, the door in front of the stairs is a guest room. *Wonder why he didn't put me in here?*

Down the hall is the family room where the TV is but it's more like a little movie theater. There are more of the oversized, super comfy looking chairs and couches, I'm starting to see a trend with the furniture here.

We walk back to the stairs and I follow him up again. He shows me the room I thought was a game room. It is. He's got all the old, good video games, and air hockey. He takes me into his office and shows me that there's a balcony that wraps around most of the house, starting at the edge down by the game room and back all the way around to the other side.

We walk past 'my' room and the door on the right is a laundry room, a nice size, laundry room. Dalton says it's for upstairs use, that there's another one down off the family room. The last door on the left, is the bathroom, which is good to know since I'll be up here. The last door in the hall, on the right, is another, even bigger, family TV room. He explains it's when his family is here, so if the adults are wanting to watch something, his nephews and other kids can be in this one watching something else. There are two guest rooms off of the family room and there's a door that goes into the bathroom from in here so you don't have to go out into the hall.

We walk back out, down the hall, but Dalton stops at my room.

"If you were wanting to get situated... I can leave you to it," he says in a forced casual way. What is he not saying that I can tell he's wanting to say?

"Okay," I say as I walk into my room.

"Ummm... okay," he says quickly, turns and walks down towards the stairs.

I stand looking at the empty doorway for a few minutes and feel tears starting to swell in my eyes.

This is stupid. Why are we acting like this? Why is it so freaking awkward? I think to myself as I turn and walk to the middle of the room.

There's a dresser directly across from the doors and yet another oversized chair in the corner to the right. I walk over to curtains in the far left corner and find another set of french doors that lead out to a private balcony. I step out and breathe in the fresh Montana evening air. The sun has gone down completely now. I turn and look at the clock next to the bed, it's 7:15pm.

I grab my bag off the bed and go put it on top of the dresser. I grab my book that I brought and pull my phone out of my pocket as I walk over to the oversized chair.

I send a message to Lucy and Emily.

Me- *It's painstakingly awkward. HELP!* 7:15pm

Thank heavens for Emily always being on her

phone, she replies almost instantly.

Emily- *Y? What's goin' on?* 7:16pm

Me- *It just feels awkward. We haven't really said too much to each other. It's like we don't know what to say now that there isn't 100's of miles between us and our phones.* 7:16pm

Emily- *Why do you feel awkward?* 7:16pm

Me- *I. Don't. Know.* 7:16pm

Emily- *OK, well chill. Where are you now?* 7:16pm

Me- *In 'my' room.* 7:17pm

Emily- *You have your own room?* 7:17pm

Me- *Yes, is that weird? I mean we've already had sex and we've had some pretty fun messaging and phone calls.* 7:17pm

Lucy- *Hey, I'm here now. Getting the kids fed, Peter's in charge for a minute so I can talk.* 7:17pm

Lucy- *Dalton doesn't seem like the type to expect you to just jump into bed with him the second you get there. Maybe he's trying to be respectful. He is the most chivalrous man I've ever heard of in my life.* 7:17pm

Emily- *Lucy isn't wrong, he's very thoughtful. I bet he put you in your own room to make you feel more comfortable.* 7:17pm

Emily- *Wait! Did you WANT to be in his room?* 7:17pm

Me- *Yes... well no... maybe... I did... I mean, I was hoping we'd... you know... while I was here...* 7:18pm

Lucy- *Just try to relax and don't put so much pressure on yourself or Dalton. Just breathe. It'll all be fine.* 7:18pm

Emily- *What did you pack for pajamas?* 7:18pm

Me- *Random... What? Haha* 7:18pm

Emily- *Just answer me.* 7:18pm

Me- *Ummm... one of my long tank tops and shorts.* 7:18pm

Emily- *Here's what you do. Change but only wear your tank and undies. Then hangout in your room for, I don't know... 3045 more mins and then go down and if you happen to see him, just tell him you needed a drink. He won't be able to refuse you wearing that...* 7:18pm

Lucy- *I don't think it's a matter of him refusing you, Lainey. But Emily's idea is a good one.* 7:19pm

Me- *Oh gosh, really?* 7:19pm

Emily- *Yeah... you guys are the only ones in the house, right?* 7:19pm

Me- *Yes* 7:19pm

Emily- *Then no problem. If you don't see him by the time you get to the kitchen, just get a quick drink anyways and then go back to your room. Wait another hour or so and go back down, and give it another try.* 7:19pm

Me- *Oh gosh... OK, I'm gonna do it.* 7:19pm

Emily- *Yay! Call or message us again if you need to.* 7:19pm

Lucy- *This is fun!* 7:19pm

Me- *Fun for you guys...* 7:19pm

I turn off my phone, get up and go back to my bag.

Why is my heart racing? Ugh! So many butterflies. This is ridiculous.

I find my tank top and strip out of my clothes except for my undies. My tank goes down to cover half of my ass. It's one of my favorite colors, coral pink. I leave my phone on the dresser, grab the blanket at the foot of the bed, and walk back over to the chair. Pick up my book and start to read. This is going to be the longest 30-45 minutes of my life.

◆ ◆ ◆

I move my legs and my book falls from my lap, crashing to the floor. I jump up, startled awake. I'd fallen asleep. Ahhh crap, I'd fallen asleep!

I throw the blanket off of me and run over to the desk, grab my phone, and see it's...

2:26am!!!! I shout in my head.

Well crap, there goes Emily's plan. Although I am thirsty, but, there is no way Dalton is still awake. I look around the room and see that the overhead light that was on earlier is off but the light on the nightstand by my bed has been turned on. Did Dalton come in here and find me asleep? Well, that's just great.

Well, I'm gonna go get a drink anyways. I walk out of my room and find the hallway is lightly lit, there must be a dimmer on these lights. The stairs are lit nicely too. I get down to the living room and it's a little bit darker but there are a couple of those little plug in lights lighting the room just enough to be able to see without running into anything.

I get to the kitchen and find it pitch black. I fumble around trying to find the light switch, but can't seem to find it on this wall. I remember the sink being straight across so I blindly walk forward but run into the island, my hands out in front of me.

"Oooof!" I say out loud. I rub my toe for a second and move around the island and stick my hands down lower so that I hopefully don't run into anything else I forgot about being in here. My hands touch the edge of the counter, I run them to the right and find the sink. There's a light above this, I know there is because it was on during dinner. I run my hand up until I find the windowsill and then run it over to the left until I find the wall and...

Bingo, a light switch! I holler in my head. I flip the bottom one.

CRRRRKKKKKKKKRRRRRKKKKKKK!

I instantly feel like I'm going to have a heart attack! It's the switch for the garbage disposal. I turn it off quickly but keep one hand on the switch so I can't lose it but place one over my heart. It's beating so fast! Cringing slightly, I flip the top one and the light turns on, quietly.

Sighing, I open the cupboard Dalton had gotten wine glasses out of earlier and find a small glass. I fill it with water and take a drink.

This is really good water. I think to myself.

"OH!" I hear from behind me, followed by a deep, slow, breath.

Chapter 13

Whirling around, I see Dalton standing there. In... his... boxers. Only his boxers. For one second that seemed to stretch forever, I can't take my eyes off of him.

MY GOD! He's way too fucking hot! Way too fucking perfect! I shout in my head. His boxers are low enough that I can see his... what's it called, inguinal crease? That could be it but it's just commonly known as the sexy 'v' shape guys have between their hip bones.

Oh shit! I'm staring! I gulp, inhale quickly through my nose, and swallow the little bit of water still in my mouth and start choking immediately. I turn back around, and grab hold of the sink, coughing my lungs up. *How embarrassing.*

Dalton walks over quickly and starts to rub and pat my back softly. The feel of his warm hand has me tingling everywhere. I lean into his hand as his rubbing starts to slow. His hand stops just above my ass.

He bends his head down so that his mouth is touching in between my neck and shoulder.

"God, I've missed you," he whispers, tickling my skin.

"I've missed you, too."

He kisses my skin, sending a shock down to my toes. I lean my head to the left a little more, giving him more access to my neck. He kisses me again, I moan and my head rolls back. Embers in my stomach flaming to life, sending heat waves to every nerve in my body.

Dalton wraps his left arm around my waist, pulling me closer against him. I can feel him hardening against my lower back, I press into him gently. A moan escapes his lips as they make their way up my neck. He kisses my ear and runs his hand across my stomach, causing the bottom of my tank to bunch up a little under his hand.

I wrap my arms around his back, grabbing his ass and squeezing tightly. He thrust forward a little and runs his hand on my stomach, up to my right breast and squeezes just as I am squeezing his ass again.

I moan and my head rolls to the right side and back to the left.

"Oh fuck, Dalton," I say, leaning into him more.

Moaning into my neck, he starts kissing down to my shoulder again. His right hand leaves the right side of my waist and travels down between my legs. Going up under my tank, he finds my warm spot instantly and starts to rub.

"Ughnah... Oh... Shit..." I moan.

I turn just as Dalton is kissing my cheek and kiss him full on the mouth for the first time in over a year. Electricity whips through me. Everything inside of me explodes in delicious, familiar flames of ecstasy!

Dalton lets go of my breast and stops rubbing my spot and turns me. He pulls me to him so that I'm as close to him as one can get to another person. I can feel his bulge pushing against me. He runs his hands up my neck and intertwines them into my hair. I wrap my arms up and around his neck.

He pushes me up against the counter, kissing me more deeply. I wrap my left leg around his leg as much as I can. He grabs my ass and lifts me up so I can wrap both legs around his waist. He takes a couple steps over to the left to find the wall and then pushes me gently into it.

"Mmmmm..." is all I can muster to say.

"Do you..." he breathes out. "Do you want to come back to my room?"

"Yes... now... God yes!" I moan.

Without hesitation, Dalton pulls me closer to him and starts kissing me more passionately but also starts walking us down the hall.

Before I know it, I'm lying on my back on his huge, soft bed. Dalton is leaning over, staring at me adoringly.

"I want to do this but if you don't… if you want another day to…"

I interrupt him, "Dalton, I appreciate that but just kiss me. I want this, I want you, too!"

With no hesitation again, he's kissing me in full force. I wrap my legs back around his waist, my arms around his neck, and pull him closer.

We both moan in unison. I run my fingers down his back, feeling his muscles tighten at my touch. He shivers.

Dalton leans to his left side and runs his right hand down the outside of my thigh and back up but finds his way under my tank. His thumb pauses a moment on my hip bone and rubs across it. He then continues up to my ribs and up still until he finds my left breast.

He gasps slightly.

It feels so good, I can't help my body's response as my back arches, pressing my breast into his hand harder. With that, Dalton grinds his throbbing bulge into my center.

I gasp, "OH!"

Dalton's hand leaves my breast, making it feel cold from the lack of the heat his hand was producing. His hand quickly finds my aching, warm spot through my undies, and he starts to rub vigorously.

After a quick minute of this, he slides his fingers into my undies and inside of me.

"Oh damn, Lainey," he moans.

"Do you have a condom?" I pant out, into his ear.

"Yessss..." he hisses. He pulls his hand away from me, causing me to whimper a little but then wraps his arms around me. He rolls us sideway twice and then he lifts me up with one arm and lays me gently down so my head is on a pillow. He reaches over to my right, where there's a nightstand. He opens the top drawer and pulls out a condom.

I jokingly raise an eyebrow at him.

"Just wanted to be prepared... better than having to scour the house for one, right?" he asks.

I grin widely, "Right!"

I start to take my tank off but Dalton does it for me. I lay back and see him staring at me.

"What?" I ask self-consciously.

"You're beautiful," he says in awe.

I can't think of anything to say but an awkward thank you, so I just smile.

He slowly takes my undies off and then removes his boxers. Swiftly, he takes the condom out of the wrapper and puts it on. He lays down on top of me again and starts kissing me deeply. Our tongues dancing and wrestling all over in our mouths.

Dalton's hand finds its way back to my breast. His fingers start to pinch and twist my nipple.

"Mmmm," I moan into his mouth.

Apparently that was the que for him to move his

mouth down to my breast and take my nipple into his mouth and start to suck it.

"Oh... shit... " I say too loudly. I place my left hand over my mouth. My right hand is gripping his left bicep.

Dalton's right hand moves down to my opening and starts to work its magic again. I thrust my hip up into him, driving his fingers deeper, causing both of us to moan.

I pull his face back to mine so I can kiss him passionately. I reach down and pull his hand back up to my breast and I position his tip to my opening. I wrap my arms back around his neck.

He slowly enters me, I arch my back.

"Oh... fuck..." I moan.

"Ughnah..." Dalton moans out.

He pulls out slowly, not all the way, and then back in. He picks up his pace, getting a nice, steady rhythm going. He starts to rub my nipple again, pinching it slightly.

"Oh! Oh god!" I scream. I slam my left hand over my mouth and put my right hand down onto my now, very, sensitive spot and start to rub in time with Dalton's thrusts.

"Oh shit, Lainey!" he moans into my ear.

"Oh!!! Fuck... Fuck me, Dalton!" I scream into my hand.

"God damn, Lainey..." he moans. He starts to

thrust harder and faster.

At the same moment, we moan in unison, climaxing together.

"Ughnah!!!" I moan.

"Shhhhiiiiit!" he moans out. It's a deep, down in his throat, sound.

After a minute, Dalton lays on top of me, panting. I run my fingertips up and down his sweaty back.

"You don't know how good that feels," he says, kissing my shoulder.

"I might have an idea," I say, kissing his cheek.

"I'm slightly embarrassed, actually," he says into the crook of my neck.

I try to see his face but he seems to be hiding.

"Why?" I ask.

"I'm not normally so... quick to finish," he says, sheepishly. "But with you... always and only with you... you're just so fucking hot, Lainey!"

"Oh... no need to be embarrassed about that, I really, really don't mind," I say, smiling. I laugh and add, "As long as I get my 'O' too, we can finish as quickly as you like... or can."

"You don't like to make it last?"

"Why make it last when we can get to the good stuff? We then have energy left over to do it again a little later."

He sits up quickly and says, "You wanna go again?"

"Well not this second and we probably need some sleep tonight but in general... yes. Multiple, amazing and maybe a little quick times, to me, is better than one dragged out, exhausting time."

Dalton rolls off of me and lays on his back, grabbing a tissue out of the box on his nightstand and takes his condom off and throws it in the small trash can under the nightstand. He then just stares at the ceiling. He glances over at me and beams his devastatingly beautiful smile.

He says, "You truly are the most amazing, unique, one of a kind woman, I've ever met."

"Why do you say that?" I ask laughing a little, quietly.

"I've never heard of a woman like you. You don't like four-play," I'm about to protest but he puts a finger up to stop me. "Okay, you like it but you say it's not necessary. And your brand of fore-play is different from typical fore-play. I've never heard of anyone liking to be softly tickled like you."

"It relaxes me and feels good. 'Typical' fore-play can be stressful and expected to feel good, it doesn't always feel good. My brand, I like and it works for me."

"Exactly. You're unique and that's a great thing to be."

"Well... thank you," I say, shyly.

"So, it's a little after 3am. Are you ready for round two or should we be responsible and get some sleep since I have to be up in less than three hours?"

"Mmmmm that's a hard one…"

"Not quite yet but it can be," he nudges me with his elbow.

"Ha-ha-ha," I say sarcastically and then truly laugh. "I think, as much as I want round two, I think we should get some sleep. We've got a lot of cattle to work tomorrow… well, today."

"We? You wanna help?"

"If you'll let me and want me to help, yeah."

"That would be great, I'd love you to help," he says excitedly. "And another plus, no need for a cold shower this evening." He laughs and rolls over so he's facing me. He grabs hold of me and rolls back to his back, pulling me half on top of him, half lying on the bed.

"Nope, no need for that," I say, and then I start kissing him.

"Mmmm if we're going to sleep instead of round two, I'm probably gonna need you to not kiss me like that while your sexy, naked body is pressed up against me," he laughs out.

"Sorry," I laugh also.

He pulls me close and sighs.

I look up and see his eyes are closed.

"Can I ask you something?"

"Mmmm, you can ask me anything, Lainey."

"Why… why were you being so weird today?"

"Me!? You were the one being all awkward and

standoffish."

"I was because you were."

"You had a guarded look on your face when you got off the jet. I couldn't figure out what was wrong. So when I asked you how the flight went, I was hoping you were going to say it made you sick or something."

"Oh... well... I...." I turn my head so it's smashed against his bare chest. *His skin smells so good.*

"What?" he asks, trying to get me to look up at him. I slide off of him so that I'm mostly lying sideways on the bed with my front still touching him.

"I saw you from the window and was blown away by how good looking you are... not that I didn't know that already. Not that I didn't think you looked good in our video chats but in person... I was instantly self-conscious. My nerves skyrocketed. And I was scared."

"Scared?"

"I couldn't imagine why you... someone that looks like you and has all of this," I wave my hand around. "Would want someone like me."

Dalton puts a finger under my chin and says, "If I do anything in my life, for the rest of my life, it's going to get you to see yourself clearly. When I saw you step out of the jet, my heart, literally, skipped a beat. I've had moments while riding a bull where I felt like my heart was going to jump out of my chest but nothing compares to when I saw you today. I actually gasped."

"I heard you," I giggle.

"You did?"

"Yeah but I wasn't sure if I heard correctly or not. I couldn't read the look on your face. I thought you were disappointed, that I wasn't what you had built up in your head, that you didn't like me anymore now that you were seeing me in person after a year."

"I was stunned... that was the look of a man that had been stunned."

"Oh, shut up," I say, nudging him.

"No, I'm serious, you looked... you are beautiful."

"I was wearing a hoodie... okay granted it was a nicer hoodie than most but still... and blue jeans..."

"And you looked absolutely gorgeous. I honestly don't know if I'll be able to handle seeing you all dolled up, like for real, for real," he says, putting on an accent at the end.

I laugh and shake my head.

"Why were you being weird today?"

"I told you, it was because you were and I couldn't figure out why. I was nervous too, you know."

"You were? Why?"

"Honestly, I don't know. I think just seeing you again, I was excited about it but then I also got nervous about if I was what you remembered."

"You are better than I remember."

"So all the awkwardness today was from you

thinking I... what... didn't like you anymore?"

I shrug, "Yes."

"There's no need for that, I like you... I like you a lot!" he says, kissing me deeply. He pulls away and says, "I feel like I've known you a lot longer than a year. It could be from the 100's of rounds of twenty questions we played. The hours we spent on the phone and all the messaging we did. I don't know if I've ever talked to someone, willingly, that long before."

"Same here," I laugh. "It's like, I feel like I know you more than I should... I don't know if 'should' is the right word but whatever... I know you more than I should for someone I've known for only a year. I know you better than I know some people I've known for years, for my entire life."

"I know exactly what you mean," he hugs me close.

"Can I ask another question?"

"Go for it," he says, laughing.

"Why the separate rooms? And why one of the furthest from you? I mean, I think I know the answer to the first but I want to be sure."

"Like I said when I took you up there first thing, I didn't want to assume you'd want to be in here with me. I wanted you to feel comfortable."

"That's what I was thinking. It goes along with how considerate you are and your chivalrous personality. And that particular room?"

"It's the best guest room I have, it's the biggest one. It has a private balcony, also."

"Did you come in later, after I'd accidentally fallen asleep?"

"I did. I came up to check on you. I was going to see if you wanted to watch a movie, but I found you asleep. I was going to wake you or move you to your bed but you looked so peaceful. So I turned the overhead light off and turned the softer, less bright, nightstand lamp on. I also noticed you had changed, so I wasn't sure if you meant to fall asleep or not."

"I didn't mean to fall asleep, I was only reading to waste time before I…" I close my mouth quickly and duck my head down into his side.

"Before you what?"

"Nothing…" I can feel my face turning red.

"Well, I can feel you face warming up, so it's not nothing… what were you going to do?"

Keeping my eyes closed, I put my head up, I say, "I was going to come down to the kitchen around 8 o'clock and if I ran into you, I was going to say I was getting a drink."

"Why's that embarrassing you? That's perfectly normal and okay behavior."

"I was in my tank and undies," I say, opening my eyes.

His eyes go big and he says, "You were going to try to seduce me by wearing that?"

"Yeah, I guess... I was going to try anyway."

"Well, you succeeded..."

"I fell asleep before I could come down and 'accidentally' run into you."

"But it worked anyways because when I came into the kitchen to find out what was going on- you were making quite the ruckus-and found you, I couldn't believe my eyes... or was that your plan B?"

"What?! No, I honestly came down for a drink when I saw it was after 2am. I figured you were zonked out but I was thirsty. The 'ruckus' was me trying to find the light switch."

"Well, when I got in there and saw you standing there, in your little tank top, I lost my breath. It felt like someone had hit me in the gut. And then you started choking, so I had to get my thoughts together so I could help you."

"I was choking on water because of you and your... boxers."

"Really?"

"Uh, yeah... I thought I had been staring at you forever and I thought you were looking at me wondering why I was just staring, so I did a weird swallow, gulp... thing and the water went down the wrong pipe."

Dalton starts laughing hysterically, "I wasn't looking at you wondering why you were staring, I was too busy staring at you and taking every inch of you in as I stared. By the way, the kitchen gets a little chilly in the evenings."

He winks at me.

"Oh my gosh, was I nipping?"

"Mmmmmhmmmm and I'm not complaining," he pulls me closer to him.

I shake my head but laugh.

I yawn, which makes him yawn.

"Should we get some sleep?"

"If I can shut my mouth and stop asking you questions," I say.

"Do you have more?"

I think for a minute, "You know, I don't. Not about today and all the awkward moments... Well, I do have a random question."

"What's that?"

"How did your pickup get to Montana if you flew yourself home last year?"

"Oh, I leave one in the hanger in La Grande and have the same one here for my ranch pickup."

"The same one?"

"Yeah, it's a nice pickup."

"It is," I say, laughing and then I'm yawning again.

"Are you happy? Are you good?"

"I'm so happy and definitely good. You?" I kiss him on the nose.

"Absolutely!"

"Then yes, we should get some sleep," I, again, yawn.

He pulls me even closer to him and I again look up at him and see his eyes are closed once again. I close mine and let his breathing and heartbeat lull me to sleep.

Chapter 14

I feel a kiss on my shoulder and a hand slide across my stomach.

"Good morning, Beautiful," I hear Dalton whisper into my ear.

"Mmmmm, good morning, Handsome," I reply. I roll my head to the right and opening my eyes barely to a squint, I see Dalton lying on his side, beside me. I roll on to my side and snuggle into his chest. He wraps his arm around my back and starts to tickle, running his fingers up and down my spine.

"Did you sleep well?" he asks.

"I did, thank you. Did you?" I ask and kiss in between his pecs.

He inhales sharply but says calmly, "Best sleep I've gotten in about a year."

I quietly laugh and say, "Me too."

He continues to tickle my back. I run the back of my left hand over his stomach and then turn it over and caress across his side, wrapping my left arm around his side, and then I start to softly rub small circles on his back. With my right hand, which is down by his lower abdomen, I run my pointer and middle fingers back and forth, slowly, lightly.

"I can see why you like this so much," he says softly into my hair. "This feels amazing."

"See, I told you," I say. I can feel a familiar tingle starting to flare up around my spot. "What time is it?"

I feel Dalton move as he turns his head to look at the clock on his nightstand.

"It's just after 5 o'clock."

"And what time do we need to be out there?"

"The guys will be bringing the cattle in around 6 o'clock but we don't need to be out there until 6:30, how come?"

I slowly run a leg over his lap, feeling his man hood hardening, and slide up on top of him.

"Well, I was thinking…" I say, rotating my hips so that I was slowly rocking on top of him.

"Oh my god, I like when you think," he murmurs, closing his eyes. He puts his hands lightly on my hips. "Mmmmm."

I reach down and grab hold of his hands. His eyes pop open and I raise an eyebrow at him as I place them over his head. I give him a look that says 'don't move'. Then, I reach over to the nightstand and pull out a condom and rip it open. I reach down and slide it over his erection and sit back down.

I look at him and he's got his crooked smile on his face.

"As I was saying... I was thinking... maybe we can get round two out of the way now? You know, just give us a little morning... " I rotate my hips so that his tip is right at my opening. I bite my lip and then say, "treat, before all the work begins?"

"Oh god," he starts to say and then I rock my hip just enough for his tip to enter me and then I sit back, letting him fill me. "Yessss"

I gasp and let out a long moan. Dalton starts to move his hands, I grab them and put them back above his head, "Tsk-tsk, nope, those stay there."

"Shhhhiiiiit," he says, interlocking his fingers and then placing them behind his head.

I start to rock my hips again, slowly. His eyes open and then roll to the back of his head. I run my right hand over his chest and then place it, palm down, on his stomach. I put my left hand behind me on his leg. I start moving faster.

"Oh... shiiit..." I say.

"Mmmmm...." is all he can get out.

I reach down and start to rub my sensitive spot, thrusting harder. I open my eyes and see Dalton's arms straining. I stop rubbing and reach up and pull his hands towards me. His eyes fly open and he eagerly takes my breasts into his hands. I go back to rubbing myself.

I start rocking faster, and faster. Dalton sits up and puts a nipple in his mouth while he rubs the other.

"UGHNAAAHHHH!!! I scream, as I'm rocked with ecstasy. I throw my arms around Dalton, holding him closer to me. I continue to rock and thrust my hips, up and down.

"Shhhhiiiiit... Lainey... I'm gonna..." he pants out... and then one big inhale and then a slow exhale when he moans out, in his very deep voice, that I'm starting to associate with orgasms, "Fuuuuuuuuckkkkkk meeee....."

I rock a minute longer and then Dalton collapses back onto the pillows, I go with him, laying on top of him, breathing heavily.

"If I can start every morning like this, I'll be a happy man for the rest of my life," he says, laughing.

"Me too," I laugh along with him.

We lay like this for a while and then his alarm starts to go off.

"It's time to actually get up now," he says, grudgingly.

"What time is it?"

"5:45am," he says, smiling up at me.

"So we have time for a quick shower, coffee, and breakfast?"

"We definitely do, but there's no way we have time to take a shower together."

Confused, I ask, "Why's that? Wouldn't it be

quicker?"

"I can barely handle you with clothes on, having you in the shower, naked with me, all wet and soapy..." he looks down at himself and says, "See, just thinking about it and I'm already getting hard, again. This is what you do to me, woman!"

I look down, "You sure that's not just left over?"

"It's definitely not," he says.

I laugh and roll off of him, taking the sheet with me as I go.

"Okay, well, then I'll go upstairs and take a shower and you take one in your bathroom. We can meet in the kitchen in... twenty?"

I wrap myself up and grab my tank and undies and turn to walk out the door.

"Lainey?" he calls from the other side of the room.

"Yeah?" I say, turning to look at him. *Gulp....* He's standing naked in the middle of his room. I've never really thought the naked male body was something too enjoyable to look at but standing here looking at Dalton, I can see the true beauty in it. *Wow, just wow.*

"I'm really glad you're here. And not just because of this," he waves his hand towards the bed. "But because I really am happy to see you and have you here."

"Thank you," I squeak out. I clear my throat and pull my thoughts away from his body, and try again. "Thank you, Dalton. I'm really happy to be here too.

But mainly because of that," I point to his bed and then at him. I laugh and then say, "No I'm just kidding, well sorta. I AM happy to be here to see you and be here with you."

He just shakes his head and laughs, "Go take a shower. Better make it a cold one, you horny woman, you."

"That's not a bad idea," I say and wink at him. I turn and walk out of his room. I'm looking down, smiling like an idiot when I walk into the kitchen. Where there's at least six guys- two older, four younger. A girl that looks a little younger than me, and an older woman. They're all standing around the island and they all look over at me. I skid to a stop.

"Uhhhhh..... hi..." is all I can say. Then I holler, "Daaaaaaltonnnnn!"

I hear him hurrying through his room and down the hall.

"What's the mat..." he starts to ask. "Oh... Val... Frank... guys, Doc, Bree... You're all here... in my kitchen..."

I look at him, he's at least got a towel wrapped around himself, he must have been just about to get in the shower.

"Yup, we sure are," one of the younger guys says, ogling me.

Dalton must have noticed him staring at me because he moves me to stand behind him, the younger girl's eyes narrow at me when he touches me.

"Junior, you best be putting your eyes right and show Ms. Lainey some respect," the oldest looking guy says. I glance over at him, since he'd said my name.

"I'm Frank, Ms. Lainey. That there is my son, Frank Junior but we call him Junior. He gives you any trouble, don't hesitate to pop him one or let me or Dalton know."

I smile at Frank, I can already tell I'm going to like him.

"We can do the rest of the introductions later," Dalton says, as one of the other younger guys was about to say something. "If you've got the cattle already brought in, why don't you all go out and start getting everything set up?"

"Yes, sir," Frank says and then he starts to usher everyone else out. The younger girl and older lady stay behind.

"Bree, I mean you too," Dalton says. The younger girl shoots him a look and then glares at me.

"Yes... sirrr," she drags out the word 'sir', in a sarcastic way. I can feel my eye starting to twitch about her.

She's going to be fun. I think sarcastically to myself.

"I'm Val, Ms. Lainey, I've known Dalton since he was just a little lad," the older lady, Val says. She walks over, ignoring Dalton's look of protest, and gives me a hug.

Had I not just been wearing a sheet, I would have hugged her better, but I say, "It's nice to meet you Val, you can just call me Lainey, no need for the Ms., part. And if you don't mind, maybe later you can tell me stories about little boy and teenage Dalton."

"Oooooh, I would love to do that," she smiles at me. She looks at Dalton and says, "I like her… don't screw it up."

"I don't plan to, ma'am," he says and then winks at me. I notice, again, he's in a towel.

"OH! I should probably get upstairs and shower," I say, turning pink again.

Dalton looks down and says, "Uh, yeah, me too."

"I'll whip up some breakfast for you two, don't you worry about that," Val says as she walks over to the fridge.

Dalton kisses my head as he walks by, I quickly swipe my hand behind me and slap his ass lightly. He jokingly jumps and turns around as he walks down the hall, he waggles a finger at me in the 'no-no' type of way and then he slowly removes his towel. I glance over at Val quickly, there's no way she'd be able to see him. I look back and he's at his door. I shake my head and stick my tongue out. Silently laughing, I turn and walk through the rest of the house hastily and run upstairs.

My shower was quick and I braided my hair in my side braid I tend to use most, if not always. I look in my bag for my baseball cap but can't find it. I must not have packed it. I throw on a sports bra, t-shirt, undies, socks, work jeans... yes I have work jeans, their holey and stained... and then my old hoodie sweatshirt and grab my boots out of the side of my bag.

When I get back downstairs, Dalton is cleaned up and leaning against the counter. He shoves off and walks over to me, giving me a kiss.

"Good shower?" he asks and winks.

"Yup, nice and hot. The water pressure is great," I say, winking back. His mouth falls open slightly but he snaps it shut quickly.

"Not nice... not fair..." he whispers into my ear.

I shrug, laugh, and walk over to where the coffee was stationed.

"I made french toast, eggs, and sausage, I hope that's okay? Dalton hasn't told me what kind of food you like to eat," Val says as she puts a plate of food in front of me and Dalton.

"I have too, I told you she's not picky and likes all foods," Dalton says defensively.

Val looks at him and then expectantly at me.

"He's not wrong, there's not a whole heck of a lot that I don't like... I like food," I say, shrugging.

"Okay, give me a couple of ideas of things you don't like?" she asks.

"Oysters... I've tried them almost every way but raw and I say if I don't like them cooked there's no way

I'm gonna like them raw, so I've never tried them off the shell. Ummm... I don't like eating anything with eyes... meaning, it can't have eyeballs when I put it in my mouth. So sardines, nope. Little baby octopus, nope.... And... yeah, I think that's about it," I say.

"Uh, interesting... I wonder if she's ever tried Land Oysters," Val says, looking at Dalton.

"She's sitting right here, why don't you ask her," he says, tilting his head at her in exasperation.

She looks quickly over at me, "I'm so sorry honey, I didn't mean to speak as if you weren't here."

"Oh you're fine," I say, smiling warmly.

"Have you ever tried Land Oysters?" she asks.

"I'm sorry, I'm not sure I know what those are..." I say.

"Testicles from when we castrate the bull calves," Dalton says.

"Ooooh, you guys call those Land Oysters. Okay, yeah, we call them Rocky Mountain Oysters. And yes, I've tried them and like them battered and deep fried," I say, smiling over at Dalton.

He smiles and looks at Val, "See, she likes food."

"Well alrighty then. You two better hurry up and eat before your breakfast gets cold," Val says, pointing to our plates.

"Yes, ma'am," Dalton and I say at the same time.

Val pats Dalton on the cheek as we walk by to go sit at the breakfast nook. His phone rings. He pulls it out.

"Sorry, it's my sister," he says. I nod him on. "Hi, Darc."

I take a bite of my food. It's delicious.

"Yeah, that's fine," he says to his sister. He's quiet for a second and then, "Yeah, she's here."

I take a sip of my coffee and another bite of egg.

"Yeah, she wants to help," he's quiet for a second and then adds, "She offered." He whispers to me, "She's asking if you're here and asked what you were going to do while we worked cattle."

I just nod and take another bite.

"No, Darcy, I didn't ask her and she knows she doesn't have to if she doesn't want to help, she offered. I've told you before, she works on a farm, this isn't going to be anything new or hard for her. In fact, I'm sure she can teach me a thing or two," he winks at me. "Yes, I would." *Silence* "If you guys had good advice, I'd take it." *silence for a second* "I'm just kidding, Darc... lighten up..."

He takes a sip of his coffee and sputters a little, "Oh whatever! I'm not that..." he rolls his eyes, Darcy must have cut him off.

I finish my plate of food and push it away from me. Dalton still has a plate full. I take a sausage from his plate and put one end of it in my mouth. His eyes go big. I suck it all in, his eyes all but pop out of his head.

"Darcy, I've gotta go. I need to finish eating my

breakfast before Lainey eats it all for me. I love you too, you guys drive safe, and we'll see you tomorrow," he hits the end button and puts his phone down on the table. "Did you just eat my sausage?"

"Yyyyup..." I say, licking my lips suggestively at him.

"Ohhh, you are an evil, evil woman," he says shaking his head but smiling at the same time. "I don't know what I'm going to do with you."

"What do you mean?"

"You're making..." he looks over his shoulder at Val, she's not paying attention to us, she's making some kind of list but Dalton still lowers his voice. "You're making everything sexy... You're sexualizing breakfast."

"Ummm no, I'm eating breakfast. I can't help it if you are overly sexed right now," I whisper back.

He eyes me and whispers, "What was that lip licking nonsense just now?"

"That was just me, licking the juice from your sausage off my lips," I whisper back, grinning.

His mouth falls open. He whisper-shouts, "See, that right there."

"It's not my fault you've got a dirty mind," I whisper. "The sausage I just ate off your plate was really juicy, what's wrong with that?"

"I'm so sure that's what you meant," he laughs out loud now.

"It was," I say and then wink at him.

Under his breath he says, "Evil... plain sexy, evil woman."

I just laugh. I know he doesn't truly believe I'm evil. I also know I was being very suggestive to him. I can't help it, it's kind of fun watching him squirm.

I sip my coffee and over exaggerate being a good girl. He eats his breakfast quickly and then downs his coffee.

"Finished?" I ask.

He eyes me, and says, "With breakfast, yes..."

I smile and get up to take our dishes to the sink. I rinse them off and put them in the dishwasher, which has been emptied already.

"Oh Sweets, don't worry about that, I can get that done," Val says from the other side of the island.

"Thank you so much for breakfast, it was delicious," I say. She comes over and gives me a hug, this time I can give her a proper hug back.

"It's my pleasure," she says. She hugs Dalton and then goes back to her list.

Dalton takes my hand and walks me back out through the living room but once we're out of Val's sight, he pushes me up against the wall and starts kissing me. He takes his right hand and wraps it around the back of my neck, his left hand goes behind my back, pulling me closer to him. I wrap my arms around his waist.

After a good few minutes of this hot make out session, he slowly pulls away.

"That's for your breakfast talk," he says and then kisses me on the nose.

"Well, shoot, if that's what I get for that, I'll talk that way more often," I say, patting his chest.

"Don't you dare or I WILL need to take a cold shower later," he says, laughing. "You really don't understand the effect you have on me!"

"You forget," I say as I run my hand down his chest, down his stomach, and grab hold of his belt and pants and pull him towards me a little. "You don't need a cold shower while I'm here."

"Damn it, Lainey... you can't talk like that," he growls and then he's kissing me passionately again. This time wasn't nearly as long but still very, very hot.

I pull away this time and look up at him. He kisses my nose and steps away from me.

"Behave," he says.

"I am," I say innocently.

"Mmmmhmmm... I think you know what you're doing."

"I'm starting too," I say. "But it has the same effect on me so I'll be good."

"Wait, what?" he says, looking dumbfounded.

I step away and start walking towards the front door. I turn around to face him and say, "You heard me."

He walks over to me with his head down and

says, "I just can't with you. Everything you say... just... sheeeiiiit!"

I laugh and say, "I promise to try to be good."

"See, when you say 'try', it takes away from the promise."

"Well I can't fully promise because what I do to you, you do to me... I just like teasing you so I say it out loud."

"Should I start teasing you?"

"No, because I won't be able to keep my hands off of you. You have better self-control than I do."

"Really?" again, he sounds surprised.

"Oh, definitely. And if you're wanting to get any work done today, we both need to be on our best behavior."

"All we can do is try," he says laughing.

"Yup... and if we fail," I say. "There's always lunch time."

"You're killin' me Smalls," he says, as he slumps through the front door. The cold air slams into me.

Chapter 15

"Brrrr... is it normally this cold this time of year?" I ask.

"No, not this cold."

"I didn't think to bring a coat."

"Don't worry, it'll start to warm up once the sun is up all the way. We'll have a fire going too."

"So, what's your definition of working cattle? It might be different from mine from back home," I ask.

"We vaccinate them all and then castrate the bull calves. What do you guys do?"

"We just vaccinate. We castrate out in the field when we check during calving season, we tag them at that time too. My father-in-law isn't big on Rocky Mountain Oysters so the dogs get them as a treat. We have a branding before we work them, to get all the calves branded, and if we missed a bull calf during calving season, then we'll do it at the branding."

"Oh, yeah we brand out in the field when we go

out to tag. Why do you guys castrate in the field, isn't that tough with momma cow snortin' around?"

"Some cause a problem but most are all bluff. We do it because it's easier to get a newborn calf on the ground than to wrestle with a couple months old calf."

"Huh...." Dalton says. "That makes a lot of sense. If we didn't make a party out of the Oysters in the evening, I'd probably start doing it your way."

"Oh, no. I like this, another reason to have a party, heck yeah. Testical Festival, whoo-hoo!" I say, laughing.

"I like that! I'm going to call it that from now on," he laughs and puts his arm around me. "You are freezing. We can go back inside and find you a jacket, I'm sure I have something that would work."

"No, I'll be fine. Like you said, once the sun is up all the way and we start working, it'll get warmer," I say, pulling him along as he slows down, acting like he wants to turn around.

"You let me know if you get too cold," he says.

"I will."

We get to the corrals where all the cattle have been brought in this morning. Frank and everyone from the kitchen are standing around a firepit, along with about seven more people. The younger girl from the kitchen, Bree, comes running over to us.

"I've got Doc all set up, Dalton. He says he's ready whenever we are," she says, looking at Dalton with undeniable desire.

Hmmmm I'm not going to like this girl much. I think to myself. Not just because she's about 5'8" and all legs, blonde and skinny. But because she was acting like I wasn't standing here, under Dalton's arm, by his side.

"Thanks Bree," Dalton says nonchalantly. He turns to me, "What would you like to do?"

"Oh, you're still here?" Bree says snottily.

Ignoring her, I answer Dalton. "Whatever you need me to do."

"Why don't you help give vaccines? Doc will get you set up on what to do," Dalton says.

"I was going to do that. She probably doesn't know what to do and it'll take Doc too long to explain it all to her," Bree protests.

"She's a farmer, she knows what she's doing," Dalton says. "You'll be pushing cattle up the alley."

"What? Ummm.. no," she says, crossing her arms across her chest.

"Bree, I don't have time for this. Either do what I say, or leave," Dalton says and then turns towards everyone else. "Doc, this is Lainey. She's going to be helping us today."

I wave. There's a murmur from everyone as I walk over to him.

"Okay, yes, everyone this is Lainey," Dalton says, rolling his eyes. "Lainey, this is Hands, John, Shorty, and you met Frank and Junior in the house. This is Sam and Lynn, Nolan and Mel, Tanner and Hannah, and Abe." As he says their names, they wave and smile a hello. I wave and smile back.

"There'll be a test later, on our names," the man, Hands, says. He then winks and smiles at me. His bottom lip sticks out a little from a wad of chewing tobacco in it.

"Come on, Darlin', I'll show ya what we're doin' today," the vet, Doc says. He starts to walk over to a table that's been set up between two squeeze chutes.

I can hear Dalton talking to the others behind us. I glance over my shoulder and see Bree glaring daggers at me. I'm gonna have to ask Dalton about that later. Was there something between them? He never mentioned a 'Bree' to me.

After being shown everything on the table, Doc hollers at Dalton that we are ready. Dalton tells everyone to get goin' to their spots. Bree, grudgingly, grabs a hot-shot and heads down one of the alley's, Junior is heading down the other. The other three girls and three guys, jump on horses and head down to where all the cattle are being corralled. Hands, John, and Shorty have all gotten on horses too but are down where we are, they'll be roping the bull calves to help control them so that Abe and Frank can castrate them. Dalton is doing vaccines on the other side. Doc is going to, quickly, make sure the cattle look good before we release them to either the pasture over or to be castrated.

Dalton whistles two loud, short whistles, followed by one long one. That must be the signal because the crew on horses down with the cattle start pushing them up the alley's toward Junior and Bree.

It takes a couple cows for me to get into a rhythm. I wasn't kidding when I told Dalton working cows was my least favorite farming activity but once I got my groove, I was golden. Working with Dalton was fun. Every time we'd meet at the table, he'd give me his heartbreaking smile.

About an hour in, Dalton asks, "How many have you done?"

"230 some... you?" I answer as I refill my vaccine guns.

"230? Damn, that's close to four every minute. At this rate, we'll be done before lunch. I don't know if that's ever happened. I've only gotten 190 done," he says, looking at me slightly awestruck.

"Speed it up, Young," I say, winking at him.

"Shall we make this interesting?" Dalton asks, raising an eyebrow at me.

"Sure," I say, pretending to holster by vaccine guns.

He laughs and then he says, "First one to 500 gets to..." He scrunches up his eyes as he thinks hard.

"Pick tonight's activities?" I suggest.

"Yes, I like that," he says.

"You know I'm close to halfway there and you're 40 behind me. Are you sure you want me choosing tonight?" I say, raising my eyebrow at him this time.

"Your ideas seem to always benefit me, so yeah, I'm okay with that," he laughs.

"Hmmmm... well maybe I'll have to think of activities that don't benefit you."

"I don't like that idea," he says, tilting his head to the side.

"Then you better beat me," I say as I turn back towards my squeeze chute.

"OH! It's on," Dalton hollers. "Bring 'em on up, Bree!"

"Keep 'em comin', Junior!" I holler too.

It's taken more than an hour, closer to two and a half since our bet because Doc had to check a couple heifers but I haven't heard Dalton exclaim that he's gotten to 500. I am only ten away. When I fill my vaccine gun up again, I glance over and see Dalton concentrating so hard, his tongue is sticking out.

Smiling and giggling to myself, I hurry back to my squeeze chute. I nod at Junior and wave him on to start back up. He quickly pushes cattle up.

The next one is in, I close the head gate. Shot. Shot. Open the head gate, she's out.

Two. Close head gate. Shot. Shot. Open head gate, she's out.

Three.

Four.

Five.

Six.

Seven.

Eight.

Nine.

Ten! I hurry and shut the head gate. Shot. Shot. Hurry and open the head gate.

Damn cow. will. not. move.

"Tssst-tssst, up cow, up!" I shout, patting her hind end. She jumps and runs out.

"500!" I shout.

"What?!" Dalton hollers. "No way!"

I turn and see him standing, staring at me. His ball cap is slightly sideways.

"Yup," I say, ginning.

"How? I'm only at 473," he says. Then teasingly, "I think you miss counted."

"Hey Junior, go ask someone back there how many are left," I holler to Junior.

"Okay!" he shouts back. He hops up over the fence of the alley and runs to the corrals. I see one of the girls ride over to him. She turns and does a quick count.

Junior nods and runs up to us. "There's 23 left."

I look over at Dalton with my eyebrows raised. "So I either have done more than 500 or you've done a couple more than 473. Which do you think it is?"

"This is crazy..." Dalton stammers. "We've never worked them this quickly before, never."

I shrug and say, "Well, let's finish them. Junior,

push 'em on up."

Shaking his head Dalton says, "Keep 'em comin', Bree."

We finish out vaccinating and then help Abe and Frank castrate the bull-calves. That takes a little bit of time, waiting for Hands, John, and Shorty to rope them. We finish and get them all secured in the pasture until morning, when we'll be trailing them to mountain pasture. We start back towards the house for lunch.

"Lainey, we'll need you to help every year. Never have we processed cattle this quickly," Doc says.

"It was because she was able to do it all by herself. I didn't have to stop what I was doing every ten minutes to help her," Dalton says.

"Hmmmmph," Bree says as she stalks past us, elbowing me slightly.

"What's with her?" I ask, starting to get really annoyed with her.

"Bree?" Dalton asks.

"Yeah, she doesn't seem to like me but I've just met her," I say.

"She's..." Dalton starts to say.

"Hey Boss, we still having the barbeque tonight?" John asks, interrupting Dalton.

Dalton looks at me, "We can talk later."

"Yeah, John, we're still having the barbeque later," he says.

"Sweet, I'm gonna run home and get my ol' lady.

What time ya think? 6 o'clock?" Hands asks.

"Sounds about right," Dalton says.

John walks his horse back towards the barn, Shorty catching up to him with his horse, and starts to talk to him.

Doc walks up beside Dalton, "My wife will be happy that we can get an earlier start to the drive. Good work today."

"Thanks again, Doc," Dalton says, shaking hands with Doc before he starts off for his pickup.

We've reached the walkway leading to the house. Hands, Abe, Frank, and Junior are all walking in the door ahead of us. I can see Bree standing just inside the doors. When we get closer, I can smell fried chicken.

"Val made fried chicken?" I ask, eagerly.

"Yeah, she makes it every time the whole crew is here for lunch. She says she can make a ton quickly," Dalton replies as he holds the door open for me.

"Thanks," I say, touching his arm as I walk inside.

He grabs hold of my hand and spins me back to him and he steps back outside, pressing me against the side of the house, just to the right of the doors. And then he's kissing me, softly at first and then more urgent, more passionately. After a minute, or two, maybe more, time doesn't mean much when we're kissing like this, Dalton slows our kissing and looks down at me.

"I'm sorry but I've been wanting to do that since we left the house this morning."

"I'm not complaining," I say, teasingly. Then my stomach growls.

"You might not be but your stomach is, let's get you fed," he says, laughing. He grabs my hand and pulls me into the house.

We take our boots off at the door and put them with the others. Everyone else has gotten a plate of food and they're sitting in the dining room at the large table. Bree glares at our hands. Dalton leads us into the kitchen and Val is waiting for us.

"Fried chicken and all the fixin's," she says as she hands me a plate.

"Thank you so much, Val. This looks great!" I exclaim. Not only is there fried chicken but she has made big fluffy biscuits, corn on the cob, mac-n-cheese, mashed potatoes and gravy, green beans, macaroni salad, potato salad, and a green salad.

"Dig in, Sweety," she says.

I load up a plate and wait for Dalton. We walk out to the dining room and take seats. Bree happens to be at the other end of the table, thankfully. I see there's pitchers of water on the table with cups stacked next to them.

We all eat in silence for a few minutes and then conversations start to break out. Val comes in with a plate and sits beside me.

"You think you'll be finished by 5 o'clock?" Val asks Dalton.

Dalton swallows his food and takes a sip of water before answering her.

"We're finished," he says, smiling at me.

"With the morning bit, yeah, but I mean with them all. I want to make sure I have plenty of time to wash the testes before cooking time," she says and then takes a bite of her food.

"No, Val, we're done," Dalton says.

Val stares at him, puts down her fork, and says, "You're telling me, you worked all thousand head? Castrated what needed castrated? Already? And it's just after 1 o'clock?"

"Yes, ma'am," he says, smiling.

Val looks at me, I smile and nod.

She looks down the table, "Franklin?"

"Yes, ma'am," Frank answers quickly.

"Dalton and Lainey are telling me you all finished working the cattle, are they pullin' my leg?" she asks him.

"No, ma'am. We finished. Ms. Lainey was a big help. She knows her way around a vac's gun," Frank says.

"So what about all the years past? You all been slacking off or what?" Val asks Dalton, laughing.

"No, ma'am. Lainey just brought us good luck for everything to go smoothly and Frank isn't wrong, I didn't have to help her once," he says, smiling at me again.

"Now, it wasn't all me. We all worked hard," I say,

not liking everyone looking at me and definitely not liking the death stare Bree is shooting me.

"Whatever the reason, we need you back next year," Hannah says. Mel nods in agreement.

"Thanks," I say. At least they're being nice. Bree rolls her eyes and gets Abe's attention. Everyone else goes back to talking amongst themselves.

I yawn.

"Nap time?" Dalton asks.

I'm about to say no, that I'm fine but thinking of the barbeque this evening has me tired already. So I say, "You know, I could use a couple minutes of sleep."

"Come on then," he whispers. He stands and grabs our plates. I grab our cups and follow him into the kitchen. We put the dishes in the sink.

"I hope you don't mind but I had Val move your bag down to my room," he says, grabbing my hand and walking us out of the kitchen and down the hall to his room.

"I don't mind at all," I say, grinning like an idiot.

We get to his room and he shuts the door behind us. I continue into his room and to his bed. I lay out across it and then roll over to my back as Dalton gets to the bed. He crawls on top of me, smiling.

"So... you won the bet," he smiles. "Have you thought of what you'd like to do this evening? Or even right now?"

"Hmmmm..." I say as I start to untuck his shirt

from his pants. "There are a few ideas I've been thinking about all morning."

I start to unbutton his shirt, starting at the top. He bends down and kisses me.

KNOCK-KNOCK

My hands freeze.

"Shhhh...." he whispers. "Maybe they'll go away."

KNOCK-KNOCK

"Dalton?" Frank's voice comes from the other side of the door.

With a deep growl, Dalton rolls over and then off the bed. He turns to me, buttoning his shirt, and whispers, "Don't move and keep thinking those thoughts." More loudly, he says, "What Frank?"

"We've got an issue... should only take a few minutes to sort out," Frank says.

Dalton reaches the door and glares for half a second before motioning Frank on down the hallway. Dalton closes the door but gives me a quick wink before it's closed all the way.

I look around his room and really take it in for the first time. When you walk through his french double bedroom doors, there's a short hallway and I had glimpsed his bathroom to the left just as you walk into his actual room. If you turn to the right and follow the wall, you'll find double sliding barn type doors, that lead into what looks like the biggest walk in closet I've ever seen. The bed is straight across from the closet, caddy corner in the corner. The oversized chair is a few feet away by the fireplace. If you continue on this wall it'll take you to the left side of the room where there's sliding glass doors that lead to the back patio. And then back to part of the wall to the bathroom and then you'd be walking back down the little hallway to his bedroom doors. His room is huge.

I roll over and grab a pillow and cuddle into it. It's nowhere near as comforting as Dalton but it's become my comfort while lying in bed alone. I yawn and close my eyes.

I'll take a quick nap, just until Dalton gets back. I think to myself.

Chapter 16

"Lainey... Laaaaainey..." I hear someone calling my name softly. I can feel someone rubbing my back, also.

"Lainey?" Dalton's voice calls softly but close to my ear.

"Mmmm..." I moan out. I roll onto my back and stretch.

"Hey, Sleeping Beauty," Dalton says, kissing my cheek.

I laugh quietly and then open my eyes. It would be completely dark in here if Dalton hadn't turned on the lamp next to the bed.

Confused, I ask, "What time is it?"

"Almost 5 o'clock."

"Oh wow!" I exclaim, yawn, and then laugh. "I was more tired than I thought."

"I'd say," Dalton laughs. "I tried to wake you up when I got back, maybe an hour after I left with Frank, but you didn't move a muscle. So I closed the blinds and laid down and took a nap with you. I set my alarm on my phone to go off at 5 o'clock."

"Whoa! It's a good thing you did. I don't know how long I would have slept."

"You and me both," he smiles. "I need to go get stuff set up for the barbeque. Do you want to sleep a little longer? I can come wake you up before 6 o'clock or do you want to help me?" he asks as he slides to the edge of the bed.

I stretch and sit up, "I'll help you."

He offers me his hand, I take it, and he pulls me up off the bed. He doesn't let go as he leads us from the room. We walk out of his bedroom and down the hall. I smell something amazing cooking in the kitchen.

"Oh my gosh, Val! What is that?" I ask as I take another deep breath.

"Well I'm not sure what you're referring to but I've baked brownies and just pulled the pumpkin cake out of the oven about 30 minutes ago," Val replies smiling at me.

I walk over and watch as she pulls the cake out of the fridge. She puts it on the counter and opens a can of sweetened condensed milk and sets it aside. She takes a wooden spoon and starts poking holes in the cake.

"What happens after you put the milk on it?" I ask. I have made a similar cake, only it was chocolate cake with strawberry glaze.

"I'll put it back in the fridge for a little bit and then put Cool-Whip on top with some candy bits and caramel syrup. Then it'll go back in the fridge until we're ready to eat it," she says as she starts to dump the condensed milk on top.

"Wow! That sounds awesome. What's it called?" I ask.

Only Dalton answers, "Better Than Sex Pumpkin Cake."

"Oh," is all I can say.

He whispers in my ear, "Whoever named it has clearly never had sex with you because there is nothing better than that." He kisses my cheek which has warmed up and is turning red from my embarrassment.

I give him a 'shhh' look and look back at Val. She is either really good at acting like she hasn't heard anything or she actually didn't. Either way, I'm thankful.

"Looks good Val, we're gonna go set up outside," Dalton says.

"Mmmmmhmmm," she replies as she puts the cake back into the fridge.

Dalton takes my hand and pulls me from the room. When we get to the entryway, where our boots are, instead of letting go and putting his boots on, Dalton gently pushes me up against the wall again and starts kissing me.

I let go of his hand and run both of mine up his muscled chest, up around his neck, and pull him closer to me.

He gasps and pushes closer and our kissing intensifies. I stretch up on my tip-toes so he doesn't have to bend down so far. Dalton slides his hands down from my back, over my ass, and places them just below it, and lifts me up. I wrap my legs around his waist and he pins me to the wall.

He moans into my mouth as he grinds his pelvic region into mine.

We can't have been making out for too long before the front door bangs open and Bree storms into the house.

Surprised, we all freeze. The look on Bree's face is the epitome of 'if looks could kill'.

I push Dalton away just enough so that I can slide down to my feet.

"What's up, Bree?" Dalton asks nonchalantly, totally relaxed.

"Just coming in to see if you were going to help with your barbeque," she snarkily replies.

"Yup, we're on our way out," he says, smiling, oblivious to her attitude.

"Clearly," she says sarcastically. She gives me a dirty once over, shakes her head, and walks back outside.

"Okay, what's her deal?" I ask.

"Who?" Dalton asks, sounding honestly confused. He bends down for his boots.

"Ummmm...," I start to say. He stands and looks at me. My palm facing up and my pointer finger pointing towards the door. I continue and say, "Bree..."

"What do you mean?" he asks but with a little more falseness to his confusion.

I stare at him for a minute and then I say, "You didn't mention you'd had a thing with someone, let alone her."

Dalton looks at me. "A thing?"

"Yeah, dating someone. She's probably not too excited I'm here. When did you guys date?"

"Never," he says matter of factly.

"Oh come on," I say in disbelief.

"No, really," Dalton says, turning to look at me after grabbing a coat for himself. "She made advances and made it clear she wanted something from me but I made it clear to her that I wasn't interested. I was... I didn't know what you and I were... are... if we're anything with a label but I didn't want to jeopardize it so I told her I was involved with you. I told everyone about you. I'm sure they're all happy to see you're an actual person, not someone I made up in my head," he laughs.

"Oh... well by the way she's been acting towards me, it's like I've stolen you from her. Like you were dating and then not because of me."

"No, I don't date people that work for me. And I've told you, I don't fool around just to fool around."

"But she's so pretty," I say.

"And that's the extent of Bree. She plays off of her looks to get what or who she wants. I won't deny that I think she's pretty, because she is but you… you are beautiful. So much more than just pretty. Your inside matches your outside, you're beautiful through and through."

"So nothing happened?"

"No, nothing happened."

"But we never agreed on being exclusive, you could have done whatever you wanted with her."

"I know we didn't but had I, I would have had to tell you, because I don't keep secrets. How would that have felt?"

I bend down and put my last boot on.

"Lainey, how would that have made you feel? Knowing I'd started seeing someone while we were talking and getting to know each other and everything that happened while I was in Oregon, when we first met?"

"Not good, okay," I exclaim a little more loudly than I meant to sound.

"And why is that?" he asks, pulling me up so he can see my face. He grabs one of his coats and offers for me to put it on.

As I'm putting it on, I sigh loudly.

UGH….

I take a big breath and say, "Because even though we hadn't talked about being exclusive, I still would have felt betrayed. Dumb, even, for thinking we were connecting like we did, even being hundreds of miles away from each other. At least I feel like we connected."

"I feel like we did too and that's what I didn't want to jeopardize. But dating Bree wouldn't have happened even if we weren't, aren't… whatever we are, because she is not what I am… was, looking for in a partner."

"And that would be what?"

"You, Lainey… I've been waiting and looking for a woman like you."

He bends down and kisses me, sweetly and softly.

My heart flutters, in the best way possible. In a way I didn't think it would ever flutter after Jayce's accident, after losing him.

BANG!

The door flies open again, banging into the wall. Frank and Shorty bump into us.

"What the hell?" Dalton shouts, catching me before I land on the floor.

"Sorry, Boss," Shorty shouts, reaching out to help me but steps back quickly as he sees Dalton has me.

"Where is it?" Frank shouts, holding a shotgun in his hand.

CHAPTER 16

"Where's what?" Dalton asks, pissed off.

"The cougar?" Shorty says, looking around.

"Bree said there was a cougar in here that needed to be taken care of," Frank says, looking between Dalton and I.

"There's no cougar in here," Dalton says, looking confused and mad.

I instantly bust out in hysterical laughter. The guys stare at me in confusion.

After a minute, I exclaim, "Me!" I choke between gasps of breath, trying to stop laughing so hard. Looking at each of their faces, completely lost, just makes me laugh even harder. "I… am… the… cougar…"

"What…" Dalton starts to ask and then laughs too.

"I don't understand," Frank says.

Shorty, who's trying not to laugh, says, "An older woman that goes after younger men is called a cougar. Bree is calling Lainey a cougar."

"Does Bree know anything about you other than you're very rich and good looking?" I ask, finally able to breathe.

"I guess not because I'm a little over a year older than you," he laughs.

"I'm sorry, Lainey," Frank says.

Shaking my head, I say, "I'll take it as a complement. Most cougars are hot older women. How old is Bree anyways?"

"26, I think," Shorty says.

"I'm going to have a word with her," Dalton says.

"No, don't, it's fine. No harm, no foul. She probably thought I'd be offended. I just think it's funny," I say as Frank and Shorty lead us out the door.

A freezing breeze blows into us.

"Holy shit!" Dalton exclaims. "It's gotten cold!"

"Still want to have the barbeque?" Shorty asks.

"Yeah, we'll get a few fire pits going," Dalton says. "And it's called the Testical Festival from now on."

He hip bumps me, causing me to laugh again.

"I like it," Shorty laughs.

"Ugh…" Frank grunts.

We get outside and walk towards the shed, where Bree and Hands are bringing out another picnic table, there is already one setup.

As we walk by, I look at Bree, who has a gloating smile on her face.

I smile at her which causes her smile to fall a little and then I bare my teeth and hiss like an angry cat at her. Her eyes go big and she starts to push the table into Hands, trying to get him to move faster.

I hear Shorty and Frank chuckle out laughs.

"Easy, Kitty," Dalton says, laughing silently into my ear as he pulls me closer to him.

"Sorry," I say. "Her smile pissed me off."

"Was she smiling?" Dalton asks.

"You didn't notice?" I ask.

"I don't notice anyone when you're around."

We step aside as Shorty and Frank take out a table and some chairs.

"Awww," I say in mock affection but I wink at him, then kiss him on the cheek. Then I add, more sincerely, "Thank you for that."

"I mean it, Lainey," he says sternly.

"I know but most guys don't."

"When... will... you... understand..." he gently grabs me and pulls me close to him. "Realize, I'm not like most guys?"

"Soon, very soon," I say.

He kisses me deeply.

"Now... I realize it now," I say, panting, trying to catch my breath.

"Better answer," he kisses my nose and then steps away. "Here, pack this out?"

He hands me what looks like a dish. I turn it and see it's a portable fire pit. He's got the stand for it in his hands plus some lawn chairs. The guy is strong.

We walk out and set the firepit up and place the chairs around it.

"Let's go get wood for this and then I need to check the barbeque, see if it's hot enough. It should be, I've had it going since before our nap," Dalton says, taking my hand.

"You go do that, just point me in the direction of the wood," I suggest.

"It's just on the other side of the shed, in the leanto," Dalton says.

When I get to the leanto, I look for kindling so that we can get the fires going and warm before everyone gets here. It's getting dark and colder by the minute. I can't find any kindling, so I grab the maul and a piece of wood and start chopping it into smaller pieces, making my own pile of kindling. After chopping up two large pieces into kindling size, I cut two more large pieces but only in half.

"What chya doin'?" Dalton asks, startling me because I didn't hear him walk up.

"Getting some fire starter," I say.

"I usually use gas or a propane torch," he laughs.

"Oh… well… we can save this for another time, but it was very therapeutic for me."

"How so?"

"Well, it was either I took my frustration out on the wood or on Bree, and that wouldn't have been productive. This was, or at least I thought it was," I laugh.

"We'll definitely use it. I'm just usually in a rush to get things going so I don't take the time for kindling."

"I enjoy it."

"You're good at it," he says as he bends down to pick up a pile.

"My wood stove at home would be useless without wood and the kids and I would freeze," I laugh.

"This is true," he admits.

"How's the barbequer?"

"Hot and ready."

"Oh, good."

We start walking back over to the set up.

"Everyone should be getting here in about 30 minutes. Frank said he'll man the barbeque this year so I can spend time with you, introduce you better to everyone," he says.

"Oh, ok! That's nice of him."

"His wife, Audrey, is the social butterfly, he usually ends up in the house reading whatever is lying around."

I laugh.

"I have a question for you," he states, putting the kindling down inside the fire pit.

"I should have an answer," I say.

"Only you would," he says, sounding timid which is weird to hear in his voice.

"What is it?" I ask, concern coloring my tone.

"Can we talk about us for a minute?" he asks.

"Sure."

"What should I call you? When I introduce you... what would you like me to tell everyone you are to me, what we are?"

"What do you want to call me?" I don't want to assume he wants to call me anything specific, so I'm going to make him tell me first.

"I think girlfriend fits accurately, don't you

think?"

I smile up at him and say, "Yeah, that would fit. So that would make you... my boyfriend?"

"I believe so," he laughs.

"That's so weird to think... I have a boyfriend... I never thought those words would come out of my mouth again," I say.

Dalton grins and steps into me, kissing me deeply, yet again. After a minute, we hear someone clear their throat. It's Frank.

"Sorry to interrupt again, but people are pulling up the driveway," he says, looking embarrassed for once again interrupting us making out like we're a couple of high school kids.

"Thanks," Dalton says.

"I'll go get some wood to pile up," I say.

"I'll help and then we can go help Val set the food out."

"Not out here?" I ask in a high pitch voice. "It'll be cold before we get a chance to eat."

"No, she said she'd have it set up inside and we can eat out here."

"Oh good."

We go back and each get an arm load worth of wood. We dump the wood off by the fire pit that Shorty has blazing away. Dalton's pile is significantly larger than mine but his arm span is at least double mine.

We walk in through the side door into the kitchen. Val already has things set out on the counter and island.

"What can we do?" I ask.

"Oh bless you Lainey! Take these to the dining room table, please," she says handing me a potato salad and a tossed green salad.

As I walk out of the kitchen, I hear Val whisper, or at least she thought she was whispering, it was just barely less loud than her normal volume.

"I like her," she says to Dalton.

"Me too," he replies, a little quieter than Val but still loud enough I can hear him.

I put the salads on the table and turn back to go get more. Dalton walks in holding an oversized baking sheet of some kind of sliced beef.

"Holy crap!" I exclaim. "That looks and smells amazing! Is it brisket?"

"Yup! Val's been cooking all day. Take a piece, it tastes better than it looks or smells."

I grab a small piece and take a bite.

"Oh... My... Gosh!" I moan.

"Hey, I thought I was the only one or thing that could make you make that sound?" he teases.

"Nope, this brisket does it too! Holy crap, it's delicious!" I reach for another piece as Dalton is putting it down but he blocks me. Instead, he picks up a piece and turns to me.

"Open up," he says.

I'm going to let him put his meat in my mouth for the first time.. I think to myself and giggle.

"What?" he asks.

"Nothing," I say and then I open my mouth, trying not to giggle again.

"Nope, tell me first," he says as he holds the piece of brisket over his head.

"Just put your meat in my mouth already," I teasingly say, as I bite my lip before opening my mouth again, fighting the urge to burst out laughing.

Dalton freezes. His eyes bulging a little and then he cracks up laughing.

Blinking rapidly, he says, "That is so not what I thought you were going to say and definitely not something you should say."

"Why not?" I ask stepping closer to him. I look up into his eyes and smile.

Dalton swallows hard and says, "Because you know what you do to me and saying things like that gets me all riled up."

"And that would be bad right now?" I ask, faking my confusion. I'm having fun with him, even though I know it's slightly mean.

"It would be if you don't want me to throw you over my shoulder and hightail it to my room."

I run the back of my hands up his thigh until they get to about my waist height and then I turn them over and run my palms up the rest of him, resting them softly on his chest.

"I don't want that?" again I ask in a fake confused tone.

Dalton closes his eyes and takes a deep breath. He drops the piece of meat onto the table. He wraps his arms around me and pulls me close. He says, "Lainey, you keep touching me like this and you'll bring me to the point of no return."

He bends his head down and kisses me.

Cough-Cough

As per usual, we got lost in our kissing and forgot other people were in the house.

"Sorry to interrupt, but I thought you two were helping me?" Val asks.

"Yes, ma'am, we are, sorry," Dalton says. More embarrassed getting caught this time than any time before, it must be because it's Val.

"Sorry, Val," I say. "We'll go get the rest of it."

Val winks at me as I pass her and I blush.

Chapter 17

We make a couple more trips in with food before we're finished.

We go back out to see who all has arrived. It's not quite 6:30pm, so Dalton doesn't expect a lot of people yet.

I can see Mel and Hannah are here and I look over at Frank, who is already fully engrossed at the barbeque, and see three guys who I think are Tanner, Nolan, and Abe.

Dalton sees Hannah and Mel wave at me and that I'm waving back so he grabs my hand and steers us towards them.

"Hi, guys," Hannah says. Mel waves another hello and smiles.

"Hi," Dalton and I say at the same time.

Two guys, who I'm pretty sure are Nolan and Tanner, make their way over to us. One kisses Hannah, and the other hugs Mel. I hadn't noticed their wedding rings before now.

"I'm introducing Lainey to everyone again," Dalton says to our little group. "So... Lainey this is Tanner and Hannah Smith and Nolan Lagdon and his wife, Melanie, but she goes by Mel. Guys, this is Elainah Richardsen."

I nod and say, "It's nice to meet you... again."

"Elainah?" Mel asks. "That's a pretty name."

"Thank you, but I go by Lainey," I smile and shrug.

"You gals want a drink?" Tanner asks.

"I'd take one," Mel says. "Whatever wine Karie has open already will do."

"Yeah, same," Hannah adds.

"I had Val pick up some strawberry lemonade beer and she found the pineapple cider that you like," Dalton suggests.

"Oooh, a cider sounds good," I say excitedly.

"We'll be back," Dalton says. He, Tanner, and Nolan walk over to where Frank is standing and I watch them open a huge cooler and Dalton grabs something out.

An older woman I haven't seen before walks up to us.

"Hi, Karie," Hannah says.

"Hey," she, Karie, replies.

"Lainey, this is Karie. Karie, this is Lainey. She's Dalton's..." Mel introduces us but then falters at the end.

"I'm his girlfriend," I say, beaming. I feel giddy.

Mel and Hannah smile hugely at each other.

"It's nice to meet you Lainey. I'm John's wife," Karie says.

"It's nice to meet you too, Karie," if I say her name multiple times, I'll hopefully remember it. I'm not good with names.

The guys make it back to us, handing our drinks over. We thank them. Dalton puts his arm around my shoulder and takes a drink of his beer.

"Karie, have you met Lainey?" he asks.

"I have! Your girlfriend seems very nice," she says, smiling at me.

"She definitely is," Dalton agrees and then kisses the top of my head.

"Not only is she nice but she can handle a vaccine gun," Mel adds.

"I heard. John was… is very impressed with you," Karie says with another kind smile.

"Oh," I shake my head. "Nothing to be impressed by, I've been working cows for years."

"So you're a cattleman?" Nolan asks.

Before I can answer, a younger cowboy walks over and hollers, "Let's get this party started! Who's taking a shot?"

"Abe, it's a little early for that, isn't it?" Karie asks.

"Not at all, ma'am," Abe says. Bless Karie for saying his name. He pulls up his hand and shows us the apple whiskey he has open.

"I'll take one," I hear Bree shout from behind us.

I must have tensed because Dalton squeezes my shoulder. I take a deep breath and force myself to relax.

I turn and see Bree bouncing over to us. She has her hair in a pony and is wearing a bikini top under an unzipped hoodie and jeans but you can see the string from her matching bikini bottoms.

Abe takes a swing and hands it to Bree, not hiding the fact he's checking out her, little, but perky breasts.

Bree takes the smallest of swigs and offers me the bottle.

"Not having any?" she asks.

"Oh, no, I want some, I love this stuff," I wasn't actually lying. This whiskey, I can drink. I take the bottle and take a big pull off of it. Not wincing, not even a little, as the slight burn makes its way down my throat.

"Daaaaamn!" Abe hollers and gives me a high-five before taking the bottle back. Bree shoots me a glare, I smile back.

"Abe, you didn't really get to meet Lainey earlier, so I'll reintroduce you," Dalton says, wrapping his arm down around my waist and placing his hand on my stomach, just below my right breast. "Abe, this is Lainey, my girlfriend. Lainey, this is Abe."

I hear Bree take in a hiss of air and I look at her

quickly as I shake Abe's hand.

"It's nice to meet you," I say.

"Same here, ma'am," he says.

Bree turns on her heels and stomps away. I look up at Dalton with my eyebrows raised.

"What?" he asks with fake confusion, again.

I shake my head and laugh a little.

"So do you guys live around here?" I ask.

"We work for Dalton, but have the houses on the other end of the valley. We're his cowboys. We're always riding. Checking cows and fixing fences in the summer," Tanner answers first.

"We feed, doctor, and do the calving in the winter and spring," Nolan adds.

"We also make sure the forest grazing land is ready in the late spring or early summer, depending on snow levels. And we make sure the winter pastures are ready by late fall," Hannah says.

I turn to Dalton and ask, "And what exactly do you do?"

They all laugh, even Dalton.

"I ask myself that all the time," he says, still laughing. "I sign the paychecks," he laughs again, louder.

We all laugh and then I see Hands and Shorty walk around the side of the house.

"'Scuse us, guys," Dalton says as he takes my hand and pulls me towards the newcomers.

"Everything looks good," Hands says before Dalton can say or ask him anything.

"Good, we're ready for the morning?" Dalton asks.

"Yup," Shorty answers.

"Keep an eye on Abe, would ya. I don't want anyone getting totally shit housed tonight. We need everyone on their 'A' game tomorrow," Dalton says, looking back over to where we were just standing.

"On it," Shorty says. I watch as he walks over and Abe overs him the apple whiskey. Shorty takes a pull but doesn't offer it back. Soon everyone is laughing at something he's said.

"Shorty is good at nonchalant control," Hands says. "Meaning, he'll have you doing something without realizing you're doing it. He's the one you want dealing with people if you think there's going to be a confrontation."

"Ahh, I see. Good one to have around," I say.

"So Lainey, are you having fun? Enjoying Montana?" Hands asks.

"So far, so good," I say, smiling up at Dalton.

"Are you guys officially a thing?" Hands asks bluntly.

I spit out the little bit of drink I have left in my mouth as I had just taken a drink of my cider.

"Yes, Lainey is my girlfriend," Dalton says, laughing at me. He asks, "Are you okay?"

"Yeah," I answer, wiping my mouth. "I just wasn't expecting that. People usually lead into asking those kinds of questions."

"Why pussy foot around when I can ask directly?" Hands asks. Then adds, "Plus, Dalton has been talking about you nonstop for the last year. I'm glad you're here."

"Thanks," I say. I like Hands, he seems very straight forward. Except, "Hey, what's your real name? Or is it Hands?"

"My real name is David but I go by Hands because of my roping ability," he answers.

"You won't find a better roper in 1000 miles," Dalton says, punching Hands lightly in the shoulder.

"Do you rodeo too?" I ask.

"I did but doing it professionally was taking the fun out of it so I decided to quit and work full time for Dalton. I'm a lot happier now," Hands answers, and then lightly punches Dalton back in the shoulder.

"Remember my best friend I told you about, that I went and stayed with when I kicked Sally out?" Dalton asks.

"Yeah..." I say.

Dalont points a finger at Hands and says, "This is him."

"Oh! Okay! It all makes sense now," I say, thinking about how blunt Hands is with Dalton and how close they seem.

"You told her about me?" Hands asks, mocking being shocked.

"Yeah, kind of on the first day we met. I told her about the day I told Sally to pack and leave. I didn't say your name specifically but..." Dalton says nonchalantly.

"It's nice to put a face and name to his best friend," I say.

"Awww, I am your best friend, aren't I?" Hands states. He steps over and puts his head on Dalton's shoulder.

Dalton playfully pushes him away.

"Don't push it," Dalton says laughing. He turns to me and says, "We met through rodeo. What... 15 years ago?"

"Sounds about right," Hands agrees.

"And what about Shorty? Is 'Shorty' a nickname because he's so insanely tall?" I ask, laughing.

"Yeah, his real name is Ray but I don't think he's been called that since he was like... 3 or something. He got the nickname, 'Shorty', at a very young age and has gone by it ever since," Hands says, looking over to where Shorty was standing, talking to Abe and Nolan.

"Foods on!" Val hollers over by the barbequer.

We make our way inside and get in line as everyone grabs a plate from the kitchen and makes their way into the dining room. Working like a buffet, we go up one side of the table and down the other.

Once we get our food and head back outside, we

stop at the barbequer and Frank plops a couple Rocky Mountain Oysters onto our plates. They are battered and then cooked on the grill, they look really good.

"So, Lainey, have you ever had these before?" Bree asks as we sit down across from her, Abe, Hands, and Shorty.

"I have," I answer.

"Really?" she asks, sounding honestly surprised.

"Yup, we have them down in Oregon also," I say, laughing.

"You know their testicals, right?" she sneers.

"I do, which is why we have them in Oregon. We have cattle there too that we work, just like up here," I say, getting a little more snarky than I usually am. Bree is starting to really get on my nerves.

Breathe, Lainey. Just breathe. She's trying to get a rise out of you.

I take a deep breath and dig into my food. It's all so delicious.

Brisket? GOOD! Tater salad? Good! Green salad? Good! Baked beans? Good! Testicals? Good!

John and Karie come and sit with us on the same side Dalton and I are sitting. They all start to break off into conversations. I just sit and enjoy my food. Honestly, it's soo good!

Halfway through eating, Dalton gets up, and goes back in for seconds. The guy eats fast. I get up and get us a couple more drinks. We meet each other back at the table. He bows his head towards the table, suggesting I sit first. Shaking my head at his chivalry, but also loving it, I sit, smiling. I open his beer and put it in front of him and I start to open mine.

"Thanks," he says as he sits down and puts a plate to the side of my plate.

"Thank you!" I exclaim. He's brought me a plate with a piece of each of the desserts Val made. I take a bite of the brownie first. It's ooey and gooey and chocolatey goodness. I get a forkful of the pumpkin cake and take my first bite of it.

My eyes close and I just sit, silent, not moving.

"What's wrong with her?" Bree asks with false concern. *Why is she always aware of me? If she doesn't like me, why is she so concerned with what I'm doing?*

"She's enjoying her first bite of the pumpkin cake," Dalton says with suppressed laughter.

"But why?" Bree asks more snark than what's needed.

"Because she enjoys food," Dalton says it like it's a no brainer.

"Oh... My... Gosh!" I say slowly.

"Good, huh?" Dalton says, elbowing me.

"Better than good! I think it's my new favorite dessert!" I say a little too loudly. I open my eyes and start to shovel the cake in, not caring how unlady like I'm being. "Mmmmm, Mmmmm, MMMM!"

I hear Dalton laugh but he starts eating. Everyone else laughs and goes back to their eating and conversations. Except Bree, she rolls her eyes and gets up, taking her half eaten plate to the garbage.

"Not hungry?" Abe asks when she comes back.

"Not really. Some of us have to watch our figure," she says, and then looks at me pointedly.

I roll my eyes and continue eating. It's a good thing I'm a grown ass woman, proud of what my body has been through, and I am happy with how I look. Bree doesn't know how to handle someone like me because she doesn't get the response she's expecting. So, she turns to Abe and starts talking to him.

Girlfriend needs to simmer on the high school snark or I'm gonna have to let her have a piece of my mind. I think in a calming voice.

"Are you finished?" Dalton asks.

"I am," I answer, as I slide my empty plates away from me.

"Are you full or do you want more?" he asks, eyeing me.

"I'm full, I promise. I can't eat another bite, I'll pop if I do," I say, patting my stomach while leaning back.

"Good enough," Dalton says, smiling. "I'll take these and then I'm going to help Val and Frank clean up a bit, I'll be back in a few minutes."

"I'll come help," I say as I start to stand up.

"No you won't... stay here and visit," Dalton

says, nodding towards Hannah, Mel, and Karie. "Just ignore Bree."

We both laugh but I sit and turn towards the conversation the table was having about the weather. They can't believe how cold it is and how the forecast is calling for snow.

After a few minutes the conversations break apart and everyone starts talking amongst themselves. I was listening to Hands tell a story about one of his rodeo adventures when Bree calls for my attention.

"So, Lainey..." she says too sweetly.

"Yeah... Bree?" I reply questioningly.

"Ummm... this is kind of a sensitive subject but I thought I should ask. Did Dalton tell you about us?" she asks, acting shy.

"No, well, yeah... but he said there's nothing to tell," I say. Her eyes harden for a fraction of a second.

"Of course he'd tell YOU that," she sneers.

The way she sounds all confident and well... bitchy... like she's about to drop a bomb on me, has me worried.

"We... well... we fucked once," she blurts out.

My mouth literally drops open.

"When?" I choke out. Trying to take even breaths. *How could Dalton have lied to me?*

"Oh... let me think," she fakes thinking for a second. Her finger tapping her chin. "The 4th of July... there were literally fireworks going off as he came."

Swallowing the bile that was creeping up my throat, I take a minute to breathe in long breaths. Collecting my thoughts. I'm confused, but only for a second.

I know what she's doing. Little bitch.

"Bree, that's enough," Mel says. She must have stopped her conversation with Karie and Hannah and heard what Bree said.

"No, it's okay," I say to Mel. I turn back to Bree and ask, "The last 4th of July? Last year? Fireworks were going off?"

"Yeah..." she doesn't sound as sure now that my tone and attitude has changed.

"That's interesting because we were video chatting during the 4th. He was showing my kids the fireworks he was watching. I don't remember seeing you anywhere in the video, let alone him cuming," I say, eerily calm.

"I... well... maybe I remembered the date wrong..." Bree mumbles out.

"When is there fireworks other than on the 4th?" Hannah asks. She looks appalled at Bree's behavior.

"Or maybe you're just trying to upset me by lying? So I'll... leave?" I ask. Okay, maybe it's more an accusation.

"I..." Bree looks embarrassed and mad, both not good looks on her.

"Dalton tells me everything, even if it's hard to

hear or hard for him to tell. You know, we act like adults, no secrets, no lying," I stand up. "I'm gonna go change into my swimsuit. Maybe you should try acting like an adult as well. You aren't a child anymore. This isn't high school. Grow up, Bree."

As I walk away, I hear Mel and Hannah start in on Bree.

Instead of walking around the house, I use the sliding glass door that's off of Dalton's room. I take a few minutes to calm down and then I change quickly. I grab a towel and wrap it around myself. I head back outside and run into Dalton just as he's getting to the sliding glass door.

"Hey! Hannah told me you came in to change. You look great! Nice suit!" he says wagging his eyebrows at me.

"Thanks," I say, blushing.

"I'll go change and meet you in the hot tub. It looked like there were already some people in it when I walked by."

"K," I say as I reach up and kiss him and then walk around him. I can't let myself kiss him full on or we won't make it back outside and I really have an issue with having sex when other people are within ear shot, unless I'm really... really... really drunk.

Laughing silently to myself and thinking about the trampoline adventure, I walk towards the hot tub.

Hannah, Tanner, Mel, Nolan, Abe, and Bree are

already in the hot tub. Hands and Shorty are just about to get in as well. It's a good thing this thing seats 12 comfortably.

I unwrap myself from the towel and get in.

"Eyes in your head, Abe," I hear Hands grunt out.

I look up and see Bree slap Abe's arm. I see him staring at my chest before he looks away quickly.

Dalton comes a couple minutes after I've gotten in, he changed super-fast. He hops in and sits between me and Shorty.

"Let's play truth or dare," Bree suggests. And then with a stink eye she says to me, "Or is that not adult enough for you?"

Well shit, I've poked the honey badger.

"Actually, it's very adult. You have to be willing to tell the truth," I say, eyeing her back.

"What's…" Dalton starts to ask but I interrupt him.

"Nothing… I'll tell you later," I whisper the last part to him.

Bree looks at us and then rolls her eyes.

"Let's draw hands, whoever picks the same as me has to pick the truth or dare of my choosing," Bree says. She counts down from ten. Everyone throws fingers up to their foreheads, Bree puts up two fingers.

Abe is the only one that also has two fingers up.

"Truth or dare?" she asks sweetly.

"Dare," Abe says, sounding drunk.

"Hmmm...," Bree thinks for a minute and then laughs. "I dare you to shake your beer and then chug it."

"Okay," Abe says.

"Lean over the edge," Dalton warns.

Abe puts his thumb over the opening and starts shaking his bottle of beer. He takes his thumb away and beer starts spraying everywhere. He tries to drink some of it but I'm pretty sure it mostly got on the patio.

After wiping his face, Abe says, "Okay, my turn... Lainey, truth or dare."

"Truth," I answer. Always safe to say truth.

"How big are your knockers? I mean no disrespect but damn," Abe says while staring at my chest that is barely visible because of the water level. But apparently he'd gotten a pretty good look when I was getting in the hot tub. And another apparent thing, truth isn't always the safest.

"Abe... manners or I'll teach you some..." Dalton says crossly.

"You don't have to answer if you're too embarrassed," Bree says with too much sweetness in her tone.

"I'm fine, Bree, thanks. Abe," I turn my attention back on him. "I wear a 36D bra."

"Nice... respectfully," he adds as Dalton throws him a look.

"Okay, my turn," I look around. "I can't choose, let's do numbers. 10-9-8-7-6-5-4-3-2-1."

I put three fingers up to my forehead. Aaaand so

does Bree.

Inward eye roll Of course she did.

"Truth or dare," I ask.

"Dare," she says with a little too much bravado.

"Crap, I'm not good at thinking up these things," I admit.

"Have her do the same as Abe," Hannah suggests.

Out of the corner of my eye, I see Bree glare at Hannah. So she must not want to do it, which means…

"Yeah, okay. Do the same as Abe…" I say, maybe a little too sweetly. This passive aggressive bullshit was starting to get on my last nerve. Or maybe I'm getting a little drunk. My patience and filter are always non-existent when I'm drunk.

Shorty hands her a bottle of beer off the table behind us. She does what Abe did but instead of letting the beer spray out, she sprays her chest.

"Oooops…" she says, running a finger down between her breasts.

Another inward eye roll, I look away and up at Dalton. He's staring at me, not paying Bree any attention. When our eyes meet, he smiles a heartbreaking smile. My heart stutters.

"My turn again," Bree says too loudly. I look away from Dalton before I attack his lips with mine. "Ummm, Lainey, truth or dare?"

"Is this turning into a Q and A with Lainey?" Shorty asks.

"Maybe," Bree says, shooting him a fake smile.

"Truth," I say. I don't trust her to choose a dare for me.

"Apparently," she says snidely. I actually roll my eyes this time. She asks, "You have kids, right?"

"Yes... is that your question?" I'm confused.

"No... they have a dad, or dads?" she asks, laughing.

"Bree..." Dalton says in a warning tone.

"No... it's okay," I say, curious as to where this is going. "They all have the same dad."

"So you're divorced? What happened there?" she asks, again feening concern.

"Bree, enough!" Dalton says in a raised voice.

"What? Is it that bad? Did he cheat on her? Did she cheat on him? OMG! Is she still married?" she throws her hands to her face, cupping both sides, faking surprise.

I swallow the lump in my throat. It's not like I haven't been asked this multiple times but it's still hard to answer sometimes when I'm asked out of the blue.

"Bree, damn it. I said enough," Dalton is pissed now.

"OMG, she is still married, isn't she... wow!" she says, sounding disgusted.

I clear my throat and say in a much smaller voice than I mean to use, "No, not married anymore, but not divorced."

"How is that possible?" she says, snarkily.

Hannah gasps, I look at her, and see her cover her mouth. She looks at me with sad eyes. Mel also looks like she knows what I mean, her face has fallen a few happy levels.

Here come the looks.

"Leave. It..." Dalton says in a scary voice, I've never heard him sound like this before now.

"But I want to know," Bree whines.

"Jesus, Bree... enough!" Hannah shouts.

Having enough of Bree, I say loudly, "My husband died in an accident 2.5 years ago. I'm not divorced, I'm a widow."

Silence.

"Oh..." is all Bree can say.

"Well... I'm done hot tubing for the night. It was nice remeeting you guys. See you in the morning," I hop out of the hot tub and wrap my towel around me quickly. I ignore the calls to wait and to stay.

I get to Dalton's room quickly, using the sliding glass door again.

Don't cry, don't cry. This isn't new. You've been dealing and processing this for 2.5 years now. Don't. Cry. I repeat to myself as I dry off. I grab whatever shirt of Dalton's is lying on the bed. I know my reality. I've known it since the day of Jayce's accident but when I get caught off guard like that, it hits me harder than if I get eased into the question. Nice people do that, Bree is not nice people.

From day one, I've hit my thoughts of denial of Jayce not being gone with a hard, cold, dose of reality. Anytime I would think, "How is this real life? How is he really gone?", I would tell myself, "This IS real life and Jayce IS gone and never coming back, he's gone."

He's gone. I think to myself. *He's gone.*

I crawl into Dalton's bed. I can hear multiple loud voices outside. I cover myself completely with the blanket and let the walls holding my tears back, break open. And for the first time in a long time, I cry for my lost love.

Chapter 18

I don't know how long I sobbed for but at some point I fell asleep.

I feel like I have an emotional hangover. This type of hangover is worse than a physical hangover from drinking because emotional hangovers are heart, mentally, and soul deep. Not cure so quickly with Tylenol and water

I open my eyes, they feel heavy and soar. An indicator that I cried hard last night. I don't even know what time it was when I came in here. I do know, I'm done being nice to Bree. Granted, she didn't know about Jayce, let alone me. But, that doesn't give her the right to treat me the way she has since I met her. I will keep my distance from her but if she says one nasty thing to me, I'm letting her have it.

I move to get out of bed and realize for the first time that Dalton has his arm wrapped around my waist. He must have held me last night.

He's so mother f-ing sweet.

I gently move his arm and slide out of bed. I grab my phone out of my bag, turning it on as I make my way into his bathroom. I shut the door before I turn on the light. As I'm peeing, my phone turns on. I see that it's 4:45am. Not too early considering- now that I'm fully awake- that I think I came in here sometime around 9:00pm.

I have three voicemails.

~Hey Lain, it's Lucy. Just calling to see how your first day there went. I hope it got better. Call me when you can. Kids say hi but they're busy playing. Love you gobs! Byeeeee.

I hit the next button to listen to the second voicemail. I have a feeling it's from Emily.

~Hi Elainah, it's Mom. Dad and I just got back to the Big Island from our cruise. We'll be home for a couple days and then we're going to take another cruise but on the other side of the islands this time. We love you and hope you're having fun in Montana with Dalton, be safe but have fun. Muah! Bye honey.

Nope, it was from my mom. I'd emailed her about my change of plans. She and my dad live in Hawaii, they retired there. Lucky for us they have a big enough house that we can stay with them whenever we visit. They've been traveling a lot now that they're both retired. Last year they traveled all over Europe, this year it sounds like they are getting to know their new home state.

Smiling at how happy my parents are, I hit the next button to listen to the third and last voicemail.

~Heeeey friend! It's Em. Just calling to check-in. I hope things have settled down. Did seducing him work? Sex as an icebreaker works wonders. Ha-ha. Okay, calling me when you can. Love ya! Byeeeee.

Oh, Emily.... Laughing and shaking my head I open our group text and send a message to Lucy and Emily.

Me- Hi guys, things are grrreat!
 Yes, Em, your seducing trick worked. Haha. We just needed an icebreaker and we already know we have great physical chemistry. LOTS happened yesterday but I'll call you later and tell you about it.
 Lucy, call me when you get this. Hopefully it's before we leave to move the cattle up to the mountain pasture so I can say hi to my little loves. I don't know when we'll get back tonight and I don't want to miss another day without seeing their faces.
 Love you both! *kissy face* 4:58am

I finish going to the bathroom, wash my hands,

and I look in the mirror and see I have dried tears all over the place and not going to lie, some snot as well. So, I wash my face as well. The water on my face feels so good, I think I'll take a shower.

I take off the t-shirt of Dalton's I grabbed last night and put it on the counter. I turn to where I think the shower is but see just a rock wall. There's an opening further down. I walk through it and around the corner and freeze. This shower... all I can do is marvel at it. It makes Emily's shower look small.

The controls for the shower aren't IN the shower. Just before walking through another little doorway, there's controls on the right. They say 'ALL' or 'ONE' and then a temperature handle. I turn the 'ALL' knob and hear a whoosh of water. I turn the temperature to slightly hotter than I normally have it but a hot shower sounds good right now. A shelf across from the controls has all sorts of shampoos and conditioners and body soaps.

Interesting....

I step into the actual shower and turn in a circle. I count eight shower heads. BIG shower heads. I walk to the middle of the room, to call it a shower seems wrong. I'm instantly soaking wet. I walk back over to the product shelf and pick out the least masculine shampoo and massage it into my hair. It smells like fresh rain.

I rinse and go back for the conditioner that pairs

with the shampoo. Again, it smells like fresh rain and I can already feel it making my hair silky smooth. I massage that into my hair but let it sit for a minute. I find a new razor head and replace the one on Dalton's razor, I'll replace it all when I'm done. I shave my armpits and legs. I then go back in and rinse my hair.

Holy crap! My hair feels amazing!

I stand in the shower for a few extra minutes after washing my body. When I feel like I've just about used all the hot water, I walk to the controls and turn them off. I grab a towel on the shelves on the other side of the products.

I grab my phone and Dalton's shirt and I walk back out to Dalton's room, he's still sleeping. I put my phone in my bookbag. I quietly get dressed, making sure to wear a long sleeve, the only long sleeve I brought, and my hoodie. I brought leggings and put them on under my jeans. If today is going to be as cold as yesterday, I want to be warmer since I'll be on horseback. I quickly braid my hair into my trusty side braid.

I crawl onto the bed and gently lean over Dalton's chest. I kiss him lightly on the cheek and then on the lips.

"Mmmm..." he moans as he wakes up.

"Good morning," I say.

"Mmmmm good morning," he says, wrapping his arms around me. And then he pulls his head back and blinks rapidly for a second. He asks, "You showered?"

"I did."

"Without me?"

I laugh, "Yeah, sorry. I hadn't planned on it but when I was washing my face, it felt good. So I decided to shower. And your shower by the way, WOW!"

"It gets the job done," he laughs at my excitement.

"So I'm curious... all that product?" I look at him questioningly.

"Every time my sister comes, she leaves her stuff here. She says it's so she doesn't have to remember to pack bathroom stuff but she always brings new stuff. Every. Single. Time. It's expensive so I keep it in my bathroom so that it's not used by a guest. Which, the only guests I really have are my sister and her family but..." he shrugs.

"The one I used smelled amazing and did crazy good on my hair."

"I can smell it and it matches you and..." he takes a deep breath. He sighs, "It makes you smell even better."

I laugh and pull away.

"What?" he asks with concern. His arms reaching for me.

"You go shower, if we get started on what we WANT to do, we won't get done what we need to do. Responsibilities... blah, blah... adulting... blah, blah," I say smiling at him.

He squints at me for a second, tilting his head to the side and then laughs. "You're right, I can see us spending all day in bed and we definitely have work to do."

"You get in the shower and I'll go get us coffee and something to eat. You like your coffee black, right?"

"Right," he smiles.

"Okay," I kiss him quickly and start to slide off the bed.

"Lainey?"

"Yeah?"

"Are you okay?"

"I am now, thanks. Sorry about last night. I didn't mean to unload an emotional tidal wave on you. I honestly don't even remember you coming in, I think I was crying so hard I wasn't aware of anything else."

"Don't ever apologize about crying or having an emotional moment. Losing Jayce is something we'll be working through for a while if not forever. I understand that and I got you," he says, sliding next to me and wrapping his arms around me.

I let out a huge sigh.

"Thank you, you're truly something else," I kiss him on the cheek and he turns into me and kisses me on the lips. The kiss intensifies, as per usual.

After some time has passed, I slowly pull away.

Taking a deep breath, but still a little breathlessly, Dalton says, "Yeah, okay, you're right. We definitely need to focus on getting through the day. But you better believe, tonight... you're all mine."

"Deal!" I say, excitedly. I smile at him as I stand up. "Go shower, I'll be back in shortly."

Not watching him, because I know what I'll want to do if I see him take his boxers off, I leave the room.

I hear what sounds like a waterfall turn on and realize that's what his shower must sound like when it's running. With all those shower heads, it makes sense. Shaking my head and laughing, I make my way to the kitchen.

I look at the time on the oven and it says it's 5:47am. The coffee is just about done percolating, it must have been set to start at 5:30am. I grab two cups out of the cupboard and the creamer-for me-out of the fridge. I search the lower cupboards for a tray and find the perfect one under all the baking sheets. I look around the kitchen and see muffins arranged on a plate. I walk over to them and find a note.

For a quick breakfast. I've made sandwiches from the leftover brisket for you and Ms. Lainey. I put them in your saddle pack, just outside the door. I'll have supper ready when you guys get back.

~V

She is the sweetest. I grab a couple muffins and

wrap them in paper towels and put them on the tray. I carry it back to Dalton's room. The shower is still running so I put the tray on the table next to the oversized chair sitting by the fireplace. I check my phone as I sit down, no new messages yet. It's 7:00am in Boise, Lucy should be awake, unless my kids have slept in this morning. Emily probably won't be awake for a while since it's only 6:00am back home and I'm pretty sure she worked late last night. She always works late, she's a hard worker.

I put my phone down on the table. I grab my book out of my bag, pick up my coffee, and take a sip.

Awwww... That first sip always warms me up. A good coffee can start the day off wonderfully.

I hear the sound of the waterfall stop and hear Dalton rustling around in the bathroom. Out of the corner of my eye, I see him walk out. I glance up and spray the drink of coffee I just took, everywhere.

"What's the matter?" Dalton asks with false concern. He's completely naked. Like nothing on. No towel. Nothing. He looks like someone the Greek's would have used as a model to make a Greek god statue out of, he's too perfect.

I can't speak for a minute and I realize I'm staring at him so I close my eyes.

"Who's the evil one?" I ask, laughing.

I hear him walking to the other side of the room.

Thank goodness. Distance is good right now.

He chuckles, "I don't know what you're talking about."

"Mmmmmhmmmm," I say in disbelief, peeking out from under my eyelashes to see if he's in his closet yet. I see his naked ass disappear through the doorway of his closet.

Shaking my head and grinning like an idiot, I take another drink and then a deep breath.

Calm down, Lainey. If you get too worked up, you guys will be late getting out of the house.

I grab the top of a muffin and take a bite. It's delicious! I don't think there's anything Val can cook I won't like, she's amazing. I take another sip of coffee, another bite of muffin, and continue reading. I can't really concentrate on what I'm reading because all I see across the page is Dalton's naked body.

Closing my eyes, I take another drink of coffee.

"You okay?" Dalton asks, more serious this time.

I look out from under my eyelashes and see he's dressed warmly as well. I open my eyes all the way and smile at him.

"Yup... I'm fine. I just can't concentrate," I say, turning a light shade of pink.

"How come? Still thinking about last night?"

I look at him in disbelief. I shake my head and say, "No, not thinking about last night."

"Then what?"

"You have no idea the effect you have on people,

do you?"

He looks startled for a second. "Me?"

"Uhh, yeah, you... Greek god reincarnate..." I say, waving my hand in his direction.

"Psh... you want to talk about someone having no idea the effect SHE has on people?"

"Oh whatever," I say, shaking my head as I stand up, putting my book back in my bag. I pick up his coffee and walk towards him.

"It still baffles me how oblivious you are to yourself. You see everyone so clearly. You can smell someone spewing bullshit from a mile away. But when it comes to yourself, nothing," he says.

I squint at him through one eye, and really think about what he's saying. He's not entirely wrong. I can usually tell when someone is being fake or they're lying. I can usually tell when someone is genuinely a nice person. But when it comes to me... I just feel like I'm me. Nothing special. Just me.

"We were talking about you," I say, as I get to him.

"Oblivious," he says as I hand him his coffee. "Thank you for this by the way."

"You're welcome. Val made muffins. She left a note, I read it, I hope you don't mind."

"I don't mind," he says as he takes a sip and looks at the muffins on table. "What did the note say?"

"She mentioned the muffins and then brisket

sandwiches for lunch. She put them in your saddle pack, just outside the kitchen patio door."

"Bless her, I don't know what I'd do without her," he says, smiling warmly down at me.

"You'd starve," I say, teasingly.

"Hey, I can cook!" he says, pretending to be offended.

"Lasagna."

"I can cook more than that. I'll cook more for you while you're here," he says. And then cocks his head to the side. "Which, we never talked about how long that would be, not that I'm kicking you out. The opposite is what I'd like, I'm really enjoying having you here."

I laugh, "I've enjoyed my time with you too. I was thinking a week or two, if that'll be okay…"

"Not as long as I'd like but I'll take it," he smiles. He bends down and kisses me softly but shortly.

I wink at him, "Good thinking."

"Responsibilities… adulting… blah-blah-blah," he says, reciting what I'd said earlier.

I laugh and walk back over to grab the tray and my coffee.

"Might be easier to keep our hands off each other, if we go out into the kitchen," I offer, walking past him.

"Lainey, I want you everywhere," he says walking up behind me.

I giggle, "Behave!"

"I'm honestly trying," he laughs.

"Mmmmhmmm," I giggle again.

We get back out into the kitchen and we sit on opposite sides of the island. We eat our muffins in silence, drinking our coffee, and enjoying the quiet. Just enjoying each other's company.

We hear the front door open and multiple voices drift our way.

"Oh, good they're here," Dalton says, half excited, half reluctantly. "It's my sister and her family. Be warned, she likes to hug."

"Dalton, do I hear you?" I hear a woman's voice say, must be Darcy.

"In the kitchen, Sis," Dalton hollers.

In walks the most beautiful woman I've ever seen. She has the same color hair as Dalton, beautiful chocolate brown. She has it braided down her back. Her eyes are emerald green and they look very kind. She's wearing a hoodie under a warm looking winter coat and jeans.

The man with her is handsome, not as handsome as Dalton, but I could be biased on that opinion. He's got sandy blonde hair, cut short, and brown eyes. He's also wearing warm clothes.

There's three teenage looking boys with them, the nephews I assume. One has the same coloring as Darcy and one the same as Phil. The other, is a mixture of the two. He has Phil's blonde hair but Darcy's green eyes. They're all very tall too. Even Darcy.

"Oh, hello," she says. "You must be Lainey, I'm happy to see you're an actual person."

She and her husband and boys laugh.

I laugh a little too and I look at Dalton, and say, "Do you have a history of having an imaginary girlfriend?"

As he says, defensively, "No!"

Darcy asks at the same time, "Girlfriend?"

Rolling his eyes and an exaggerated sigh, putting on an act of annoyance I'm guessing, Dalton says, "Darcy, this is Lainey, my girlfriend. Lainey, this is my annoying but best sister, Darcy."

"I'm his only sister," Darcy says, winking at me. She walks over to me with arms wide, asking for a hug. I stand up and hug her.

"Which makes you the best," Dalton says teasingly.

Darcy steps back from me and glares at her brother.

"Lainey, this is my husband, Phil," she gestures towards who I had figured was Phil. He steps forward and shakes my hand. She points to each of her boys as she says, "These are our boys. This is Craig, Liam, and Tony."

The boys step forward one by one.

"Craig," Craig, the one that looks like Phil, says as he shakes my hand. "Nice to meet you Ms. Lainey."

I nod and smile.

"I'm Tony," the one that has a little of each of his parents in him, says. He winks. I laugh a little and shake my head. He seems to be a cocky little thing.

"I'm," the boy that looks like his mom, Liam, shyly starts to say. "I'm... Liam."

After shaking my hand, he steps back quickly.

"It's nice to meet you all," I say, smiling at each of them.

There's a knock at the patio door off the kitchen, Dalton stands and opens the door.

"Hey Dalton, Ms. Lainey. Oh and Ms. Darcy and men," Hands says, tipping his cowboy hat towards me and Darcy. "We've got everything about ready."

"Sounds good, we'll get our boots and coats on and meet you by the barn," Dalton says.

Hands tips his hat at me again and then turns and walks away.

"We'll head out and get our horses unloaded," Darcy says. She waves at me and starts ushering her husband and sons out the patio door.

"Ready for some cowgirling today?" Dalton asks, smiling at me with his crooked smile that makes my knees go weak.

"Sure am," I say with a little shake in my voice, a mixture of reaction from his smile and anticipation to riding.

"I know you're worried about riding but I have

the perfect horse for you, she's really gentle. She'll go but she's easy going and doesn't have a ton of speed," he says leading the way to the front door.

"I'll be fine, it'll just take a few minutes to get my saddle bearings again," I laugh.

We get our boots on and Dalton helps me with his coat that I'd worn last night.

"If this weather keeps up, we'll have to run into town and get you a coat that fits you better. Mine swallows you up. Which isn't a bad thing, maybe my guys will be able to focus better with you all bundled up," he laughs out a deep belly laugh.

Shaking my head I open the front door. We step out and are greeted with what feels more like dead of winter air rather than late spring, early summer air. A shiver runs down my spine, not the good kind either.

"Brrr... what the crap?" I ask.

"Yeah, this isn't typical weather up here so don't base your opinion on us from this," he says jokingly. He bends down and picks up his saddle pack and pulls out a bottle of water and two granola bars. He hands them to me and I put them in my coat pockets. Luckily it's big enough there's plenty of room. "Those are in case you get hungry or thirsty along the way and if I'm not close enough for you to get anything from me. And we get a late winter storm every once in a while but this is a little too late in the spring for this nonsense."

"We get them too, every once in a while. This

isn't tainting my opinion," I laugh. "But this is..."

Bree's walking up to us.

"Bree," Dalton says, warningly.

"I just want to apologize. I'm sorry about last night. I didn't know," she says, looking embarrassed.

"Which is why we've been telling you to think before you speak," Mel says, walking up behind her.

Bree rolls her eyes.

"Dalton, need your help over here!" Hands hollers from across the turnaround, on the other side of where the barn is located.

"Shit... I need to find out what's going on, I'll be back to get you saddled up, hold tight," Dalton says.

Before he can get more than a couple steps away, Bree says, "I can help her."

He looks at her doubtfully, "Really?"

"Yes," she says.

"Alright... put her on--" he starts to say but he's interrupted.

"Boss, need you now!" Hands yells.

"I know, I know, just go," Bree says, motioning for him to go.

"I'm gonna go check mine and Nolan's horses one last time, make sure we have everything packed that we'll need. You'll be okay?" Mel asks me, looking at Bree pointedly.

"Of course she will," Bree says, putting her arm through mine.

Okay, a person can't do a complete 180 degree turn-around in less than 12 hours. What's going on?

"I'll be fine," I say.

Mel nods, looks at Bree again, but more sternly and walks away.

Bree rolls her eyes, sighs, and says, "Sheesh, what's everyone's problem?"

Maybe it's because you've been a class 'A' bitch to me since you met me?

I shrug.

We get to the barn and she leads me past a buckskin that's already saddled and to a stall. There's a beautiful bay horse munching away on a little hay.

"Lainey, this is Stormy. Stormy, this is Lainey," Bree says as she opens the stall door.

Stormy picks her head up and looks at me. She shakes her head and then her body.

"Hi girl," I say as I step towards her. I let her smell my hand before I pet her muzzle. "Aren't you a pretty girl?"

"I take it you can't ride?" Bree asks.

"Why do you ask that?" I counter ask, sounding defensive.

"Oh just by the way Dalton was acting," she says nonchalantly.

"I can ride. Like make a horse go and stop but if one takes off on me, I panic. And don't get me started on if they start to buck, I'm no bronc rider."

"Stormy will treat you right, won't you girl?" Bree says, patting the horse's neck. Bree grabs the halter and reins hanging up outside Stormy's stall and puts it on her. She leads her out and ties her while she goes into the tack room and grabs a saddle. I help her saddle Stormy up and I make sure everything's nice and tight. I don't fully trust Bree has changed her attitude towards me completely and I wouldn't put it past her to make my cinch loose.

"Hop up and I'll adjust the stirrups," Bree says.

I put my foot in the stirrup and pull myself up with ease. Thank goodness, I didn't want to give Bree any ammo to use against me.

She has to bring the stirrups up a couple notches and then she pats my leg.

"All set," she says.

"Thanks," I say, still confused about her behavior.

Bree walks over to the buckskin and pulls herself up into the saddle.

"This is Chico, he's another one of Dalton's horses but I usually ride him. He's got a little more go in him than what people usually like," she says, sounding more like herself.

I just nod and kick Stormy to start walking. She does with ease. We get outside the barn and we're hit with that cold ass wind again. I follow her through the gates, into the pasture where all the cattle are rounded up and ready to go.

She nods to Hannah and Mel, who then turn and nod towards, I'm guessing Nolan, he's too far away to see for sure, especially since everyone is bundled up for the cold weather. I hear a whistle and everyone starts whistling and saying things to get the cows to start moving. We're up towards the front.

"Up cows, up!" I holler. It's what I'm used to saying when we move cows back home. I whistle a couple times and then, "Up cows, up!" again.

I look to the left, over Bree, and see Dalton looking over at us.

Is he pissed? I think to myself.

We're almost to the edge of the forest and I see Dalton is making his way towards us, and yup, he looks royally pissed.

"Why's Dalton look so mad? Do you know what Hands needed him for this morning?" I ask.

"Nooo, I don't know," Bree says with too much falseness in her tone. I look over at her and she has the evilest smile on her face. She sneers out, "Hold on tight, cowgirl!"

"Wha---" I start to ask and then she slaps Stormy on the ass.

Instant chaos. Stormy starts bucking and then one of the cows hits her and she takes off like a bullet from a gun.

That lying piece of shit! I scream in my head. My

mouth is clamped down tight. Every muscle is clamped down tight.

I hear everyone yelling for me to hold on tight.

Like I'd just let go!?

We zoom through the trees. I'm getting smacked in the face with little limbs, luckily I have Dalton's huge coat on or my arms would be torn up as well. I'm not sure how long we've been running but my face is starting to sting from all the little cuts but I hold onto the reins and saddle horn with everything that I have in me.

WHAAAM

A large, low hanging tree branch, catches me right in the chest. I imagine I look like a character in a western when they get knocked off their horse in this way. My body curls around the branch for a fraction of a second and then topple over backwards, off the horse.

THUD

I hit the ground on my stomach. Trying to regain the breath that was just knocked out of me, not once but twice, has me gasping in the contents of the forest floor.

I hurt, I hurt all over.

Darkness comes and I pass out.

Chapter 19

I feel wetness hitting my face lightly. I slowly take in my bearings before opening my eyes.

I'm on my stomach and my chest hurts. My left wrist hurts and my face. I try to take a deep breath but I'm met with extreme pain, that I imagine is from broken ribs. I wince.

"Okay... I can't... lay... like this... forever... turn over," I pant out, talking to myself. I open my eyes.

Holding my breath because that actually feels better than breathing, I use my right hand and push myself, as stiff as I can make myself, to my side. I stop and take as deep of a breath as I can, which isn't that deep. I then push myself the rest of the way to my back.

"UGH!" I scream. Pain, so much pain. Being on my stomach was so much better. I can't lay like this for much longer either. I move my head around to see where I'm at and I figure out what the wetness is that had woken me up.

Snow.

It's starting to snow and it looks like it was significantly lighter than when we first came into the forest.

Speaking of we, Stormy is nowhere in sight. Poor thing. She has to be terrified.

"Fucking... Bree," I say out loud. No one is around to hear me so why not talk to myself. It's better than the deafening silence of the forest.

I tilt my head back and look behind me. I'm less than a foot away from a large tree trunk.

"Okay... that's our... destination... We can do this... It's going to hurt... like hell... but sitting up... has to feel better... than this agony..." I pant out again.

I roll myself back to my side, and then onto my hand and knees. I'm pretty sure my wrist is broken, any pressure almost makes me blackout again. I crawl-hop, which causes excruciating pain from my chest, the little ways over to the tree. I put my left shoulder against it and use it as support as I turn my body and slump against it.

"Fuuuuuuuck!" I cry out. Trying to catch my breath, I realize that this does feel better than lying on my back but not quite as good as lying on my stomach, for whatever reason.

I finally relax and look around again, now that I'm in a sitting position. It all looks the same. Nothing but dense trees. I'm surprised Stormy was able to run through here. I lift my left arm up and gently pull the sleeves back. Comparing it to my right wrist, it's already swollen three times its normal size. So broken for sure.

I push my sleeves back down and rest it on my lap. Using my right hand, I reach up and touch my face, and feel a large, sensitive, goose egg on my right cheek. Probably where I hit the ground. I can feel multiple cuts and scratches on my face, too many for me to count. All from the tree limbs that slapped my face as we flew through the trees before the big bastard that hit me in the chest, knocked me off Stormy.

CRUNCH-CRUNCH

I hear the crunching of something walking nearby.

"Stormy?" I call out, hopefully.

The crunching stops.

GGGGGRRRRRRRR

SHIT! Not Stormy.... Animal... and it sounds big and pissed. I silently scream in my head.

And then I see it.

Oh god! Oh god! Oh god! Oh god! Oh god! Oh god! Oh god! Oh god!

It's a big grizzly bear. *Sit still. Don't move. Be one with the tree. FUCK MY LIFE!!!!!*

SNOOORT

"RAAAARRRRGGGGGRRRRR!" the bear bellows out with rage.

Fuck me! I think, as adrenaline helps me slide up to a standing position, still using the tree for support. My fight or flight response takes over my body and mind functions, flight being the most prominent feeling. But I know that you're not supposed to run from a bear. I'm in too much pain to lay down like you're supposed to do. I start to inch my way around the tree, trying to put it between me and him. I'm not sure if it's male or female but using 'he' seems appropriate.

He stands up on his hind legs and mine about give out on me from the sheer terror now locking around my mind and heart. This guy is HUGE!

"RAAAARRRRGGGGGRRRRR!" he bellows out again, this one hurts my ears and I can feel it vibrate in my chest. He pounds back to the ground, back on all fours, jumping towards me and now kind of hissing at me. I'm not sure how else to describe that sound. It's not like a cat, it's more horrifying.

I move quickly behind the tree, turning so I can keep my eyes on him. He moves quickly too and is close enough that when he swipes his massive paw out, he catches the tree. I feel bark hit my face, slicing me in the cheek. I duck behind the tree and move to the other side. He swipes again, but misses the tree completely this time.

I hear running hooves.

Has Dalton found me? I think hopefully.

But it's not Dalton, it's Stormy.

She comes snorting into the area. She hits the surprised bear with her hind end. She turns and rears back on her hind legs and kicks out at the bear, like she's boxing him. She gets back on all four legs, turns again, and kicks back with her hind legs and connects with the bear's head. He's still shocked to see her, that he doesn't have time to react. He falls down to the ground by her kick, is stunned for a couple seconds, turns and runs off. He sounds like he's whimpering, or crying. It's hard to describe that sound as well.

Stormy paws the ground with her right hoof, snorting still.

"Oh Stormy, girl!" I call out with so much love, she turns her head towards me.

She snorts once and walks over to me. She's breathing hard.

"Easy, girl, easy," I say. She gets to me and bows her head down. I start rubbing her muzzle and make my way up her head, into her mane, and down her neck, she leans into me gently. "What a brave girl you are, thank you!"

She turns her head to me, like she truly understands me. I kiss her nose and hug her. She wraps her neck around me, like she's hugging me back.

After a few minutes of just holding her and feeling her warmth, my adrenaline eases and I can feel the pain in my body returning.

I let out a slow, soft moan. Which causes Stormy

to pick her head up and look at me.

"I'm okay, I just hurt... all over," I say. *I'm talking to a horse like she can understand me... I guess that's better than talking to myself... maybe...*

I look around us and see it's started snowing harder now.

"Crap... We need to get out of here but I know if you're lost in the woods, you're supposed to stay put and let the search party find you... crap, crap, crap," I say. Stormy just kind of snorts out a small breath. I take that as an agreement. "I'm going to need a blanket."

I look around and obviously don't see one, except...

"Okay, Stormy. I know, now, that you are a little skittish and don't like sudden touches but I need you to stand still and not freak out, okay? I'm going to take the saddle off so I can use the saddle blanket but I can't lift the saddle off so it's going to fall to the ground by your feet. Pllllease, don't jump or run off," I say to the horse.

Please, please, please, stand still.

I grab the cinch and, trying to ignore the pain from the protest in my chest. I pull up with my right hand and loosen it and let the strap fall to the ground.

"Good girl," I say lovingly, patting Stormy on the neck. "Okay, this is the hard part. Stand still."

Holding my breath, I slide the saddle off, away from me. It falls to the forest ground with a thud. Stormy twitches but stands still otherwise.

CHAPTER 19

"Oh, good girl! You are such a good girl!" I say, patting and scratching her neck. I kiss her on the jaw. I slide the blanket off towards me and lean back against the tree.

"Okay, sweet girl, I'm going to sit down now. Don't freak out if my legs end up under you, okay?" I say, not feeling ridiculous about talking to her anymore. It's actually really comforting having her here. I slide down the tree, back to sitting. I feel better instantly.

Stormy paws the ground, but she doesn't come close to my feet that are directly below her stomach. She moves over to the side, and starts to bend down, and then she's lying beside me. She's as close to me as she could have gotten had I helped her down. Her head is facing the way the bear had taken off. By coincidence or as a self-defense, defensive way, I'm not sure but it puts her neck in the perfect place for me to rub it and her body is next to my leg. I can feel her warmth starting to warm my leg she's touching. I throw the saddle blanket over my legs and pull Dalton's coat into me.

"You think our guy will be here soon? You think he can find us?" I ask her. No response, no surprise, she's a horse.

I feel something running down my neck and reach up. When I pull my hand away, I see red. Blood. The tree bark must have really gotten me. I wipe it away with the sleeve of the coat.

"I'll have to buy him a new coat after today."

I can feel it running down my neck again. I unzip my right pocket and put my hand in to see if there's anything in his coat I can use to stop the bleeding. I feel something and pull out napkins. They're crumpled up so I'm not sure if they've been used or not, but it's better than letting my cut bleed all over me. I also find the granola bars Dalton gave me. I open one and eat half, not knowing how long I'll be out here, I need to ration it. Thank goodness this coat is so big, I can pull the left side over so I can get the bottle of water out. I'm sure landing on it didn't help me. I open it and take a small sip. Again, rationing it.

I talk to Stormy throughout the afternoon. Listening intently for the sound of our rescuers or the bear coming back for round two. But I never hear a thing. Before I know it, it's dark. Darkness that I have never experienced before now. I camp but we have a campfire going, flashlights, and lanterns to light the area. This… this is pure darkness.

"Have I mentioned I'm afraid of the dark?" I ask Stormy. "Well, I am. I know I'm a grown ass woman but I like being able to see. I like being able to see when danger is coming. My mind tends to run away with itself with every little sound."

Stormy twitches a little, in agreement? Maybe, but she has better hearing and animal instinct on her side, so maybe she'll know real danger rather than my imaginary kind.

"I'm hungry and tired. How about you?" I ask, as my stomach growls. I eat the rest of my first granola and take another sip of water.

I yawn and lean my head back against the tree.

"I'm going to close my eyes. Wake me if there's danger nearby, k?"

She snorts and I take that as her understanding me.

I close my eyes and pretend I'm back in Dalton's room, sleeping.

◆ ◆ ◆

Snort

I'm startled awake. Other than being cold to the bone and wet, really wet, I had forgotten where I was while I slept. I look around and see that it's daylight, just barely but still light enough to see everything. And it looks like it snowed throughout the night. Everything is covered in snow, including me and Stormy.

She snorts softly again and I realize it's her snort that woke me up.

"Good morning, beautiful girl," I say, rubbing her neck.

She moves like she's going to stand. I slide my legs a little away from her and then she rolls up onto all four legs. She shakes herself and the snow that was covering her goes flying. I cover my face with my arms to keep the snow from hitting my face. I'm welcomed with pain.

"Shit!" I call out. My ribs and muscles must have tightened up while I slept and my wrist starts to throb even worse.

"Stormy girl, we're gonna need to get out of here," I say as I force myself to stand, I use her reins to help pull myself up, as I use the tree for support still. "I have no way to build a fire and I'm soaking wet and freezing."

My teeth start to chatter as I'm now standing and don't have her body heat to keep me warm.

"Can you bend down so I can get on you?" I ask as I gently pull her reins down towards the ground. I'm sure she's never been trained to do this but she lays down onto her legs. "Good girl!"

I slide the reins over her head, place the saddle blanket just behind the reins, towards her body. I put my right leg over her neck- I figure when she stands, I'll slide down to where I need to be, and then I don't have to adjust myself too much. I hold my breath against the pain in my, well... entire body now, and pull up on the reins. She jostles around for a second, her hind legs coming up first.

I use my right hand on her neck, and every sore, screaming muscle in my body, to keep myself in place. Squeezing my left arm into my chest so I'm not tempted to use it.

Shit, this fucking hurts!

In another second, she stumbles around, but then she's up on all four. I relax and take short, excruciating breaths.

"Good... girl... Stormy," I pant out while patting her neck down to her front right shoulder.

I take a couple minutes to catch my breath, or what I can catch anyways, my ribs are really screaming at me now. I put the saddle blanket over my legs and grab hold of the reins.

"Okay girl, take us home. Find Dalton, get me back home to my kids," I say as I give her a gentle kick.

She turns and starts heading in the direction behind us. I'm so turned around I'm not sure if she's leading us further into the forest or if she actually knows where we're going.

"I trust you sweet girl, go home," I say as I relax my legs and loosen up the reins more.

I spend the next few minutes talking to Jayce.

"Jayce, I know you're here. I know you're doing all you can to protect me. I have to get home to our kids. They can't lose another parent. They can't lose the last person on earth that loves them as deeply as I do. A mother's love can't be replaced, nor can a father's. They've already gone through so much in their short little lives, more than a little kid should have to go through. A child shouldn't lose a parent, let alone two in a short amount of time. Pllllease, get me home. Jayce, please, watch over me and get me home to our babies! Lead Stormy in the right direction. Help me find my way back to Dalton and the others. I know it's probably not fair for me to talk to you about Dalton. But I never thought I'd ever feel this way again after losing you. I never, ever, thought I'd be lucky enough to find you, and now, I think I've found a good guy that could love me like you did. I love you and miss you, and I always will. Please help me."

I'm bawling now, which hurts my ribs. I try to take deep breaths to calm myself but that makes it hurt enough more. Stormy turns her head towards me and snorts.

"I'm... okay..." I pant out. I relax my body and take as deep a breath as I can, without feeling like I'm being stabbed all over my chest. They aren't very deep but they're enough to get my breathing back under control.

After a while, I let the reins go all together and run my fingers through Stormy's mane and I start humming a song. The trees are either thinning out or the clouds have begun to part because I can tell it's getting lighter. Looking around, it doesn't look like the trees are any less sparse than before, so it must be the clouds moving overhead, letting some sunshine through.

Gurgle-Gurgle

I put my hand over my stomach.

"I could really go for one of those brisket sandwiches that Val made for us yesterday," I say, scratching Stormy's neck. "When we get home, I'll make sure you get some delicious apples and oats, and all the goodies."

I take my second, last, granola bar out and eat half of it. I also take my eater out and take a bigger sip of it. I have, maybe, half of it left.

After what I think has been a couple of hours, my eyes start to get tired.

"I'm gonna shut my eyes, and maybe take a nap. Don't let me fall off," I say, patting Stormy's shoulder.

I wrap the reins in my right hand as tight as I can without pulling on it and close my eyes. I let the rocking and soothing motion of Stormy's walk, lull me into sleep.

Chapter 20

MmmmmRrrrrrrr
	A soft horse sound wakes me up. I blink my eyes rapidly and look around. It's dark again, but not pitch black yet.

"Holy cow, how long was I out for?" I ask, as I again pat Stormy's neck. The temperature has dropped more than just a couple degrees. I pull the saddle blanket off my legs and swing it painfully around my shoulder, one handed, but I push through with clenched teeth. It works well enough, that I'm able to grab the other corner over my left shoulder but just barely. I pull it around, adjusting it so it's covering both shoulders better. I lean in closer to Stormy for heat.

"MmmmmRrrrrrrr...MmmmmRrrrrrrr..." Stormy 'says' and then she stops walking. I can see her ears twitching and turning, hearing something I can't.

"What is it, Stormy?" I ask. "Danger or our rescuers?"

As she starts to walk again, she turns to the left a little more than the direction we had been going. After what feels like hours, it's gotten much darker, but I see a faint glow in the distance.

"What is that?" I ask, excitedly.

Snort- Stormy's response.

I keep my eye on the glow. It looks like Stormy is taking us straight to it. After a few more minutes, I can smell smoke.

"A campfire?" I exclaim, even more excitedly. And then wince, pain shoots across my chest and ribcage. I rub in Stormy's mane, scratching down her neck, and say softly, "Good girl, Stormy."

When we get closer, I can see a small clearing with two tents set up, and seven horses tied nearby. The fire in the middle has six people sitting around it.

"Ohhhh," I cry in relief. I can see Hands, Shorty, Mel, Hannah, Darcy, and… "Dalllltooon!"

I holler his name as loudly as I can. I've never been so happy and relieved to see someone in all my life. And in so much pain from saying a name.

"Dalton!" I hear Hands shout.

Dalton's head snaps up from whatever he's looking at on his lap. He looks at Hands, who's standing up, and already starting to walk towards me, but he's pointing in my direction. Dalton looks to where he's pointing and his mouth drops open and then the most heartbreakingly relieved look settles on his face.

"Lainey?" he shouts.

"Dalton!" I yell again, as loudly as I can, what my body will allow without causing excruciating pain.

Thank you, Jayce! Thank you!

"Lainey!" Dalton's on his feet-a big piece of paper falls to the ground, a map?-and he's running to me. "Lainey!"

When he gets to us, Stormy stops and backs up a little.

"Easy girl, easy," I say as I pat her neck. She still instantly at my words and touch.

"Oh my hell, Lainey! Are you okay?" Dalton asks, reaching for me. Stormy isn't as tall to Dalton as she is to me. He puts his hands under my armpits and starts to lift me up and off of the horse.

"Aaaargh!" I exclaim in anguish.

"What?" Dalton asks, stopping halfway from pulling me down. "What's wrong?"

"Don't... stop. Get me... off... Stormy first..." I pant out and through my teeth.

"Shit, sorry," he says. He pulls me the rest of the way off and gently lets go.

Hands, Shorty, Darcy, Mel, and Hannah have reached us now too.

"Lainey!" Mel and Hannah exclaim together.

"She looks like hell," Hands says.

"I got Stormy," Shorty says. I haven't let go of her reins. "You can let go."

But I can't bring myself to let go.

"It's okay, Lainey. I got you now. Let Shorty take care of Stormy, she has a couple wounds on her chest," Dalton says, wrapping an arm around me.

I lean away and look. She does have some scratches on her, they don't look too awfully deep but you can see they've been bleeding. How did I not notice before?

I reach out and massage down Stormy's neck, down to her shoulder. I wrap my arm around her neck, she puts her head against my back, and I whisper into her, "Thank you."

I hand the reins to Shorty and let him walk her back to camp. I see she's limping now.

Had she been limping while I was riding her? I hadn't thought so.

"Here you go, Sweety," Darcy says, as she takes the saddle blanket off of me and wraps a sleeping bag around me.

"Thanks," I say, through chattering teeth.

"You must be freezing," Mel says.

"I... hadn't... noticed... how bad... 'til now," I say, trying not to bite my tongue off. My teeth are really starting to chatter hard.

"Maybe she's going into shock now that she's safe," Darcy suggests.

"Maybe," Hands says.

"Let's go get some food warmed up for her," Mel

says.

"Come on, Lainey. Let's get you by the fire. Can you walk?" Dalton asks.

"I… think… so," I say, taking a tentative step forward. I'm wobbly but Dalton holds me tight. I lean into him for support, like I did with the tree. We walk back slowly. Mel, Hannah, Darcy, and Hands going ahead of us to get things set up for me.

By the time we get to the fire, Mel has some soup warmed up and Darcy has another sleeping bag ready for me. She's warming it up a little by holding it up to the warmth of the fire.

"Can you sit?" Hannah asks as she grabs a chair.

My chattering teeth are easing a bit, I must have just been really cold, the sleeping bag is definitely helping. I say, "Maybe one a little more sturdy, I'm not sure I can get out of that one."

"I don't know if we brought anything else," Hannah says, looking around.

"Hold on… Hannah, come help me," says Hands. They walk away for a minute. I hear a chainsaw and a second later, Hands is rolling a large chunk of tree-a log-towards us and Hannah is carrying the chainsaw. He turns the log up on its end once he gets close to the fire. He comes and stands by me, using his hand to mark on his chest how tall I am to him. I barely meet below his shoulder.

I laugh.

He walks back over to the log and marks about where my head would hit it. He reaches for the chainsaw, Hannah gives it to him. He cuts off two feet of excess wood. He then lays the log back down and roughly but quickly starts to cut into it.

"Here Lainey, while we wait for Hands, eat some of this," Mel says, handing me a cup of soup.

I take it from her and blow on it first, then take a sip.

"Mmmmmm," I moan. I start to gulp it down. It has been, maybe, 32 hours since the last time I ate anything of real substance. I really don't know how long, I don't know what time it is but this soup tastes amazing. It has chunks of veggies and beef.

"Done," Hands says.

We all look over at him and start to laugh.

"Brilliant," Dalton says.

Hands has cut me out a chair. There are armrests and a high back. It even looks like he's intending me to use the small piece he cut off the top as a footrest.

Dalton walks me over but before I can sit down, Darcy says, "Hold on."

She wraps the warmed sleeping bag around the one I'm already wrapped in and then she runs over to the side of a tent. She comes back with the saddle blanket I had been using. She folds it in half and pushes it down into the wooden chair. Dalton lowers me down. I have to hold my breath as my body screams in agony.

I let out a slow breath as I sit all the way down. Dalton helps lift my legs and puts them on the makeshift leg rest. He carefully tucks the sleeping bags in around me.

"Do you want more soup?" Mel asks.

"Yes, please," I answer. "It's really good."

"One of Val's," Dalton says, winking at me. His playfulness doesn't meet his eyes. I tilt my head a little to the side, trying to read the look on his face.

"Here Bubs," Darcy says, handing Dalton a folding lawn chair.

"Thanks," he replies while taking it and setting it up beside me.

I look at him with a questioning look and ask, "Bubs?"

"My nickname she calls me," he chuckles.

"I like it," I say, sticking my right hand out so he can hold it.

He instantly takes it. He squeezes gently, I squeeze back.

"Okay, so what hurts?" Darcy asks as she comes to my left side. "Besides the obvious."

"The obvious?" I ask.

"Well, your face, Deary, it's pretty cut up... Ummm, are those claw marks?" she asks with extreme worry.

"What?" Dalton asks, leaning over to look too. "What the hell!? What happened out there Lainey?"

I take as deep a breath as I can and start to tell them my story. Starting at the beginning. Bree pretending to have changed her mind about me. Her picking Stormy for me and being sweet. Bree slapping Stormy on the ass. Flying through the trees. Getting knocked off Stormy. Waking up from being knocked out. The bear.

"A fucking bear?" Hands shouts.

"Yeah," I say. "I didn't think he got me when he swiped at me, I thought he had hit the tree and it was tree bark flying by that hit me. But thinking back now, the way he swiped out, there's no way it was tree bark, my head was to the side but behind the tree, his claws would have hit me before he hit the tree."

"Oh my gosh," Mel says.

"Lainey!" Hannah states with surprise.

I look at Dalton, he looks extremely pissed off right now. So I hurry and carry on with my story. Stormy saving me and fighting the bear away. Stormy keeping me warm and safe through the night. I told them how she let me take the saddle off and how she let me get on her. How I told her to take us home and she started walking. She kept me safe while I slept and led us to the campfire.

"Damn," Darcy says, looking at me with something that looks like awe.

"Holy shit, Lainey," Hands says.

"Are you okay?" Mel asks, she's got tears in her

eyes.

"Yeah, I'm okay," I say, trying to reassure her.

"Of course you aren't, but you will be," Dalton says, squeezing my hand.

"Okay, back to your injuries. You said your ribs, chest, and wrist hurt?" Darcy asks.

"Yeah, I'm pretty sure I have some broken ribs and my wrist is broken," I answer.

"Mel, will you go get my medic bag out of our tent?" Darcy asks. Mel nods and heads to one of the tents. "Can I see your wrist?"

I nod and pull my left hand out from my cocoon. She gently pushes my sleeves up and gasps.

"Ugh, yeah, I'd say it's broken," she says. She gently pushes her fingers down in a couple spots which causes me to breath in sharp breaths. "Sorry, Honey."

Mel's back and places a big black duffel bag beside Darcy.

"What do you want first?" Mel asks.

"Let's splint this, it might ease the pain in your hand, if we do," Darcy says, looking up at me.

I nod. Anything for some relief of any kind is welcome.

Mel pulls out the things Darcy will need for a splint and hands them over when Darcy asks for them. In no time at all, but with some pain and apologies from Darcy, my wrist and hand are splinted and wrapped nice and snug.

"Better?" Darcy asks.

"Yeah," I say. My hand and wrist don't hurt nearly as bad anymore and I feel like I can relax my muscles from holding it in the least painful position.

"Okay, now some alcohol wipes. Let's take a look at these cuts and scrapes. I'm worried about the claw marks causing an infection but we should be able to get you some antibiotics as soon as we get home," Darcy says. Mel hands her some opened alcohol swabs. "This is going to hurt a little, sorry."

I laugh out a short, sarcastic laugh, "Pain? What's that?"

She laughs and says, "Right? A little sting won't compare to the pain you're in but I just want to prepare you."

"I know, thank you," I say, smiling at her. I look over at Dalton, he still looks upset.

I decide to wait until after Darcy is done cleaning me up before I talk to Dalton about what's wrong. It doesn't take long for her to clean up my face. There was A LOT of stinging. She worked on a couple spots really hard, probably really dirty from when I'd been lying on the forest floor.

"Boss?" Shorty asks, quietly. He's come up behind us without me hearing him. I jump a little. "Sorry, Lainey."

I smile at him and shrug, which I'm rewarded with a shot of pain. I bite back my exclamation from that pain. I don't want Dalton to get any more upset.

"Yeah," Dalton says.

"I think I should get Stormy back to the barn. I know my way back, I can take your horse and lead her back, along with Sarg. Then I'll bring the side-by-side back. That might be easier for Ms. Lainey than trying to get her back up on a horse, riding back home, and then off again," Shorty says. That thought has me wincing, which Dalton notices.

"Yeah, that's a good idea," he says, squeezing my hand.

"Make sure Stormy gets some treats, I promised her once we got home, I'd make sure she'd get some," I say.

"Might be better to wait a day to do that. She hasn't eaten for a couple days, she needs some hay and water," Shorty says.

"At least an apple or some carrots... something. She took such good care of me, she deserves something to know she's a good girl," I plead. My voice is starting to rise. I don't know why Stormy not getting a treat is causing me so much anxiety.

"It's okay, Lainey," Dalton says, turning and patting my arm while squeezing my hand reassuringly. "Shorty, ask Val for a couple apples and carrots, it won't hurt her to have those."

Shorty nods and then tilts his hat towards me. He walks away.

"He won't get lost?" I ask, worried about Stormy being lost in this forest another night.

"No, he knows his way around here really well. We aren't too far from home anyways," Dalton says.

"We aren't?" I ask, surprised.

"After you and Stormy took off, Hands, Shorty, and I tried to follow you but that mare can run. We tried to find her tracks but after a little ways into the forest, we lost them. We went back to the beginning and told them to keep moving the cattle, we were almost there anyways. I told them that Hands, Shorty, and I were getting supplies and then starting the search for you. Darcy, Mel, and Hannah insisted on coming. We went back to the house and you should have seen how distraught Val was, she'll be over the moon to see you," Dalton pauses to smile at me. "She really likes you."

"I like her too," I say, smiling back.

"So, we packed for a couple nights, we weren't sure how far you and Stormy would get, I was hoping she'd calm down. But the further we got into the forest, the more panicked I got. The first night-"

I interrupt Dalton, "Wait, first night? You make it sound like it's been a couple. Tonight is only the second night, right?"

Dalton looks at Darcy, I look over at her. She turns my face back to Dalton so she can finish cleaning the wounds on her side of it.

"Dalton?" I ask.

"You lost a day or two in there somewhere, last night was the second night," he says.

"I'm confused... What time is it?" I ask.

I feel Darcy remove her hand, I look at her, and she looks at her watch.

"It's 4:23am... Wednesday morning... So technically, three nights..." she says.

I stare at her, dumbfounded. I slowly look back at Dalton.

"It's Wednesday?" I ask in disbelief.

"Yes, apparently. I wasn't aware of the time," he says.

"Okay, I'll process and figure that out later. Finish your story," I say, still stunned.

Dalton looks concerned but continues, "It snowed a little the first day, Saturday. We think Stormy was on her way back because we found her tracks in the snow but we could see where she turned and went back into the forest. We weren't sure why. We lost her tracks when the snow melted but we kept going straight, using a compass and map, hoping it was the direction she had gone. They talked me into stopping when it got too dark to see anything. I reluctantly agreed. We set up camp but as soon as it was light enough-Sunday morning-, we were moving again. We continued on our straight path, again, hoping we'd find you and/or Stormy. It started to snow again. We were slow going, we didn't want to miss anything, hoping to find a hoof print or something to indicate we were going in the right direction. We made camp again in the pitch darkness. And again, once it was light enough-Monday morning-we were moving. It had started to snow again. Then, Shorty went about 50 yards away and way to the right of us, for a bathroom break, when he found Stormy's hoof prints. As far as we could tell, they looked fresh. I was hopeful you were nearby. We started hollering for you, but we didn't get a response so we kept following her tracks. We could tell she started running, and then from the way she was digging in, she had to have been running really fast, to what, we don't know."

"I bet it was when the bear was attacking. She came in like a rocket," I say. "She might have heard the bear."

"Horses don't run towards danger, especially Stormy. As you know from your experience, she's skittish," Hannah says from across the fire. "We were all surprised to see you even sitting on her, let alone riding her, when you came out of the barn."

"I don't know about other horses, but I know Stormy came to my rescue," I say.

"True, there's no denying that," Hannah admits.

"So you were tracking her?" I ask, urging Dalton to continue.

"Yeah and then we lost her tracks again because the snow melted and it was like she was flying through the forest. There wasn't a broken tree limb or anything. Like I said, we were slow going, looking for any signs. So we set up camp for the third time. Darcy forced me to eat, I was racked with stress and worry," he looks at me with something in his eyes, I can't tell the emotion.

I wish we were alone so I can ask him what he's feeling.

He continues on, "So we start back up again at the first sign of light-Tuesday morning-but we were greeted with a ton of snow. I was really worried. You had gone three and a half to four days without anything substantial to eat but that muffin we had for breakfast Saturday morning and only the one bottle of water and a couple granola bars, since I had the lunch pack on with me. And it was freezing and snowing. We pushed on though, no tracks to follow this time but we kept going in the direction Stormy had been going. We kept following the compass well after dark, tonight... errr, last night... but finally stopped and made this camp not too long ago. I was just marking on the map where we'd been when Hands shouted my name and pointed you out. You looked like a ghost riding in from the dark. But then when I hollered your name and I heard your faint reply of my name, I knew it was you."

"You guys must be exhausted," I say.

"Us?" Dalton asks, incredulously. "You've just spent that last four days in an unfamiliar forest, after getting knocked off a spooked horse, a bear attack, sleeping on the ground, snowed on, and sleeping on a horse while you trusted her to lead you home. And you're worried about us?"

"Ummmm… yes?" I answer with a question. I look around at all of them, they're looking at me like I'm a different species. "What? You guys have been out here the same as me. Sleeping on the ground. In the snow. Riding on horseback for four days."

I look at Darcy and see her grinning ear to ear.

Are they not used to people who care about others? They all seem like caring people, to be out here looking for me.

Ignoring them, I stare into the fire. After a few minutes I see Mel and Hannah stand up.

"We're gonna go get a few hours of sleep before we head back, since we've been up for almost 24 hours," Mel says.

"I'll join you girls," Darcy says.

"Night," Hannah says to me and Dalton. Darcy and Mel wave at us. We wave back.

After a few minutes of silence and staring into the fire again, Dalton stirs beside me.

"Are you warming up?" he asks, tucking the sleeping bag around me more. He stands up and throws another good size log onto the fire.

"Yeah, I think I'm thawing out," I chuckle. Dalton doesn't smile. "What's wrong?"

He looks at me and stares. His eyes start to get

watery.

"Dalton?" I ask, really concerned now. I haven't heard or seen him cry in the year that we've been getting to know each other.

He gruffly wipes at his face and grunts out to clear his throat.

"It's nothing," he says.

"Dalton... talk to me," I plead.

"I thought..." he clears his throat again. "I honestly thought we weren't going to find you and if we did, I was expecting something much worse than this. Don't get me wrong, what you went through is horrific. But..."

He takes my hand back into his left as he sits back down but he shakes his head and then puts his right hand over the top half of his face.

"What?"

"I didn't think we were going to find you alive... I'm not doubting your ability to survive. I know you're smart and resourceful but with how cold it got at night, the snow, lack of food and water, and not knowing if you were injured... The strength it took for you to get back on Stormy, the trust you had to muster to even do that, and then to keep her moving... I don't know anyone else that could have done that, you're amazing."

"Stormy kept us going. I didn't have the reins in my hands until I got here. She led us to you. I think she was on her way back to you guys when she turned around and started back to find me. I don't know if she made a loop or if she went by me at one point while I was knocked out. From your story and me knowing how long I've been awake, it sounds like I was out for the rest of Saturday, all that night, all day Sunday, all that night, and a good chunk of Monday. But anyways, I think Stormy knew where I was but also knew you guys were coming. She was doing her best to keep close enough to both of us, to keep you coming in the right direction and for her to get to me if I needed her and it's a good thing she did because I did need her. Dalton, you should have seen her. The way she took on that bear, it was incredible. Stormy saved me. She got us here."

"I believe it but I think it was more than that."

"Well, I do too. But…"

"But what?"

"I talked to Jayce," I say. Dalton looks at me with concern. "Not like in person or that I saw him or his ghost. I mean, once I got back on Stormy… I talked to him. Asked him to get me back to you. To help get me back to our babies. I don't know if you believe in that kind of thing, but I felt comforted after talking to him."

I shrug. I'm sounding like a nutjob, Dalton must think so. But he squeezes my hand again, I look up at him. He leans forward and kisses me gently on the cheek.

"I think you're right. I think Stormy used her instincts to get both of you back to us and I think Jayce was there helping her and keeping an eye on you."

I tilt my head towards him. He leans closer to me.

"I want to say something and I don't need a response or reply but I need to get this off my chest," he says after a few minutes of silence.

"Ooookaaay," I say, hesitantly.

"I love you, Elainah," he says. "I knew it before we left the house Saturday. Staring at you across the island, I knew it then. Being able to sit with you in silence and just enjoy your presence, your company, I knew I loved you. When I realized I might have lost you... in the final, permanent way, I couldn't breathe. I couldn't eat... not until Darcy forced me to have some soup. The pain of thinking I'd never see your warm smile, never feel your touch, your warmth- physically, and the warmth that comes from you, was deep and gut wrenching. It was downright crippling but I had to keep looking, I had to find you. I knew that if I felt this way, felt like I couldn't handle life without you, I knew I loved you. I know I love you. I never felt this way in any of my past relationships. Thinking back on those relationships, I realize that when I was just thinking of breaking up with whomever I was dating, it was a relief thinking our relationship would be over soon, and that's not a good thing to feel when you're dating someone. You should want to be with them and the thought of losing them should hurt, at least a little, if you have true feelings for them. The thought of not being with you, that's pain. It's to the core, pain. It's through the heart, soul, and mind. I know it doesn't come close to actually feeling the loss of the person you love. What you've felt after losing Jayce and still feel today, but I have a better understanding of it and I'm going to do my damnedest to help ease that pain for you, anyway I can."

I wipe a tear away and lift my head from his shoulder and kiss his cheek.

"Thank you, I say," I wipe another tear from my cheek. "I love you too, Dalton, I really do."

He turns his face and kisses me softly on the lips. My heart races, my breathing picks up a notch, and then I gasp from the pain in my chest.

"Ouch," I moan.

"Sorry," he says.

"It's okay, I just get overly excited when you kiss me."

"Me too, Lainey, me too."

"Oh, I owe you a saddle and a new coat..." I mumble out in my sleepy state.

"How do you figure?" Dalton chuckles out quietly.

"I got blood on the sleeve of your coat when I was trying to get my face to stop bleeding. And I had to leave the saddle after I pushed it off Stormy," I say, remorsefully.

"Don't worry about any of that, those things can be replaced, you can't be replaced. I'm just so damn glad you and Stormy found us," Dalton says, kissing my head with a little force, it didn't hurt but I think he's trying to put meaning behind the gesture.

I put my head back down on his shoulder and close my eyes. Finally, feeling safe, warm, and happy. Dalton starts to hum a song and I feel myself starting to drift off to sleep.

"Rest, Lainey, I'll wake you when Shorty gets back with the side-by-side and then we'll head back and get you to a doctor."

"Mmmmm," is all I say before sleep takes me.

Chapter 21

I wake up to the sound of growling.

"AHHHH!!" I scream, jolting to a standing position.

"What! What?" Dalton says, half sleepily, half on high alert. He jumps to his feet also.

"Bear! Bear!" I screech.

I hear the scramble of tent zippers being ripped down and crashing as the occupants of the tents stumble out.

"Where?" Dalton asks.

Hands pulls up a shotgun and I hear him load a shell into the chamber.

Pain, so much pain.

"Aarrgh," I moan, wrapping my right arm around my rib cage.

"Lainey, did you see-" Dalton starts asking but then stops and cocks his head to the side and listens.

"That sounds like the side-by-side coming. Is that what woke you?"

I try to listen through the ringing in my head. And I hear the 'growl' that had woken me, only it's not a growl, it's the sound of an engine making its way towards us.

"Yes," I pant out. "Sorry… I must… have… been… sound… asleep…"

"It's okay. I'm just glad there isn't an actual bear around. You can lower the gun now, Hands. False alarm. She heard the side-by-side and it startled her awake."

"Gotchya," Hands says. He lowers his shotgun and unloads it.

"Dalton?" I ask, breathlessly.

"Yeah, Lainey?" he asks in return, worry thick in the tone of his voice.

"I don't feel so good," I say, swaying.

"Darcy!" Dalton hollers as I start to fall to the ground. He catches me before I can move more than a couple inches down.

"Coming!" she shouts from over by the tents.

"Deep breath… in… and out… Breathe, Lainey," he says.

"I… can't…" I say. I'm just now noticing that it's starting to get light out but I can see black dots popping around in my eyesight. I see Darcy's face come into view.

"What's wrong with her? She says she can't

breathe," Dalton says, panicking.

Darcy unzips Dalton's coat I'm still wearing, and feels up under my hoodie. I wince.

"She could have punctured a lung... I don't know. That's something she needs a scan for, I can't 'feel' that. Her breathing isn't so labored that her stomach is collapsing while she's trying to breathe in... Lainey, do you think you're having a panic attack?" Darcy asks as she pulls her hands out from under my hoodie, rezips the coat, and puts my cocoon back around me.

"Poss...ibly," I gasp out.

"Close your eyes and listen to me. I want you to take a steady breath in through your nose and when I get to five, breathe out your mouth. Can you do that?" Darcy asks.

"Yes... but... probably... not to... five," I say.

"Okay, we'll try it first and if it's too deep of a breath for your ribs to handle, we'll shorten it, deal?" she suggests.

I nod.

"Okay, deep breath in, through the nose," she encourages.

I do as she says.

"One... two... three... four...," she barely has the word four out of her mouth and I'm wincing in pain, breathing out quickly. "Okay, okay, okay. Easy. We'll try again, but we'll just go until three. Ready?"

I nod.

"Deep breath in," she says again and I comply. In a very calming voice, she continues with, "One... two... and three... let your breath out through your mouth, slow and steady. Okay, and again. Breathe in... three... two... one... and out, nice and slow. Good."

We do this a couple more times and I feel my breathing becoming more normal. I feel my heart starting to calm as well. Dalton has been holding me in his arms the entire time, gently but tightly.

"How do you feel?" Darcy asks.

"Much better, thank you," I say.

"You can probably put her back in her chair now," Darcy says to her brother.

"I prefer her in my arms," Dalton says, tightening his hold on me, just a smidge.

I open my eyes and see him smiling his crooked smile.

"I'm good here, if you are," I smile back.

"I am," he moves to sit down, and adjusts me ever so slightly and with so much care, it's like he's barely touching me. I see that he's sat down in 'my' chair. I rest my head on his chest and just breathe in his smell. His jacket smells like him, it's become a comforting smell. Darcy puts the sleeping bags-that had fallen to the ground when I jumped up-on me and Dalton.

"Thank you," he and I say at the same time.

"Shorty's about here. I'll start getting things packed up and we'll head back," Hands says.

"We'll help," Mel says, who was a lot closer than I thought.

I open my eyes and watch Hannah hop up from a chair nearby. Darcy pats my shoulder and squeezes Dalton's and then she starts to help get things packed up. It doesn't take long. The tents come down a lot easier than I remember tents coming down. They fold the chairs back up and start loading the horses with stuff. They're done by the time Shorty pulls into the clearing and drives right up to us. He hops out and brings two cups to me and Dalton.

"Val sends these," he hands the cups over. I smell delicious coffee. "She also wanted me to give you a hug but I'm guessing that might hurt. I told her you were injured but I didn't know the extent of it. She was already in a hissy when I showed up with Stormy who was hurt, so I didn't want to worry her more by telling her everything that was hurting you. It took a good few minutes to get her calmed down enough to tell her you were okay, Lainey. She's excited to see you, it's all I could do to keep her at home. She said if it weren't for her needing to stay home to let your sister and friend know you were okay, she'd be coming out."

"My sister and friend? How did they find out? How did they get a hold of Val?" I ask, concerned. I know Lucy and Emily-I'm assuming it's Em- must be worried sick.

"They hadn't heard from you so they called Bill

the Sheriff, who called Val, who told him to give her number to the girls. They've been checking in since Monday," Shorty says.

"Oh man," I say. "They must to be so worried."

"We'll get you home soon," Dalton reassures me.

"Thanks for bringing us the coffee and the side-by-side. How's Stormy?" I ask Shorty before he leaves to go mount up.

"She'll be okay, I think. I called Doc. He's back from visiting his daughter. I guess she and his wife told him to go home, something about the daughter's house being too small and the daughter feeling cramped. But, I waited for him to show up. Which is what took so long, it's starting to snow pretty good back at the house. He had a hard time getting into the lane, nobody there to plow. I guess once Nolan and Tanner got back to their houses, their lane got drifted shut as well and since the plow is at the home place, they're stuck until we get back. I told them not to worry, to sit tight, and we'd dig them out soon. Hope it's okay that I told them that, I figured with the cattle on the mountain and snow in the valley, there wasn't a huge rush for anything right now."

"Nope, that's great," Dalton says. "Ready to head back to the house?"

"Hhhhell yes," I say, excitedly. I lean forward carefully and stand up from Dalton's lap.

"Okay?" he asks.

"Mmmmm," I lie. My entire body hurt. Muscles. Skin. Probably even my hair.

I can't fool him for a second, "Liar."

I chuckle.

We walk a couple of feet to the side-by-side and Dalton reaches forward and opens the door for me. I stare for a minute and then look up at him.

"I don't know if I can get in, it's a little higher than I think I can manage," I say.

Shorty looks around and says, "Ah-ha!"

He runs a short distance away and comes back with a rock. He places it down in front of me so I can use it as a step.

"Thank you," I say.

"No problem," he says, smiling. "Okay, I'm going to mount up and start back with the others."

Dalton just nods, he's watching me intently. I step up on the rock and carefully, ever so carefully, turn myself and sit down. I slide around so I'm facing forward. Not as much pain as I thought there would be, I might have this moving thing down. He grabs the sleeping bags on the wood chair and tucks them around me.

"Thank you," I say. He winks at me and smiles.

Swoon. Get a hold of yourself. If you get too excited you'll be rewarded with pain. Simmer. Down.

"Hey Shorty?" Dalton shouts, now that I'm safely inside the side-by-side.

"Yes, sir?" Shorty stops and turns around.

"I'm going to be going slow on the way back so that Lainey doesn't get jostled around too awfully much. Make sure everyone gets something to eat when you all get back, okay?" Dalton says.

"Can do," Shorty says, hustling to the last horse tied to the tree nearby. The others were just barely out of earshot. He unties his horse, hops on, and trots away.

Dalton walks around, gets in, and puts the side-by-side in reverse. Once we're facing the direction Shorty came, he puts it in drive and slowly pulls away from the clearing. I can feel the tension and fear sliding off of me. I'm going to leave it here. I don't need to bring any of that back with me.

After a few minutes of driving, Dalton starts to sing.

"I love it when you sing," I say, adoringly. He stops singing. "Tsk... I didn't want you to stop. I actually do love it when you sing. You have an amazing voice."

"I never notice when I start singing, it's something I do out of habit," he says, smiling.

"It's starting to be a sound of comfort for me."

He reaches over and grabs my knee. He can't hold my hand as it's in a splint. I reach over with my right hand and pull his hand into my lap as I hold it. He then starts to sing a very sweet and calming song. I close my eyes and listen to him. After that song is over, he starts singing the song, "You Won't Ever Be Lonely" by Andy

Griggs, the one playing on the radio when we went up to Wallowa Lake.

"You remember?" I ask.

"There's not a lot I forget and I think of you when I hear this song, ever since that day," he says, he leans over and kisses my head, I lean into his kiss.

He starts singing again. My heart fills with more love than I ever thought I'd possibly ever feel again.

Thank you, Jayce. I say with all the love I have for him and the love I'm starting to be filled with for Dalton.

I keep my eyes closed and listen to my personal concert. Dalton sings just about every genre. He has me start picking songs, the guy is like a walking jukebox. He makes me chuckle-full on laughing hurts too much- when he performs a rap song. I'm not sure how much time has passed, it's been quite a few songs, when I feel a difference in temperature. Apparently, the trees were keeping us protected from the wind. I burrow down into my sleeping bags. I open my eyes and see white. Nothing but white.

"Damn..." Dalton expresses with surprise.

"It's been snowing a lot since we left," I say.

"I'd say. More than what Shorty said. I wonder how much has accumulated since he left to bring us the side-by-side?"

"Will this thing make it through?"

"Yeah but I'll have to pick up speed so we don't

get stuck. Ready?"

"Yeah, let's get to the house."

Dalton pushes on the gas pedal and we plow through the snow. I stiffen against the jostling. Trying not to make a noise. I know if he knew how much this hurt, he'd slow down, and we need to get to the house. It's a full on blizzard out here.

We make it to the pasture by the barn in a couple of minutes, and thankfully, to the house in a couple seconds later. Dalton pulls around back, on to the patio, which is bare because of the cover. He parks and turns it off. Before he gets to my door, the door opens and I see Val standing there with her hand over her mouth.

I wave at her and she starts to cry.

"Oh, Val… don't… I'm okay!" I say, trying to get out as quickly as I can to get to her so I can comfort her.

"Lainey, slow down," Dalton says, sternly.

"But Val," I say.

"She'll be fine, I don't want you hurting yourself even more," he says as goes to get a crate that's by the kitchen door. I hear him say in a sweet, calming voice, "She's okay, Val."

Dalton puts the crate in front of me and with his help, I slide out onto it. I try hard to hold my facial expression in place so that they don't see how much it hurts getting out and stepping off my makeshift step.

Val holds the door open as we walk in, she gives me the gentlest of hugs.

"Lainey, I am so so happy to see you. Overjoyed," she says, with tears in her eyes still.

"I'm happy to see you as well, Val," I pat her arm. Again, trying not to show how even that gentle hug hurt. My muscles are just really sore, I guess.

"Let's get you both something to eat," Val says. We walk down the little hall past, the dining room, and into the kitchen where Val starts bustling around. "Darcy said you weren't eating much, Dalton."

"Hard to have an appetite when you're filled with worry," he says, squeezing me.

"Well, you're both home safe. Let's fill you up with some food," she says. "Go into the dining room, they're all in there now. They've got the horses all boarded up and fed. I told Mel and Hannah they were staying here tonight, the road is completely drifted in, Doc is stuck here too," she rambles on and on while she works with the food on the stove and counter, and island.

"Were you planning on feeding an army?" I ask, jokingly.

"I cook when I'm stressed and worried," she says and wink at Dalton. "It'll all keep for a couple days and it looks like we'll have extras in the house for that amount of time, so it all works out."

Val takes my sleeping bags from me, I smile at her, and then I let Dalton lead me into the dining room. And sure enough, everyone is in here. Even Phil and the boys. They were all surrounding Darcy like she was their sun. It was sweet.

A mother's love, I tell you what.

I look around the room and then freeze. Bree.

Dalton looks at me to see why I've stopped moving and then his eyes follow my line of sight and sees Bree too.

"Bree I told you-" he says but she interrupts him and runs over to us.

"I just wanted to-" she starts but I interrupt her.

"Don't," I say as I raise my hand, palm out to her, while trying to keep my breathing and rage in check. "Don't say another word. Don't say you're sorry. I don't want to hear it."

I turn from her and walk around her, and sit in the nearest chair, which happens to be next to Hands. He gently pats my shoulder.

"I told you to leave and to not be here when we got back, I wasn't joking. After hearing about what happened in the barn and how Stormy took off, you're done here," Dalton whisper-shouts but that never works, we can all hear him.

"I didn't do anything to that old bitch of a mare," Bree hisses.

I leap out of my chair and I'm in her face before I even know what I'm doing.

"Don't you dare... Don't you fucking dare say another damn thing bad about Stormy. You lying piece of shit..." totally in a rage, I rear back and punch her as hard as I can in the face. My hand connects with her nose and I hear multiple crunches. Some from my hand and the other, her nose.

"AWWWW! You crazy bitch!" she says. Now I've got Mel and Hannah jumping up but Shorty and Hands are holding them back.

"You're the bitch, you cun-" Hannah starts to say but Mel is screaming over her.

"Say that to me, Bree," Mel screams.

"I'm calling the Sheriff," Bree whines, pointing her finger in my face. "I have witnesses! You're going to jail."

"Witnesses to what?" Abe says, walking over to stand next to me. "I saw you pull on the door as you were leaving and it was stuck from the wind, so you pulled harder and it finally flew open and hit you in the face."

"Yeah, I saw that too," Mel says, seething.

"Me too," Hannah agrees, glaring at Bree.

Everyone starts shouting their agreements with Abe. I start feeling my adrenaline leaving my body and it's replaced with agony but I'll be damned if I let Bree see me in pain.

"You want to call the Sheriff, Bree? Fine, call. I have Bill's number in my phone. When he gets here, he can hear how you knew Stormy was skittish and you still spooked her, knowing full well that Lainey wasn't an expert rider. You're lucky she's skilled enough to have stayed on as long as she had but I'd wager Bill wouldn't have any problem with charging you with something because of what you did, it caused all of Lainey's injuries. So yeah, call Bill, I actually wouldn't mind having a chat with him," Dalton says, putting his arm around me.

"Dalton, please," she starts to plead.

"No, done. I'll mail your check to you, you have until Friday to get out of the cabin. If you aren't, I'll be calling Bill myself," he's fuming mad now.

"Laney, please, I'm so-" she turns to me but before she can finish talking, I turn from her and walk back to the table.

I hear her splutter and burst into tears and then she runs from the room. I glance over and see Val standing just inside and to the right.

"Can't say I'm sad to see that one go," Val says walking towards us. I burst out laughing. Hearing sweet, old Ms. Val say something not very kind about someone, is hilarious to me, apparently.

"Ow... ow... ow..." I say in between laughing. Everyone else starts to laugh, too.

I slowly catch my breath and stop laughing as Val puts my plate of food in front of me. A little bit of everything. Pancakes. Waffles. Strawberry crepe. Fresh fruit. Scrambled eggs. Bacon. Sausage. Ham. It looks so good.

"Now, don't get too carried away and eat it all. You've been gone a couple days and who knows what you had to eat. Don't make yourself sick thinking you have to eat it all. I put a little bit of everything on here so you can eat whatever sounds or tastes good," Val says, patting my shoulder as she turns and walks away.

I look at Dalton's plate and see ham, pancakes, eggs, and bacon. I ignore the new pain in my right hand and I take a bite of the eggs. So good. I put some peanut butter and syrup on my pancake and waffle and take a bite of each. So, so, good. I take a little bite of everything and as per usual, it all tastes amazing.

All I hear for the next few minutes is eating utensils hitting plates and people eating their food. Slowly, conversations pick up and soon it's all I can hear, one jumble of voices. I lean against Dalton and just look around the room. I just met these people but they all, or most, came looking for me. They went from strangers, to friends, to family all in less than a week. And that's how it works sometimes. When you connect with someone, you connect. These people are good people.

Dalton asks where Frank and Junior are at and Abe tells him that they went home before the snow got too bad and before the driveway got drifted shut. Abe was saying he was feeding the horses when Shorty showed up with Stormy. He helped Doc with her once he got here. Then he sat with her after Doc went into the house, until the riders got back. The horse Hands rides, Knightly, is the only horse that calms Stormy down but even with him back, she wouldn't stop pacing her stall and neighing. I had thought at that moment, I needed to go see her but my tired body had me slumping into Dalton even more.

"Hey, you want to go take a shower and then maybe Doc can look at ya. I think he's got something to close up the claw marks on your face," Dalton says.

I hear a gasp behind me and I turn to see Val standing there, she's holding a stack of plastic cups and a pitcher of orange juice.

"I'm sorry, but did I just hear you say 'claw marks'?" she asks, shocked.

Dalton looks at me with big eyes, grimaces, and turns back to Val and says, "Yes, ma'am."

She puts the cups and juice down on the table and takes the seat at the end.

"Lainey?" she looks at me.

"Yes, ma'am?" I ask too innocently.

"By claw marks, does he mean what I think he means?" she asks, putting her hand to her chest and grabbing onto her shirt there.

"Well, what do you think he means?" I ask. I don't want to worry her, I really am okay.

"Wild. Animal," she says shortly.

"Ummm, well, yeah... that's what he means," I say.

"Tell them the story," Darcy says.

"She doesn't need to do that," Dalton says.

"I want to hear it, Uncle D, please," Liam asks and then looks at me and blushes.

"No Li-" but I interrupt him.

"In my experience, it's best to talk about the hard things. The scary things. The things that might give you nightmares. If you talk about them, they can't hang out in your head and take hold," I say, touching his arm. He smiles at me and puts his hand on mine.

I turn to Val and start my story again. Starting from the beginning like I did back at the clearing. As I'm telling it, I look around the room at everyone. Even those that had heard it before, are listening intently. When I get to the bear attack, Val gasps and puts her hand to her mouth. Craig cusses which earns him a slap to the back of the head by his mom. I continue on with my story until I get to us pulling in here.

It's silent for a few minutes. I look around and finally land on Dalton, he winks at me, leans in, and kisses my head.

"That's fu-" Shorty starts to say but changes it since Craig just got in trouble by Darcy. "-reaking insane!"

"That's incredible," Phil says. "I've heard of people surviving bear attacks but I've never met one in person before, you're a brave little thing aren't you?"

"She's a lot of things wrapped in an amazing little package," Dalton says, winking at me again, which makes me shake my head.

"Honestly, I just did what my instincts were telling me to do, except run. I wanted to run from that bear but I knew that was the wrong thing to do. Luckily Stormy came when she did because I don't know if I could have waited him out before he got bored of me and left," I say, shrugging.

"Well, we don't need to think about that," Dalton says, even though he shivers at the thought.

Val stands up and walks over to me. She bends down, puts her hands carefully on my face, and says, "You... you are something special."

She kisses my forehead and then hugs me tightly. I hold my breath and my expression. She pulls away, pats my shoulder and leaves the room. I let out a long, slow breath.

"You okay?" Dalton asks, looking at me in concern.

"Yeah... just... hurts to... be hugged," I say, moaning.

"Go get cleaned up, I'll come have a look at chya when you're done," Doc says.

Dalton stands up and helps me stand. I've gotten stiffer while sitting. I walk slowly from the room, everyone saying their good nights and goodbyes.

Chapter 22

Luckily, Dalton's room isn't too far away, and extra luckily it's on the first floor. He leads us in, turning lights on as we enter the room. We get to the bathroom and he hits a couple switches. One for lights and the other says 'FL HT'.

"What does that switch do?" I ask.

"Heats the floor."

"Ooh that'll be a welcome feeling to my frozen toes."

"Do you want a shower or bath?"

"A bath would feel amazing but I don't think I can sit down in it or get out of it. Probably safer and better for me if I take a shower."

"Do you need help with your clothes?" he asks. I look at him with wide eyes, pretending to be shocked. "No! I don't mean in any way other than you might hurt too much to do it yourself."

I wink at him and say, "I know, I'm just giving

you crap."

Shaking his head, he chuckles, "You do that well."

I shrug and then start to unzip the coat. I try to reach up with my right hand but find it's hurting really bad now.

"Hmmm... maybe hitting Bree wasn't the best idea," I say as I look at my hand. My little pinky knuckle is swollen, as well as over into my ring finger knuckle. I can't make a fist anymore. Dalton comes over and looks at it.

"Looks like you might have a boxer's fracture," he says, turning my hand over in his hands. "You did hit her pretty hard. She deserved it and more, in my opinion."

"Has she always been like this?" I ask. Dalton helps me take the coat off. Taking the hoodie and long sleeve off are going to be the most painful. "Do both the shirt and hoodie at the same time. They should come off easy enough, that way I don't have to raise my arms twice."

"Good thinking... and no, she's never been that rotten and vindictive. What pisses me off the most is that you didn't do anything to her. You've been nice and way too understanding towards her. What she did is unacceptable. It takes someone truly evil to do that."

"I don't think she's evil but she's a very entitled person."

"You aren't wrong there."

"So it was me that brought that out in her?"

"No, I mean, yeah, she was the worst with you but she's always had a hint of it there. You just helped show her true nature. I've noticed that with everyone you come into contact with though. Shorty and Hands seem a lot more mellow and respectful when you're around. Mel and Hannah sure like you and they have kind of became their own little duo. They all really like you."

"I like all of them also."

When he's gotten my shirt and hoodie off, he takes a sharp breath in, and puts his right hand to his mouth.

"What?" I ask in concern.

Shaking his head, he doesn't say anything but turns me and shuts the bathroom doors. There's floor to ceiling mirrors on them. My breath catches as well. I have huge bruises all over my body. The biggest one is directly below my bra line. I'd say it's four to five inches wide and is the whole length of my ribs.

He helps me with my pants and leggings, and again, he gasps. I look down and see what looks like angry red stripes all over my legs. Must have been where tree limbs had hit me when Stormy and I were flying through the trees. I look at my arms and see some marks but they aren't as bad. Luckily, the heavy coat I was wearing saved my arms.

Dalton unclasps my bra strap and I let it slide off my arms. He kisses my shoulder.

"Umm.. you can't do that," I say, shivering but not because I'm cold or in agony.

"Does it hurt?"

"It will if you don't stop."

"Why is that?"

"Because I won't want you to stop and there's no way I can do what I'll want to do if you keep kissing me."

"Oh!" he says catching on. "I'll behave then, I don't want you in pain."

"Thank you," I say.

He helps me take my underwear off, which should feel weird but it doesn't.

He turns on the water and I walk in and let the waterfall of showers hit me. It's so warm and soothing. I turn and see Dalton walking in naked.

"Umm... that doesn't help anything," I say, pointing at him, head to toe.

"I figured you'd need help shampooing and washing your body. This is strictly a shower. No hanky panky, no funny stuff. I promise."

I eye him doubtfully but he looks completely serious.

"Okay," I say. "I believe you."

He shampoos and conditions my hair like a pro and rinses both times. He then finds a loofa and uses it to wash my body. It's weird letting him do everything but also relaxing in a way too. I move out of the way so he can shampoo his hair and wash his body.

I take a quick look at his junk and see that he's semi-hard. He's turned on but he's trying really hard to not let it get too carried away. He's such a good man.

Dalton finishes his shower and turns the water off. He grabs two towels from inside a hidden cupboard. They're warm, like fresh out of the dryer, warm.

"What the heck?" I ask as he wraps me up in the warm, and oh so soft, towel.

"This is a mini drier meant for exactly this, to warm up a towel. Had I known you were going to take a shower the other day, I would have shown that to you."

"I like it!"

"I thought you would."

He helps me dry off and then wraps me into a cocoon with the towel. He reaches into a drawer and pulls out a bottle that rattles. I look at him questioningly.

"Tylenol... It's the only pain reliever I have and even if I had something stronger, I know you wouldn't take it. You prefer the over the counter meds," he says as he shakes the bottle.

"Thank you," I say, again.

He smiles at me and then helps me out into his room.

"Hmm... you need something to wear for pajamas. One of my button ups?"

"Sounds good to me."

"Can I get you a pair of your undies?" he asks.

"Yeah, they're inside my bag to the left."

He grabs one of his shirts from the closet and then goes to my bag and grabs a pair of my white undies. He comes back and holds my underwear so I can step into them. He then helps me into his button up.

"That's much better than holding my arms over my head," I say as he buttons the third from the top button and then stops.

"I think one more button would be good, especially if Doc is coming in to do an exam," I suggest.

"Oh fine," Dalton says in a jokingly reluctant way. "You look better in this shirt than I do."

"Oh whatever, not even close," I say I walk over to the bed. "Hmmm… Do you have a step stool?"

"Nope, but if you let me pick you up, I think I can lay you down gently enough," he offers.

"We can try, I guess."

Dalton proceeds to pick me up so gently that I don't even feel like he's holding me, I feel like I'm sitting in a chair. He lays me down very carefully. Nothing hurts, or at least nothing hurts worse than it already did. He covers me with the sheet and blanket. He goes back into the bathroom and I hear the faucet turning on and then off. He comes back out with a small glass of water. He then opens the Tylenol bottle and dumps out a couple pills and then hands them to me, along with the water. I take them in one gulp.

"Want me to brush your hair?" he asks.

"Sure, my brush is in my bag."

He grabs it and brushes my hair gently. He puts the brush back when he's done.

"I'll go get Doc," Dalton says.

"Umm... Dalton?" I ask.

"Yeah," he replies.

"You might want to put clothes on, at least shorts, maybe..." I say, pointing from his head down to his penis and then circling my finger around there for a minute.

"Oh! Yeah, good point."

"I mean, I'm not complaining but the others might be seeing more than they'd like... Although, the girls probably wouldn't mind seeing you naked. But they're married, so I'd guess their husbands wouldn't like that very much," I say, laughing.

Dalton shakes his head and mumbles something under his breath. He then goes back into his closet and comes out wearing pajama bottoms and a navy t-shirt.

"Better?" he asks.

"No... I liked you better naked," I say as I waggle my eyebrows at him. "But for the people out there, yes, much better."

"You have to stop talking like that... I like it too much," he says, chuckling, as he walks over to me. He kisses my forehead and continues to say, "I'll go get Doc, you relax, and behave."

"I'll try," I say mockingly and then remember I wanted to call Lucy. "Oh, Dalton?"

"Yeah," he says as he turns, he's halfway between the bed and the door.

"Can you grab my phone for me?"

"Sure thing, where is it?"

"In my bookbag."

Dalton walks over to the chair against the other wall and grabs my bag off the floor. He reaches in and pulls out my phone.

"Here you go," he says as he hands it over.

"Thank you," I say. I catch his hand and pull him down to me and give him a quick kiss.

"Any time," he says.

He cups my face with one hand and stares into my eyes for a minute. He stands, turns, heads back to the door, and leaves the room. I settle back into my pillow, and get more comfy.

I turn my phone on and wait for all the notifications to finish dinging. I don't bother looking at them. I'm sure it's all the same. Worry. Anger. Worry. And more worry.

I hit the video chat option for Lucy. It rings twice and then it says *'connecting.'*

"*Lainey!?*" Lucy screeches over the phone. She looks like she has slept about as good as I have the last couple of days.

"Hi, Sis," I say, waving.

"Oh Laine! I've been so worried. When you didn't call Saturday, I thought maybe you just got busy with everything going on there. But when you didn't call or answer my calls or messages all day Sunday, I knew something was wrong. I knew something was really wrong when Emily called me asking if I'd heard from you. I waited until Monday morning to call the Sheriff there in Missoula as it's the biggest city near where Dalton's ranch is located. He said that he had five messages from Emily waiting for him when he got to work. She'd called as soon as she got off the phone with me Sunday. He said he would call Dalton and see what was going on. Next thing I know, the Sheriff is calling me back and giving me Dalton's housekeeper, Val's, phone number. I knew then that something was seriously wrong. I made Peter take the kids out for ice cream so if I had to have a meltdown, I could do it without them here. When she told me all she knew, I thought I was going to have a heart attack. I called Monday night and she said she still hadn't heard anything. She sounded so tired, I felt bad for bothering her again, but she was my only line to you. I called again Tuesday morning, still nothing. Tuesday night, nothing. Emily and I were blowing each other's phones up, seeing if either of us had heard anything. She was calling Val also. When my phone rang this morning a little after 5:00 and I saw it was Val, my heart fell to my stomach. I answered. She was laughing and crying. She said they had found you. She said you were hurt but you were going to be okay. She said you'd be *home before lunch but you'd need to eat and probably sleep before you'd have the energy to call. Oh Lainey, I'm so happy to see..."* she pauses, wipes her eyes with her free hand, and actually looks at me. *"Oh my gosh! Lainey! What happened to you?"*

I can kind of see my face in the little window of what she sees from my phone. I just see some scratches. I turn my face so my left side is showing more, still hard for me to really see, but the marks look longer and wider. Lucy gasps and puts her hand to her mouth.

"I'm okay, Luce, I promise," I say, trying to give her a reassuring smile.

"Don't give me that crap. I know you're downplaying how hurt you are because you don't want me to worry but Lainey, I'm already worried. Tell me everything."

So I once again tell my story. My sister is a good listener and doesn't say a thing until I'm done talking.

"Holy shit..." she says barely above a whisper. My sister doesn't cuss so I know she's in shock. I also know she's in shock because she's so quiet, she's not the quiet one in our sister duo.

"Yup, so the last couple of days have been interesting. How are you my kiddos doing?"

Lucy still has an open mouth-shocked-look on her face for a few more seconds before she blinks rapidly, shakes her head, looking a little bit like she's in a daze, but says, *"They're fine. You know kids. As long as they're having fun, they don't notice much. Time means nothing to them. And I wasn't going to tell them anything until I found out more."*

"Yeah, don't tell them. Can they stay a little longer with you? We're snowed in up here and I'm not sure when I'll be okay enough to fly. Shouldn't be long but knowing Dalton, he'll want me checked out by a human doctor and get the okay from them to travel."

"Human doctor? What other type of doctor is there? And of course they can stay. They can stay as long as you need. All summer, if need be. You know I love having them here," Lucy laughs.

I roll my eyes and laugh too.

"I meant a doctor who works on humans, people. Dalton went to go get his animal doctor, who was here looking after Stormy. Doctor Thomasen. Doc is out in the dining room eating. And I don't think I'll need all summer but maybe another week or two."

"Have you eaten?" she changes subjects quickly when she's anxious.

"Yes, Luce, I've eaten. I took a shower and now I'm lying in bed. Waiting for Doc to come check me over. Then I'm taking a nap. I'm really tired. But I wanted to call you so you could see that I'm okay."

"Do you want me to call Emily?"

"No, I'll call her real fast. I don't know what's taking Dalton so long." And then I hear shouting from somewhere in the house.

"What's that?" Lucy asks.

"I don't know, it sounds like people arguing but I can't tell about what," I strain my ears to try to make out some of the words but I can't. "I better call Emily real quick and let her know I'm okay. Lucy can you do me a favor?"

"Anything, Lainey."

"Give my kids big hugs for me. Hold them tight and tell them the hugs are from me and that I love them so very, very much?" I say as tears start to fill my eyes.

"Of course I can do that, no problem."

"Thanks Sis, love you."

"Love you, too. Bye."

"Bye."

I hit the end video chat button and scroll to Emily's number. I hit the video chat option and it rings a couple more times than Lucy let it ring but then it says *'connecting'*.

I can't see Emily because it looks like she's standing in a dark room.

"Emily?" I ask, confused.

"*Mmmmhmmm,*" she says and sounds like she's crying.

"Oh my gosh, Emily! Are you okay? What's going on?"

"*I'm... just... so... glad... to... see... your... name... show... up... on... my... screen,*" she says between crying and trying to breathe.

"Oh Emily. I'm okay. It's okay, take a deep

breath."

She does and it takes a couple more before she's done crying. I haven't seen or heard her cry like this in a really long time.

"Better?" I ask.

"Yeah."

"Good. Now... where are you? I can't see you."

"Oh! Hang on..." it sounds like she's fumbling around and then the light comes on. She's standing in what looks like a cleaning supply closet. *"I'm at work, you know I have to keep myself busy if I'm stressed or worried. When I saw you were calling, I told Pam I had to take the call. I had told her you were missing for a couple days. She told me to step in here."*

"Oh, I got chya. I see you now, hi," I say waving at her with my left hand.

"What the fuck, Lainey!? What's up with your hand? And... do I see a bunch of cuts on your face?" She brings her phone closer to her face to see me closer I guess.

"Okay, remember you're at work so don't freak out when I tell you the story, okay?"

"Ooookay," she says skeptically.

I dive into the story and tell her everything, just like I did the other times I've told it.

"Oh my hell!" she shouts as I get to the bear attack. She covers her mouth and the door to her supply closet flies open. *"Sorry, Ted. I didn't mean to startle you.*

I'm just on the phone. Yeah, thanks… Sorry, Lainey, keep going."

I continue on with the story all the way up to now.

"So that's what's been going on," I say.

"You were attacked by a mother fucking bear?" she whisper-shouts.

"Yyyyup…"

"And before that, you were knocked out for how many days?"

"The rest of Saturday, which was most of the day since we were on horseback by, I think, 7am. All of Sunday and a good part of Monday. So, maybe two and half days."

"Have they checked you for a concussion?"

"Not yet, I'm waiting for Dalton to come back with Doc. He was in another room in the house. I don't know what's taking so long," I stop talking for a minute and can still hear yelling. "Somethings going on. There's been a loud argument going on for the last 5-10 minutes."

"You punched that bitch, Bree? For real?"

"Yeah"

"Good."

I laugh.

"How are you feeling for real?"

"I'm sore but honestly just really tired."

"You said you talked to Lucy?"

"Yeah."

"*Good.*"

I hear footsteps, well more like stomps, coming towards the bedroom.

"Hey, someone's coming. It's probably Dalton but I better get off here so I can find out what the yelling's been about and you need to get back to work. I love you, Em."

"*Love you too, Lainey. Call me or text me after your nap.*"

"I will... bye."

"*Bye.*"

I hit the end video chat button when Dalton walks through the door and I can see him shaking.

"What's wrong?" I ask.

He takes a deep breath and says, "If I say nothing, will you believe me?"

"No."

"Of course not. You're too perceptive."

"I could hear shouting."

"Oh."

"What's going on?"

"Bree's back."

"What?" I shout and then wince instantly.

"Shhh, it's okay," Dalton says, coming to sit beside me.

"If she's here, it's definitely not okay."

"She can't leave."

"Uh, like hell she can't."

"The lanes drifted in, remember?"

"Oh crap," I say. I had forgotten about it being drifted shut.

"I mean, I can make her leave but she'd probably freeze to death in her car once it gets stuck in the first drift it comes to but..."

"No, I don't like the girl but I don't want her to freeze to death. Maybe get some frostbite but... no, not even that. Where is she staying?"

"Hands and Shorty took her out to the bunkhouse which is just rooms on the upper level of the barn."

"Is that where Shorty lives?"

"Yeah, him and Abe. Before we built the cabins and the houses across the valley-that Mel and Nolan, Tanner and Hannah live in-they all lived in the bunkhouse. It was getting cramped and when they all got married, I decided those two couples needed a little more privacy and I didn't want to lose them if they decided they couldn't handle living in the bunkhouse anymore. So we built those two houses and four cabin type houses, they're just smaller, more for one person than multiple people. Frank and his family live in the old farmhouse."

"That was kind of you."

"It's hard to find good help and even harder to find ones that'll stay on for an extended amount of time. I figure, if I treat them right, they'll stay."

"You're a good boss."

"They're good workers... for the most part," he laughs.

"So is Doc coming? I feel kind of sleepy."

"Yeah, he was waiting for Darcy to get her medic bag since it's got people medical supplies in it, he figured you wouldn't like him using his vet kit on you."

I laugh out loud, "Ow... but that's funny."

"I love that you have a sense of humor."

"Thank you, I love that you can make me laugh."

"I love you," Dalton says, leaning forward and kissing me softly on the lips.

"Mmmmm, I love you too," I reply, around his lips.

Our kissing deepens and we slip into our own little world.

Chapter 23

There's a knock on the door. We jump apart, interrupted. I wince from the pain of moving so quickly and mentally kick myself for getting so worked up while making out with Dalton... again.

"Come on in," Dalton says, a little breathlessly too.

Doc and Darcy come in. She's holding her bag and Doc's got a bunch of bandages and what looks like rolls of something, in his arms..

"How are you feeling?" Darcy says as she puts her bag on the floor beside me and stands next to Dalton, who's gotten up and moved a little out of the way.

"Tired," I answer.

"Understandably so. Even though you were getting some sleep out there, your body was on high alert, just a natural reaction to stress and trauma. Add in the injuries, I'm surprised you've lasted this long. I would have been zonked out while we were eating," she laughs. I smile at her and chuckle too.

"Okay, so you aren't an animal but wounds are wounds. I'll be able to get the cuts and abrasions on your face cleaned up and closed. I have a portable x-ray machine that Hands is grabbing out of my truck. I'll take that splint off and we'll have a look at it again. We can also check your ribs and see how badly they are broken. I'd like to make sure you don't have any splinters floating around that might puncture a lung," Doc says as he sits his arm load of stuff beside me. He holds up the rolls, "These are quilted leg wraps meant for horses but I'm going to make them work to wrap around your rib cage to get you some support and hopefully some relief from that pain."

"That worrrrrrks for me," I say 'works' with a horse type sound in the middle. Dalton busts out laughing instantly hysterical and then Darcy and Doc join in also.

"She's funny too?" Darcy asks, looking at Dalton. She walks over to her bag and starts pulling out the little packets of pre-soaked alcohol pads.

"She's a hoot," Dalton answers, looking at me adoringly.

"High complements," Doc says, smiling at me. He comes and sits on the bed beside me. "Can you turn your face to your left?"

I do as he asks. Darcy hands him gloves and puts a pair on herself. She then opens a couple of the alcohol pads and hands one to Doc. He starts to wipe at my face, it stings but not too terrible.

"These are healing nicely. I'd still like to put some ointment on them, just to try to ward off any infection that might be starting. Turn to the right," he instructs. I do. He breathes in sharply, "These are from the bear?"

"Yeah, I guess. I haven't really looked yet," I say.

"I'll get them cleaned up and put some stitches in, which will sting since I don't have any human numbing ointment," Doc says, looking at me with concern.

"Are they that bad?" I ask.

"They aren't awful, but they aren't good," he says, taking an alcohol wipe from my temple and wiping down to my chin. I feel a sharper sting.

"I think I have some mouth numbing gel in here, would that work on her skin?" Darcy asks as she digs into her bag. "Ahh-ha!"

She pulls out a small, brown, glass bottle. She holds it over for Doc to read it.

"Yeah, that should numb it a little, not completely but it should take the majority of the sting away," he says, nodding at Darcy.

He spends the next ten or so minutes wiping and cleaning the left side of my face. I can feel where the claw marks are, and they hurt, they hurt bad. Hands came in and put a tote looking box that-I assume-has the x-ray machine in it, at the foot of the bed. He tipped his hat at me and then left. Darcy has the numbing gel ready and Doc dabs some on a sterile gauze pad and smears it around my claw wounds.

"I'll give that a couple minutes to soak in before I start to stitch these together. Let's have a look at that hand," Doc says, as he reaches for my left, but I'm offering him my right.

"Oh, your right hand is hurt too?" he asks.

"It is now," I say, slightly embarrassed. Now that my adrenaline is gone and Bree is out of sight, I feel bad about punching her.

"It's from when she socked Bree," Dalton says. He, on the other hand, sounds proud.

"Awww," Doc says in understanding.

"That was a good punch and she definitely deserved it," Darcy says, winking at me.

Doc turns my right hand in his and Darcy leans in for a look when he offers it to her.

"Boxer's fracture?" Doc asks.

"That's what I was thinking," Darcy says.

"Let's get your left hand unwrapped and I'll stitch your facial wounds up. Then we'll use the x-ray machine and take a look at both hands and then see what you have going on with your ribs," Doc says.

"Sounds good," I say as I move my left hand across my body so he can take the splint off.

As soon as the wrapping is off, I can feel my arm

trying to overcompensate to keep it from hurting too much. I wince and hold my breath. The splint had taken so much of the pain away from my wrist, I forgot how much it was hurting before I got to Dalton, when Darcy doctored me up.

"Okay," Doc says. He looks a little concerned but he sets my hand down, gently, onto my lap. Darcy hands him the stitching stuff and he looks at me with an unhappy look. He says, "Now remember, that numbing gel isn't going to be like getting a shot but it should have worked enough to make it a dull pain. If this is too painful, you let me know."

I nod and close my eyes. I feel pressure but no pain. I open my eyes and look at Doc.

"No pain, just pressure," I say.

"None?" he asks in surprise.

"Nope," I say.

"Good, that'll make this easier and quicker," he smiles. He gets back to work. It feels like I'm sitting here for a good while before he puts his hands down and moves my face from my right and then to the left and back to the right. "Looks pretty good, if I do say so myself."

"I agree," Darcy says, nodding as she hands Doc a small tube and I can see it says *'antibiotic ointment'* printed in big red letters. Doc smears the ointment pretty much all over my face.

Do I have that many cuts or is he just being a little

generous with the stuff trying to fight any infection that might be starting already? I think to myself.

Darcy hands Doc a big gauze pad and she starts ripping pieces of tap.

Doc starts to cover what he just stitched up, when Dalton says, "Hang on. Don't cover it yet. I think Lainey needs to see it before you do that."

"Oh good thinking," Darcy says. She reaches into her bag and pulls out a little mirror and hands it to Dalton.

"You should call that your Mary Poppins bag," I say chuckling.

"It definitely has just about anything a person can need," she laughs.

Dalton hands the little mirror over to me and I look at my face for the first time, up close.

I gasp just like everyone else had, my hand goes to my mouth. I say, just a little higher than a whisper and then gradually get louder, "Oh my... Holy shit... I didn't think I looked this bad. I definitely don't feel as bad as I look, I promise. No wonder you all thought I was trying to hide how hurt I am. I look awful!"

I turn my face to the right so I can see my left side, my bear claw side. Sure as shit, standing out against all the little scratches and medium cuts from the tree limbs, I have three large cuts going from just below my temple to the middle of my cheek. I turn my head back to the left so I can compare the two sides. I reach up and touch the goose egg and bruise I have on my right cheek bone.

"From when I hit the ground?" I ask.

"Probably. That could be why you were knocked out. I don't want to x-ray that but I can say pretty certain, your cheekbone is broken. There's not a lot we can do for that, even in the hospital," Darcy says.

"Damn..." I say.

"That was our reaction," Dalton says.

"Shall I cover them up now?" Doc asks, holding the gauze pad up.

"Sure," I say, lowering the mirror.

He quickly covers my slashes from the bear and Darcy hands him pieces of tape. They make a good team. In a couple minutes, he's finished. He gently grabs my chin and turns my head to the left and to the right and back again, and then turns it so it's straight ahead.

"I think that's as good as it's going to get for now," Doc says.

"Couldn't have done it better in a hospital, Doc. Those stitches are top notch. I doubt you, Lainey, will have scars," Darcy says, smiling at me and Doc.

My face falls a little, "What? No scars? What's a bear attack story without the scars to back it up?"

"Oh, you'll have scarring but I really don't think it'll take away from your beautiful face. Doc did a great job but you did get your face slapped by a bear, there will definitely be evidence of that on your face," Darcy says, laughing at me.

I wink at her to let her know I wasn't entirely being serious but kind of, maybe a little, wanting scars. I did want to have something to show for what I went through. Scars help tell a story, they're important to have, sometimes.

Doc walks to the foot of the bed and grabs the big tote looking box that I'm still assuming has the x-ray machine in it and walks back. He opens it up and pulls out a blanket looking thing and hands it to Darcy. He then pulls out something that looks like a camera but bigger and bulkier.

"Lift your arms, Honey," Darcy says as she holds the blanket thing towards me. I lift my arms as she asks and she lays the blanket on top of my chest and stomach. It's heavier than I'm expecting it to weigh. "Okay, now put your left arm about where your sternum is and your right arm where your belly button is on your stomach."

I do as she asks. I'm trying to be a good patient.

"This is my portable x-ray machine. Super handy but pretty finicky, so I need you to lay as still as possible, okay?"

I nod and then lock my muscles into place. Doc puts the lens part of the x-ray to my right hand and pushes a button. There's five clicking sounds and then a faint buzzer type sound. He looks at the screen for a second and taps another button and I hear something in the tote box making a sound.

"Good. Now we'll do the left," he says. "Keep laying the way you are, you're doing great."

He puts the lens to my left wrist and again, pushes the button, and then the five clicking sounds, and then a faint buzzer. He looks at the screen and again, taps a button, and then I hear the same sound from the tote box.

"Okay, so we'll do your ribs now and then take a look at the results after all the images are done. If you aren't comfortable with me taking these next x-rays, I can show Darcy how to use this, it's quite simple," Doc says.

"I'm fine, Doc. Once you've seen a boob, I'm sure you've seen 'em all, right?" I ask, trying to lighten the mood. Darcy and Doc laugh.

Dalton laughs but says, "That's not entirely true."

"You hush," I say glaring at him in mock annoyance. I then wink at him.

Darcy beams over at him. She looks thrilled at our little interaction. She then looks back at me and steps forward and removes the blanket thing. It must be to protect from radiation like in the dentist office. She pulls my actual blanket down to my waist and then the sheet.

"Do you mind if I unbutton your shirt?" she asks.

"Go for it... but I'm going to keep my eyes closed

until all this part is over. I feel like making eye contact with you or Doc might make it more awkward," I say with a chuckle.

She laughs and nods while shrugging.

I close my eyes and she starts to unbutton my, well Dalton's, shirt. I feel the air hit my bare chest as she pulls my shirt away.

"Christ almighty!" Darcy exclaims. My eyes twitch but I keep them shut.

"What?" I ask.

"She's just seeing your bruises," Dalton says. "They've gotten more purple and darker since your shower."

"Oh good," I say sarcastically.

"No wonder you're hurting," Doc says. "That was a big branch that knocked you off."

"Felt like it," I say, smiling.

"Okay, so for these. I need you to take a breath in and hold your breath when I say 'now' and then when you hear the little buzzer sound, you can exhale, okay?"

"Yup," I reply. I can feel Doc getting into position.

"Now," he says.

I breathe in and hold it.

Click-click-click-click-click-BZZZZZ

"And exhale," Darcy says.

I let it out slowly. It hurts.

I feel Doc move the lens to a different spot, not close enough to be touching my skin but I can still feel it in a way.

"Now," he says again.

Another breath in and hold.

Click-click-click-click-click-BZZZZZ

"And exhale… Good job, Lainey," Darcy says, patting my shoulder.

"I think that's it," Doc says. "You can button her back up."

I feel Darcy start to button my shirt back up. When I feel her put the sheet and blanket back over me, I open my eyes. It's hard to do, I'm starting to get really sleepy.

Doc has sheets of paper in his hands now. Or maybe it's large picture paper. He brings them over to me and hands me the first one.

"This is your right hand. You can see clearly where it's broken," Doc says, pointing to my pinky knuckle area that is definitely broken.

Darcy looks over Doc's shoulder and says, "From what I can see, I don't think you'll need surgery but you'll definitely want to get in to make sure."

"Here is your left wrist," Doc says, handing me

another large picture.

I look and see a bunch of lines everywhere.

"I can't figure out which lines are supposed to be there and which ones are the lines from the breaks," I admittedly say.

"Darcy, why don't you show her," Doc says, stepping out of the way. "You are way more familiar with the human skeletal system than I am."

As he stands up and Darcy sits, he hands her the rest of the pictures.

Using what looks like a popsicle stick, Darcy points to the x-ray picture and says, "This is your Radius and Ulna, this line that goes across both of them isn't supposed to be there. You've broken both of those bones. And in this area," she points to the spot just above my wrist. "There isn't supposed to be that many pieces. Your carpals are all broken. It looks and sounds bad but usually these types of breaks don't necessarily need surgery to fix. Again, you'll want to be seen to make sure and to get a proper brace or cast. A splint will help immensely but you may need something else. Keeping it elevated will help too. Once we get both hands splinted, we'll get them nice and high for you, but comfortable," she adds with a smile.

I nod, staring at the image of all the little broken bones. No wonder it hurts so bad.

"And here's the source of all your pain," Darcy says as she hands me one of the pictures of my ribs. She holds the other in her hand, while pointing with the popsicle stick with the other. "Your 6th, 7th, and 8th ribs on both sides are broken. As well as your sternum. That branch took a clean whack straight across your lower chest. Add in the speed that Stormy was no doubt traveling, I'm surprised to not see any splinters floating around in here but there aren't any. They're all clean breaks. We'll get the braces put on and that should help stabilize the bones, and you should heal nicely. Ribs are a long process but you'll heal. And again, get checked. Don't just take mine and Doc's word for it. The big machines in the hospitals might be able to see something we can't. These portable machines are amazing and great but they don't have the digital greatness that the big ones have now."

"I'll take her in as soon as the lane and roads are open," Dalton says.

"Good," Doc says. "Now shall we get you wrapped up?"

"Yes... please," I say. I was starting to hurt, even with the Tylenol I took. Not having the splint on was really making my hand ache.

"We'll have to sit you up and take your shirt off," Darcy says.

"That's fine," I say.

Dalton steps forward and helps lift me into a sitting position, putting a hand up high, on my back.

"Paaaaaahhhh," I breathe out. I'd gotten in a

comfortable position, my ribs weren't bothering me much, but now. Ouch!

"We'll be quick," Darcy says. She leans in front of me and starts to unbutton my shirt again. I close my eyes. Soon, Dalton's hand leaves my back, I tense to hold myself in place. I grimace at the stabbing pain. I feel my shirt being taken off and set beside me. "Arms up, Lainey. Just to shoulder height, you don't need to raise them over your head."

"Good... because... I didn't ... put any... deodorant... on... and this... pain... is making... me sweat..." I pant out.

I hear them laugh.

I feel the quilted wraps go around me, one isn't quite big enough. I feel-I'm assuming-Doc, stop and pull away.

"I think I'm going to have to use two... Your... your bust size is impressive but causes for one more wrap," Doc says shyly. My face turns red instantly.

"Gee, thanks," I say. I laugh with embarrassment and shake my head. Thank goodness my eyes are closed.

"Sorry," he says, remorsefully.

"Oh it's okay... you aren't wrong..." I say, causing Dalton and Darcy to laugh again.

"Dalton, if you'll crawl onto the other side of Lainey, I'll have you hold one in place. Darcy, I'll have you hold the other one and then I'll use the Velcro straps that come with these, to hold them in place,"

Doc says, back to business.

I feel the bed move a little as Dalton gets on and crawls over to me. I feel a wrap go back around me. Then another.

"Okay, Lainey, we have to make it a little tighter, just to make sure you have good support. Let me know when it hurts, okay?"

"K," I answer. I feel Dalton and Darcy start to tighten their wraps towards each other. And then, "Okay, Okay, there… there… that hurts."

"Okay, guys, back them off slowly, Lainey, tell us when the pain is gone," Doc says.

They do as he asks and loosen the wraps slowly. In a second the stabbing pain is gone but it's still throbbing. I think that's good though.

"There, stop there," I say.

"Are you sure?" Dalton asks. "I can tell you're still hurting."

"It's bearable and I want these to be as tight as I can stand. I'll be able to handle this," I say. I feel Dalton's body moving next to me. "Did you just shake your head at me?"

"No," he says but it sounds like he's smiling.

"Oh, he totally did," Darcy says, laughing.

I feel Doc start to put the straps around me. Luckily those are really long, he has to go around me two and half times with each strap. He pulls them a little tighter than what Dalton and Darcy had the wrap but not by much, it actually feels better at this pressure. He puts three more straps on and then I feel someone trying to put my hand through the shirt again. Soon it's back on and Dalton is helping me lay back down.

I force my eyes open and look at him.

"Better?" he asks.

"Oh, so much better," I say. I take a tentative deep breath in and breathe deeper than I have been able to in days. "Oh, that's nice!"

"Makes my heart happy to see that," Darcy says, patting my shoulder. "Let's get your hands wrapped and then we'll get out of here."

"Can you handle the splints?" Doc asks.

"I sure can," Darcy says.

"Great, I need to call and check in with the wife," Doc says. He pats my foot and says, "Get some rest."

"Thanks, Doc," I say with as much gratitude as I can put into my tone. He nods and walks out the door. "Darcy, you mind if I close my eyes while you splint my hands? I'm awfully tired."

"Go right ahead, Sweety," she says as she digs for things in her bag.

Dalton leans over and kisses my forehead. My eyes close at the touch of his lips. He says, "Get some rest. I'll be right here when you wake up."

"Mmmmkay," I sigh out before I fall into the best sleep I've had in a couple days.

Chapter 24

The next couple of days are a blur. I've spent most of the time sleeping. Eating whenever Dalton, Val, or Darcy brought me food. While I ate, I'd wake up enough to call Lucy and talk to my kids and send a message to Emily, letting them know I was doing okay but really tired. Whoever brought me food would help me to the bathroom and back to bed. Dalton helped me shower in the evenings but I'd go right back to bed and to sleep as soon as I was lying down again.

My broken bones are better from the wrappings around them, it's my sore muscles giving me a hard time. It hurts to sit. It hurts to move. I feel like I worked out with the heaviest weights known to man and I should have been using five pound weights. When I say every muscle hurts, I mean, every. muscle.

I have just been woken up to the sound of a pissed off horse. I hear men shouting, the horse neighing in frustration, something hitting tin or metal. More shouting. More upset neighing. I feel like I know that horse's neigh.

I instantly feel sick to my stomach.

"Stormy?" I shout. I slowly push myself out of bed and walk to the window. I can't see anything but the beautiful view. The barn is on the other side of the house. I grab the flannel of Dalton's that's lying on the chair and I carefully put it around my shoulders, and slide my arms through.

I walk out into the hall and all I hear in the house is silence. But I hear Stormy neighing again out front. I continue through the kitchen, no Val. Past the dining room, no one. Through the empty living room and get to the front door. I slip on my boots, luckily Dalton had put me in my sweatpants last night or I would be going out in only his shirt-a fresh one-and flannel, and my boots. What a sight that would be.

I open the door and step outside for the first time since being brought back from the forest. First time looking outside even. The snow is completely gone. There's a ton of mud and puddles everywhere but there's not a snowflake or mound of snow to be seen. The sun is shining and I have to shield my eyes from its glorious brightness. Stormy's protesting neigh has me moving again. I look towards the barn and see Hands, Shorty, Dalton, and Frank trying to load her into a trailer.

"Hey," I holler. My voice cracks a little but I try again, trying for more volume, "Hey!"

"Lainey?" Dalton turns and looks at me confused. He hollers, "What are you doing out of bed?"

"What are YOU doing with Stormy?" I shout back. Almost as soon as she hears me say her name, she calms down, and whinnies. Shorty, who's holding her lead rope, looks at her and then at me. A strange look comes across his face, I'm not sure what it is, exactly. A lot of surprise, a little expectant, and a ton of reluctance.

"She won't eat, hasn't eaten anything since I brought her back. No one can get on her. She was a hard one to ride before her run in with the bear, I think she's too traumatized," Shorty says, sadly.

I get to them and I put my hand out to Stormy. She sniffs once and then starts bobbing her head up and down, and whinnies again. I rub my hand up her muzzle, up between her ears. The stretching hurts but in a good way.

"Shhh, girl, shhh, it's me... I'm here," I say. I step to the side of her and rub down her neck. She settles down and wraps her head behind my back like she had in the forest and pushes me into her. I laugh, "I missed you, too. I'm sorry I haven't been out to see you."

"Incredible," Frank says.

"Where's an apple?" I ask.

Hands runs to the pickup and comes back with a

couple in his hands plus some grain.

"We've been trying to get her to eat anything but she won't, at least not for us," Hands says, handing me one of the apples. "Here, you try."

I take the apple and offer it to Stormy. She sniffs it and snorts a little, and then sniffs at my splinted left hand. I take a bite and offer it to her again, while saying, "I'm okay, just a broken wrist. This is just an apple but it's delicious, you'll like it. Come on, take a bite."

She sniffs my hand again and then the apple but then takes the apple and starts munching on it. Hands offers me the grain and I offer it to Stormy. She sniffs and snorts again.

"Nope, I won't be taste testing this, you just have to trust us that it's good for you and eat it," I say, petting her neck, offering the bucket again. I shake it a little, which makes her ears perk up. I shake it again. She dips her head down and into the bucket and I hear munching. I look up and see the guys' awestruck looks. I ask incredulously, "So, you were doing what with Stormy?"

"I was taking her to the sale," Dalton said, still in shock.

"I'll buy her," I say. "I'll have to borrow a pickup and trailer to get her back to Oregon, but I'll pay for fuel and mileage."

"You won't buy her, she's staying. You two obviously bonded out there but I want a trainer to work with her before you get on her again," Dalton says, sternly. I glare at him. I don't like being told what I can and can't do. And he knows it. He sees my look and says, "Now Lainey, it's only out of the safety for you that I said that, you know I wouldn't tell you what to do unless I thought it was unsafe."

"She's not unsafe, not for me," I say.

"Lainey-" Dalton starts to say but I have already started to pull down on Stormy's lead rope. She bows, I loop the rope under and around her neck and make a makeshift halter and I carefully throw a leg over her neck and she stands up. I'm jostled just a little and try to hide my wince. I smile instead. Dalton's eyes tighten, I can't fool him.

I click my tongue and nudge Stormy with the heel of my boot and she starts walking. I relax into our walk around the pickup and trailer. When we get back to where the guys are standing, Junior comes running out of the barn, yelling.

"I'm coming! I'm coming!" he's not paying attention and slams the barn door behind him and a loud clap of wood and tin rings out through the barn lot.

The guys all jump like they're going to try to catch me but Stormy just stands here. Her coat shivers a little but that's all the reaction we get out of her.

"Remarkable," Shorty says. "Any other day, any other rider, she would have probably flipped her lid but with you Lainey, she's as cool as a cucumber."

"Can we not press our luck?" Dalton asks. He

looks like he's about to come undone with worry. "Stormy is doing amazing. She's a completely different horse with you around, Lainey, but you are just now, obviously, starting to feel better enough to be up and around, I don't want something to set her off and have you get injured again. Can you please get off now?"

"Oh alright," I say, sympathetically. "But she's fine."

"I know, I know... You're just stressing me out," Dalton says. I slide my legs over Stormy's neck and let Dalton help me down. It was nice being close to him like this, my body reacts like it did before my pain obliterated all feelings besides agony. Now, I feel that familiar flame stirring in the pit of my stomach. Don't get me wrong, getting off Stormy hurt, but not nearly as bad as before, and this feeling for Dalton was starting to intensify.

"Hi," I say, looking up at him. His expression changes when he sees the way I'm looking at him.

"Hi back," he says sweetly, even his tone of voice has changed. His hands cup my face, softly, and he kisses me even softer. The moment our lips touch, electricity shoots through my lips, down my neck, my spine, through my stomach, down my legs, to my toes, and back up again, settling in my lower stomach.

We both gasp and pull our lips apart and just stare into each other's eyes.

Cough-Cough

I put my head into Dalton's chest as he looks away, towards the person who interrupted. I'm embarrassed yet again at our ability to forget that there were other people standing just feet away.

"Just wondering what you want us to do with Stormy, Boss," Shorty says, repressing laughter.

"Put her back in her stall, make sure she has fresh hay and water, she might eat now that she knows her person is okay," Dalton says, looking down at me. I look over and see Stormy start to resist Shorty's encouraging words and pulling on her lead rope.

I step away from Dalton and walk to Stormy. I rub her nose and give a kiss and say, "It's okay. We're okay. I'll come out and see you soon, I promise."

With the quietest of whinnies, Stormy lets Shorty turn her and lead her back to the barn. I turn to Dalton and smile.

"That horse loves you," Frank says, smiling at me.

"I love that horse," I say.

"It's good to see you, Ms. Lainey," Frank says, patting my shoulder as he walks by, towards the barn.

"It's good to see you too, Frank," I smile even wider at him.

"I'll get the pickup and trailer put back and then

Junior and I will head to the shop and get to finishing the tractors," Hands says, walking towards the driver side door. "Get in Junior."

Junior runs by, waves as he gets into the passenger side, and Hands fires it up and drives off. Dalton walks over to me and puts his arm around my shoulder. I put my mitt of a hand-because of the splint-around his waist.

"So you're feeling better?" he asks.

"Much better in some ways but in others, still the same," I answer.

"How so?"

"Well it's not just the pain... the soreness... that has my attention anymore, which is good. But I'm still pretty sore, which isn't all that great. Although, I feel like the more I'm up and around, the more the soreness will go away. But I'm still feeling pretty tired."

"That's good. You're tired because your body is healing. And hey, about telling you, you couldn't get on Stormy, you do know I only said it because I was worried about you getting hurt? Not knowing how she was going to react."

"Oh yeah, I know. But my reaction to that is to do what I want to do."

Dalton kisses the top of my head, a zing of electricity flies down to my toes, even from that little gesture. He says, "Yeah, I'm realizing that more and more."

"Is that a bad thing?"

"Not at all. I want you to be you. And you are a strong, independent woman. But I think it's good for you to have someone that'll look out for your safety because I feel like sometimes you put others before you, to the point of no self-awareness as far as what danger is waiting for you. You put your needs second and everyone else around you, first. I think it's good for you to have someone that will make sure your needs are met as well."

"Huhhh..."

"What, no arguing?"

"Well, you aren't entirely wrong."

"Not entirely?"

"Okay, not at all. But again, is it so bad to put other people first?"

"Not at all. It's one of the things I love about you, you care deeply about other people. I'm just saying, while you're off making sure everyone else is happy and getting what they need, I'm going to be here to make sure you are taken care of, that your needs are met, and that you're happy."

"I am happy," I say, squeezing him.

"I'm glad, so am I," he says, kissing my head again. Another zap of electric spark zings its way down to my toes and back to my stomach. We're back at the front door, I'd left it open in my haste to get to Stormy. We kick off our boots, and Dalton shuts the door behind us. "Hey, you wanna go for a ride with me in the morning?"

"Sure, where to?"

"One of my favorite places on the ranch."

"Wait, what time is it?" I ask, looking around confused.

"Just after 4 in the afternoon."

"I'm so lost on time and days right now, is it..." I think for a minute. "Is it Saturday?"

"Yeah, it's Saturday," he says. "It's been a whole week since your ride into the forest."

"Oh, you're right. It doesn't feel like it, probably because I've been asleep for 99.9% of it," I laugh.

Dalton laughs too. We've walked into the kitchen. There's still no one around.

"Where is everyone?" I ask, sitting at what's becoming my seat at the island.

Dalton grabs some sandwiches out of the fridge and some glasses. He puts the sandwiches on the island and then gets us some water. Then grabs the bag of chips sitting in the corner.

"Let's see, once we got the driveway opened up, Bree left like a bat flying back to hell. That was Thursday late afternoon. Mel and Hannah went home that night, after Shorty got their driveway opened up. John and Karie stopped by yesterday to check on you. Sam and Lynn also stopped by last night. Those four were all part of the crew that got the cattle to the forest land and were able to make it back and home before the snow hit. Junior has been in and out, always asking if you're feeling better. Darcy, Phil, and the boys ran into Missoula to get some things. Val also went to Missoula to go get some groceries."

"When did the snow melt away?"

"Most of it was yesterday, but the bluebird sky, and super warm sun did away with the rest today. It's supposed to be another beautiful day tomorrow."

"Perfect for our drive."

"Sure is."

I've eaten half of my sandwich when I yawn.

"Time for bed?"

"I didn't think so but now that I have some food in my tummy, my eyes are thinking they're heavy and needing to close."

"If you want to go lay down, I'll finish up here and then clean up and then I'll be in to snuggle with you."

"Mmmmm that sounds nice," I say. I walk by and kiss him on the cheek. "See you shortly."

I get to the bedroom and take off the flannel and my sweats. Dalton's room is feeling warm. I carefully slide under the covers, which are thankfully, nice and cool.

❖ ❖ ❖

"Lainey... Laaainey..." I wake to my name being

softly called.

"Mmmmm," I mumble out.

"Lainey, wake up beautiful," Dalton's soft voice filters in through my sleepy mind.

"Mmmmm, Dalton?"

"I've got coffee," he says. My magic words. I open my eyes and at first I'm confused.

"It's dark?"

"Yeah, I wanted us to get an early start."

"How early?"

"It's 4:30am."

"Wasn't it just after 4 in the afternoon?"

"It was... yesterday. It's Sunday now. Come on, get up. Do you still want to go for a drive with me?"

"Mmmmm, yes," I say as I try to stretch. I had been sleeping on my back with my arms prompted up on pillows and it's starting to make my back sore, not that I needed any help in that department. I sit up and turn my body so that my legs are dangling off the bed. "Did I fall asleep before you got in here last night?"

"Yeah, you were out," he chuckles.

"I'm sorry. This bed is so comfy and I've been so tired."

"It's okay, you're still healing."

"Yeah but still," I say, yawning.

"I'm putting your coffee over here by your chair so you have to get up and go get it if you want any of it. You get 10 minutes to sit and enjoy it while you wake up but then we need to get you dressed."

"Thank you," I say lovingly. He knows how to wake me up- sweetly and with coffee. I stand up and walk to... my chair? "Wait, my chair? Why is this my chair?"

"Because you've used it more times than I ever have, so it's yours now, if you want it."

"Heck yeah, it's a great chair. Perfect for reading."

"I thought so," Dalton chuckles. "Can I lay some clothes out for you?"

"Sure... are you trying to rush my 10 minutes?"

He laughs, "No, I'm just excited to show you one of my favorite places. We haven't gotten to do a lot of fun stuff and tomorrow I'll be taking you into the hospital to get new x-rays done, so I'm hoping to have a fun filled day today."

"Oh, well in that case, I can drink this on the go. I don't have to wear anything fancy, do I?"

"Nope, just maybe something warm. The mornings are still a little chilly, nowhere near the cold you've experienced so far but it's still 'hoodie and maybe a jacket' cold."

"Sounds like my perfect outing," I say as I put my coffee down and start to fumble with the buttons on the shirt of Dalton's I had worn all of yesterday and apparently all night. He steps over and helps me and then slides it back and off my shoulders.

"Your straps look a little loose, hold still and I'll tighten them," Dalton says as he walks behind me. He pulls on each Velcro strap, tightening them a little more than they had been. "We'll be in the side-by-side, I want you as snug and supported as possible."

"Oh, speaking of support, will you help me get my bra on and clip it in the back for me?"

"Sure will."

I grab a fresh bra out of my bag and put my arms through it and then turn my back towards Dalton. His fingers slide up my shoulders, looping under my bra straps, and pulling them up higher towards my neck. His right finger continues up my neck and back down. Goosebumps appear all over my right arm. An electric bolt runs through my right arm down into my stomach. His fingers slowly slide down my back until he finds the clasp. He slowly clips it together and then runs his fingers over the top part of my bra strap, up my shoulder straps and onto my shoulders. He leans in and kisses my neck.

"Ugh, I miss you," he whispers into my ear.

"Mmme too," I stammer out.

"You let me know when you're ready."

"You'll be the first to know."

He turns me gently and kisses me. After a minute, I pull away, shaking my head.

"I stop breathing when you kiss me like that," I say, breathlessly.

"You take my breath away too," he says, taking in a slow deep breath.

"Will it bother you to help me getting dressed?"

"Not at all. Helping you is enjoyable on a whole different level. When you're healed up completely, helping you in and out of your clothes will have a different effect on me but right now, I know how much you need that help, and I love that I can offer that to you."

"You... you are just simply the best. I can't think of a better word but you are, you're the best."

"What do you need help with? New undies and socks?"

"Yes, please," I say, not missing the way he changed the subject away from himself. He does that all the time.

He grabs a fresh pair of socks and undies from my bag and brings them over to me. He slides the undies I had been wearing off and I step into the fresh ones. I sit in my chair and he puts on my socks. He then brings my jeans over to me and helps me pull them up.

"It'll be really nice when I have full use of my hands again."

"I honestly don't mind."

"I know, but I'm just ready to have my hands back."

"I get it."

He reaches into my bag and pulls a tank top out

CHAPTER 24

and slides it over my head. Then grabs my last clean hoodie and helps me pull it over my head. It takes a minute to get my splinted hands through the arm holes.

"Val packed us a light breakfast. She said since you're feeling better she's going to make lunch a special to-do."

"She's another absolute best person."

"That she definitely is, without a doubt."

Dalton waits for me to drink the rest of my coffee. Then grabs my mitt of a hand and leads us from his room. We get to the kitchen and I see our large lunch box. There's a note on it.

Enjoy, my lovelies.
~V

I smile at her note. "She is just the sweetest person I think I've ever met."

"You've never met yourself."

I laugh and shrug him off.

He grabs the lunch box and we walk to the front door. We put our boots on and he takes a new, smaller jacket, off a hook.

"I hope you don't mind but I had Darcy pick up a jacket that'll fit you better,," he offers the coat to me, holding it so I can put it on.

"Oh, thank you Dalton, but you didn't have to buy it for me."

"Well, I did."

"It fits great, thank you, again," I say, reaching up on my tip-toes and kissing him on the cheek as he put his coat on.

"You're welcome."

We get outside and the morning air is a little cold. Dalton is right, it's nothing near what it had been last week. The side-by-side is parked at the end of the walkway. We walk to it, Dalton opens my door and I get in. Dalton runs around to his side and gets in. He reaches into the back seat and pulls a blanket up front and hands it to me.

"This thing has a heater but sometimes it's not enough. I thought you might get chilly, do you want this?"

"Yeah, I'll take the blanket, thank you."

Dalton starts the ATV up and puts it in drive and away we go. The sun is just barely starting to shine light up into the sky, far in the distant horizon. It looks like we are driving straight to it. We go through a couple pastures. Some hay fields. We cross a creek and a couple bridges.

"It's so beautiful here," I say, smiling over at him.

"It's not so bad," he smiles back.

We're quiet again for a few more minutes and then Dalton clears his throat.

"Lainey, can I ask you something?"

"Sure, you can ask me anything."

He chuckles and then asks, "Could you see yourself living here? Would you ever consider it?"

I take a minute to think of my answer.

"It's definitely something I've thought about, especially if we continue our relationship. But there's so much to consider."

"Like what?" he asks encouragingly.

"Like my kids. I won't move them away from family, friends, and the school. At least, not right now. I feel like we've finally got back into a stable routine again and I don't want to throw them for a loop by moving states and schools. For now, I'm feeling like maybe when they're all out of school, I'd consider moving up permanently. I have to think of my shop. It's been a great addition to the community. I wouldn't want to close down but again, I don't know how I'll feel year in the future. How I feel right now, I'd like to keep it up and going."

I can see that Dalton's thinking hard.

"You said you'd consider moving up permanently, does that mean you might be open for partial residency here for a little while?" he chuckles.

"I mean, spring breaks and summers would be a lot of fun here. I know Max would have a blast and the girls would love all the horses. Maybe every other major holiday... I'd still do things with Jayce's family because they're my family too. So that would have to be considered. What about you?"

"What about me, what?" he asks back airily, like a weight has been lifted off of his shoulders.

"Would you consider moving down to Oregon?"

"I've been thinking about it. Winters are really slow up here, not a whole heck of a lot to do. Spring and summer are usually my busiest times of year. Fall only because we gather the cattle out of the forest land and bring them back home to graze the hay fields and pastures before we have to start feeding them. And even then, that's Frank and the guys' job to do that. I wasn't kidding when I said I just sign the checks and make decisions. I can do all that over the phone," he smiles at me.

My heart starts to race. *Are we planning a future together?*

Trying to not let my mind get away from me, I focus on the scenic beauty in front of us. We start to follow a creek and a line of trees for a few minutes before Dalton starts to slow. The sun is starting to lighten things up just enough that I can follow the creek up a ways and I see a beautiful, covered bridge.

"Oh wow, that's gorgeous," I say, pointing towards the bridge.

"It's the oldest bridge on the ranch."

"That's amazing."

Dalton comes to a stop. Too far away for the bridge to be our destination, unless he was thinking we were walking to it, which on a normal day would be fine but I don't think my sore body and broken ribs will

CHAPTER 24

make it that far. Dalton comes around and opens the door for me.

I'm about to leave the blanket, but Dalton says, "You can bring it if you're cold."

I grab it back up and start to wrap it around myself, Dalton helps me. He's got a look in his eye, and again, I can't figure out what it is. I'm about to ask him what's wrong but he grabs my hand, and we start walking. Not towards the bridge like I had thought, but towards the tree line. We walk through a couple trees and just as we're getting to a little meadow type field, the sun shines through, I see a tree in the opening that is leaning over slightly. It's the most beautiful sunrise I've ever seen.

For a second, my mind goes back to one of the nights Dalton and I were talking on the phone, playing 20 questions. One of his questions for me was what my favorite time of day was, I had told him, sunrise or sunset.

I love the way the sky turns colors, how it changes. How the sunrise's beauty is a reminder that a new day is beginning and what a beautiful gift it is to be able to have another day. The sunset's beauty is a way to reflect on the day we had and be excited for the beauty of tomorrow. He had said he wasn't expecting that answer but he said he really liked it.

He had mentioned there was a place he wanted to show me on his ranch, that if I ever came up to visit, it would be one of the most beautiful sunrises I'd ever seen. This must be the place.

I look to my side, expecting to see Dalton standing beside me but he's not there. I look behind me and see him kneeling. The sunrise's golden, reddish, and orange light is shining on him and making him look like the Greek god I always teased him to be. But he's kneeling and has something in his hand.

"Elainah Richardsen, I want to start every beginning of every new day together with you. I want you and I always will. I don't want any more of our yesterdays, to not have each other in them. I want us to be in the rest of each other's todays and tomorrows. I want our futures to be together. I want your kids to become my own. I know I'll love them dearly because I love you beyond anything I could have imagined. I love you, Lainey, with everything that I am. Will you marry me?" Dalton cracks open the little box he's holding and offers me the most beautiful ring I've ever seen. I can tell it's an heirloom by the unique build of it. It doesn't scream modern, it whispers tradition and love.

In a flash of a second I can see our life together. I can see us being happy and in love. I can see my kids running to him and him hugging them with the love a father has for his kids. I can see him and Max doing father and son things. I can see Nelly and Janey taking turns getting piggyback rides when they get tired when we've gone for a walk. I can see the love they all have for each other. But in another split second, I see Jayce's face. My heart breaks ever so slightly in that second. But I hear in my head, *"It's okay. Allow yourself to feel everything good that this life has to offer. Allow yourself to be loved and to love again. Allow yourself to be happy, Lainey. You are loved, let yourself be loved, he is that love."*

I blink back tears, I know only a second has gone by. My little 'episode', or whatever you want to call it, isn't noticed by Dalton. I wipe away my tears and smile at him.

"Yes, Dalton, I'll marry you, of course I will."

◆ ◆ ◆

DEAR BELOVED READERS,

I wasn't sure if I was going to include this here or not but in the end, I thought someone might like to hear how I came up with this story.

My husband was killed in an accident in January 2020 and for the months to follow, I had a lot of dreams. Still have them actually. Some good, some bad. I have vivid dreams and dream in color. I can think through them as well, for example- if I were having a nightmare, I could think, "I don't like this, this needs to change," and my dream will change to something a lot less scary. Weird. Strange. I know. All of my 2020 dreams, I wrote down. When I write things down, I don't think about them as much anymore.

The morning of September 1, 2020 I woke up from having a very vivid dream. It was the first time the leading male role wasn't my husband. I thought it was pretty interesting since I had no idea who the man was in my dream. I had never seen him before in my life. I couldn't stop thinking about it. I tried to ignore it but the more I tried to ignore it, the more it persisted to dominate all my thoughts that day. I didn't think about writing it down that morning because it wasn't about my husband and I figured I would forget about it throughout the day. Boy, was I wrong. So lying in bed that night, I decided to write it out. Except when I started writing, the dream didn't stop where I woke up, it continued on. I wrote the first two chapters of "Along Came You" that night. The next day, September 2nd, I wrote three more.

When I had this dream, I was in the process of writing a sequel to my fantasy fiction book, "Emma Hart and the Demi-gods". Once I started writing "Along Came You", I couldn't stop and I couldn't focus on Emma. I told a friend of mine it was like having two children fighting for my attention. "Along Came You" needed my attention more than Emma's 2nd book. So I put her way and really started working on Lainey and Dalton's story.

"Along Came You" was very therapeutic for me. I like to think that I'm a good listener, a good friend. I feel like I can help my friends and family talk out an issue or problem or feelings they might be having and we can find a solution. But when it comes to myself, I tend to just tell myself to not worry about it or push it off to the side. I used the character of Lainey to work through some of the big feelings I was- and still am- having about losing my husband at a young age and having our young children to raise alone. Having conversations between her and her friends, sister, and Dalton, helped me look at myself from the outside looking in, in a way. I think it really helped me process and heal.

So, I hope you enjoyed reading this as much as I enjoyed writing it.

Thank you so much for reading, "Along Came You".

With all my love,

A.L. Stephens

A SPECIAL THANK YOU TO MY BETA READERS:
Stephanie Mays, Danielle Martin, Jane Wisdom, Lacey Wisdom, Melissa Kendall, Pam Maxwell, and Lacey Grende.
Thank you for taking the time to help me work through this more emotional writing experience. I truly appreciate you all, so very much.

Made in the USA
Columbia, SC
15 March 2021